The Key to Enniskillen

by WYATT TREMBLAY

Raspberry Press

For Bonnie, *my partner in the adventure of travel.*
And for my siblings, who have supported me
in this journey.

THE WINDOWS

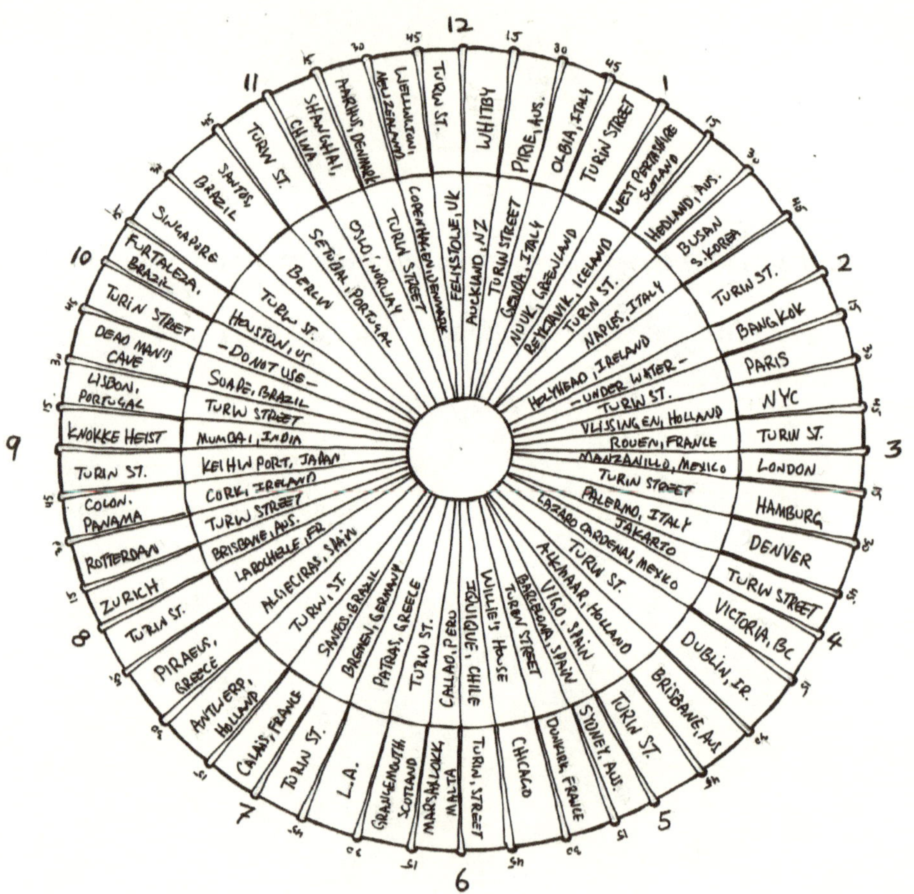

12
1
2
3
4
5
6
7
8
9
10
11
15
30
45
TURN ST.
WHITBY
PIRAE, AUS.
OLBIA, ITALY
TURIN STREET
WEST PERTHSHIRE, SCOTLAND
HEDLAND, AUS.
BUSAN, S.KOREA
TURIN ST.
BANGKOK
PARIS
NYC
TURIN ST.
LONDON
HAMBURG
DENVER
TURIN STREET
VICTORIA, BC
DUBLIN, IR.
BRISBANE, AUS.
TURIN ST.
SYDNEY, AUS.
DUNKIRK, FRANCE
CHICAGO
TURIN, STREET
MARSHALLOKK, MALTA
GRANGEMOUTH, SCOTLAND
L.A.
TURIN ST.
CALAIS, FRANCE
ANTWERP, HOLLAND
PIRAEUS, GREECE
TURIN ST.
ZURICH
ROTTERDAM
COLON, PANAMA
TURIN ST.
KNOKKE HEIST
LISBON, PORTUGAL
DEAD MAN'S CAVE
TURIN STREET
FURTALEZA, BRAZIL
SINGAPORE
SANTOS, BRAZIL
TURN ST.
SHANGHAI, CHINA
AARHUS, DENMARK
AUCKLAND, NEW ZEALAND
TURIN STREET
COPENHAGEN, DENMARK
FELIXSTOWE, UK
AUCKLAND, NZ
TURIN STREET
GENOA, ITALY
NUUK, GREENLAND
REYKJAVIK, ICELAND
TURIN ST.
NAPLES, ITALY
HELYHEAD, IRELAND
— UNDER WATER —
TURN ST.
VLISSINGEN, HOLLAND
ROUEN, FRANCE
MANZANILLO, MEXICO
TURIN STREET
PALERMO, ITALY
JAKARTO
LAZARD CARDENAL, MEXICO
TURN ST.
ALKMAAR, HOLLAND
VIGO, SPAIN
BARCELONA, SPAIN
TURIN STREET
WILLIE'S HOUSE
IQUIQUE, CHILE
CALLAO, PERU
TURIN ST.
PATRAS, GREECE
BREMEN, GERMANY
SANTOS, BRAZIL
TURIN, ST.
ALGECIRAS, SPAIN
LA ROCHELLE, FR.
BRISBANE, AUS.
TURW STREET
CORK, IRELAND
KEIHIN PORT, JAPAN
MUMBAI, INDIA
TURW STREET
SUAPE, BRAZIL
— DO NOT USE —
HOUSTON, US
TURW ST.
BERLIN
SETUBAL, PORTUGAL
OSLO, NORWAY

"Never forget, kiddo, everyone has a story; some they write with their bad decisions, and others just get handed a Shakespearean tragedy. It's not always their fault."

- Felix Montgomery Ames

ONE

A severed sparrow head lies between my feet, its dark, startled eyes staring up at me as its tiny yellow beak twitches involuntarily as if trying to ask me why – why did I kill it?

The thing is, I didn't. I tap my cellphone's camera app and stare at my face, staring at the screen in my hand.

"Morgan, I'm recording this because I don't know what the hell is going on, and you're not going to believe me without seeing what I'm seeing."

I flipped the phone around so it recorded the door I had stumbled through a few minutes earlier. The door severed the tiny bird's head as it closed, but there was no sign of blood on the doorframe or anywhere else. Maybe sparrows don't have much blood, and maybe this isn't the horror movie it feels like to me.

The rest of its tiny little body is nowhere to be seen.

I'm standing on a platform not much larger than a real porch, with only a doorframe attached to the back edge. The front edge has narrow steps leading down to knee-high grass. The entire thing looks like a porch waiting for the rest of the house to fall out of the sky and complete the image my brain expects to see. I flip the phone around and see this wide-eyed and stressed face – mine. I can feel my heart beating wildly in my chest. Who wouldn't be stressed if they'd just walked through an innocent-looking closet door and ended up wherever this is?

I have an antique key in my hand, and I think it brought me here somehow. I hold it close to the camera. It's not that big, maybe twice the length of a normal house key, but it looks massive compared to my head in the image.

"So, this is no lie. I used this old key to open the closet door in the study on the third floor of my grandfather's house, and I think it killed a sparrow. I mean, I think the door killed it."

I pause, staring at the screen. The pain of my grandfather's death was still close.

"Well, uh – it's my house now. Gramps is dead, but you know that."

I look away, swallowing hard and then exhaling frustration between my clenched teeth. The porch-waiting-for-a-house is at the back of a small paddock inside a much larger one. Several black-faced sheep have gathered at a rail fence in the stone wall that separates us, bleating, pleading with me, I assume, their little black eyes looking expectantly. Maybe it's feeding time. I don't know farm stuff. I'm a city kid.

"I think this is called a skeleton key, though I don't know why it's called that. You probably know, Morgan. I used this to open the closet door."

I flip the phone around to show the weathered, old door on the porch, then flip it back.

"All you see around me here appeared in the closet after I opened it. I was standing in my grandfather's house – in my house – and these sheep and fields and those trees over there are like in my closet. And the bird flew into the study, and I ducked and stepped through the doorway, and the door closed, killing the poor sparrow as it tried to escape."

I sweep the phone a full circle around me, then down at the little head on the porch, then return it to my face.

"I think I'm trapped here, and there's no cell reception, and I have," I squint at the phone, "I have 31% battery left."

I tapped the recording off and lifted the device above my head again, hoping for even the slightest shade of a bar that would give me the tiniest glimmer of hope. Nothing.

"What the hell," I bark at the growing number of sheep. They bleat plaintively in reply.

Okay, don't panic. I picked the sparrow's head up by its now still beak and gently let it fall into the grass at the edge of the strange porch. I sit on its faded edge, away from the sad makeshift gravesite, my socked feet resting on wooden steps, grey from sun and weather. What exactly happened? How would I explain what had happened to Morgan, who, of course, would pester me for every detail – if I made it back?

I had only flown from Calgary and gotten to Turin Street in Kingston, Ontario, the night before. I inherited the house after my grandfather suddenly died of a heart attack two years earlier. I was sixteen when he died, and now, I was in Kingston to attend college. I could have pursued post-secondary education in Calgary, but the house meant free rent, and along with the almost two thousand dollars a month from his estate, it just made sense. This morning, I explored the third floor. I had not been back since my grandfather's funeral, and he had never allowed me into the room nestled in the peak of the house when I had stayed with him during the four summers before he died. But now his house was mine, and I wanted to see what the mystery had been all about.

When I entered the room, I was immediately disappointed and quickly felt the layers of mythology my young brain had created melting away like an ice cube on a hot sidewalk. The room, or as my grandfather called it, his 'personal study,' spoken by him in metaphorical large capital letters no doubt, was long and narrow, with one window looking out over the mundane happenings of Turin Street and one closet door about halfway along the left wall. I had expected books, shelves, and leather furniture, but the room only had a middling oak desk, a wooden swivel chair and a coat rack with one of my grandfather's fedoras hanging from it. He liked fedoras, and honestly, he looked cool with one perched askew on his head.

The plainness of this Gramps-only space was strange and unnerving. Then, of course, there was the diary. I found it in the desk drawer with a wallet that held a credit card issued from the Chase Manhattan Bank, a bunch of foreign bills of various denominations, and an old skeleton key tucked in among the bills. I pocketed the key, thinking it might be important. It obviously had been to him. I flipped through the diary pages and was surprised and troubled by what I found. It contained the hand-written, meticulously documented journeys of his daily continent-hopping travels. Something I was sure he had never done. I was certain my grandfather could not have gone to Paris, London, or Zurich as often as the diary suggested. According to his numerous point-form entries, he sometimes travelled to and from London or Paris several times a week. My grandfather was a retired elevator repairman. He was not wealthy enough to travel as often as he'd written down, and surely, some of these flights would have been several hours long. I doubted he'd be able to sit still that long.

What happened next, then?

I tucked the peculiar diary under my arm and proceeded to the closet. The door was odd. It seemed much older than the rest of the already old house. It was unlocked. I pulled it open and stepped inside, hopeful of anything that made me feel like my grandfather had a reason to keep me from this room. However, like the crushed myth of the rest of the third floor, the strip of closet held nothing spectacular, just dust bunnies and depressing darkness. I closed the door and noticed the odd-looking keyhole beneath the tarnished brass handle. The hole was designed for a skeleton key. A lock on a closet was odd, and I wondered what he would have needed to lock inside it or keep people from getting into it.

I slipped the skeleton key out of my pocket and looked at it. Was it for this door? My grandfather carried it around, so it must have been important. I pushed it in, gave it a turn, and felt the mechanism move. I gave the handle a twist and a pull to ensure it was locked and was surprised to see the door opening. Of course, that was nothing compared to the surprise I felt at seeing an unexpected burst of light and sound erupt from the closet. I pulled the door fully open.

I saw the black-faced sheep first.

Then, the hills, the towering fluffy clouds, and the sun dipping down to a horizon that shouldn't be inside the closet. None of this should have been there.

Then, several small birds flitted by. One of them, startled by my sudden appearance, veered into the study, almost hitting me in the face. I jumped and stepped backwards into the closet, struggling to comprehend what was happening. The bird panicked, swooped around the desk, and then saw the open closet door and the paddock behind me and quickly angled towards it, hoping for an escape. The door suddenly closed, slamming forcefully as if someone had been in the study and pushed it shut. The poor sparrow's severed head bounced off my chest, dropping to the boards at my feet. I was trapped with the sheep. Of course, I grabbed what looked like a completely different doorknob, twisting it and throwing the door open in utter panic, but all I saw was more of the paddock and the moss-covered stone wall of the enclosure.

I panicked, feeling unsure of what to do and who wouldn't. My house, my inheritance, included a closet that was a one-way portal to a sheep enclosure and could cut little heads off.

"Okay, Aidan, relax," I mumbled to myself and the universe. "There's got to be a logical explanation for this, right?"

I tapped the record button again and centred my face on the screen.

"I think I'm hallucinating.."

TWO

I stared at the sheep, who mostly ignored me with a weird mammalian indifference and decided I wasn't hallucinating. I pushed my way through the grass around the structure to its backside. There were no steps, but the frame the door was set in was securely anchored by two long timbers embedded into the dirt of whatever this little enclosure of weirdness was. I reached up and grasped the handle on this side. It felt jiggly and loose, likely worn from use, but I pushed the door open. It swung easily toward the front side of the porch and what I had seen from my grandfather's study, only from a lower vantage point. I pulled it shut to keep things as they were, then returned to the front, taking the steps onto the porch. I tried the door again, and it swung open with the same result.

I examined the lock. The keyhole was identical to the one on the closet door, designed for the skeleton key that might have somehow been responsible for bringing me here. I slipped it out of my pocket and inserted it. Now what? The door was already unlocked. What if I locked it? Would that make whatever had happened with the closet happen again? I turned the key, the deadbolt clicking easily into place. I could see a sliver of the bolt in the gap between the edge of the door and the door jam. Nothing crazy happened. On a hunch, I turned the knob and pulled on the door.

The locked door opened, followed immediately by a flash of light and a rush of air that buffeted my body. Incredibly, instead of seeing the enclosure through the door, I was looking at a small, dimly lit room with muted daylight dribbling through two narrow, dirt-streaked windows on one wall. My heart sank. I pulled out my cell and hit record, turning it to record this new location.

"Un-freaking-believable. The key opened the door to somewhere else."

I stepped to the side of the porch and peered behind the structure, positioning the phone so it could see what I saw – a closed door.

"You won't believe this, Morgan; the door isn't open on this side. That's not possible. How could it still be shut on the backside?"

I closed the door, unlocked it, then opened it. The room was gone, replaced by the enclosure. Curious, I shut the door, locked it again, and cranked it open. The scene had changed!

This time, I was looking out into murky darkness. The rectangle of light from this side revealed a short set of wooden steps down to a narrow boardwalk, which was swallowed up by the blackness of night and my retinas not having adjusted yet. I could hear waves crashing on a shore in the distance, and moist air licked at my face as I inhaled the scent of the ocean. As my eyes adapted, a brilliantly star-lit night sky and a half-moon began to reveal themselves. There was a smattering of brightly coloured lights in the distance. Boats? The sluggish tempo of waves was in strange contrast to the pastoral sounds of where I was standing.

"This is crazy," I said, letting the phone record the new location.

I leaned around to the backside of the structure, holding the phone out so it recorded the bizarre sight of a door that was open but not open. Feeling a relentless fear crawling in my stomach, I shut the door and tried again, but this time, it opened on the same nighttime scene. Each time I did this, more than a dozen times, the same boardwalk presented itself.

I tapped the recording off. I had 23% battery left. Damn.

How was this possible, and should I be afraid of being cut in half like the poor, unfortunate sparrow? I flopped down on the edge of the porch and thumbed through the journal. There had to be an answer in it somewhere. There were dates, times, and places, some familiar and others I'd never heard of, and nothing about losing one's head. The entries seemed completely random, without any clear schedule, and nothing with an arrow and words that said, *You are here.*

I leafed through the pages, hoping to spot a pattern, any clue as to what my grandfather had meant in these short excerpts about what had been actual travels. Angry, I slammed the journal shut. I couldn't concentrate; my mind was still trying to grasp what had happened. How could an empty closet do something like this?

Feeling desperate, I inserted the key and tried the door again. Suddenly, I was presented with a narrow, dimly lit alley framed by high cinder block walls and a new set of odours. A dozen or more large black plastic bins in various states of cleanliness, some with lids and some without, were lined up on either side of the alley. Between these were empty wooden and plastic crates stacked in creaky towers that reached higher than my head. Further away, where the alley intersected a busy road, I could see a river of light from a torrent of vehicles and motorbikes. The din of city noise suggested that I was not even close to home. And, it wasn't night yet in Kingston.

I glanced at my cell; the time read 2:01.

I had been stranded for at least an hour. Unsure of what to do, I pressed record and filmed the alley, which was somewhere else, far away from where I was in the sheep enclosure. Should I walk through or close the door and try for what I assumed would be a different destination based on what I had already experienced? There were narrow and pitted concrete steps with a rusting, unpainted pipe rail on one side of the door that descended to the alley, and I desperately wanted to step out onto them.

A grime-streaked door suddenly screeched open a few metres away on my right, letting light stream into the dark alley. An elderly man in a heavily stained apron emerged. He slopped the contents of a plastic bucket into one of the bins a few steps from the door and then turned. Our eyes met. His mouth dropped in surprise as I leaned into the door to close it.

"Ames?" he called. There was obvious excitement in how he said my last name.

It was my turn to be surprised.

"Excuse me?"

"Ames! You return, yes?"

The man spoke with an accent as he took a step toward me. In the bright daylight behind me, I realized that my silhouette was all he could see of me. He thought I was my grandfather.

He quickly wound his way through the maze of crates, stopping near the bottom of the stairs while shielding his eyes. He was slightly built and probably in his seventies, with thin, spidery-white hair and wrinkles that tracked across his face like a city road map.

"I'm Aidan Ames. You knew my grandfather, Felix Ames?" I asked, pausing the recording. I wasn't sure if he'd be offended if I kept filming our encounter.

"Ai-dan?" he pronounced slowly, "Ah, Ames' grand-son, yes? Where is Ames?"

He leaned toward one side to look behind me.

Scrambling to grasp the fact that he knew my grandfather, I replied.

"I'm sorry, he passed away two years ago. You were a friend of his?"

He nodded slowly.

"Ah, his death is sad. I would have," he paused, struggling to find a word. "I am sorry, I do not speak English very much since Ames stop coming."

"You knew my grandfather well?"

He nodded vigorously.

"Yes. Yes. Ames and Boon Nam," he touched his chest with his free hand, "we were friends for many years. Many times visit, and we play pai gow. Ames lose many American dollars."

He rested one hand on the railing and pointed curiously around my legs.

"Your ban. What is in ban?"

I wondered if he was about to walk up the steps and push past me.

"Your ban," he insisted, pointing. "What is in there?"

"Where is this?" I asked, deflecting his question while gesturing in the general direction of the street I could see, hoping he would turn to look. "Where am I?"

He regarded me with a quizzical expression.

"Bang Phlad."

"Where?"

"Bang Phlad. District of Bangkok. This is Bangkok — very big city in Thailand. Many people," he said, sweeping a hand towards the alley behind him. "You do not know where you are, Ai-dan, Ames' grand-son?"

This was Thailand? This man knew my grandfather but didn't know how he had travelled.

"Thank you."

I stepped back, my stomach twisting with apprehension and quickly secured the door. It was rude of me to do this to a friend of my grandfather, but I needed to calm down and think.

My grandfather travelled the world through a closet. What the hell? I sat down with my back against the door, running my hands through my hair, half expecting to hear knocking from a perplexed old man, but none came. Before me were sheep and fields and rock-strewn hills; over those, a bright sky was giving way to evening. Behind me was a door that looked normal but wasn't, that opened on one side but remained closed on the other. I rubbed my feet, wishing I had worn my running shoes before exploring the study.

I had no idea where I was or how to explain what had happened. I thumped my head on the door behind me in frustration. How could I possibly explain this? I was trapped, without my wallet and identification and roughly fifteen Canadian dollars in my pocket. My cellphone had no service and was running low. I looked at the antique key that opened at least the closet door and this one. Should I start walking down the dirt road outside the enclosures to find some help, or keep opening the door, hoping that one of these things my grandfather called a window would eventually open onto the study?

"Breathe," I said, taking a few long breaths like before a 100-metre sprint. Focus on the stretch of track before me, not the finish line.

Reluctantly, I opened his journal again. There had to be a clue somewhere, and I needed to find it quickly. I had about thirty minutes of daylight remaining before it became difficult to read, and I'd have to use my cellphone flashlight, which would surely deplete the battery. I began searching through the pages again.

Times, places, and events were all meticulously recorded, with no apparent instructions, not even a hint to explain why or how this was possible. My grandfather knew how it worked, yet he had seen no need to leave directions for his unsuspecting grandson. He may have been doing this for years, living this secret life and journeying to the places he had so time-consciously documented.

"Oh," I said aloud, startling a handful of sheep still pondering my intrusion from the gate.

The key to the mystery was in the times in his entries.

A quick search revealed that he always left for London at 3 p.m. He would return to Kingston within a few hours or sometimes a day or two later. On March 3rd, the year before his death, he'd left for London, then later that evening caught the 9:15 p.m. window to Lisbon and then the 10:15 p.m. window home again. Why that particular time, and what time zone was it referring to, and how did he know it would take him back to Turin Street? Still, despite the gazillion questions running through my head, it was clear that every quarter of the hour led to a specific destination, and all I had to do was figure out which one would eventually take me home. I'm not a big fan of puzzles.

My watch said it was 2:18. If the 10:15 p.m. listed in the journal meant I could return to the study, I had a long wait ahead of me. It had been about ten minutes since my conversation with the elderly man in the alley. Had the destination on the other side of the door changed? I got up and inserted the key, turning it. Light flashed, and I felt air ripple past me from behind the door. Suddenly, the knob pulled out from the lock assembly, slipping from my hand and falling to the porch at my feet.

"Damn."

What do I do now? The door was open a sliver, and I could see a different shade of light coming from behind it, but should I open it and look? I decided against it. Whatever combination of things I was doing to make these windows open, now wasn't the time to be taking chances. I could get stranded here. I pushed the door shut and retrieved the knob from where it had landed at my feet. The other half had fallen into the dense grass on the other side. I quickly retrieved that. The porch side knob had the spindle end, so I slid that back through the square aperture in the door's lock, pushing it securely into the outside knob. I searched for the screws that would have connected the two halves, but they were nowhere to be found. Why was this door in such poor repair? The last thing I needed to do was break something. I carefully put the key in, turned it and slowly edged the door open as the obligatory flash of light flared around the opening.

I faced a brightly lit area across from a glassed-in and unoccupied security booth. I could hear rain tapping on a nearby window, but I was reluctant to put my head through the opening and look. However, what I could see didn't feel North American. A sign, which was attached to the window frame of the booth, had bold white print on a dark red background that read 'Sécurité.' There was no English subtitle, so wherever this was, while it might be in Quebec, it was most likely somewhere else. Ah, there was a clock inside the booth. It read 8:15. I scoured the journal. Paris was listed at 2:15.

I let out a subdued cheer. It was 2:22, according to my phone, and France was six hours ahead of Ontario. That meant the times in the journal were in Eastern Standard Time, which made sense if my grandfather's base of operation was out of the closet in Ontario. I gently closed the door, ensuring the two halves of the door knob remained intact. Feeling a slight hope, I rifled through the journal until I found a destination for 2:30 p.m. He had visited New York City at that time on the clock. That would bring me closer to Kingston. I watched the minutes count down along with my phone's battery life.

2:30.

If the journal were accurate, this would get somewhere close to home. I inserted the key and opened the door. There was the flash, a rush of air, the strange mixture of odours, and something I recognized immediately — the Brooklyn Bridge. I could see a portion of it through a dirt-streaked window in the far wall of a shadowy room. The distant landmark was partially hidden behind large brick buildings. I had never been to New York but had seen enough movies to know I might be looking toward the East River and Lower Manhattan. Sun streamed feebly through the panes, playing with the swirling dust disturbed by my intrusion. New York was in the same time zone as Kingston. I was getting closer to home.

"Wait," I said.

I held the door open with my shoulder and read through the full entry on his visit to New York. He had stayed one night, visited someone named Alex, and then caught the 3:30 window to Denver and then the

3:45 home again. I had to make a decision. I looked at the fields, the sheep, and the sun steadily tracking toward the horizon. I was east of Ontario, possibly in the British Isles or the European continent. However, there appeared to be nothing here that could immediately help me, and civilization might be hours away on feet that didn't have shoes. If I walked through the door and became stranded in New York with no passport, I would be closer to home than I was now.

Slipping my cell out of my pocket, I swiped it to record.

"All right, I've found one of these windows that connect to New York City. Yes, *the* New York City."

I flipped it around so the lens captured the view of the Brooklyn Bridge, then turned it back to my face.

"I'm going to step through. Gramps' journal says he took this route a few years ago and got home. Let's hope I don't lose my head."

I swiped the phone off, noticing 19% left on the battery. Taking a deep breath, I exhaled slowly, removed the key, and jumped across the threshold into the empty room. The door slammed shut behind me like every door slammed shut in every slasher movie.

THREE

I was twelve when my parents brought me to spend a summer alone with my grandfather. Quite short and broad like a character from The Hobbit, he smelled of grease and mechanical things and had a laugh that grabbed you in the chest. He always wore a fedora – everywhere. During that summer, our relationship unexpectedly jumped the generational divide, evolving from that of a grandson and grandfather to that of friends. We got along so well that my grandfather, or Gramps as he said I should call him, invited me to spend every summer with him after that, four in all, before he unexpectedly died.

There might have been an age difference of sixty years between us, but that didn't matter. Our shared curiosity for people and learning and exploring always led to conversations with anyone of any age who lived on his street or to rummaging through the nicknacks we'd find at garage sales and second-hand stores, hoping to find anything that would spark a sometimes silly conversation about the object's real or imagined purpose. On rainy days, we would hang out around the table in his tiny kitchen and talk about the books we read or the places we'd seen in the many travel magazines he bought. He had a peculiar fondness for locations near the ocean, though he had never lived on any coast as far as I knew. I would tease him sometimes about how he should have been a sailor instead of an elevator technician, and he'd howl with laughter and then regale me with a fantastical story about blood-thirsty cannibals, chests of cursed pirate's doubloons, and secret tropical island hideouts.

However, he had never mentioned that he travelled the world using the closet in his study. I spun around as the door slammed shut. No gust of wind had been coming from behind me, forcing it to close; it was as if stepping through prompted some kind of reaction. Of course, none of that mattered at the moment.

I whipped out my phone and hit record.

"I'm in New York City. This is crazy!"

Laughing with nervous relief, I panned the phone around the room.

"The room's about the size of my bedroom in Gramps' house and doesn't look like it's been used for a while. There's only this aluminum stool."

I swiped the phone off and crossed to a dirt-streaked window that looked out onto a city in a country I had just illegally entered. I rubbed a patch of the grime away to see better the fenced storage yard beneath me filled with dozens of orderly rows of shipping containers.

How was any of this possible? My grandfather had been an elevator technician for most of his life, and I was pretty sure that the science behind that hadn't advanced to the level of instantaneous transportation. I walked over to the door. It was old and rubbed bare on the leading edge from years of use, but it had one difference from the two that had brought me this far. It had a working deadbolt and a separate lock for the skeleton key.

So far, I have seen five different places through the Windows. Well, six, if I counted the one where the door knob fell out of the lock. I hadn't seen what was behind that door, but there had been something. How had he paid for all this if there were different destinations every quarter-hour? My grandfather had left me the house and a generous amount of money, but it was not enough to finance whatever science made this work.

I approached the entrance, turned the deadbolt and pulled open the door, revealing a walkway that overlooked a dimly lit warehouse. A staircase on my right descended to the murky floor below, which held row upon row of crates and items covered in tarpaulins or wrapped in broad plastic bands. Dozens of dirty windows high above, from which shafts of light pierced into the gloom like low-watt searchlights, encircled the enormous expanse of the building.

As far as I could tell, I was alone.

I propped the door open with the stool and then began to explore, mindful of my lack of shoes. There were several doorways along the length of the walkway, all of them locked. The door closest to the stairs had a large window on the wall next to it through which I could see a normal-looking office. It was Sunday, and the place was shut down, but I did not doubt that it was filled with workers any other day of the week. I found the reference to New York City again in the journal. It took just a moment to figure out that his trip would have been made mid-week and that the owner of the building, or at least any security, must have known that he'd be coming and going.

My cell suddenly chirped with an incoming email. The device had found a carrier. I dug into the system settings and turned the roaming feature off. I didn't want any extra charges. I noticed the time indicated I had close to 50 minutes until the next leg of the journey to Denver and then home, hopefully.

I returned to the room, shut the door, inserted the key, and activated the window. There was that explosion of brilliant light, but this time, a blast of frigid air buffeted me. I was presented with yet another compact space. This one had a window with a broken pane. It looked out on an unpleasant, featureless grey landscape. The floor was partially covered with a fan of snow that had spread from the damaged window. I felt the chilly air assault the room in New York with each new icy blast that swirled out of this forlorn room.

Where was it winter? Antarctica? I closed the door, brushed the snow off my pants, and sat on the stool to wait, rubbing my feet to create some warmth. I wondered if my grandfather had been here and done this too, but I was sure he was smart enough to travel with his shoes. I opened the journal and began reading it again, hoping it might contain a roadmap to whatever he had been doing. Every site listed was completely random, but the times were unwaveringly consistent.

At 3 p.m., I opened the door and saw another plain room shrouded in darkness. A quick flip through the journal indicated that this site was in Kensington, England, where my grandfather would visit a couple named the Sellars. I shut the door and plopped back down on the stool to wait impatiently, my feet tapping a mindless rhythm; time wasn't moving fast enough for me. If 3:30 wasn't Denver, I wasn't sure what I would do next.

There was no way I would call my father in Calgary and explain how I ended up in the US without my passport or shoes.

Finally, my cell's digital clock mercifully tumbled over to 3:30; it was time to go. I put the deadbolt into the locked position to keep things as they were when I'd arrived and then waited another thirty seconds just for insurance. I swiped my phone to record, tucked the journal under an arm, and inserted the key. The brilliant light flashed as it had the other times. I quickly removed the key and walked through. I should have waited, though I doubt it would have made much difference. Denver's elevation is considerably higher than New York's. My eardrums protested painfully as air whipped around me until the door slammed shut.

"This is so unbelievable," I said for the recording while grimacing in pain from the change in air pressure. I panned the phone around the room I was now standing in. "I'm in an apartment in Denver, I think."

If my grandfather's journal was accurate, it was Denver. I flicked the light switch next to the door, bathing the room in a subdued glow from a single light overhead. Someone was still paying the electrical bill.

"Okay, there's a kitchenette, a single bed and what looks like a separate washroom." I angled the phone so the lens captured the two narrow windows near the ceiling. "This is a basement apartment. I wonder if Gramps lived here sometimes?"

It occurred to me that Silverstein's law firm, which had administrated my grandfather's estate until I turned eighteen, might know something about these sites. I'd visit him when I returned.

A warning flashed on my phone – 10% *battery*. I had to wait about ten minutes before the next window, so I powered it down. I might need to call someone for help if this door didn't open to the study. I wasn't sure who that someone would be, certainly not my father. It felt eerie standing in the silence of the apartment, waiting for time to march forward to my hopeful destination, so I rummaged through the cupboards. They held a few pots, dishes, and an electric coffee pot. There were cans of corned beef and a tin of ground coffee. I popped the plastic lid. The coffee had compacted into a rigid mass but smelled surprisingly fresh. A gleam of something metallic caught my eye. I dug my fingers into the dark grounds and pulled out a key. It was a duplicate of the skeleton key in my pocket. I left it in the can and made a mental note to look for spare keys if any other locations listed in the journal had kitchens.

I chuckled. I was already thinking about exploring whatever this was, even though I had no idea what it was.

I became aware of faint sounds above me, voices and music. I crossed over to the door and examined it. The lock setup was the same as the one on the other side of the continent in New York, with a functioning deadbolt and a lock for the skeleton key. I unlocked the deadbolt and opened the door to find a long white hallway with several doors along its length. A sign on my right pointed the way to a laundry facility, and there was a set of stairs off to my left next to an elevator door. Besides the sheep paddock door, my grandfather preferred unassuming or secluded places. It made sense. You wouldn't want to draw attention if you were in a country illegally.

I closed the door and inserted the key – waiting. Surely, ten minutes had passed. I tucked the journal under an arm and turned the key, remembering to plug my nose to help with the drop in elevation, and then pulled on the door.

A blast of light, a rush of wind, and my ears struggled with the changes in elevation between Denver and … but it wasn't home. I was looking at a small furnished office space, but this one had no windows. I swore. Had I opened it too soon? I held the door while I flipped through the pages of the journal to where he'd written about Denver. Yes, he'd gone back to Kingston at 3:45 p.m. Now what? Wait, did I need to close the door and open it again? That seemed to be a pattern: two destinations for each fifteen-minute spot. I pushed the door shut, pulled the key out, inserted it back in, turned the key and yanked the door open as my heart pounded in my chest.

The atmospheric pressure between Denver and Kingston equalized brutally. A cloud of debris from the basement apartment in Denver, thousands of kilometres away from the third floor on Turin Street, swirled through the doorway, a mini dust storm propelled by a blast of pressure-driven air. The body of the sparrow, laying forlornly at the door sill, rocked gently with the onslaught. I gingerly but quickly stepped over it.

I was home.

FOUR

Scroll back two years.

The unexpected legacy of my inheritance began on a stormy night, as all good mysteries must. Rain was lashing against my bedroom window, thrown in unwieldy splashes by one of those mid-summer evening prairie storms that stumble off the Rockies onto the Alberta foothills like an uncoordinated toddler. I had been bored with my science homework, peering through the window's rain-streaked glass, my eyes focused on the muted glow across the street from Morgan's bedroom window. She was also struggling through an end-of-term Earth Sciences project. We could have been doing it together, but we knew better. Being in the same space would have led to laughter and conversation, and very little work would have gotten done.

I texted her.

[how's it going?]

She replied with an animated weeping emoji. I laughed. Then there was the knock.

Its intrusive, abrupt sound startled me. It was my father, of course. He always rapped three quick hits, perfectly spaced, like a metronome. Let. Me. In. I lived in his house, and he could have easily just walked in, but we had come to a detente, with his knock being the non-nuclear option.

I groaned and slid my phone underneath my pillow. He would criticize me for using it while studying. I dropped my eyes in exasperation to the laptop resting in the cradle formed by my crossed legs.

I probably answered harshly; that was our relationship before everything happened.

"What?"

He slowly pushed the door open, stopping halfway to lean into the room as if my unorganized space might be toxic to his organized mind. He had sighed through his nose like he always did when my music was too loud, or too crude, or too whatever.

"What?" I demanded, toning my voice down a notch while slowly raising my eyes to meet his. As much as I disliked his intrusions, I hadn't felt like engaging in one of our heated and circular confrontations.

"Your grandfather died."

He had said those three words in an emotionless voice as if he were commenting on the weather, but his eyes had been red and hollow. He had been crying, not something I had seen since the death of his mother. I did not reply. My mind was stunned, slapped by those cryptic words.

"Aidan?"

"What did you say?" I remember hearing a tiny, disbelieving voice ask.

"My father died last night."

There, he'd said it – *my father*.

Then I saw the anguish in his eyes, or anger maybe, I didn't know which, and I hadn't cared. My grandfather might have been his father, but he had been my friend. I turned away, focusing my numb mind on the wet blackness of the night beyond my window. My birthday was in two days, and my grandfather had told me over the phone that I would have a celebration I'd never forget. He was flying in from Toronto to hand deliver my gift.

There was a moment when I became aware of my father's presence again and glanced at him over my shoulder. His face was dark, waiting for a response. I looked away again, not willing to acknowledge his pain. I hadn't considered this to be rude. I did not wish to share how I felt, especially with him.

"You're not the only one who loved him," he said, his voice finally conveying a hint of the loss he must have been feeling. The door had clicked loudly shut before he had finished speaking.

The next few moments are a fog. I might have keyed in the last couple of paragraphs of my report on the declining habitat of the Pacific tree frog, or was it the decline of coastal habitats because of climate change? I can't recall. I may or may not have shut my laptop, but I remember texting Morgan.

[need 2 c u]

I walked out the front door into the driving rain without my coat to cross the glistening street. Her startled face greeted me after I tapped my fingers on her first-floor bedroom window. Only then, as she let me in the back door and held me, did tears finally come.

My birthday was not a celebration. My father had flown to Ontario to direct the funeral preparations, which was just as well; he always seemed out of place at family events, like he was unsure of the concept of celebration and fun. Mom made a cake – chocolate, I think – and my sister Amelia hugged me longer than she normally would have.

Four days after my birthday, we boarded a plane and flew from Calgary to Toronto. My father met us at the airport, and we drove the 401 to Kingston and then to 27 Turin Street, where my grandfather lived – had lived, I bitterly reminded myself. The house seemed to tremble in his absence as though it knew he would never return.

The funeral was held in a small chapel that grew out of the side of a wood-panelled, squat mortuary. The room's glaring white decor woefully attempted to create a feeling of a happy place. It had fake windows, backlit to appear that the calming light of day offered comfort for the mourners gathered before the shiny coffin. I kept telling myself that my grandfather, or just his body, was in that coffin surrounded by urns choked with gaudy bunches of flowers that seemed too bright and cheery for such a sombre occasion.

I had never been this close to a coffin before, and what was funny, in a macabre sort of way, was that he had joked about them a week before I'd returned home that last summer, calling them "Pine boxes for stiffs whose tickets had been punched."

Now, he had become one of those stiffs in a pine box.

Other than my family, I remember there were about a dozen people at the funeral, none of whom I knew. Before the service started, Amelia and I cautiously approached the open coffin. I was immediately struck by the strangeness of the face of the man who lay in the box. There had to have been a terrible mistake. We had travelled all this way for the funeral of a stranger. I had been sure of it. This man was pale, unsmiling, and wore a suit. My grandfather never wore a suit, just jeans and plaid shirts from the sale rack at whatever shop was selling cheap or used clothing and an old brown, tweed jacket he boasted he'd found lying in a back alley. And where was his fedora? He wouldn't be caught dead without his hat askew on his head. The thought caused me to chuckle.

"What?" Amelia had whispered in my ear. She had been holding tightly to my arm.

"Nothing," I had whispered. I hadn't felt like sharing my dark humour with her.

The service was mercifully short. There was a lofty but terse prayer from a man wearing a minister's collar, followed by an insipid eulogy from my father about the vast prairie skies and how they were like his father's childhood and other nonsense. I ignored him, not letting my eyes leave the coffin. There was another prayer, and suddenly it was over.

Now what, I had wondered? My parents wandered to the back of the chapel, mingling with the few people that had come. Amelia sniffed, blew her nose into a tissue, and mumbled about finding a bathroom as she walked away. I suddenly felt alone and wished Morgan had come. I had texted her earlier, but she hadn't yet responded. I had told my grandfather about Morgan Vogel the first summer I had stayed with him four years earlier. He had listened intently to me, as he always did, as I described this girl who was my age and had striking green eyes and could outrun me – and I was fast. He had teased me, of course, but I could tell he approved of her because I did. In contrast, my father hadn't ever spoken a complete sentence to Morgan, even though she and I had been inseparable since we were about ten.

Amelia had returned then, slipping quietly into the chair beside me, reaching for my hand. I had taken it, appreciating her thoughtfulness as we stared at the coffin.

"That was weird," she had said in a whisper as she leaned into me.

I shrugged a non-reply.

"Dad was arguing with some guy back there."

I shrugged again. That hadn't surprised me; he was always upset about something or angry at somebody, usually me.

Amelia touched my arm and leaned close to my ear.

"That's the guy."

Out of the corner of my eye, I caught a glimpse of a tall man I had never seen before that day. He looked stiff, and his dark suit suggested he was someone important. He nodded to my father, then approached our row of chairs. He shuffled sideways along the row, noisily knocking a few with his long legs. Mumbling an apology, he sat beside me and cleared his throat. I ignored him. He then touched my arm, and I reluctantly acknowledged his presence. I didn't want to talk with anyone, especially people I didn't know. He was bony, thin, balding and smiled in a way that made me uneasy.

He spoke, his voice deep and creepy sounding.

"Hello, Aidan. My name is Arnold Silverstein. I am your grandfather's lawyer."

He offered a slim but thickly veined hand. I eyed his fingers like they were diseased but grasped his hand, shaking it like an adult.

He smiled, trying, I thought, to appear sympathetic.

"I am sorry for your loss. Felix was a good friend."

Felix?

That was when I understood that my grandfather had a name other adults called him by. I remember feeling angry that this stranger would know something about him I hadn't. I wanted him to leave, to go away and argue with my father, but he leaned closer, and I could feel the unwelcome heat of his breath.

"And a damn fine poker player, if I may say so, having lost a small fortune to him."

He had sniffed, clicked his tongue, and looked away as he cleared the emotion from his throat. This man had been my grandfather's friend. I hadn't thought of him as having a friend other than me. I looked at this man's face and wondered what kind of relationship they must have had. Did they go exploring as he and I had? I sniffed at my childish thought. Of course not. Gramps was an adult; they probably did adult things, like play poker and have adult conversations, something I'd never have the chance to do now.

"Aidan," he continued, interrupting my thoughts while letting his pale eyes rest on mine, "tomorrow morning, we, your parents and you and your sister, will meet in my office. It won't be a long meeting. Your grandfather requested that you be present when I read his will."

He leaned forward to see Amelia on the other side of me.

"I can tell you, miss, that he set aside funding for your continuing education, which I understand from your father that you are actively pursuing."

I could feel Amelia nod and heard her whisper yes beside me. I stole a quick sideways glance at her face. She smiled at me and then looked down at her hands resting on her lap.

Silverstein tapped me lightly on the arm, and I turned to him. He smiled slightly then and winked, and a chill crept down my spine like a spider was crawling down my back, but I nodded blankly and turned my attention back to the coffin. If I sat up straight, I could just make out the profile of the man lying there.

"I'll see you there, then," Silverstein said as he rose and fumbled out of the row. I saw my father standing off to the side, a few rows back, his expression rigid. He had been watching and frowned as our eyes met. I turned away.

That evening, after strangers had placed the coffin in a hole in the earth far from the familiar comfort of my grandfather's home, I had curled up in my bed in the room my grandfather had told me would always be mine. In the stillness and safety of that sanctuary, I wept. It might have been hours before I fell asleep; I don't remember, but I do recall accepting that I would never see him again. I suppose it was mature to understand that, but I hated the thought.

The next day, we drove to Silverstein's small, cluttered office. After polite greetings and arranging us in a tight semicircle on a smattering of mismatched chairs before his document-strewn desk, he read the will of Felix Montgomery Ames, my grandfather. It took less than twenty minutes, and though the things he said were a jumble of language and jargon I did not fully understand, I knew the words that tumbled from his thin lips would forever change my life. An all too familiar mood enveloped my father, who, after a moment of fussing with the creases on his pant legs, sniffed that loud, familiar inhale of air that signalled his displeasure. As he exhaled through tight lips, he stood up, shoving his chair back, its feet scratching like nails on a chalkboard, and pushed his way out of the office.

I had just been given a large amount of *his* father's money and the deed to *his* father's house. I was sixteen years old, and my grandfather's house was legally entrusted to me. I should have been happy, but it seemed unfair. I would gladly have traded it for one more summer with my grandfather.

FIVE

Monday, the day after I discovered the impossible function of the closet, I should be at St. Lawrence College for my official orientation day and to pick up my course syllabus and meet instructors. Instead, I spent the morning examining the closet, the closet door, and the door frame. I took the door off its hinges and stood it up against the short end of the desk, with the keyhole side facing me.

"Day two," I said as I recorded with my phone. "There are no electronics, no futuristic-looking controls, and, uh, you know, no magical, occult symbols. (I chuckled) This thing my grandfather calls a Window, uh, there's no logical reason it should do what it does."

Would the portal work with the door off its hinges? I piled up magazines on the desk's rolling chair and wheeled it around so it faced the door and me. I propped my cell up with more magazines and then hit record. I took the key and inserted it into the hole, slowly turning it. I could see the tip of the deadbolt pushing out from its borehole at the edge of the door. Suddenly, a blast of air ruffled my hair. A window appeared centimetres behind the door, partially embedded in this end of the desk.

"Shit!"

Yes, it worked while off its hinges, and the opening, which was wider than the width of the desk, had cut through the solid oak it was made of.

No, the desk looked undamaged; the opening was an incredibly thin slice a few centimetres inside the desk at the same angle as the propped door.

I pulled the key out, but the bizarre juxtaposition of wherever this window had opened and my grandfather's desk remained.

"Damn."

I walked around to the drawer side of the desk, and as I did, the window disappeared. All I could see was the old door propped up against the side of the desk. Thinking the portal had closed, I walked around again, but it was still open. The open window could only be seen from the side I opened it on. Could it be moved?

I grabbed the door and lifted it away, but the window stayed where I had opened it, continuing to be lodged in the desk. I propped the door against the wall next to the closet opening. The portal had opened on a windowless office space lit by light from this side. I grabbed my cell and angled it towards the strange sight.

"This is crazy. The key and the deadbolt definitely make this thing happen, and it seems once the Window's open, it stays open even if the door is removed."

Why was the Window staying open, though? It had shut immediately every time I walked through one yesterday or if I opened and closed the door immediately. Either of those two actions ended the magic. I grabbed a large stack of magazines and threw them through — nothing changed as the magazines splayed out on the floor on the other side with a thump. I walked around to the back of the desk to see if it still disappeared with the door frame gone. The window blipped out of existence from that side but came back into view as I walked back to face it.

"Interesting. The portal is there, but only visible from the side I open it on. That's freaky."

I waited for it to close, eventually pushing the magazines off the chair to sit and watch.

About fifteen minutes later, the window suddenly and quietly vanished. Startled, I jumped up just as the portion of the desk the window had sliced through shuddered and fell over at my feet. The side of the desk looked like a relief cutaway drawing, with two very thin segments of legs still supporting the heavy oak.

"Oh. Oh, that's not good."

I panned the phone along the side of the desk, capturing the cut-open sides of two drawers and the internal wooden structure that held the desk together.

"Wow. That wasn't in Gramp's journal."

I stooped and lifted the slice of desk lying on the floor. It was a wedge, about six centimetres at its thickest, and the cut was flawlessly smooth, with an almost finished look, like it had been sanded with fine-grit sandpaper. I turned the phone back to me.

"O–kay, that was unexpected. Note to self: don't get caught in a closing portal," I paused, thinking through what had just happened, "And, whatever makes this thing work, I think it requires a large mass, like my body, passing through it to make it close, or closing the door without going through seems to make it shut down, too. Otherwise, I guess – " I thought for a moment, " – I guess it stayed open for about fifteen minutes."

I laughed as a thought occurred to me.

"That explains why the times in Gramps' journal are broken up into fifteen-minute segments on the hour. It also explains why the doors I have seen have additional locks. The key doesn't lock or unlock anything; it activates the magical door or, as my grandfather called them, Windows."

Excited about my discovery, I swiped the phone off, reassembled the handle into the door, reattached the door to the frame, and checked to see that the magic still worked.

It did, revealing another windowless and furnished office space not much larger than a living room. I shut the door.

"Okay, I think I'm ready to tell you, Morgan."

I ended the recording and looked at the time. Morgan was in Victoria and probably in a class, but she would want to know about this, and I had the video to prove what would surely sound like delusional ramblings. I was about to quick-dial her when I remembered that I'd seen Victoria listed in my grandfather's journal. I could show her the Window.

I leafed quickly through its worn pages. He had gone to Fifth and Bay Street in Victoria on Tuesday, May 15th, three years ago, at 4 p.m. Then he had returned home by catching the 5:30 Window to Chicago, followed by the 5:45, back to the study in Kingston. Why he was in Chicago for only fifteen minutes was uncertain, but it meant I could go to Victoria and get back home. It also suggested that the 45-minute mark on at least the third and fifth hours on the clock always connected back to Kingston. That was convenient.

At 3:58, I faced the closet holding my grandfather's fedora. I could sense its history in my hand as I brushed the rim with my sleeve. Then, I placed it casually on my head. It fits perfectly. I held my phone in front of me, recording, and turned the key.

I blinked at the burst of light. A furnished apartment materialized in the closet. A single sliver of dazzling sunlight edged through curtains that didn't quite meet, creating a narrow strip of light that flowed across furniture, carpet, and into the study where I was standing. I pocketed the key. It was 1 p.m. in Victoria.

I stepped through and turned quickly to record the door shutting. It was super fast, like an editing glitch in a film. I stopped the recording and replayed at half-speed what had just happened. The image seemed to jump or flicker, and in the span of two frames, the old, white closet door with its creaky old door knob became a dark, wood-grained modern door.

I turned around, reached for the wall beside the door, and flicked the light switch. I was in a furnished living room. A leather couch flanked by two leather chairs faced a low coffee table and the curtained window. A small open kitchen had a microwave and coffeemaker. Seeing the latter reminded me to look for a tin of coffee and a spare key. There were two other doors in the room, both closed.

I crossed to the window and whisked the curtains open. A shower of dust cascaded down. Coughing and brushing my arms, I looked down a narrow street lined with older houses whose front yards boasted colourful flower gardens and dense manicured shrubbery, which my mother would have been envious of. Like serene giants, elm trees towered over the vehicles parked along the street.

I turned around to gaze at the apartment. What was my grandfather doing in Victoria? I wandered over to examine the entrance. Besides the doorknob with a keyhole for the skeleton key, this one had a deadbolt and a security chain, both still in locked positions. I slid the chain out of its slot and unlocked the door. A hallway had numbered doors, two across and one beside me. Brass numbers were tacked to my door - 2B. I was on the second floor of an apartment building.

I closed the door and explored the other two rooms, a bathroom and a bedroom. The bathroom had a soap bar on the edge of the sink that had been left in a pool of water after its last use and had fused to the porcelain. My grandfather had washed his hands with that soap! The bedroom had men's clothing neatly folded in the drawers of a dresser, and an empty suitcase sat in the closet where a light jacket and several shirts and pairs of pants hung.

Returning to the living room, I slid into one of the chairs, calling up Google Maps on my phone to see where I was in relation to Morgan's address. The result indicated I was on Fifth and Bay Street, on the edge of a busy commercial district, and she was about a twenty-minute bus ride away. First, I'd call to let her know I was in Victoria, then find a bus. I left the apartment, went down a flight of stairs to the main lobby, and out through the building's entrance, barely containing my excitement. I heard the door lock automatically behind me and suddenly realized I didn't have a key to get back in. I foolishly hadn't even considered needing one. I had left the door unlocked to the apartment since I didn't have a key for its functioning lock. In desperation, I pulled the skeleton key out, hoping this door might also be keyed to work as a Window. It wasn't, and I ended up dropping it on the ground. As I stooped to retrieve it, the door opened, its pane butting against my head. I stumbled backward, falling and landing on my backside on the sidewalk, the key and the journal landing on the concrete beside me. My grandfather's hat was crumpled down over my eyebrows.

"Oh, sorry! Are you all right?" a voice asked through the discomfort.

I grabbed the key and journal as I struggled to my feet. The fedora had taken most of the blow, but my head still throbbed. I pried my hat loose and looked in the direction of the voice. Three young women stood in the entryway. I vaguely recognized two of them, but the third was Morgan Vogel.

My heart skipped a beat, and I felt my face heat up. Morgan stood before me, her raven black hair dancing slightly across her face in the breeze. She was holding the offending door open and looking at me with confusion and surprise on her face. A teasing smile began to grow across her full lips. She was slightly taller than my five-foot-seven inches, and I quickly recognized she was even more beautiful than the last time I'd seen her in early summer. Her eyes, a dazzling mix of greens and browns framed by black-rimmed glasses, began an all too familiar squint. I suddenly felt unprepared. I hadn't expected to find her this soon, and my mind was racing with a list of possible answers to the questions I knew would follow.

"I'll be okay," I managed to say.

"Well, Aidan Ames. What are you doing here?"

"Um …" I began, but then my mind went blank. I had come to Victoria to show her the mystery of the closet. I was going to show her the recordings I had made. I was about to interrupt her busy and complicated life as a med student with something completely out of this world. Then it struck me, what was she doing in *this* building?

"Having problems working the tongue?" she asked, amused.

"Uh, yeah, no. Umm, I dropped my key. The wrong key," I held the key up. Her eyes fell on it, and she frowned. I babbled on, hoping I didn't sound like an idiot. "Couldn't get in. Left it, the other one, I mean, in the apartment."

The other two women, who I now realized had been friends of Morgan in high school, struggled to keep from laughing.

"Apartment? Are you here? In *this* building?" Morgan asked incredulously, eyeing the key in my hand.

I felt compelled to answer.

"2-B"

"Huh, we're in 1-B," she offered. Then she thrust out her arms, intending to hug me.

"It's so good to see you."

I awkwardly reached out, and we hugged briefly. When she pulled away, I felt the lingering warmth of her familiar embrace.

"Aidan, you remember Kelli Jamison and Brittany D'Angelo from high school? They were a year ahead of us."

She pointed to the muscular blonde woman on her right, whom I remembered from the track and field program, and then to the tall, dark-haired woman on her left, who had been on the long-distance running team.

"Yeah," I said, gripping their hands in turn. "I remember you from track and field, Kelli. Shot put, right?"

She nodded and then turned to Morgan.

"You two were a couple, right?"

I felt my face grow hot.

"Um – "

"We're just friends," Morgan interjected hastily.

She looked away, a slight smile on her face, and I immediately felt an odd feeling of disappointment. We were *just* friends? We had been very good friends and could have been more than that, but time and life had gotten between us. Still, she was the first person I wanted to tell about the Windows.

Kelli rescued the awkward moment.

"You still live in Calgary?"

"Uh, yes, no," I stammered, scrambling to regain my composure. "Uh, I'm in Kingston, mostly."

"So, which is it?" Morgan asked.

"Which is what?"

"Calgary or Kingston, or here?"

Oh shit.

"Uh, yes, as you know, Morgan, I'm going to school out East, um, at St Lawrence College… Kingston, uh," I said, gesturing at Kelli and Brit, "Um, we're just visiting. Uh, 2-B."

"You and your parents? You're all here?" Morgan asked, one eyebrow rising in doubt.

It was more of a statement and less of a question, and she said it slowly like she knew something wasn't right.

"Uh, yeah," I struggled as I tried to sound truthful, "uh, Gramps rented this apartment."

She frowned, her eyes reflecting her disbelief.

"Still?"

I nodded, thinking quickly.

"I mean, his estate still rents it. Uh, Mom and Dad used to come out here occasionally. We're, uh, just here for the weekend. Man, it's amazing to see you. Imagine running into you in *this* building."

"We live here," she said slowly, continuing to frown.

"Oh?"

I was confused. She was staying with her aunt and had been working in a coffee shop in Victoria for most of the summer to help cover the cost of university. She knew that I had her aunt's address in my cellphone contacts.

"So, uh, staying at your aunt's didn't work out?" I asked, desperate to change the subject.

She laughed, and I realized how much I had missed her.

"No. We only just moved on the first of the month. It wasn't working out with Aunt Shirley," she shrugged. "I just needed to be alone. You know, no family."

I understood what she meant.

She threw her arms around the girl's shoulders, and they all laughed.

"And I invited these lovebirds to split the rent with me."

"You're a couple?" I directed to Kelli, eager to divert the conversation from how and why I was in Victoria.

"Since high school," she responded, reaching around Morgan and playfully teasing Kelli's long hair.

I nodded and shrugged, and then Morgan frowned again.

"Hey, where's your mom and dad?"

I groaned silently. Morgan knew something wasn't right, and I was a terrible liar.

"Oh, uh, they went out. Down to the harbour."

Her frown deepened.

"Haven't classes commenced at St Lawrence?"

"Uh."

I felt trapped. I had planned on telling her everything, but her friends were hanging on to every word I said. My big surprise reveal wasn't going to happen as I had imagined. Morgan and I had always shared every sorrow and joy, and my grandfather's Window travels had to be shared with her. But how?

"I was heading off to grab a bite. Do you know any good places?" I asked, turning my body towards the street.

I caught Morgan's look. She knew I was avoiding something.

"Well," she began, glancing at her wristwatch, "the girls were going to drive me to the Uni. I have a class at three."

Kelli nudged her in the arm and smiled at me.

"C'mon, it's your boyfriend. Let's have a quick catch-up. We'll get you there before the class ends."

The sun was warm, and a light breeze filled the air with the distinct scent of the Pacific. Kingston didn't smell like this, and neither did Calgary. The three led me to an odd little place about five minutes from the apartment. The menu was a fusion of Japanese and European cuisine. You could order salmon sushi and German hot potato salad and then follow that with a pot of green tea. We ordered what we could afford from the Sunday Specials.

Morgan was the girl next door, or, more accurately, she was the girl across the street and my best friend for eight years. We had many of the same interests: running, reading, and griping about our parents' withering relationships. You know, the usual teenage angst. We grew into a close, comfortable friendship, and until high school graduation, we spent more time together than either of us spent with our families. We were great friends, and while there was always a hint that it could evolve into a romantic friendship, we flirted relentlessly at times, but it never did, except for that one kiss last May.

There was a final end-of-season track meet in Red Deer, and we had to take a bus to the event and back. While returning after a long and exhausting day, Morgan had fallen asleep on my shoulder with her arm linked to mine. She had done that before on other road trips, but this time, I was keenly aware of the warmth of her body against mine and the steady rhythm of her breathing. It felt wonderful and mature, like we were more than friends, like a couple. Many of our friends had paired off over the last year of high school, and suddenly, it felt like that. When we arrived back at the school, I knew she had been awake for some time but hadn't bothered to move away. Something unexpected and wonderful, I thought, had ignited between us. My mother picked us up from the school for the ride home, and Morgan and I sat shoulder to shoulder in the backseat, talking about our wins at the track meet. When we arrived, she leaned over and kissed me quickly – on the lips. I was surprised and excited all at once.

Then she drew back, and we looked at each other intently, trying to fathom what had just happened. Then we both started laughing.

We never said a thing about the kiss to each other after that, though I think it created a kind of weirdness like we'd gone somewhere in our relationship neither of us had thought through. Then, we were suddenly going our separate ways: Morgan to Victoria in June to work and university in the fall, and me to Kingston in September, about as far apart as possible. She had left within a week of graduation, and I had seen her off at the airport, where we had hugged goodbye and tried to act like this was just a part of adulting and our friendship would carry on like it always had. Two months later, I had hopped a bus to Kingston, and now I was painfully aware that I had pushed my feelings for her to somewhere I didn't have to think about them.

As she talked, my longing for her ached in my chest. I loved how her mind worked and stayed positive even when terrible things happened, like her parents' divorce. She had this quirky way of squinting when she smiled, and she always adjusted her glasses with her pinky finger, and she had a habit of tilting her head as she flicked an errant strand of hair away from her face with a single swipe of her slender fingers. Why had that kiss been so awkward? We could have easily slipped into a romantic relationship. We enjoyed being together, and eight years of friendship had proven that.

"Isn't it odd that we would rent an apartment in the same building as your grandfather?" She asked as the waitress brought us our orders.

I had been wondering about that myself. It was a somewhat implausible coincidence.

"How did you happen to rent it anyway?"

She shrugged.

"It was a cold call from the building manager. I was living with Aunt Shirley, and I could have tried harder to make that work, but, well … out of the blue, this guy calls, saying that the University had given him my name as someone looking for a rental. I guess they do that. It's a pretty good deal for renting in Victoria, and I knew Kelli and Brit were looking for a better place to rent than the hole they were in. I'd say it worked out pretty well in my favour. And I got to see you again."

And then she looked away, smiling.

See me? Again?

Had she just flirted with me? I felt a rush of excitement, like the night of the kiss, but pushed it down, distracting myself by turning to her friends and asking them a few questions.

Kelli was studying criminology, and Brittany was in a pre-architectural undergraduate program. Kelli explained they had worked for a year after high school and moved to Victoria to attend university early in the spring, but their housing situation had become difficult.

"We were sharing an apartment with two other girls, but some people still get knotted up about a couple of lesbians," Brittany said, "even here."

So when Morgan contacted them on social media and invited them to share the apartment, they jumped at the opportunity to move.

"Which," Brittany said while winking at Morgan, "means we have to babysit and keep her out of trouble, you know?"

I could sense Morgan watching me, tapping her fingers lightly on the table. It was unnerving because I knew something was bothering her when she did that. Could she tell I'd been lying? And, hadn't I come here to tell her about the magical closet? Yes, I had, but her friends were with her, and I wasn't prepared to tell them.

"How is your family doing?" she finally asked in a lull in the conversation, her eyes momentarily betraying what she knew about them and the friction that shrouded my parent's marriage like a dark cloud.

I shrugged and answered.

"Mom's okay. Dad, well, you know my father."

She nodded and briefly touched my hand. We didn't have to say anything further. Many a moonlit prairie night had been disturbed by our mutual grumblings over our parents' stormy relationships. Morgan's home hadn't been much more peaceful than mine, but at least her parents had decided to end the misery of the emotional quagmire they had called a marriage.

"Amelia's cool. She just started a shadow position at the Foothills ER. I think she's happy. She's sharing an apartment with another nursing student near the hospital."

Time passed too quickly, and we had stepped back into that safe oasis that friendship creates. It was unexpected, even exhilarating, and could have gone on for much longer, but I looked at my phone.

I had just over five minutes to get to the Window before it cycled to the next site, Chicago. This was not working out as I had hoped. I had come to Victoria to tell my friend about the Windows, but I had run out of time. Besides, it felt weird now. Something had changed between us, and I couldn't quite put my finger on it.

"Uh, sorry, Morgan. I gotta go."

It was as if a fire alarm had gone off.

"What's the rush?" Morgan asked, standing up with me.

She didn't want me to go. I could see it in her eyes. I wanted to stay but couldn't. I didn't dare, not yet.

"Hockey game!" I suddenly burst out, remembering I hadn't seen a television in the apartment. I grimaced apologetically at Morgan as I turned and hustled out of the bistro.

"Hockey? It's just pre-season." I heard Kelli call after me.

I crossed the street and began sprinting back to the apartment building. I wanted to stay but was afraid I might not know how to return to Kingston if Chicago wasn't the way back. Morgan was suspicious of my evasive answer, and to remain in Victoria another day might lead to her wanting to see the apartment, and then I'd have to explain why my parents weren't there or why there wasn't a television so I could watch my lame excuse of a hockey game. She knew I wasn't a fan of televised hockey games. I was already lying to her, and I knew how much she resented liars.

I wasted precious time pressing call buttons on the panel outside the apartment's entrance until someone answered and buzzed me in. That worried me. If my grandfather rented the apartment, it must have keys somewhere.

"Stupid," I muttered angrily as I entered the apartment and slammed the door shut, locking it.

I shouldn't have come. What was I trying to do? We weren't kids anymore; this wasn't show 'n' tell. I had no idea what the hell this Window thing was or how it worked, or even if it was safe. There could be dangerous radiation pulsing into my body every time I walked through a Window.

I looked at my phone. There was little time left, and I wasn't absolutely certain the fifteen minutes between locations were consistent. I inserted the key into the lock and was about to turn it when someone knocked at the door. I jumped, my heart slamming into my ribs.

"Aidan?" A muffled voice came from the other side of the door. It was Morgan.

I clenched my teeth. I didn't want to answer her. If I missed this opportunity, could I get back to Kingston? I could look in the journal; maybe my grandfather had other routes to take him back. Morgan knocked again.

The journal!

She knocked harder.

"Hey, I have the book you were carrying."

I unlocked the door and yanked it open. She was standing in the hall, breathlessly holding one hand to her chest and clasping the journal in the other.

"You forgot this," she said. "Since when do you watch hockey?"

I took the journal. Time was counting down in my head like a swiftly falling executioner's axe.

"Sorry," I said stupidly, then attempted to shut the door.

She caught it with the edge of her hand, holding it open.

"When do you fly out?"

"Today, tomorrow morning, my parents, uh …."

"Which is it?"

"Um, tomorrow. Yeah. Wanna do something later on, after I'm, uh, done here?"

She frowned even deeper, not believing a word I had just said. She knew me, and she knew I wasn't being honest.

"Uh, sure. I should be back from the Uni by seven, but after that, maybe a movie?"

"Okay, sure," I replied a little too quickly.

I didn't know what to say, so I pushed against the door, and she let it close.

"Hey, thank you suddenly not in your vocabulary?"

She was right. I couldn't just leave without thanking her. I edged the door open again.

"Hi."

She stared at me, her eyebrows knit together in suspicion.

"Hi? Are you all right? What's going on?"

"I'm okay, Morgan. Thanks for, uh, returning my book," I stammered in reply as I pushed the door shut again and locked it.

She said something I couldn't make out as I turned the key. This little drama would be difficult to explain if she was still interested in talking to me. I whisked the door open.

Dust swirled around my feet, and I felt a sharp discomfort in my ears this time.

A bare room appeared where Morgan should have been standing. It was small, windowless and dark. The only light source was coming from behind me, in Victoria.

I flicked the apartment light off and quickly walked through into the darkness.

"Damn," I spat as the Window shut behind me. I had wanted to tell her about what was happening to me, but I realized I didn't know what to tell her. I mean, one day, I find the crazy closet and the next, I'm using it to visit her clear across the country. And now, two minutes later, I'm in Chicago? How the hell do I explain this?

It took a moment to locate the wall switch. A naked bulb surged to life overhead, revealing a small empty room with all the necessary plugins and wall sockets for an office. The door had two locks, one for the skeleton key and a push-button lock. One locked the door, and the other let me instantly traverse the planet.

I could hear noises coming from the other side of the door. Pressing my ear against it, I listened for a few minutes, trying to decipher the faint sounds. Movement and conversations were going on, but I couldn't understand anything. Finally, I slowly turned the knob and edged the door open just enough to look. There was a vast, brightly lit, carpeted hallway with groups of people walking back and forth. A few glanced at me, but only with indifferent curiosity as they passed.

However, a football player-sized security guard about three metres across from me did not ignore my sudden appearance. He rose quickly, banging his knees on the underside of the small table he'd been sitting at, tipping a cup of liquid onto a magazine. A small monitor on the edge of the table jigged dangerously. He grimaced in pain and surprise, but his eyes never left mine, not even as brown liquid cascaded off the table onto the expensive-looking carpet. I immediately shut the door, ensuring the button was pushed into the locked position. I was somewhere in Chicago, in a place open for business on a Monday evening, and I had become the centre of this man's attention.

"'ello?"

A muffled voice suddenly spoke from the other side of the door.

I felt a wave of fear as a key was pushed into the lock from the other side. Quickly, I pressed my thumb against the lock button, preventing him from unlocking the door. I slid my key into the keyhole reserved for closet travel.

"Eh," the voice said, "who are you?"

Keeping the button depressed, I pulled my phone from my pocket and thumb-swiped it open. I had another seven minutes before opening the door, not just once, but twice, to get it to open on Kingston. I was sure the guard would have broken the door down by then.

More banging.

"Eh, open the door. Who are you?"

"This is my office," I yelled back. "What do you want?"

"Who are you?"

I didn't reply. For whatever reason, this guy was intent on getting into the room. Why? Surely, if a Window opened into this space, it belonged to my grandfather, or at the very least, he rented it. The guard tried several more times to use his key, but I kept my thumb firmly in place. Then, silence. Had he given up? I kept my phone in my other hand, waiting, watching the clock.

A few seconds after 5:45, I turned the key. There was a flash of light, and my grandfather's study blinked into existence. I walked quickly through the doorway, realizing that I had been holding my breath as the door slammed shut behind me.

What the hell was that about?

SIX

I took the train into Toronto and then a taxi to Bloor Street to meet Arnold Silverstein at his office. Until my eighteenth birthday, he had been the executor of the estate I'd inherited from my grandfather. He was waiting for me as I entered his office. I instantly remembered him from the funeral. He was still slender and bookish, his hands still bony and thin. He ushered me into the same cluttered room where he'd read my grandfather's will three years earlier.

"Please, sit down. I appreciate your call, Mr. Ames. You may be here for other reasons, but first, I have been holding onto something your grandfather left with me the week before his passing."

He cleared his throat and sat across from me as he pushed a small, black metal box across the desk toward me, the size and shape of a necklace case.

"I was not permitted to give this to you unless your grandfather instructed me to or he was no longer living. In which case, it was the latter, and I was to wait for you to contact me or for your nineteenth birthday, whichever came first."

I looked at the box, feeling a sudden wave of emotion. This was yet something else my grandfather had left me. I fumbled with the hasp for a moment and then opened it. It held a polished skeleton key, nesting in a bed of purple velvet. It looked identical to the one I had been using, only newer. I held it up so Silverstein could see it.

"What does it open?" I asked but felt quite sure it was another key to the closet.

Silverstein shrugged.

"I'm sorry. This is the first time I have seen the contents of that container. Perhaps it's for a desk or a cabinet of some sort."

Or, a closet, I thought.

"Why couldn't you have just sent it to me and the other keys when I assumed the estate?"

Silverstein nodded, his forehead wrinkling up like an accordion.

"It was a stipulation attached to his will that I, of course, am bound to comply with. Either way, you would have received the case upon your nineteenth birthday, which, I believe, is fairly soon."

He smiled, and I had a disturbing flashback to the funeral.

I turned my attention to the key; it had a word and a number etched in it – *Closet 2*. I was sure that the house didn't have any other locking closets.

"Thanks," I offered, feeling mystified. "I'll see if it fits something back at the house."

Silverstein nodded slowly, his eyes on mine.

"Now, you have a reason for your visit today, Mr. Ames?"

I nodded.

"Did my grandfather ever talk to you about his house?"

He frowned, his head cocking to one side.

"Do you mean other than as your inheritance?"

I hesitated, noting the curiosity in his eyes.

"Uh, did he mention anything unusual?"

"Unusual? How so?"

Clearly, he was not privy to the bizarre function of the closet.

"Oh, nothing, really. Maybe it's just the age of the place. Plumbing. You know. Strange noises at night."

"Haunted?" He smiled. I shivered, and he laughed nervously and sputtered, "I apologize. That was inappropriate, considering the nature of your grandfather's death."

"The nature of his death?" I echoed, "What do you mean?"

Silverstein's eyes grew large.

"Why, he, uh… you don't know?"

"Know what?"

The lawyer grimaced and fidgeted with a ring on his finger.

"I'm sorry, Aidan. You know your grandfather took his own life, don't you?"

"What?"

He continued to frown, alarm clearly on his face.

"No one told you?"

My mouth felt dry.

"I… no."

He blinked several times, his hands clasping and unclasping.

"I'm sorry, Aidan. I assumed you knew."

"I was told he died of a heart attack."

Silverstein seemed perplexed.

"I do not know why you were told that. Perhaps because of your age at the time, but no, he was found in his study. He had shot himself in the chest with a pistol."

I was stunned. My father had lied to me.

"Odd thing, though," Silverstein continued, "for all the indications of a suicide, there was no note, and the evidence suggested two bullets had been fired from the gun, probably in fairly close succession."

"He shot himself twice?"

He shook his head.

"That's the mystery. One bullet was in his body, and the other was never located."

I felt my chest constricting. Why had I not been told how my grandfather had died?

"I-I'm sorry, Aidan. I'm sorry you had to find this out from me," Silverstein said.

I turned my head away, willing myself not to cry. Besides, I was too angry to cry.

The two-hour train ride back to Kingston was agonizingly long. I wanted to call my father from my cell phone, but I waited until I arrived back at the house, where I could be loud if the conversation escalated with emotion. It was late in the evening in Alberta, and I woke him up.

"What's wrong? Are you okay? Do you need money?" He shot-gunned me with questions.

I pulled the cell away from my mouth, but not far enough so he wouldn't hear my frustrated sigh. He knew I didn't need his money.

"No, Dad. I have a question about Gramps."

Silence. I knew he wouldn't respond, so I continued.

"I met with Arnold Silverstein today, and he told me how he died."

More silence. I waited. He finally spoke, his voice surprisingly soft.

"Aidan… I'm sorry."

"Why didn't you tell me?"

"I, I couldn't."

"Why?"

I could hear him groan.

"Aidan, please."

I didn't care if this was hard for him. I needed to know.

"Why, Dad?"

"You loved him," he said quickly. "I didn't want you… to hurt any more than you already were."

I was surprised. I had thought he had withheld this information as a way of knowing something about his father that I didn't. I hadn't thought my father cared enough for my feelings to want to protect me.

"Why would he kill himself, Dad?"

"I don't know, Aidan. He had the beginning stages of prostate cancer, but many men his age do."

"There was no suicide note?"

"No."

"What about his journal?"

He hesitated.

"Oh, that. What about it?"

"Did you look through it?"

"Of course."

"Well?"

"Aidan, his mind, he was seventy-eight."

His voice sounded awkward, as if he didn't want to offend me. This unexpected compassion for my feelings troubled me even further.

"I understand," I replied slowly. "It is a bit of fiction, isn't it?"

"Aidan?"

"Yeah."

"I'm sorry. I should have told you. I had planned on telling you, but, well, you were suddenly heading off to Kingston and I – "

I was at a loss for words. I could not remember my father apologizing for anything he had said or done in our fractious relationship. Once upon a time, I had adored him, but that seemed so long ago now.

"It's all right, Dad. I get it."

We said our goodbyes. Our relationship felt a little less anemic somehow.

SEVEN

After a morning of stumbling around the St. Lawrence campus to figure out where the three classes I was taking this semester were, I stuffed my coursework into my backpack and caught transit back to Turin Street. Once home, I grabbed some of my grandfather's tools from the garage, a drill, a level, and some screws, and managed to reattach the side of the desk sliced off by the Window. I didn't do a great job, and the drawers were a struggle to open, but the top was somewhat level, and it could still be used.

I downloaded the video clips on my phone from Monday's travels in the closet to my laptop and began splicing them together. The end result was like one of those found footage movies where student filmmakers stumbled across something evil, and death and mayhem ensued. The images were jumpy, and it was clear that I was freaking out. Who wouldn't be?

I felt a growing anger over how I had lied to Morgan. Friends don't do to each other what I had done to her. We had a long history, though, and I hoped that would be enough to repair any damage I had caused. I wanted to invite her into the mystery of the closet, but there was still too much uncertainty. I still had no idea if it was dangerous. It was clear that I walked from one place to the next by stepping over the threshold, but what was happening scientifically? Were my molecules being deconstructed and reconstructed?

I quickly finished the video and saved a shareable copy to my phone. I was feeling angry and frustrated about what to do next. I had two keys now to add to the mystery of what my grandfather had left me. I climbed the creaky stairs to the study and sat at his desk. It was an unusually cool, late-September day, and rain pelted the window in a discordant rhythm of plops and splashes. I yawned; the rain was putting me to sleep. I pulled open the middle drawer and retrieved sheets of lined paper and a pencil. Opening my grandfather's journal, I attempted to plot the dates and times, writing down each time and associated destination. There was no clear pattern other than the times, and the few details he'd written about the places he'd gone often lacked helpful information. Travelling through the closet was normal for him, and he hadn't needed to add minute details for his grandson.

The hours passed, the sun began to dip behind houses along Turin Street, and my frustration grew. I picked at day-old pizza, tapping my pencil on the desk as I tried to visualize some flow to the sites he had listed, but it was like building a house without architectural plans.

I glanced at the key to *Closet Two*, nestled in its case where I'd placed it on the desk, a Rubik's Cube begging to be solved. It had fit the closet lock but wouldn't turn. This key was obviously for another door, but where? I laced my hands behind my head as I leaned back in the chair and swivelled gently back and forth, my mind pondering the room, trying to envision how travelling through the closet would have been a normal experience for my grandfather. If Closet One was in my house, was it fair to assume that Closet Two would also be somewhere in the house? But where? The only lockable closet was in this room.

"Oh," I groaned. "Of course."

A possible answer had been right in front of me the entire time. Only one of the two long walls of the room had a door, but both sides had space behind their walls. I jumped up and crossed to stand in front of the wall without the closet door. No obvious entrance was visible, and the painted baseboards ran the length of the wall without any clear sign of a doorway. There was simply nothing out of the ordinary. I rapped my knuckles against its hardness. The sound was hollow. Of course, it would; there was space behind the wall, with a less-obvious way to get to it, short of ripping off the panelling.

Then I saw what I had failed to consider as anything but ordinary: a single light switch mounted in the centre of one of the panels about halfway along the wall. Why was there a switch on this wall? The switch for the study's single light was over by the door. I tried to flick the switch up, but it didn't budge. It was fake. Then I noticed that the plate was attached by only one screw, with slight circular scratch marks on the dark panelling on either side. I grasped it by its sides and wiggled. It moved. I pushed it, rotating it completely, revealing a brass keyhole flush with the wallboard. The keyhole was old and tarnished and should have been on an equally old door, not attached to a wall panel in my grandfather's study and hidden by a fake light switch. I pulled the key to *Closet One* out of my pocket and slid it into the keyhole, turning it. Nothing happened. I then snatched the *Closet Two* key from its polished box on the desk and slid it in, turning it slowly.

A second later, a flash of light briefly outlined the section of panelling before me. It shuddered, popped towards me about a hands-width, and stopped. Curious, I pulled on its edge. The panel swung effortlessly into the study. My shadow from the light behind me jutted out onto a concrete floor flush with the base of the wall.

I grabbed my cell from the desk and set it to record.

"I found Closet Two. You'll never believe it, Morgan. It was in the study all along."

I turned the lens to capture my face, then paused as I caught my ridiculous grin. What was I doing?

"This is stupid," I said, hitting the pause button.

Who was I kidding? I couldn't bring Morgan into this, and recording moments of discovery as if she were here with me was just, well, lame. If and when I invited her to experience this, it would take more than a bunch of video clips to convince her; it would have to be on her terms. Morgan was like that. She would fully research the pros and cons of a decision before committing to it.

I would record everything for me for now because it was too unbelievable anyway. Sure, I'm alone, and having Morgan with me would have been fantastic, but I enjoy long-distance running, and that's definitely a solitary act. Still, whatever this thing was that my grandfather had been doing, it just felt like it was something you wouldn't do alone. Travelling is an experience better shared. I unpaused the recording.

"Okay, the air is muggy, like in Victoria."

There was an electrical buzzing sound as columns of florescent tubes on the other side flared to life.

"Whoah, lights just came on."

The sudden illumination revealed hand-hewn rock walls, a concrete floor whose edges flowed along the natural contours of those walls, and heavy vertical timbers supporting horizontal ones overhead in an otherwise empty corridor that was wide enough to drive an SUV through.

I cautiously poked my head through, hoping not to trigger the Windows' closure. I had no wish to have my head severed by a closing portal. An oversized, arch-top wooden door was at the far end of the hallway, much further than where the back of the house would be on this side. Large colourful stones were mortared in place up each side of the door frame, meeting at the peak of its radius. Wherever this was, it was like the sites in Closet One – elsewhere.

"This is unlike any place I've seen so far. The hallway is cut out of solid rock, like a tunnel, and the door over there looks like something you'd see in a castle," I said.

I slipped through, turning to watch the door close, but it didn't. I reached through the opening, grabbed a wooden handle on the panel's backside and pulled it shut. This had an astounding effect. The handle disappeared, leaving my hand grasping at the air. The panel was replaced instantly by an arch-top doorway like the one at the end of the hallway. There was an ornate brass keyhole plate and a large porcelain knob, one above the other, in the centre of its rich dark panels. Holding my cell so the camera would catch the effect of the Window, I slipped the key in and turned it. The usual flash of light happened as I pushed the door open, revealing the study. However, this door suddenly disappeared, replaced by the backside of the panel in the study with its plain wooden handle. The key was still in the lock, which was now just the brass keyhole plate. This instantaneous transformation was startling, like a magician's sleight of hand trick. I repeated the process several times until my eyes were stinging.

"So, that's something new," I said for the benefit of the recording. "It appears this door provides access between the study and wherever this is. It doesn't want to cycle shut like the other Windows seem compelled to do."

Leaving the opening ajar, I removed the key, pocketed it, and then walked to the door at the far end of the hallway. I placed my hand against it. It was solid, made of dark hardwood, but it had no keyhole, just a heavy latch on the right. I lifted it and pushed against the door, the hinges squealing unpleasantly. A mist of dust sprinkled over my head and shoulders as I pushed the door wide. I paused, brushing myself while staring aghast at what I'd found.

"My god," I managed to croak, but the immensity of the space swallowed my voice.

I was in a massive hall with towering walls that reached up into the darkness above me. One of those walls, far across from me, was almost entirely made of three columns of arch-topped windows stretching upward to just below the curved ceiling. They gave the impression of being in an old English cathedral. As my eyes adjusted to the dim light, I could see this wasn't a hall but a large cave transformed into a livable space. The dark rock walls curved gently up from a floor of colourful flat stones. Light filtering through the windows was from a deep blue sky, giving the cave a church-like feeling of reverent awe. Two large, slowly spinning fans had been built into the rockwork on either side of the windows, about two-thirds of the way up the front wall of the cave. Sunlight flickered through the fans, illuminating a kaleidoscope of sparkling dust particles in the air.

I took a few steps, slowly turning, to let the phone capture the scale of the place. There was a modern-looking kitchen with an enormous rectangular dining table surrounded by at least a dozen chairs to my right, a grouping of chairs and a television at the centre of the cave, and an imposing fireplace far to my left with its own semi-circle of furniture. About a half-dozen doors of varying sizes were set in the walls throughout. An electrical service box with a row of light switches was mounted on a beam next to the entrance door. I flicked them all up at once, and the shadows fled, bathing the cave in light from dozens of fixtures mounted overhead and a dozen or more accent lights a few metres up around the cave's perimeter.

"Wow. Apartments and storage rooms, those I get, but this? I didn't expect anything like this."

Hanging between the doors were tapestries and swaths of heavy, colourful cloth designed to hide the dark and uninviting rock. The tapestries depicted various scenes, violent battles, stunning gardens, and intricate geometric patterns; many were enormous, four or five metres long.

The centre area of the cave was a jumble of mismatched, overstuffed leather couches and high-backed chairs resting on a mess of rugs, looking like castoffs from a furniture store. Just as ill-matching were small tables and old steamer trunks serving as end tables, providing space for antique oil lanterns, small statues, goblets, and other unrelated items. This brought back memories of the thrift stores I used to explore in Kingston with my grandfather. A squat entertainment centre complete with a flat-screen television faced the furniture. I laughed. He had refused to allow a television in the house, but here was one. I stopped to see if it worked, pressing the "on" button on a remote next to one of the chairs. It flared to life, but I couldn't find any channels. I turned it off, taking note of the rows of DVDs in the cabinet beneath it.

There was way more history here than my grandparents could have had, and this was definitely not the summer cottage of someone who had once made a living repairing elevators. So, where was I?

I approached the windows where a ship's steering wheel and a brass bell were mounted on separate podiums a metre or so out at the centre of their span. The bottom sill of all three columns was at knee height, allowing for a spectacular view of a cove. Gentle waves lapped at a crescent-shaped beach made of light-coloured sand, but my attention was drawn to the remains of an old schooner caught in its crystalline waters a half kilometre out near its narrow mouth. A large section of the bow jutted above the water, and a single mast and spars, tangled in tattered rigging, reached upward like a bony finger pointing futilely to the sky. It was centuries old, ravaged by the elements, and draped in a rotting cloak of sea flora.

I realized I had been holding my breath and drew in a lungful of humid air. Was this the pirate ship of the many swashbuckling tales my grandfather had told to entertain me? I turned to the ship's wheel and gripped one of its smooth handles. The device felt old and rife with forgotten stories but spun freely on its spindle, and the bell sang alarmingly loud as I gave the clapper a slight pull. *Seagull* was hammered into the aged brass surface. My gaze returned to the ancient vessel in the cove, wondering if this was the name of the ship that had tragically come to rest in this watery grave.

On the other side of the windows, a stone walkway wide enough for two or three adults was blocked in by a knee-high stone wall carrying the same signature of skilled stone craft as the wall that held the windows. On either side of the cove, gulls and egrets nested in cliff walls that quickly angled down to merge with lush foliage and a spit of sand that marked the entrance not far from the wreck. The sand bar, formed by years of unforgiving tidal action and rising sea levels, was cluttered with debris and almost pinched the cove shut. Beyond that, white breakers marked where an unseen coral reef shredded the surf, and further still, a vast and empty body of water stretched to the horizon.

An imposing wooden door to the right of the windows gave access to the walkway. Keeping my phone in play to capture everything, I unlocked the door and pushed it open. A blast of warm, humid air and the chorus from the bird population hit me as I crossed to the walkway's stone wall and looked down. I stood atop a wall that sloped about three metres to the beach below. I assumed it was a breakwater in case a storm tide ever surged to the cave. A stone staircase on my right, anchored to the sloping hill that framed one side of the cave's front, provided a way down. I sat on the wall, looking up at the windows and the stretch of cliff face above them. The windows towered above me, like lancets in a medieval cathedral, impressive in size and as solid as the rockwork they were built into. The entire front of this large cave had been closed in with stone, iron, and glass, and it looked like it had been done long before either of my grandparents was born.

I should have explored the cove, maybe looking for some indication of where I was, but I returned to the cave, fortress, or whatever the hell something like this was called, locking the door behind me. I remained still for a moment, looking out the window at the strangeness of the cove, feeling overwhelmed by the implication of this place. The cave was meant to be used and filled with people; it felt that way.

I suddenly noticed a distinct handprint on the glass. Did it belong to my grandfather? I pressed my hand against the pane beside the palm print, ensuring the cellphone captured the moment.

"Shit, Gramps," I said quietly. "Why would you kill yourself?"

A faint whistle of wind emanating from the fireplace pulled me from my thoughts. As I approached, I realized it was the largest fireplace I'd ever seen. The wide chimney crawled upward from the mantel over the firebox, seamlessly incorporating the irregular bumps and divots of the cave until it disappeared through an obviously human-made opening in the arching cave wall. The whistle came from the air being drawn through it, playing its lonely tune and serenading the forlorn lifelessness of the cave like a giant flute. The mantle, made from a single, thick slab of polished marble as long as I was tall, held an array of books and framed pictures, colour and black-and-white images of people I didn't recognize and ones of my grandparents, my parents, and when Amelia and I were younger. I swept the phone along the mantle so it captured all the photos.

"It looks like people have been living here a long time, but how are my grandparents connected to this?"

I turned towards the sitting area facing the fireplace and caught my breath. A shoebox-sized present wrapped in blue paper sat on a low table facing two high-backed leather chairs. A white envelope was attached to the top, and my name was written in large, black letters on it. I stared in disbelief for a moment at the dust-covered gift. Was this the present my grandfather would have brought with him to Calgary if he hadn't – what – killed himself?

I swiped my phone off, wiped the lounger seat closest to the present with my hand, and sank into it, turning the box towards me. It was a strange moment, holding a gift meant for me that had sat here unopened for almost three years. Carefully, I slid the card out of its envelope.

It was of a cartoon pirate brandishing a cutlass, with words in bold red letters that read: "Argh! Birthday salutations, M'hearty!"

I chuckled as tears stung my eyes. I would have turned sixteen then, yet he still enjoyed playing the pirate's line with me.

Inside the card, he had written:

To my grandson,

May we have many more adventures together, especially now that I have told you my secret.

Gramps.

I wept.

How could he have done this to me? He had every reason to live. Brushing tears away, I peeled back the edges of the wrapping paper and slid the box out. It was a shoebox, but it didn't contain shoes. Inside were three business envelopes marked with the numbers One, Two, and Three. Beneath these were a leather, zippered booklet and a thin wallet that held two credit cards, both black and with my name on them. The envelope marked with the number One had lettering across the top with the words *Universal Holdings, Zurich, Switzerland* embossed in gold. The other two envelopes had my name on them, written in my grandfather's sprawling handwriting. I laid the items on the table, spacing them apart in the order I had removed them from the box and stared at them. My heart was pounding in my chest.

The Universal Holdings envelope contained a quarterly financial statement for the *Enniskillen Group*. The dates were from around my grandfather's death, and the pages detailed income totalling just over 455 million U.S. dollars. The zippered booklet was surprisingly heavy. It contained a dozen or more plastic pages with six pouches on each side of each page, each pouch holding a modern-looking key and an accompanying business-sized card describing the name and location of the buildings the keys were for. The last two pages held safety deposit box keys for several financial institutions. These also had pull-out cards with the institution's names, addresses and security information to access the boxes.

I opened the second numbered envelope. It held copies of documents I remembered my grandfather had me sign the final summer I had visited him. He had been a little vague about what they were for then, but he had assured me they were for a trust fund or something like that and would be important to me one day. I should have asked what they were at the time, but, well, he was my grandfather, and I trusted him. It also had a sheet with a long list of charities and institutions that had received grants from the Enniskillen Group.

The third numbered envelope contained a handwritten letter to me.

Happy Birthday, Kiddo!

Welcome to Enniskillen!

You have a million questions, and I'll answer them over time. First off, we're on an island in the South Pacific, east of Papua New Guinea. According to local lore, the Polynesians abandoned the island several hundred years ago. They referred to it as el Ojo del Diablo. The Eye of the Devil. That might have been because of the bright effect that occurs when a Window is opened. It's been a tradition to call them Windows because that's how they appeared to William McPhie and his crew mates — as a window opening into other places. They were shipwrecked on this island in the seventeen hundreds. The cave used to be littered with pieces of dark rock, which spectral analysis suggests came from a meteorite. It reacts with the volcanic iron already present here, causing the Windows. We'll talk more about this later.

The locks and keys are made from these two different sources. William was a rather unsavoury character who used the unique abilities of the Windows to rob people. He and his descendants built Enniskillen and the company you now own. Don't worry, you are not the heir to a gang of thieves. His descendants, Marianne and her son Ian, made the Enniskillen Group respectable, and it shall remain that way.

All of this is yours now. You may remember that I had you sign a pile of documents when you came this summer. It must have been close to a dozen or more signatures, but you were very patient. Well, those weren't just for savings accounts or your trust fund, as I told you. Today you have complete control of the properties and investments of the Enniskillen Group. The last of the McPhie line, Ian McPhie, gave all of this to your grandmother and me, and now I have given it to you.

The Key Wallet holds the keys to the locks of all the properties the Windows are currently installed in. You and I will visit each site, and it'll be the most fantastic adventure we've ever had. I use an international financial company, Universal Holdings, to manage the hundreds of properties that the Group owns. Next week, we'll visit Reinhold Bonk, the company's president. I've worked with him for a few decades, and he's eager to meet you. He does not know about the Windows, and it should remain that way. He'll bring us up to date on how things are faring, and together, we'll manage your holdings and investments.

I won't be around forever, Kiddo, so I want you to have all this now so I can teach you how to protect the greatest secret in the world.

I love you, Kiddo.

Gramps.

I slowly reread the letter, letting his voice fill my mind as if he were sitting across from me, telling me all this in person. This was my friend, my grandfather, talking, and these were his last words to me, and they didn't sound like the words of someone intent on ending their life.

A voice suddenly called out, making my skin crawl with the unexpected intrusion.

"Aidan, you, uh, you in here? Wherever the hell this is."

"Shit."

I hadn't closed the door between the house and the island. The voice belonged to Dane, and I had completely forgotten that he and his twin brother were arriving in Kingston today. Before leaving Calgary, I gave them a house key, as I wasn't sure if I would be at the house or in class the day they arrived. I quickly shoved everything back into the shoebox and stood up.

Dane, a large aluminum travel mug dwarfed by his equally large hand, was standing on this side of the entryway, his mouth agape as he looked towards the enormous wall of windows and then at me. Dane's a big guy with thick, round arms and a solid chest that had developed over the years while working alongside his parents on their ranch. He looked oddly small as he stood in the doorway.

"Over here," I called, barely able to control the anger I felt at his unwanted intrusion. He was suddenly in my new world. I hadn't let Morgan in on my secret, and now Dane had walked right into it uninvited.

"I don't think we're in Ontario anymore," he said slowly as he approached, his eyes taking in the expanse of what my grandfather had called Enniskillen.

"I'm sorry," I said as even-tempered as possible. "I forgot you guys were arriving today."

Dane nodded slowly and took a swig from his mug as he playfully slugged me in the arm.

"Uh, yeah, arrive in Kingston, not wherever this is."

He gestured back toward the entrance door.

"You knew about this place?"

"No. I just found it today."

He turned to look at the fireplace, his eyes following the chimney up into the cave's ceiling.

"It's not possible for this to be in your house."

I gripped the shoebox tighter. He shouldn't be here.

"You seem awfully calm about this," I said, perhaps with too much edginess.

He turned to me, his eyes narrowing slightly at the not-so-well-disguised tightness in my voice.

"Well, I don't think I'm hallucinating. Where is this place?"

"We're in the Solomon Islands on an island called Enniskillen."

He nodded slowly.

"Right. The South Pacific. Ennis-what?"

"Enniskillen. It's Irish, I think," I explained as I caught sight of Bill poking his head from around the door. His eyes were wide. I felt my jaw clenching. They shouldn't be here, in this sacred place, but I couldn't just toss them out and expect them to forget what they'd just seen.

"My god, how the hell is this possible?" Bill's voice echoed as he pushed through the door, his head twisting this way and that. "Where is this place?"

"The Solomon Islands!" Dane called over his shoulder, his eyes not leaving my face.

Bill blinked several times, his eyebrows reaching up for his thatch of dark hair as he turned to look back through the door he'd just walked through. He placed his hands on his head and turned to me, his mouth wide open.

"How the hell is this possible?"

"I don't understand," Dane said as he walked toward the towering windows. "How are we in the Solomon Islands by just walking through that wall panel back there? Is that a pirate ship?"

Bill quickly skirted around the centre grouping of furniture to where I was, stopping to tap me on one of my arms, his excited face turning from me to his brother. He's as physically impressive as Dane but slightly taller, somewhere over six feet, so I'm always looking up at them. Even that simple fact of our genetics was making me angry.

"How is this possible?" he asked again, barely containing his excitement.

"Uh," I started, feeling perturbed. They shouldn't be here.

Not waiting for a reply, he followed after his brother, who had stopped before the windows, gazing up at their impressive height.

"Those are crazy tall windows. It's like I'm in a church. Is this a church?"

I reluctantly followed until we all stood before them, the cove's glistening waters before us. They both turned to me, their faces expectant. I sighed, willing the anger to leave like I'd done when my father and I were heading to a verbal collision. It wasn't their fault I had given them a key, and that they'd found the panel I'd left open.

"Gramps left all this to me. He wrote a letter explaining everything," I finally said. "The opening in the study is a portal that comes here, to this island. It has something to do with pieces of a meteorite found in this cave a few hundred years ago by the sailors on that ship," I gestured to the *Seagull,* "and with a guy called William McPhie. He and his descendants used the meteorite material to make these things they called Windows."

"Windows?" Bill echoed, gesturing to the windows before us. "These?"

"No," I said, "the one you walked through back there in the study is one of these Windows. They're like holes in the air, and I guess when the sailors first saw them, it was like looking through a window. Any Windows I've gone through have been in a physical door, like the one back there that brought you here. I found that one just before you guys showed up. The closet door in the study goes to other places, but not here."

Bill gasped.

"The closet door does this, too?"

"Not to this island, but it does go to other places all over the world. I was in Victoria a few days ago and Chicago. I think they might be dangerous, though. A sparrow's head was cut off as the Window closed."

"What?" Bill exclaimed.

I told them about the paddock and the unfortunate bird that had flown into the study and then tried to escape as the Window collapsed and then about the end of Gramps' desk getting sliced through.

"But you're okay," Bill said, quickly looking me over.

I nodded.

"Aidan," Dane said, raising his hands, "how is any of this even a possibility?"

I smiled reluctantly. It wasn't possible, yet it was. I had lived the impossible since my first step through the closet door. So, I told them everything from the beginning. The words tumbled out of my mouth, and though I felt angry at being forced to tell them, it felt surprisingly good. I wasn't alone anymore. When I finished talking, Dane was frowning at me.

"I'm sorry, we shouldn't be here," he said. "I'm sorry we just walked in."

I shrugged, turning my face to the cove.

"It's okay."

Dane is the more empathetic of the brothers, and I could tell he didn't believe me.

"Would you like us to leave?"

I shook my head as I fought back tears. The brothers had been good friends, my only close friends, except for Morgan. We could figure this out together, and I would eventually tell Morgan – if she was still talking to me.

"It is okay, honestly," I said, feeling somewhat truthful.

Dane nodded slowly as his gaze settled on the shoebox in my hand.

"Uh, what's that?"

I lifted it, placing a hand over the lid, feeling the weight of its revelation.

"A gift for my sixteenth birthday," I said quietly. "From my grandfather."

Bill touched my shoulder.

"Should we go back to, uh, Canada?"

I didn't know what to say. I looked at the two of them, their eyes on me, and took a deep breath.

"I'm okay. I'm actually glad you guys are here. I don't know what my grandfather left me or what or how any of this could possibly work. It's all a little crazy."

Dane guffawed.

"I bet."

"I'm also a millionaire," I said.

"What?" The brothers gasped in unison.

I lifted the lid of the box.

"Gramps planned to bring me here on my sixteenth birthday and tell me about the Windows. I own this island and have hundreds of millions of dollars in bank accounts. And, then, there's these."

I slipped the lid under the box and held up the credit card wallet.

"This one has credit cards." I passed it to Bill and handed the larger Key Wallet to Dane. "This one has keys to dozens of buildings."

Dane leafed through the Key Wallet.

"These are from all over the world, Aidan."

"I know," I said. "I guess I own them all."

Dane handed it back as Bill suddenly exclaimed.

"Your name is on these cards."

I nodded as he returned the wallet.

"I met with my grandfather's lawyer. He told me he didn't die of a heart attack. He says my grandfather killed himself."

"What?" Dane's mouth dropped. "But that's not what your dad told you."

"No, it isn't. I asked him about it, and he said he didn't want to tell me the truth. He didn't want to hurt me."

"You've talked to your dad?" Dane asked. "Did you tell him about these, uh, Windows?"

"No, I haven't told him anything. I called him after talking to the lawyer."

Bill gestured to the vastness of the space around us.

"I don't know how you could tell anyone about this. I mean, this eliminates air travel, hell, any kind of motorized travel."

"I guess," I said. I actually hadn't thought what the implications were yet.

"You say you were in Chicago?"

I nodded.

"Yeah, and Denver. Not for long in either place, though."

"Why? Do these Windows force you to leave?" Bill asked.

I laughed.

"No, I just don't know how to use them yet. My grandfather's journal has times and dates for places in dozens of countries, but it's just vague notes, so I was flying blind."

Dane shook his head and turned his eyes to the cove.

"Wow, Aidan. You can bypass sovereign borders. This is all, uh, really illegal."

"What? I didn't make these Windows." I replied, feeling the anger at their intrusion frothing up again.

He flinched, and I realized he was only thinking practically. That was one of his greatest strengths.

"I'm sorry," I said quickly. "I hadn't thought of that."

Dane nodded.

"Of course, I'm sorry, too."

And then he said what I had been thinking.

"But this doesn't make sense. Why would your grandfather kill himself if he had this planned for you?"

"I know," I replied as I looked out the window, "it makes no sense."

"Hey, look." Bill was holding his cell phone. "There's reception."

Dane pulled his cell out of a pocket and looked at its screen.

"You're right. There is, and it's not password protected. My phone automatically connected to it."

I pulled my phone out and saw the reception bars on the screen. I swiped through to where I could see cell providers and saw the name ENNIS. Was that for Enniskillen? I hadn't thought to look for cell service when I first arrived; it just didn't seem like a place that would have any. Were there people living on the island?

Dane slipped his phone back into his pocket and pointed to the door leading to the walkway.

"I guess that goes outside?"

Glad for the diversion, I gestured to the door.

"It does. Why don't you guys go find out what's out there? I want to read my grandfather's letter again."

Bill didn't need any prodding, but Dane frowned thoughtfully and looked at me.

"Are you sure you're okay?"

I smiled reassuringly, but I could feel the tears begging for release.

"I'm good," I answered, hoping it was true. "It's all, just," I shrugged, "a lot crazy."

"Yeah," Dane said as he turned to follow Bill, "no shit."

"Hey!" I called after them. "Don't get eaten!"

They laughed as they pushed out onto the walkway, closing the heavy door behind them. I walked over to the muddle of furniture in the middle of the cave and pushed and pulled one of the heavy wingback chairs so it sat beside the ship's bell. It just seemed like it should be there. I wiped the chair off with my hand and sat, placing the shoebox on my lap.

Bill was right; my grandfather's suicide didn't make sense.

EIGHT

I slipped my earbuds on and set the music app on my phone to shuffle, playing a mix of classic R&B while slowly rereading the letter. How had something so out-of-this-world been kept a secret for so long? What the Windows did was the stuff of science fiction. What if one of them suddenly broke down, stranding me somewhere? How was I supposed to take care of whatever this was? There were too many questions and too few answers.

I slid the letter back into the shoe box and placed the lid on it. I knew very little about managing a single property, which was one reason the brothers were the ideal choice for roommates for the house on Turin Street. They knew how to fix stuff. But what about the scores of locations worldwide? Who was doing the upkeep on those? Reinhold Bonk's name and his phone number in Zurich were prominent on some of the papers, I would have to contact him.

I closed my eyes and leaned back into the chair, letting my mind wander to the last summer I'd spent with my grandfather. He'd been oddly mysterious those four weeks, spending hours in his study, which, now that I knew what was in it, probably meant he hadn't even been in the room, or on the Continent for that matter. He had been elsewhere on the planet, travelling while I read a book or played a video game. What was I supposed to do now?

A hand suddenly touched my shoulder, startling me. I jerked upright and pulled the buds out of my ears. I had fallen asleep. Bill was leaning over me, a huge smile on his face.

I yawned.

"Geez. I didn't hear you come back in."

He laughed as he turned and walked away, gesturing for me to follow.

"Oh, sorry. You've been out for about three-quarters of an hour. You've gotta see what we've found."

He headed to the back of the cave. I placed the shoebox on the chair and followed him. Dane was already at the back wall, his hand on the edge of a door to the right of the entryway.

"There's a room behind here, too," he said.

"What do you mean?" I asked.

"Well," Bill stopped by the grouping of chairs and pointed in a sweeping motion, "you see all these doors. There are rooms behind them; they're like adjoining caverns that have been turned into functional spaces."

He pointed to the right of the fireplace to a set of double doors.

"There's a sign on one of the doors, if you can believe it, that says West Wing. It leads to a group of bedrooms."

"Over there," he pointed to a door at the back of the kitchen area, "there's a bathroom behind that one, though it's pretty basic, just a compost toilet, a hand washing station and an industrial first aid kit, like back home on the ranch."

"Over here," Dane waved to us. He was holding a door open to the right of the one he'd just been looking through.

"It looks like a meeting room."

He disappeared through the door, and Bill and I followed. Behind it was a wide passageway through the solid rock, connecting to a rectangular-shaped chamber. Like the main cave, its walls held several beautiful tapestries of varying widths and lengths. They were hung along with assorted track lighting from a mesh of heavy beams anchored into the rock at least two metres overhead. At the centre of the room was a long table, its exquisitely carved legs matching the handful of antique, leather-covered chairs surrounding it. The table centre was adorned with several large leather-bound books of varying size and thickness sandwiched between two tarnished brass sextants. However, as impressive as the table and its centrepiece were, the object on the room's back wall caught my breath. A large disc rested in a natural indentation between two tapestries, brilliantly illuminated by several lights from the lattice of beams above.

The disc was made of thick dark wood, about a metre and a half in diameter. A circle of heavy, yellowed paper was fitted to it with the words *The Windows*, written in block lettering above it. We were looking at a diagram of a circle within a circle, each drawn to resemble the dial of a clock face. Spokes radiated out from the centre through both circles to the edge of the diagram, marking each hour, three-quarters, half-hour, and quarter-hour. Each 15-minute segment created a pie-shaped wedge in each circle and contained handwritten names of places.

"What is this?" Bill asked.

"I think it's a map of sorts," I said as I skirted around the table. "It's in my grandfather's handwriting. He must have drawn this." I swallowed hard. Here was further evidence of the time he had spent on the island. "Look, here on the outer circle is the apartment in Victoria, where I was on Monday, and there's Chicago at the 5:30 mark."

"Wow," Dane said from behind me. "They're all written in capital letters."

"Yeah, his handwriting was terrible," I said, recalling the little instructional sticky notes he sometimes left me when I thought he'd been in his study. They were notes I usually couldn't decipher.

"These are places where the Windows are located?" Dane asked as he leaned around me.

I shrugged.

"I guess. Look," I tapped the disc in several places, "every quarter hour on the inner circle and every three quarter on the outer circle have Turin Street written on them."

"It's a chronological map, with the segments corresponding to specific destinations and times," Bill mumbled as he slipped his cell phone from his pocket.

"Do you mind if I take pics?" he asked.

"No, go ahead."

As Bill began taking photos, Dane pushed a chair aside and sat on the table's edge, resting an arm on the back of a chair.

"So, does this mean there are two destinations for each time on the map?" he asked.

"I think so," I answered.

This confirmed what I had experienced that first accidental trip through the closet.

"Look at this," I said, "at four o'clock on the outer circle, I can go to Victoria and then return to Turin Street anytime after that on the next quarter past the hour. I didn't know that. Because of what I'd read in my grandfather's journal, I thought I had to go to Chicago at 5:30 on the outer circle and then return to Kingston at 5:45. If I'd known that, I could have avoided that security guard in Chicago."

"Security guard?" Dane asked.

I told them about the odd behaviour of the guard in Chicago.

"He kept asking who you were?"

I nodded.

"Through the door. I didn't let him in. I told him it was my office space."

"You have an office in Chicago?" Dane asked, laughing.

I shrugged.

"I guess so."

I turned back to the map. The confusing notations in my grandfather's journal made sense now. Both circles represented a twelve-hour clock, giving me two opportunities for each destination within a normal twenty-four-hour day. I could go to Victoria at 4 a.m. or 4 p.m. My earlier assumption had been correct; the journal and this chronological map, as Bill had called it, were definitely in Eastern Standard Time. Other than the constant of time moving forward, the placement of destinations was completely random, as if names had been pulled out of a hat and then written down.

Many were places I'd never heard of, and the ones I did recognize seemed to be located near water. A few had been marked with cryptic warnings such as *Do Not Use!* or *Danger!* One stated *Underwater*.

"There's a lot of places on this map," Bill said as he scrolled through the images he had taken.

He was right. I quickly did the math. Not including the two times per hour I could return to Turin Street and the three listed as places I should not visit, there were sixty-nine destinations, not counting the island, which seemed to exist outside the map. Whatever the Windows were, they represented far more destinations than I had seen so far.

Dane slid off the table's edge and gestured toward the room's entrance.

"You won't believe what else we've found."

NINE

To the left of the fireplace was another set of double doors. Dane, grinning as if he'd just found a chest of gold doubloons, turned both handles and pulled them wide open. The passageway behind was large enough to drive a small car through, and the cavern it connected to was significantly larger than the Map Room; that's what I decided I would call it unless my grandfather had given it another name.

The scent of machine oil and battery acid rested heavily in the air. Along the length of most of the wall to our left was a sturdy, tool-laden workbench and several wooden shelves filled with lumber and what I supposed were the things required for maintaining an island fortress. On the bench were drill presses, vices, grinders, and all manner of wood and metalworking machinery, along with stacks of dark wooden drawers. The bench and its collection of tools had the same feeling as my grandfather's garage, where anything and everything could be fixed, reused, or repurposed.

Bill walked over and pointed at the closest stack of drawers.

"Look at this," he said, pulling out a drawer on the bottom row.

A paper label in a brass frame had the words *Enniskillen Keys* written on it. A half dozen keys were lying in it. They were identical to the one Silverstein gave me, all stamped with *Closet Two*. I pushed the drawer shut and turned around, letting my gaze take in the history of this room. This island had been lived on for a long time.

"What are those?" I asked, pointing to rows of large car batteries sitting on wooden pallets.

"That's the 12-volt power setup," Bill said excitedly as he crossed over to a sturdy metal rack holding modular electrical panels marked with *Battery, Wind,* and *Solar.* "No gas here; it's all renewable."

"And, take a look at that," Dane said excitedly, tipping his chin towards the cavern's shadowy back wall.

I followed his gaze and immediately burst out laughing. A modern elevator with an accordion-style door was shrouded in shadows at the back of the room. It seemed out of place in contrast to the feeling of a long and old past around us, but it was a clear indication of my grandfather's influence on that history.

"It's probably the newest thing here," he said as we walked towards it.

"Wow," I responded with genuine awe. "It makes sense, though. Elevators were my grandfather's business."

Its concrete support structure rose straight up the wall, hugging it until it pierced through the rock ceiling above us. It must have been no small feat of engineering for my grandfather to install it.

I slid the door open, stepped into the cage, and looked up through its open top. I could see cables and metal tracks alongside the walls and the bottom of counterweights catching the light from whatever room was above us. The brothers followed me in, and Dane slid the accordion door shut.

"Mind if I press the button?" he asked.

There were two lighted buttons on a metal box on the steel frame beside the door, one with an up arrow and the other with a down arrow.

"Is it safe?" I asked.

"We rode it down," Dane said, grinning.

"Down from where?"

He continued to grin, his head bobbing with excitement.

"You'll see. There's a switchback staircase carved out of the rock on the far side of the front of the cave, to the right of those windows, that leads up to a plateau."

He chuckled as he pressed the up button, and the lights dimmed momentarily as an unseen motor, somewhere above us, whirred to life, pulling from the stored electricity in the batteries. The elevator began to rise smoothly upward, causing dust to shower over us as we crept toward the light.

"I don't think it's been used much for a while," he said, brushing dust from his shoulders.

I nodded briefly as counterweights passed silently by on one side. I didn't want to seem ungrateful, but my grandfather should have been the one who was showing me the secrets of Enniskillen. I kept my emotions to myself, looking up at the rapidly approaching flare of light above us. A few seconds later, the elevator lurched to a stop, emerging at the back of a substantial garage. Sunshine poured in through two open doors, causing me to squint. Dane pushed the cage door open, and we stepped out. The air was muggy and hot, and I immediately began to feel perspiration forming across my forehead and in my armpits.

"Wild, eh?" Bill yelped as he approached one of two white electric golf carts parked just before the elevator. Each had faded striped canopies that looked like they'd seen better days. A large aluminum boat secured to a trailer perched next to these against the garage's wall. A sleek outboard motor was mounted in a cradle on the edge of a well-organized workbench beneath a window in the garage's opposite wall.

"We were pretty happy to find there was an elevator," Bill said. "That was a brutal climb up the staircase from down the beach."

I chuckled.

"I bet. My grandmother probably insisted on it."

"Did I ever meet her?" Dane asked.

"I don't think so. Once they moved to Kingston, they only returned for short visits, and then my grandmother was gone."

Dane nodded in reply, then gestured to a ladder anchored to one side of the elevator's thick concrete walls.

"You'll like this."

Dane began climbing, and I followed until we passed through the plywood ceiling and emerged in a small room, the walls completely covered with dark curtains. I could tell from the glow along their bottoms that they were covering windows. Even with most of the tropical sunshine blocked, the air was stifling, and we quickly pulled them aside and unlatched the storm windows behind, pushing them all outward, their hinges catching and locking in place. Two blue Adirondack chairs with a small three-legged table between them allowed for a comfortable viewing of the stunning scenery. A coffee mug sat on the edge of the small table, a solitary reminder of the man who had sat here, relaxing as he gazed out upon this world – his world – his paradise. A set of old binoculars hung by a leather strap from a peg on one of the window frames triggered a thought that made me smile. My grandfather had given me a pair for my thirteenth birthday.

It was surreal gazing out at this place that had obviously been a second home to my grandparents. The lookout was the highest point on the island, sitting on the edge of a gently sloping plateau, the erosion-filled bowl of what was left of a long-extinct volcano. It had formed this island out of the depths of the South Seas. From here, I could see that the island was roughly crescent-shaped, about five or six kilometres long and about two-thirds that in width, a tropical oasis surrounded by an ocean painted from an artist's palette of blues and greens.

From our vantage point, we could see where the sandbar at the mouth of the sheltered lagoon separated it from the vast open ocean. To our right were the slowly spinning tines of a wind generator perched atop a steel tower with a couple of dozen solar panels mounted on a wooden structure at its feet. To the left of the solar array, the cave's chimney loomed like a great stone monolith, rising high above the grass-covered ground. Near this, a large satellite dish and a cell tower with two flat antennas facing opposite directions explained the cell reception we'd noticed.

"The dish must link to a satellite, and those are the transmitters," Dane pointed out.

I wondered how often my grandfather had called me from the island, maybe even from this room, as he watched a South Seas sunset.

The island's north was mostly dense jungle, interrupted here and there by little clearings and bald, wind-swept rocky hillocks. One of those clearings was a small graveyard with a scattering of crosses and monuments.

"There's probably about forty or fifty graves over there that I can see," Dane said as he adjusted the binoculars, focusing on the graveyard. "People have been living here for some time."

"Huh," I responded, feeling perturbed that he had thought using my grandfather's binoculars was okay.

The dirt road leading from the front of the garage swept around the building to follow the natural southern outflow from the bowl of the plateau. It was almost immediately concealed beneath a sea of towering trees and foliage that undulated gently in the warm breeze. Several atolls off in the distance to the south and east were like velvety green outcrops in a turquoise sea. Other than these, the island stood starkly alone.

"Quite the view, eh?" Bill said as he joined us.

I nodded in reply, a sudden wave of weariness sweeping over me. I felt cheated and robbed of what should have been the greatest day of my life, my grandfather introducing me to my inheritance. It was so unfair.

"I'm tired," I said to no one in particular.

Dane touched my shoulder.

"We can go back to Kingston. This has been quite the … uh … I don't know what the hell to call this day."

"Bizarre?" Bill chimed in. "I mean, we flew out of Calgary this morning."

I glanced at their faces, seeing their excitement for the new reality that had been thrust upon them. It hadn't been fair for them either.

"Thanks. Right now, I want to go home and shower. It's really hot here."

It would have been an unbelievable sixteenth birthday.

TEN

I barely slept. It felt like my life was rushing madly off in a direction I had no control over. In less than one week, I had gone from moving to Kingston to attend college to discover a centuries-old secret that the McPhies and my grandfather had kept from the world. I finally rolled out of bed around seven. The brothers were already up, mining through bowls of cold cereal and drinking coffee. It was Friday, and we had classes at St. Lawrence: orientation for the brothers and two classes for me. I couldn't quite remember which ones.

College? How could I focus on whatever I had planned for my future with a South Sea island a step away from Turin Street? I knew my parents would not be pleased if they learned I was skipping classes. Did it matter? I hadn't asked either of them for help coming to Ontario. Moving had come about through my efforts, from working after-school jobs and stashing away most of the monthly trust fund money from what I thought had been the bulk of my grandfather's estate. How could I possibly learn how to protect the secret of the Windows and Enniskillen and still attend college?

I took a cautious sip of the strong coffee one of the brothers had made as I sat with them to eat. I was split over how I really felt about them knowing my secret. On one hand, it would have been difficult to keep it from them, especially if I started disappearing for days, exploring the sites listed on the diagram in the Map Room. On the other hand, they had grown up on a ranch and knew practical things about maintenance and machinery. I would have to spend hours scouring the Internet to find answers to my questions and even more hours putting them into practice. I chuckled at the thought of me repairing the elevator if it broke down.

"What's funny?" Bill asked, a spoonful of cereal halfway to his mouth.

"Nothing," I replied with a shrug. "Hey, do you guys want to skip orientation day and hang out on the island? I could use your expertise."

Bill looked at Dane, grinned, then nodded.

"Hell, ya."

The island was under the dome of brilliant and disturbingly unfamiliar stars. None of us had travelled in the Southern Hemisphere until the day before. We rode the elevator to the garage and stood for a moment in the inky darkness of the plateau, staring up at the cosmos, pointing out star formations we thought we recognized from books. It felt like being on another planet.

Websites I'd perused while eating breakfast indicated there were poisonous snakes in the Solomons. The deadly Coal Snake was the chief concern, but it preferred the dark and didn't usually nest in people's houses or, as in my case, island fortresses, I hoped. That gave me one less thing to worry about regarding the connection between the two sites. However, the ecosystem on the many islands in the chain did boast thousands of reptilian species, from skinks to frogs, and a large contingent of spiders, tarantulas specifically.

After an hour of clearing debris and emptying and restarting several dehumidifiers peppered around the cave and in every auxiliary room, the brothers asked if they could take a look at the utility systems in the fortress. While they wandered off, talking excitedly, I entered the Map Room and began writing down the destinations and times on the wall map in a notebook. My grandfather's journal was far too confusing and incomplete to use as a guide. It was written by someone who had travelled the system for years and knew it well. Partway through, I noticed that the Window connecting to Zurich, Switzerland, would open within the next half hour. I found the brothers in the Utility Room, which is what they were calling it, and they encouraged me to go. I crossed to Turin Street and quickly changed into clothes a little more suitable for a business meeting if one happened today. Surely, there were things I needed to do as the Enniskillen Group owner. Reinhold Bonk could enlighten me on what those might be.

The Window opened to a large and luxurious bathroom. I stepped through and turned in time to watch the aged closet door on Turin Street replaced by a solid wooden door with an elegant door handle. Above the handle was an oval-shaped keyhole designed for a specific key – my skeleton key.

I opened the bathroom door and entered the main room of a large, stylish hotel suite that immediately made me feel like I didn't belong. The large raised bed, the wall-mounted flat-screen TV, and the full-sized brushed aluminum fridge all screamed at me: you can't afford this. I crossed to the richly draped windows and parted them in the middle. I was on the third or fourth floor, overlooking a wooded area crisscrossed with paths and gardens touched by the last days of a European fall. The sky was overcast, and little drops of rain lightly peppered the window's glass, tapping out a song of quiet solitude. The entire room was quiet.

A black cradle phone was sitting on the bedside table, and a slim digital clock indicated that the time was just past three, making Kingston seven hours behind. A room keycard was tucked neatly into a leather folder, which seemed unusual, but perhaps my grandfather had arranged for this. Installing a lock for a skeleton key in the room's main entrance might have looked suspicious.

I had no idea where I was in Zurich. I could have used my phone, but I had turned off the roaming feature before stepping through the Window. I found a glossy leaflet, emblazoned with Hotel Herrlich, lying beside the phone. The benefits of staying at the Herrlich were listed in several languages, including English, alongside photos of the hotel and the surrounding area.

Wherever the hotel was in the city, it was time to contact Reinhold Bonk. I sat on the bed, lifted the receiver, and wondered if I should dial zero when a voice spoke in French. I have high school French but understand more than I can speak. I panicked and dropped the receiver back onto the cradle. Now, someone would know I was in the room. I looked at my cellphone, wondering if it was worth racking up significant roaming charges if I used it to call Bonk.

The room's phone rang. I jumped. It quit ringing just as I was about to answer. I waited a moment, uncertain, but it didn't ring again, so I lifted the headpiece and listened.

At first, there was only silence, then a click and a male voice spoke.

"Bonjour?"

This was followed by a rapid-fire staccato of French, only some of which I understood.

"English," I said hopefully. "Do you speak English?"

"Yes, yes," he said with a slight accent. "Bonjour, Mr. Ames. I am André. The concierge did not inform me of your arrival, for which I apologize. How may I make your stay with us more pleasurable?"

Mr. Ames? Did he think I was my grandfather?

"Uh, I need to make a phone call. Thank you."

"My pleasure. May I have the number, please?"

"Oh, one second."

I rummaged in my pack for the letter marked with the number One and then quoted Bonk's telephone number to the concierge.

The man apologized again, and I assured him in that self-deprecating Canadian mannerism that it was "not a problem, really."

He connected me, and a moment later, a woman's voice answered in German.

I certainly didn't know German. Maybe she knew French.

"Uh … je ne parle pas très bien le français," I managed to say, but then said, "Do you speak English, please?"

There was a brief silence, then, "Yes, Monsieur, I speak English."

I cleared my throat, feeling frustrated and totally inadequate. I was worth 455 million US dollars, according to the papers my grandfather had left in the shoe box, but how does a person translate that reality into an appropriate manner of behaviour?

"My name," I began, as my lips suddenly felt numb, "is Aidan Ames. I'm from Canada. I believe someone there named Reinhold Bonk worked for my grandfather, Felix Ames."

The woman replied immediately.

"Yes, one moment, sir."

I was briefly treated to a muted stringed orchestra over the phone, then it abruptly ended, and a man spoke.

"Mr. Ames, you cannot imagine what a pleasure it is to hear from you finally. Are you in Zurich?"

My heart leapt into my throat. I hadn't thought this through.

"Uh, no," I replied a little too quickly. "My grandfather left instructions for me to contact you."

"Yes, indeed. It would be an honour to welcome the owner of the Enniskillen Group to our offices. I trust Universal Holdings is still meeting your requirements in a satisfactory manner?"

I wasn't sure how to respond, so I laughed, trying to sound aloof, and said, "Yes, uh, I would like to meet with you."

"Of course. It is a great privilege to manage the properties of the Enniskillen Group. I had great success in my dealings with your grandfather, and I'm quite certain our relationship will be just as positive."

He paused, and I could hear tapping – a keyboard, I presumed.

"When will you arrive in Zurich, and will you be staying at the Hotel Herrlich?"

I hesitated. Did he know I was already here? My panicked mind calmed enough to realize he was only being thorough.

"I can be here, um, I mean, I can be there on Monday," I said, my voice sounding foolishly high-pitched to me. "And, if I may ask, is the Herrlich the best place to stay?"

He laughed lightly.

"Why, I should hope so. The Enniskillen Group is, of course, a partner in the hotel's ownership."

This was the reason for the Window in the bathroom door. I owned part of this hotel, so I had a way to enter Zurich.

Bonk indicated that Monday would be suitable, but the only way I knew how to keep the appointment, at present, was either at 3 a.m. or 3 p.m. Zurich time, so I suggested that we meet shortly after three. He agreed, and I asked for the address, telling him I would catch a taxi from the airport.

"My apologies, Mr. Ames, taxicabs are scarce in Zurich and quite expensive. You can shuttle from the airport to the Herrlich, and I'll send a car to pick you up from there."

I thanked him, trying to sound like I belonged in his world, and hung up, feeling like I didn't belong at all. This world I had suddenly been thrust into was foreign and strange. How was I to know taxis were scarce in

Zurich? What else would I discover that would make me feel inadequate and unable to measure up to the task my grandfather had left me? I know I've lived a privileged life; I can't complain. I've never once wondered where my next meal would come from or where I would sleep, but the magnitude of this inheritance gave me a privilege far beyond what I had known. I flopped back onto the bed and glanced at my phone. I had roughly twenty minutes before the three-quarter-hour Window connecting to my house in Ontario. At 3:45, I entered the bathroom, shut the door, inserted the key, turned it, crossed an ocean to Kingston, and then crossed seventeen time zones to Enniskillen.

ELEVEN

My grandparents met Ian McPhie in the Canadian Tire store parking lot off Princess Street in Kingston after backing into his rental car, according to the newest journal on the table in the Map Room. After exchanging insurance information, Ian insisted on buying them lunch. This was the unlikely beginning of a friendship that spanned five years, leading to my grandparents' unexpected inheritance of Enniskillen and the Windows.

As their friendship grew, so did their time together, meeting weekly to play card games and sample Kingston's diverse culinary scene. But that relationship changed dramatically when Ian McPhie was diagnosed with inoperable brain cancer. During one of their weekly get-togethers, Ian convinced my grandparents to accompany him on the long drive to a Port of Thunder Bay warehouse at the head of the St. Lawrence Seaway System. He introduced them to the secret heritage he and generations before him had been keeping. He had no children, and as simple and as random as their chance meeting was, that was how Felix and Mariah Ames inherited the keys to Enniskillen. This was six years before I was born.

This journal was broken into sections divided by card stock dividers, and one of these discussed the possible science behind the Windows phenomenon. The section wasn't very detailed, but the handwriting was my grandfather's, which I found surprising. My grandfather had never expressed any interest in cosmology to me, but he had written out several conversations he'd had with Ian McPhie before he died. Ian speculated that the relatively new understanding of wormholes might explain what was occurring between the two types of ore. My grandfather agreed. Ian also believed the permanent door to the island resulted from the meteorite ore interacting with the iron ore in the cave, which he felt was supercharged by the meteor's impact long ago. I scanned through this journal quickly. I was looking for something specific: how and when did all this begin?

Another of the journals, the leather soft and worn, contained what I wanted to know. William James McPhie entered the world in April of 1701 in Fermanagh County in Ireland. Affectionately called Willie, he was the youngest of seven born to a mother of Irish heritage and an English father who died when the boy was six. At age eleven, he was apprenticed to a ship's master, a cousin of his father's, and the young McPhie began the arduous life of a seaman. He worked his way up from cabin boy to ironsmith, serving aboard the Seagull, a sturdy merchant vessel that plied the South Seas, trading coal for the lumber and spices of the Solomon Islands. During one of these island-hoping excursions, the ship was caught in a fierce storm and ran aground the shoals off a small remote island in the spring of 1719. Willie was one of seven of the ship's complement of twenty-two who survived. According to the account in the journal, he considered himself lucky. However, he soon learned that the harbour of their salvation had a frightening mystery.

Strange lights flashed deep from within a large cave at the foot of the steep slope of the extinct volcano that had formed the island in the distant past. Locals from nearby islands were aware of the crew's plight but refused to assist the sailors because they believed the lights were the work of evil spirits. Willie, a first mate by this time, was curious about the lights and determined to discover what they were. The journal described window-like openings of various sizes that appeared randomly in midair, sometimes at strange angles or partially embedded into the cave's walls and floor. Forests, beaches, mountains, and farmlands could be seen as these openings appeared and disappeared day and night. They looked like windows to Willie, so he named them Windows.

It didn't take him long to determine that the effect was caused by two types of iron ore lying about on the cave floor. Most of the pieces were small, one light in colour and plentiful, appearing to come from the indigenous rock of the cave's volcanic walls, and the other dark and rough in texture and fewer in number. If the rocks happened to be touching, as dozens of them were, the Windows they formed flickered on and off every fifteen minutes, creating a dazzling display, especially at night. Spooked by the magic of the place, the crew avoided the cave, but Willie began to wonder if the phenomenon could give them a way of escape. He began to take note of the locations that appeared when a Window opened and would throw driftwood and stones through to see what happened to the objects.

Convinced that he could use the Windows to leave the island, he explored ways to make the effect less disturbing. He made his first Window using a door and doorframe salvaged from the Seagull, smelting components for the lock from the light-coloured ore and making a key from the dark ore. After some experimentation, adjusting the quantities of ore between the key and lock, he managed to confine the effect within the doorframe.

On a stormy day in October 1720, the sailors escaped the island, passing through Willie's Window and arriving on a hillside near Montpellier on the coast of Southern France. Willie also left the island with two separate grain sacks filled with the two ores. Once back in Ireland, he spent several months perfecting the Windows, building different sizes of locks and key combinations and fitting them to various door styles. During this time, he discovered that any Window he made also connected to any others he had made as long as the lock remained intact. The only place they didn't connect to was the door he had built on the island where his adventure had begun. Two years later, he embarked on a career that would mark the beginnings of the centuries-old legacy of Enniskillen.

Willie reinvented himself. He refined his speech and mannerisms and created a false identity and backstory. He presented himself as a professional locksmith for the wealthy upper classes, providing advice and well-built lock systems that he claimed were resistant to tampering. His scheme gave him access to estates and palaces of influential and wealthy people across much of Europe. His method was simple: offer his services to the wealthy owners of a site he had targeted and replace the main entrance lock with his own, including a key fashioned from common metals of the time. Each site then became another link in his system of Windows, and using a key made from the dark ore, he had access whenever he wished. When he learned his targets would be travelling or residing elsewhere, he would return through the Window, murder any servants left behind, and strip the residence of valuables. Before escaping with his loot, he would damage a servant's entrance or coal door to make it appear as if that was how thieves had gained entrance. Months later, he would return using regular transportation as a courtesy follow-up to his prestigious locksmithing service. Then, he would quietly remove the lock and replace it with a duplicate mechanism made from normal iron ore.

After a decade of building his empire and establishing more than a dozen permanent sites, something unusual happened with a Window he installed in a grand door in a palace in Stuttgart, Germany. While testing the device to ensure it worked, it opened on the South Sea island where the Seagull had run aground. The Window would open nowhere else. Not questioning his good fortune, Willie quickly removed the lock, installed a copy, and retreated to Ireland.

Following this, the island became the hub of his empire, which he named after Enniskillen, a castle in the County Fermanagh of his Irish homeland. He continued expanding the Window's network while building villas and warehouses in shipping ports across Europe to create a legitimate-looking business empire.

The generation that followed him carried on the family tradition, restricting the number of those aware of the secret to their immediate family. Their victims suspected nothing, for the McPhie family had become adept at using disguises, aliases, and fake businesses as they were about their duplicitous occupation. The world was their treasure house, and they pillaged it with impunity.

It wasn't until Marianne Isabel McPhie inherited the McPhie legacy that Enniskillen began to take on a different purpose. Born in 1899, she was the oldest of three sisters whose parents met their untimely deaths along with two uncles during a botched robbery in an estate in Belgium when she was fifteen. Marianne immediately and dramatically changed its nature and future. She took it from a secret den of thieves who profited from the theft and slavery associated with colonialism to the more noble vocation of travellers, explorers, and philanthropists. Through their newly formed company, the Enniskillen Group, she negotiated the island's purchase from the British in the last decade of the nineteenth century and, with her sisters, continued to reshape Enniskillen to reflect a higher sense of morality and charity.

As much as they were able, they sought out the descendants of the family's ill-gotten treasures, made restitution, and donated much of what could not be returned to museums and art galleries. Using their company and the belief that men owned it, the women began to diversify the family's investments in markets around the globe as a means to ensure the health of its financial future. Women in business, to such an extent as they were, were a rarity, but they hired male lawyers, accountants, and realtors to act upon and further their interests. The sisters carried on the tradition of dismantling old Windows and creating new and less conspicuous ones in properties the company purchased, which enabled them to be more discreet as world travellers.

Another of the older journals detailed descriptions of the sibling's journeys and how they used their unusual inheritance. Unfortunately, Marianne's younger siblings were killed in a boating accident in Brazil, leaving her alone to care for Enniskillen. However, she was not alone for long. She met an American soldier during World War Two, and they eventually married. Following the McPhie tradition, she kept her family name and passed it on to their two children, a daughter and a son, who continued to improve on the legacy. In time, the sister passed, and Ian McPhie became the final conservator, continuing to bring Enniskillen into the twenty-first century.

The journal indicated that Ian had been married, but his wife had been unable to conceive and had fallen into depression. She died at the age of fifty-three, and he never remarried. At this point, the journal's handwriting changed to my grandmother's and my grandfather's, listing many of their travels and repairs to the system. It also revealed something I hadn't known: my grandmother's ashes were spread on the cove's waters.

The journal's final written page ended with this sentence.

I believe Aidan is ready.

I stared at the words for a long while before closing the book and pushing it away from me.

Was I ready?

TWELVE

On Saturday, the brothers and I took transit to a home furnishing store and bought bedding and the necessary equipment to clean the apartment in Victoria. I also used the Chase Manhattan card to purchase a large flat-screen television from an electronics store and sleeping bags and pads from an outdoor gear store.

I found a key in the Key Wallet that corresponded to a card with the address of Morgan's apartment building. I showed it to the brothers, and Bill wondered if I was the owner of that building and if that meant I was Morgan's landlord.

"That'd be complicated," I replied, laughing and grimacing.

Sunday afternoon, we stuffed our backpacks with extra clothing and an assortment of non-perishable foods and caught the Window to Victoria, Dane and Bill carrying the TV between them as they hustled through the portal.

The brothers were excited about their first real trip through a Window. Technically, getting to the island was through a Window, but this was different; the door closed behind us. Dane spent some time looking at the lock, taking video on his cellphone as he opened and closed the Window, and Bill began exploring the plumbing and electrical in the apartment. As I watched them, I was even more grateful they were a part of what was happening.

The apartment, for the most part, just needed a good cleaning, and as the three of us swept away the dust and neglect of the last few years, I became aware of how good it made me feel to do this. I was taking ownership of what my grandfather had left me. I might not know how to fix the elevator on the island, but I knew how to swing a broom and mop.

Then, the inevitable happened. We were hungry for something other than junk food. I thought the possibility of running into Morgan was high; she may have already heard us from her apartment below, and I didn't know if I could face her. I had betrayed our friendship with my lies. I suggested we order in, but the brothers wanted to eat out. A Google search identified a Thai restaurant a few blocks away.

This time, I had a key to the main entrance. It was dark in Victoria and slightly overcast, with an ocean-flavoured wind blowing in from off the Pacific. At the restaurant, we had a serious conversation about the future. They, too, faced the implications of how this discovery would change their lives. As we talked, it became clear that they had concerns. How did the Windows work? Was there radiation? Would there be any long-term health effects from moving through the wormholes if that's what they were?

"How do we even keep something like this a secret?" Bill asked, shaking his head as he dug into a noodle box.

"And," Dane said, "we've all been taking pictures and recording everything. What if I lose my phone and someone gets into it, or I get hacked, and they see what we've been doing?"

I shrugged.

"It's been a secret for over three hundred years."

"Yeah," Dane replied, "but it sounds like it was that way because it was kept to one family. Now, there are two families, and this is not something you can forget."

I frowned.

"What do you mean?"

"What if I get married someday — "

Bill laughed.

"To who?"

"Whom," Dane corrected and then continued. "My point is that the number of people who know about this could exponentially grow if we bring a partner into it. And, in the *modern* world of social media and the prevalence of CCTV cameras, it's only a matter of time before someone somewhere figures it out."

"He's got a point, Aidan." Bill said while raising his hands. "You're probably going to tell Morgan, right?"

I stared at him for a moment. I had almost told her and probably would have if her roommates hadn't been with her that day. I nodded and answered.

"Yeah, I was thinking about it."

"See," Dane said, shrugging, "that's three. Three separate families and all their connections."

"Okay," I countered. "We'll go digitally dark. We'll stop taking pictures and videos on our phones. Any pictures we take must be on a non-connected device, like a simple digital camera, so there's no accidental posting to social media. We can set up a central laptop that's isolated from WiFi and only used for archiving what we're doing on the island or whatever else. We keep Enniskillen to ourselves, and if we bring others in, we have to all agree on it."

Dane's eyebrows shot up.

"So, we're partners? We all have an equal say in *your* inheritance?"

I shrugged.

"Well, you're a part of it now."

Bill nodded slowly.

"Yeah, I'm sorry, but I almost wish we hadn't known about this."

Dane nodded in turn as I stared at both of them.

"Hey, it's too late for that, and besides, I need you guys. I want you to be a part of this, whatever *this* is. We'll figure it out as we go. My grandparents did this for over twenty years, and no one knew about it."

There was silence for a few moments as we picked at our meals, but Dane finally spoke, a smile slowly spreading across his face.

"Thanks, Aidan. This is pretty cool, you have to admit. I might even change my elective to weird science stuff."

Bill laughed and nodded.

"Yeah, I'm okay too. It's weird as hell, but who wouldn't want to be a part of this? I didn't expect this when we flew out to Kingston to – " he made air quotes, " – go to college."

We laughed, and I knew we would be all right. A short time later, we walked back to the apartment building and headed up to the second floor just as Kelli, Morgan's roommate, emerged from her apartment. She did a double-take when she saw me. My heart jumped.

"Back so soon?" she called after us.

I could feel the chill in her voice. Morgan must have told her about the outcome of our last conversation, how it ended, about how peculiar I had been. On top of that, I had left Victoria without saying goodbye.

Her question, however, was met with silent stares from the brothers. I didn't know what to say, and they had no idea what was transpiring. Morgan suddenly appeared behind Kelli.

I gave her the biggest, most sheepish grin I could muster.

"Uh, Hi."

She glowered at me, both angry and confused, and I felt terrible.

"Hi," she replied curtly. "I see you brought the McHale Sandwich with you this time."

I chuckled. In high school, Dane and Bill always seemed to walk one on either side of me, and Morgan had quipped one day that it made us look like a sandwich. Two thick slabs of ranch boy with a thin slice of city boy between them, the McHale Sandwich. It might have been funny then, but she wasn't smiling now. I looked up the stairs and seriously contemplated heading up them to disappear into the safety of the apartment, but I couldn't. We were friends.

"Look, I'm sorry."

She stood beside her friend, raised an eyebrow and smiled thinly.

"Sorry about what?"

I shrugged.

"About last week, about not getting together later, um, and about the hockey game."

Her eyes didn't flinch. She knew I had lied.

"Oh, the game you love so much. If you didn't want to talk to me, you should have just said so."

I felt awkward. I had to deflect things quickly before I was forced to lie again. I didn't want to lie, but I couldn't tell her the truth, not in front of her friend anyway. I stepped back, bumping into Dane, who sidestepped out of the way into Bill, who gripped his brother to keep them from falling over. I would have laughed if not for the deadly serious look on Morgan's face.

"Coffee?" I asked.

"What?"

"Coffee. Do you want to get some coffee and talk?"

"With you?"

Ouch, that hurt.

"Please. I'll explain."

"Aidan?" Dane whispered beside me.

I turned to him. "It's ok," and then back to Morgan. "Just the two of us, okay?"

She looked from Dane to me.

"Okay."

"Why don't you guys watch some TV?" I said to the brothers.

"We don't have cable," Bill stated, eyeing me curiously. I could tell he was wondering if I would tell Morgan about the Windows.

"You don't have cable?" Kelli said.

"Well, we don't live here. We only visit on weekends," Dane mumbled.

"Visit on weekends? From Ontario?" Morgan said, her voice heavy with skepticism.

"Not every weekend," Bill added hurriedly in an attempt to smooth over the blunder.

Morgan wasn't buying it.

"Right. Just some weekends."

"Hey, guys," I turned to them, "just do something. Go for a walk, or whatever. Morgan and I need to talk."

I grabbed her arm, pulling her towards the entrance.

"But – " I heard Bill stammer.

"We have cable," I heard Kelli say.

Bill smiled and shrugged, looking from me to Morgan.

"Sure," he grinned.

"Don't get any ideas," I heard Kelli say as I headed for the entrance. "I've got a girlfriend."

Outside, Morgan pulled her arm away and positioned herself as far away from me as the sidewalk would allow.

"Why did you do that?" She finally asked.

"Do what?"

"You're being evasive."

I stopped.

"What?" she looked at me, confused or irritated. I wasn't sure which.

I didn't like this. I wanted her friendship, and I knew she felt the same way, but I found myself, yet again, wondering what to tell her and if I should tell her anything. Last week, I had come to Victoria, full of excitement, ready to spill everything, but now, I didn't feel I was ready, and I didn't want to lie either. I probably wouldn't have even told Bill and Dane if I hadn't left the door open to the island. I felt like my life was suddenly moving a million miles an hour, and I couldn't make it stop.

"What, forget something?" She placed a hand on one hip.

God, she's beautiful, even when she's angry.

"A lot has changed for me," I said.

She pursed her lips, eyeing me deliberately.

"Like what?"

I grimaced.

"Some things are happening in my life, and I'm not sure how to tell you."

She frowned.

"Like what? What's going on, Aidan?"

I shrugged.

"That's what I mean. I don't know what to say."

"First one word, then the next."

"Hah, hah, it's not that easy."

"Well, you're up to something. You and the twins could not afford to fly from Kingston just for the weekends, even with your inheritance."

"Well," I began, "that's exactly it. This is about the money from my inheritance."

"Good. That's the first thing you've said that doesn't sound like a lie."

"I need to tell you something."

"I'm ready to hear it."

"Let's find someplace to sit first," I suggested.

I'd noticed a corner coffee shop earlier and led us back there. Only a few people were in the shop, and a guitarist was quietly playing classical music on a corner stage. We didn't say much until after we had ordered coffee and found a table. Morgan sat across from me; the expression on her face was one of focused expectation as she took a sip from her cup. I cringed inside. I didn't want to say too much or too little, so I did my best to look honest and to spin a believable version of the truth.

I began with my grandfather's suicide. She was horrified, and her eyes softened a little, reaching out to hold my hand. I told her about the shoebox birthday present he had left for me, saying it was hidden in a drawer in his desk, and how that was when I discovered how much money I actually had. As I talked, it surprised me how easy it was not quite to tell her the whole truth. I would have never done this before the discovery of the Windows. Had I really changed that much in the two weeks?

I didn't tell her about the Windows. I wanted to, and if she could have heard the gonzo back-and-forth argument going on in my head about whether to tell her or not, she would have thought I'd lost my mind. I was worried the Windows would disrupt her life like they had the brothers and me. She was already moving forward with her new life, forging her way toward her dream, and I was suddenly going to say to her, 'Hey, look what I found!' It didn't seem right to do that to her, at least not until I knew we were safe using them and I had time to figure out what this meant to my future, and maybe hers, if that was something she was interested in. I mean, before, I was just her best friend who lived across the street; now, I was more than that, much more than that. I was wealthy, I could be somebody.

"This is amazing, Aidan," she said after I paused, my eyebrows raised, wondering what she felt about everything I'd told her.

Our conversation began to feel like it was before graduation, like we were walking home from school or hanging out in the park down the street. She reached across the table and slipped her hand into mine again. My heart skipped, and I realized how much I loved her, and I regretted that I had never told her that, and then I felt lower than pond scum.

And then she asked me what I hoped she'd forget.

"But why lie to me about the hockey game, and what was all that weirdness at your apartment door last week?"

"Um – ?"

"After you shut it in my face, and there was that flash of light from under the door? I stood there knocking, feeling like an idiot. What was that all about?"

A flash of light? She had seen it! I wanted to tell her everything, but could I? The Windows were reshaping my future, and I had no idea where it was taking me. What would it do to her or us if I told her?

"Can I ask you something?"

"Sure," she answered confidently.

"We've been good friends, right?"

"Closer than you and the Sandwich?"

I chuckled.

"You're a lot more attractive, but, yeah, closer than that. Do you trust me?"

"Normally," she replied, her eyes twinkling, but her brows creased slightly.

"How do you feel about us?"

"We're holding hands," she teased.

"I know – "

"Quit smiling!"

"Can you trust me?"

This time, she frowned.

"What are you getting at, Aidan?"

I hesitated, my stomach twisting inside me.

"It's not just the inheritance, and there's something else. It's not bad, " I added hastily.

"Do you have a girlfriend?"

"No."

"Well, what?" she asked slowly.

"I, um, I'm not sure I can say just yet. "

"You ask me to trust you, but you don't trust me?" she interrupted, the pain in her voice edging back.

I shook my head.

"It's not that, believe me. It's not that at all. My life is just nuts right now with this inheritance. If it seems like I'm acting sort of, well, strange, could you just overlook it?"

"I don't know what you mean." Her hand grew stiff. "Strange, like how?"

"Strange, like last week."

She pulled her hands away.

"You mean winning the inheritance lottery makes you, what, a jerk?"

"God, no," I said, the warmth of her hand lingering like a raindrop. "I want to explain, I just need some time."

She nodded slowly, and I felt a heart-wrenching loss.

"I guess you have changed, Aidan. We used to tell each other everything. God, you and I even – "

She looked away briefly and then focused on my face again.

"Tell you what, I'll make this easy for you. I suppose we've always only just been friends. I don't owe you anything other than that, and you don't owe me anything, either. Thanks for whatever it is we had, but if there are some things you need to keep secret," she waved an arm in the air, "like, why you couldn't answer a knock on the door, pretending you weren't there, then, I guess I'll just have to live with that."

She stood up, the anguish in her eyes ripping my heart.

"I hope *you* can live with it, too."

Oh, how I wanted to tell her. I had to, but no, I couldn't. Not yet. I felt the joy in my heart extinguishing like a flame in the rain. We had gone from hot to cold in a matter of moments.

"When you were knocking, I wasn't there," I said quickly, standing as well. I had to tell her.

"You weren't there? Right. I saw you, Aidan."

"I know."

I had to tell her. No, I couldn't. I didn't know what I had stumbled into. Bill and Dane's lives might already be ruined by their knowledge of the Windows and the demand for secrecy it placed on them. I couldn't drag someone I loved into this.

"I was, but then I left."

"How? Out the window?"

Well, yeah, in a manner of speaking.

I sighed, feeling grimly fatalistic.

"I can't explain."

"Can't? Or won't?"

I felt my face heat up as I became aware of heads turning in our direction.

"Why is it such a big deal?" I asked, looking around. "Why can't you just trust me?"

"Why is it such a big deal? I thought we had an honest friendship, Aidan. Obviously, we don't anymore."

I reached out to touch her arm, to make some gesture of contrition, to salvage the thread of friendship that was rapidly unravelling between us, but she pulled away.

"I'm sorry your grandfather killed himself, Aidan, but you lied to me. You lied about some stupid, fictitious hockey game and your inheritance. How about trusting *me*? You would never have done something like this before!"

Before the Windows.

She stared at me intensely, waiting for an answer, but I had none. I had foolishly hoped she would accept my vague answers and not ask questions, but that wasn't Morgan; trust had been a massive issue for her all the years we had known each other, and I had blown it.

"Thanks for returning my journal," I said weakly. I couldn't think of what else to say.

She sighed, closed her eyes briefly, and then turned away from me, shaking her head.

We walked the two blocks back to the apartment building silently, a vast, lonely chasm between us. The words that had spilled over earlier seemed cheap all of a sudden, even stupid. What had I expected? Life had changed for both of us.

Gramps, you have really screwed up my life.

THIRTEEN

R einhold Bonk met me as I exited a crowded elevator on the 12th floor of Zurich's Van Buren Exchange building. He was a middle-aged man dressed in a dark suit who immediately made eye contact with me. I knew who he was, even though I was confident I had not met him before. He held out his arms as he approached, and I had the impression that he would hug me, but he stopped short, cupping his hands around the one I offered. He shook it vigorously as though he and I had been best friends.

"Mr. Ames, " he said, with a slight accent, "Welcome to Zurich and the Bahnhofstrasse, the financial district. You will want to acquaint yourself with the many shops and restaurants while you are in our wonderful city, but for now, it is such a pleasure to meet Felix's grandson! The limousine was satisfactory, I trust?"

I had never been in a limousine like the one that picked me up from the Hotel Herrlich, long and cavernous, but I nodded, trying to appear sophisticated like I always road in them.

"Yes, comfortable ride."

"Excellent," he replied.

I silently chided my comment. Whom was I trying to fool? I wasn't ready for this life, I couldn't even muster enough courage to tell Morgan the truth.

"How long are you in Zurich?" he asked as we walked.

I shrugged.

"A couple of days, I guess. I want to look around while I'm here."

"Indeed. Zurich is the financial capital of Switzerland, but it also has a history back to Roman times."

He said this as we entered a vast hallway with large double-glass doors at the far end. *Universal Holdings – Zurich* was stylishly etched with gold lettering on the glass. He pushed them open, waiting for me to walk into an outer office where a woman around Bonk's age sat behind a well-organized desk that dominated the room. She was wearing a telephone headset on one ear, smiled politely at me, and then nodded at Bonk as he greeted her.

"Everything's ready for you, Reinhold," she said briskly. I recognized her voice from the telephone call I'd made at the hotel.

"Thank you, Elle." Then he turned toward me. "This is Aidan Ames, Felix's grandson. Elle is my wife and business partner of many years."

I would have shaken her hand, but she didn't offer it, nodding once instead and lowering her eyes to the paperwork before her. I thought I detected a hint of a smile on her face.

"Would you care for some tea Mr. Ames, or coffee, before we begin?"

"No, thank you, but maybe a glass of water," I said.

My mouth was dry from the tangle of nerves in my gut.

"Your grandfather was a remarkable man and a close friend. Please accept my family's belated condolences," he offered.

His wife lifted her face and smiled briefly.

"Thank you," I replied.

"Very well then. Come this way, and we shall begin to update you about your properties."

Bonk pointed toward a set of doors on his wife's left, which led into an office that instantly made me feel inadequately dressed. A massive mahogany desk was in front of tinted wall-to-wall windows that overlooked the Limmat River. A dozen large flat-screen monitors ran the length of the two side walls, providing what looked like moment-by-moment global market updates and the latest international business news. A lounging area along one side of the room was furnished with a soft leather couch and chairs, and an etched glass table in the centre was adorned with business journals. This office was designed to reflect the success of Universal Holdings. It succeeded.

Bonk crossed to a small glass-fronted cooler and retrieved a bottle of water, which he handed me with a tall glass.

"Thank you," I said, my eyes wandering around the impressive room.

He then positioned a rolling leather chair for me behind his desk, and we sat. Three computer screens were sunk into the desk's dark, polished surface, tilted upward, forming a semi-circle around us.

"Let us begin, shall we," he said enthusiastically as I took a quick drink of cool water.

Using a keyboard, he began to scroll through charts and graphs, rattling off numbers, figures, and trends pertaining to various stock and investment portfolios. My mind began to blank as he followed this with more charts detailing the names and locations of the Enniskillen Group holdings that he felt were prime to be sold and other properties he believed were prudent to purchase. The words 'rental' and 'lease' were on several lines. I was the landlord of dozens of properties. I nodded politely but understood little, except that it seemed the Group was global, and it was Bonk's commission to manage and oversee them. Pressing on like I understood everything he was saying, he pulled up a chart showing the disbursement of *my* wages into Chase Manhattan and Bank of London accounts, along with several investment institutions. Highlighting another browser window, he informed me that the Group holdings' value had grown to 4.2 billion US dollars depending on current market trends. I gasped. Bonk paused, frowning, obviously confused by the growing expression of shock on my face.

"You are surprised by this?"

"Yes," I stammered, gesturing at the screens.

"How much exactly had your grandfather told you about the Enniskillen Group?"

I stared at him, feeling oddly like I was sitting in my high school principal's office and might be in trouble.

"Nothing," I answered hesitantly, "he died before he told me anything. He left me a birthday present I had just found, with some papers with your name on them. That's why I contacted you last week."

Bonk sniffed through his nose.

"I see. So, may I assume you know nothing of the Enniskillen Group?"

I nodded slowly.

"I think he was going to tell me on my sixteenth birthday, but he died."

His eyes narrowed, seeming almost annoyed at my ignorance.

"Nothing in your grandfather's papers made mention of the complexities of the Enniskillen Group?"

"No," I replied.

"Ah. However, this does explain why you have only just contacted me. Frankly, I was becoming concerned. The Enniskillen Group is a very diverse and rich portfolio, and you are quite young."

I don't know how to take his comment.

"I'm almost 19," I countered, trying not to sound miffed. But I was. I might look barely old enough to be out of high school, but I'm not stupid.

He raised a hand.

"Please, do not take offence, Aidan. Typically, I met with Felix at least quarterly. He preferred a hands-on approach to the Group, and it has been more than two years since his passing. I have had to make decisions in absentia. Nothing major, mind you. My contract with the Enniskillen Group provides me with some flexibility; however, I greatly prefer the agreement I had with Felix."

"That's okay," I assured him. "I want to do things the way my grandfather did."

"Well," he nodded, "let us start from the beginning. What would you like to know?"

I didn't hesitate.

"How large is the Enniskillen Group?"

He smiled, and I wondered if it was an immature question to ask.

Bonk began explaining what he assumed I had known. He talked at length about stock portfolios, transportation development, shipping, clean tech, responsible resource extraction, and commercial and residential real estate investment. He explained that the company also had a vibrant philanthropic side, focused on climate, housing, and income equality issues.

He paused, smiling as he caught the wide-eyed look on my face.

"You manage all of this for me?" I asked.

He chuckled.

"Yes. The Enniskillen Group is the sole client of this branch of Universal Holdings."

"Oh," I stammered. "Shouldn't I have a board or something? Isn't that what companies do?"

Bonk shook his head.

"When your grandfather came to me over two decades ago, Enniskillen was an internationally incorporated business with him and your grandmother as the sole owners and managers. They were not managing very well, and I say this with the greatest respect. Neither had a financial background, and they struggled to, as you can imagine, keep track of all the moving parts, and there are many. That they sought out a company such as Universal Holdings is to their credit, and, fortunately, together, we brought some order to what is a very successful organization."

I nodded and wondered why Ian McPhie thought an elevator technician and his wife, a librarian, would have known what to do with such a vast company. For that matter, why did my grandfather think I could have handled this?

"How many – ?"

"How many properties do you own?"

"Yes."

"At the moment," he quickly pulled another chart on a screen.

"Four hundred and sixty-one. Universal Holdings manages them independently through local contractors and property management agencies."

Four hundred and sixty-one? There weren't that many Windows or keys. The Enniskillen Group was much larger than just the sites the Windows occupied.

Bonk went on.

"You own land and buildings on every continent except Antarctica. Forty-six countries in all."

"Are they all warehouses?"

Bonk smiled politely. I had asked another ignorant question, obviously.

"Oh, no. Your real estate portfolio is quite diverse. Not to be too general, but there are agricultural holdings, storage facilities, warehouses, office buildings, residential dwellings, rental flats – "

"Rental flats?"

"Yes, you own rental properties in several countries."

"Any in Canada?" I asked hopefully.

"As a matter of fact, yes."

"In British Columbia?" I asked, barely containing my excitement.

He clicked a link on one of the screens and then scrolled through a document.

"Yes, in Victoria. It is an older building, but it is a sound structure and well-maintained. You are unaware of this site?"

"Aware of an apartment building in Victoria?"

Bonk nodded.

"Yes, your grandfather left instructions to hold one of the units for a, er – " he quickly pulled up another file, moving it to a less cluttered screen, "– yes, a Miss Morgan Vogel, a friend of your family. It was to be held on the occasion of her eighteenth birthday until such time she needed it."

He saw the shock on my face, frowned and leaned back in his chair, placing the fingers of his hands together.

"I assume you know nothing of this arrangement, then?"

I shook my head slowly, barely believing what I was hearing. My grandfather had planned for Morgan to rent an apartment in a building he owned, which now made me Morgan's landlord. How could he have planned for something like this? He had died without meeting her, and how could he possibly have known about her plans to attend university, specifically in Victoria? I had certainly talked about her often enough to him. I may have mentioned our post-secondary education plans.

"Was it you who contacted Morgan about the vacancy?"

"No. Not me directly. It was the property management company for the building. They had a standing order per your grandfather's instructions to contact Miss Vogel once she enrolled in a certain university."

"Wait," I interrupted him, "how would they know she had enrolled?"

Reinhold smiled.

"It's common practice for rental companies in North America to apprise educational institutions of available rental stock prior to the beginning of a school year, especially for students who travel from afar."

"Oh."

That explains the cold call from the building manager Morgan said she'd received.

"I apologize that you were unaware of this arrangement. Your grandfather was very specific about Miss Vogel and her desire to further her education at this particular institution."

Morgan had planned and talked about going to Victoria as early as Grade 9, but how could my grandfather have known this?

"You and my grandfather were friends?"

"Yes – " Bonk paused, lifted his teacup to his lips, and chuckled.

"Well, truthfully, Elle and I have worked for many wealthy clients over the years, but Felix was one of a kind. Wealth didn't matter much to him or your grandmother. It was, however, important to them to be responsible with how they used it. That's why the Group owns no mansions, has no private jets or yachts, and has one of the largest philanthropic portfolios I've ever enjoyed managing."

His gaze drifted to the view of the river beyond the windows.

"I miss both of them still. They were more than clients."

"Why do you think he would kill himself when he had all this and – "

'And you?" Bonk finished, levelling his gaze on me.

I nodded.

He set the cup down.

"Felix spoke with great affection for you, Aidan. I was alarmed when he informed me that he was signing over control of the Enniskillen Group to you, then almost sixteen. His desire was legally possible despite the variety of countries you have properties in, but you were and are still quite young. But I also trusted Felix's instincts. He felt strongly about this, and I believe he made a wise choice. Despite your lack of knowledge of the Group, I believe, based on our meeting here today, that you are more than capable."

"Thank you. That's kind of you, but why would he, you know – "

"Why would he kill himself? Please forgive me if I am too forward, but I am not convinced he took his own life."

I should have felt shocked at the statement, but his words only echoed my suspicions.

"You know this for a fact?"

Bonk nodded.

"I believe I do. After his death, and out of personal interest for our friendship, I hired private investigators, the best in North America. The official police report concluded that his death was self-inflicted, but I do not believe this is true."

"I don't think so, either," I said quickly. "What do you think happened?"

Bonk shrugged slightly, watching my face.

"I do not know for certain. However, it was confirmed that two shots were fired from the pistol found in his hand, but only one bullet was recovered. He was found on the top floor of the house you mentioned earlier, yes?"

I nodded once.

"In Kingston."

"Yes, well, to further confuse things, the report described blood droplets trailing from an adjacent storage room to the desk where he was found. It would appear that he shot himself in this storage room, then proceeded to the desk where he died."

He lowered his hands to his lap, his fingers playing with the creases of his pants.

"Yet, there was no evidence of the pistol being fired in the storage room where the blood trail indicates he had come from. He was shot from a great enough distance that there was no additional residual gunpowder at the site of the wound. In effect, absolutely nothing would suggest he was shot on those premises. It is all very peculiar."

The closet. He had been shot somewhere in the Window system.

"However," Bonk continued, smiling conspiratorially while raising a finger, "there was gunshot residue on his right hand and the sleeve of his shirt, indicating blowback from the weapon having been fired by him."

"What does that mean?"

"It means he fired the pistol, not the bullet that killed him, even though it came from the weapon. The bullet that killed him had to have been fired several metres away. Something he could not have done."

"So someone shot him with his gun?"

Bonk frowned and shook his head.

"Not technically, the pistol was not registered to Felix, but to a deceased American living in Chicago, in the United States."

"Did he – "

"No, Felix did not kill this man nor, I am certain, could have known him. The gun was sold to a pawnshop from an estate liquidation sale and somehow ended up in your grandfather's possession. Felix had seemed agitated during our last meeting, about a week before his death, but he would not speak of the reason. I'm sorry, Aidan."

I suddenly felt cold. Someone somewhere in the interconnected world of the Windows had murdered my grandfather. It might have been good that I chose not to let Morgan in on the secret after all.

"What do you suggest I do now?" I asked.

Bonk shrugged.

"That I can't say. The best that we can all do is to continue living. Based on what he has left you, your grandfather would want that. If he was murdered, fate has a way of bringing the evil and good of life full circle."

A silence fell between us for a moment until Bonk cleared his throat.

"I believe we have discussed enough for this visit."

He reached into a side drawer and pulled out an official-looking folder with the words Universal Holdings etched across the front.

"Take these, look through them, and we can talk more when we get together next."

I nodded and took the folder, feeling mature, but also very much like an imposter.

"What should I be doing now? I'm not going to pretend I know what I'm doing. I feel overwhelmed. A week ago, I thought my grandfather had left me a house and some extra cash to help get me through college."

He leaned back in his chair and frowned.

"Indeed, since you knew nothing of the Group, our conversation here would be overwhelming. What should you do now? Due to the nature of your holdings and our company's long relationship with the Enniskillen Group, there are very few problems. There is the occasional hiccup, which is easily resolved if we stay in contact."

He tapped a finger to his lower lip before continuing.

"Do you have your grandfather's Key Wallet?"

I nodded, pointing to my backpack.

"It would be of immense help to both of us if you were to follow in your grandfather's footsteps and familiarize yourself with the holdings represented by the keys in the Key Wallet. The Group has many more holdings and partnerships, but these were of interest to your grandfather. I receive constant updates from the companies that manage your properties on the ground, and while I trust them, perhaps it would be useful for you to visit some of them in person. Do you have time to travel? Are you able to take a leave of absence from this college you are attending?"

Time? I had plenty of that. Travel? Going to college was definitely out of the question for now.

"College can wait a year, and I've always wanted to travel," I laughed and then followed it with a lie. "This is the first time I've been to Zurich."

Bonk smiled as he rose. I stood up as well.

"Very good, then. I'll notify the various companies and property management agencies to expect you over, say, the next six months?"

"It'll take that long?" I asked, also standing up.

"Oh, yes, if you visit all the sites in the wallet. I trust you enjoy air travel? This venture will require a considerable amount of that."

I grinned and shrugged.

"I'll get used to it."

"Excellent," he said as he laughed softly, reaching out to shake my hand.

I shook it firmly, like a billionaire businessman who had stopped by to check up on his investments.

"Do you have a cell phone?" he asked.

I pulled it out.

"May I enter my personal line for you?"

I swiped it open and navigated to my contacts before passing it to him. He created a new contact and entered his address and personal phone number.

"You have a sufficient roaming package for your cell?"

"Yes, I just got one before flying here."

It was only a half lie. After returning to Kingston from the mess I'd made with Morgan in Victoria, I purchased an out-of-country unlimited roaming package. I needed to get away, to not put myself in a situation where I was lying to someone I cared for. I was beginning to see why my grandfather had never once hinted at the secret of the Windows. Protecting it turned you into a liar. If the brothers hadn't accidentally stumbled onto the island, I'd be lying to them, too.

"May I make a suggestion?" he asked as he returned the phone.

"Sure."

"Felix was not a big user of technology, but you are, of course, a member of the technology generation. A few years ago, I encouraged your grandfather to use a satellite phone so he could contact me wherever he might be, but he never took to it. May I suggest you purchase a satellite-based Wi-Fi access point? That way, you can use your cell and its GPS functions should you need them?"

I blinked.

"Is that like a WiFi Hotspot?"

"No. A satellite Wi-Fi access point," he explained. "It's a small device that acts as a Wi-Fi access point for your cellphone, giving you reception just about anywhere in the world. Some of your properties are in areas with poor cell reception, and should you need to contact me, you can do so."

I swiped the notes application open on my phone and typed the name. I needed to go shopping.

"Thanks, I'll do that."

I said goodbye to his wife as Bonk accompanied me to the building's entrance and the waiting limo. I should have been excited over the wealth and the adventures awaiting me, but I sank into a brooding silence as I rode back to the hotel.

I was alone, more alone than I had ever felt, and something dark and dangerous was waiting for me in the world behind the closet door.

FOURTEEN

I remained in Zurich for the rest of the day, following the ebb of tourists who wandered through shops along cobblestone streets and winding alleys. I was surprised to see scores of people from all walks of life riding bicycles and catching crowded trams and buses. The city was unlike Calgary, where every shopping mall and neighbourhood seemed distant and accessible only with a vehicle. Feeling adventurous, I found a map kiosk and randomly picked one of the many quays on Lake Zurich to visit. I even managed to catch the correct tram that dropped me off along the Limmat River, where the quay hosted several restaurants and shops in buildings far older than anything I'd ever seen. I walked awhile before finding a restaurant whose seating spilled out onto the quay. I ate a light meal there before returning to the Herrlich. It was early evening in this time zone, but my head was aching from the meeting with Bonk and my restless sleep from the night before. I took a quick shower and fell asleep in my reserved room in a hotel where I was part owner. I woke in the middle of the night and tried watching television, but the programs were unfamiliar, and my mind was much too occupied with a chaotic mix of future possibilities and dread. I finally drifted off again, more from exhaustion than from anything else. It was early afternoon when I awoke, feeling somewhat refreshed.

Later, I caught the Window back to Kingston. I realized I had begun using the language my grandfather had in his journal, referring to the process as *catching* a Window, like catching a plane or a bus. It was pre-dawn in Ontario, and the brothers were asleep. I crossed over to the fortress and checked my email while sitting on the steps that led down to the cove. The gentle sound of waves coursing up the beach was relaxing. I could get used to this, I thought.

I had a voicemail. The phone must have picked up a call when I was sleeping in Zurich.

It was Morgan.

"Hi, Aidan. Look, I'm sorry about yesterday. I know you have classes and everything, but if you're ever back this way, you know, on your chartered jet, we could talk. Okay?"

I had stopped breathing as I listened to her voice. My heart was pounding.

"I meant what I said. I really am sorry."

The message ended. I played it again and saved it. We were still friends, and besides, I knew we still cared for each other. A few lies couldn't change that, could it?

I dialled her number from my cell. It rang four times before voice mail clicked in. I hung up and tried again. Who knows, she might have been in the shower. My heart jumped when the call picked up. I hadn't thought about what I would say if she answered. It wasn't Morgan.

"Hello?" The sleep-heavy voice grumbled.

I held the phone motionless, wondering if I'd accidentally hit the wrong phone number on my cell.

"Hello?" The voice repeated. It was Kelli. She didn't sound pleased.

"Uh, hi. This is Aidan, Aidan Ames. This is Morgan's phone, right? Is she there?"

I felt sheepish.

There was silence, except for a sharp sniff, and then, "Yeah, this is her phone. She must have left it in our room last night. We were watching a movie. She's asleep. Do you know what time it is?"

I paused, thinking, and then mentally kicked myself. It was almost four a.m. in Victoria.

"Oh, geez, I'm sorry. I'm calling from Ontario."

There was dead silence.

"Don't wake her," I continued apologetically.

"Don't worry. I won't."

"Can I leave a message?"

More silence.

"Hello?"

"Yes, yes," she answered, sounding more annoyed. "What do you want me to tell her."

"Thank you. Please tell Morgan I'll be travelling for a while, but I'll call her, okay?"

"Fine."

She ended the call before I could say anything else, but I already felt stupid. I should have considered the time difference, but the sun had been shining over Zurich. I needed a watch that would show multiple time zones. I needed to go shopping.

The Window to Manhattan is at 2:30. The warehouse I had accidentally found on my first adventure with the closet was bustling with mid-morning activity as I stepped out onto the walkway. I passed through the building, barely glancing at anyone, but every face that met mine left me wondering if they might be the person who had killed my grandfather.

It was overcast in New York, and the sun struggled to burn through the shroud of fog that hunched over the murky Hudson River. The card that matched the warehouse in my grandfather's Key Wallet had a taxi service number. I dialled and asked for a cab. As I waited outside at a side entrance, I was amazed by the depth of sound that hung in the air, coming from everywhere, all at once. I thought Calgary was a noisy hub of activity, but this city had an underlying resonance that seemed to transmit through the ground into my body. Finally, a sedan pulled up, and it suddenly occurred to me that my grandfather had probably waited like this.

A middle-aged cabbie watched passively as I slipped into the back. The plastic card containing his photo ID mounted to my side of the marred Plexiglas partition introduced him as Manuel Rodriguez. Alex McGuire was the name written on the back of the company card from the Key Wallet, but when I called the dispatch, they informed me that Alex was no longer with them.

Manuel continued to observe me in the rear-view mirror as I fastened my seat belt and wondered if such a law was in effect here.

"Where to, kid?" he inquired.

I leaned forward, reading his ID tag.

"Uh, Mr. Rodriguez, I want to hire your services for the morning."

"Sorry, kid. I only do point-to-point hauls. What you need is a limo or an Uber."

"Oh, well, I need to go to a bank or an ATM and find someplace in Manhattan to buy some decent clothes. I'll pay you double or triple what you normally get."

Man, it felt exhilarating to say that!

He looked at me in his mirror, eyeing me thoughtfully.

"Like I said, kid, I don't do that. I have a contract to haul point-to-point. I'd lose my job."

"My grandfather used to do this kind of thing with a driver named Alex McGuire," I persisted.

Manuel shrugged.

"Sorry. I don't know anybody called McGuire, but if he had an arrangement with your grandfather, it was his business. This is my business, and I don't want to mess it up. Got kids to feed, you know?"

I was undeterred.

"How much do you make in a day?"

"Enough."

"No, c'mon, how much?"

He turned away, rubbing his brow thoughtfully, and then turned back.

"One fifty on a good day. Why?"

"I'll triple that."

An eyebrow arched up.

"I'm serious!" I insisted.

"You got money, kid?"

"Enough."

He smiled at that, obviously amused by my answer.

"Well, kid, I'll take you to a bank, but I'll need to see some cash."

"Take me to the bank."

"I meant, now."

I had fifty-five dollars Canadian in my wallet, two twenties, a ten, and a five. I passed them through the slit in the Plexiglas, and he rubbed them between his fingers as though he expected them to be counterfeit.

"You from Canada?"

He passed the ten back to me.

"Yeah, Kingston."

"What're you doing down here on the docks?"

"I own this warehouse."

Of course, he wouldn't believe me, but it was thrilling to say it.

He angled around to look me over, suspicion clouding his face.

"Uh-huh. Okay, kid, to the bank. Anyone in particular?"

"Uh, any that has money. Oh, wait, I have a Chase Manhattan card. Is there one here?"

He smiled lopsidedly and shrugged as we set off. It took about 20 minutes to navigate through traffic. Manuel used the time to ask questions along the way. The warehouse was far from any tourist hotels, and I was dressed in jeans, a T-shirt, and a light jacket and was carrying a small shoulder pack. I stuck to my story, answering vaguely until he got the idea that I wouldn't tell him anything more than I wanted to. Besides, I was trying not to gawk at the stunning maze of buildings, which towered over us on either side as we drove. This, after all, was my first trip beyond the warehouse in New York City. Manuel double-parked near the First National Bank of America and promised to wait for me.

"Cause I got a kid about your age, and I wouldn't leave him alone, even in Manhattan," he said with a wink.

I liked him. My size tends to make me look much younger, like a fourteen-year-old. I wondered if he thought I was a runaway.

There were several ATMs in the foyer. I withdrew a thousand US dollars from the Chase Manhattan account. The receipt didn't give the account balance, but where the available daily limit should have been printed was the word "Unlimited" in bold block letters. I folded the printout and stuffed it into my pocket as a memento.

Back in the taxi, I held five crisp one-hundred dollar bills against the Plexiglas.

"Still doing just point to points?"

He stared fixedly at me.

"Where'd you get that?"

"I told you, I have money."

"You don't look like you got money, kid."

"That's why I'm in New York. I need some new clothes."

He stared at me for a moment and then shrugged.

"I get all kinds, kid, but if you've got the money – "

I shrugged. What could I say? I had the money!

He took the bills and folded them, slipping them into his shirt pocket, before calling his dispatcher and clocking off for the rest of the day.

"You can call me Manuel, kid," he said, shaking his head and chuckling.

"And you can call me Aidan."

I sat back, smiling. This was the first person in my entire life I had hired to do anything for me. It was a strange feeling of power, giving me a rush that felt exciting and foolhardy at the same time. I was wealthy beyond anything I had ever imagined. Even my father would be jealous, but at the same time, it was almost as if I had found a wad of cash, and instead of finding its owner, I was quickly spending it all before I was forced to give it back. As Manuel slipped the taxi back into traffic, I chided myself. This was my inheritance. I deserved this.

He took me first to Ralph Lauren on Madison Avenue and then to several shops along Fifth Avenue. I tried to get him to join me, but he wouldn't leave his cab. So, he dropped me off and then either waited or drove to where he could legally park. When I was finished in a store and needed him, I texted his phone, and he picked me up. I'm sure he thought I was one of those spoiled rich kids. In a very short time, I had spent over seven thousand dollars on clothing, shoes, a leather wallet, an unbreakable carry-on-sized suitcase and a smartwatch, which could be programmed to show multiple time zones on its face. This would be the first time in my life that I'd worn a watch.

When I told Manuel I needed satellite phone gear, he drove to a high-end tech store off 51st Street. I purchased a new cellphone as the most powerful Global Smartphone Access or GSA I could get was incompatible with my old phone. The GSA was about the size of a paperback novel. I bought two spare rechargeable batteries and a 20W solar panel array for remote charging. All of this came to just over three grand, including a subscription to the Iridium Satellite Network, providing me with cell service just about anywhere on the planet.

As the salesperson transferred the contents of my old cell to the new one along with the GSA app, he asked where I planned on travelling.

I grinned, my head buzzing with the elation of being able to purchase whatever I wanted.

"Around the world," I answered, perhaps with too much enthusiasm, "I'm going to travel the world."

He laughed and said, "Well, don't use the GSA for web browsing. I see you have a good roaming package on your cell; use that first. Use this," he said smiling, tapping the box the GSA came in, "when you're like totally off-grid."

I texted Manuel from my new phone and met him on the street. It was almost seven, and I hadn't eaten since Zurich. I asked him to take me to his favourite restaurant, and he drove us to a burger place, where he ordered the house special for both of us. We sat in his cab and ate while Manuel told me about his wife and their two teenage children and what living and working in New York City was like. He occasionally asked about my life. I kept my answers simple: I had inherited money and property from my grandfather and was taking some time to travel before going to college. He didn't need to know more.

I wasn't ready to go back to Kingston yet, so Manuel took me to what he said was the ritziest place in Manhattan, the Plaza Hotel on Fifth at the foot of Central Park. He said he'd hauled a lot of rich folks there and that, with my new clothes, I'd fit right in. When we pulled up front, I offered to tip him an extra two hundred, but he flatly refused, promising to return at my request at nine o'clock the next morning. I had thought of staying a few days in New York City, but a world awaited me.

A clerk looked up casually from behind the imposing front desk as I approached with my suitcase and shopping bags. He gave me a quick once over and barely concealed a sigh. I assumed it was the age thing. That usually doesn't bother me, for, as Morgan says, when I turn sixty, I'll look forty, whatever that'll look like. However, the clerk's manner irritated me, and I took great pleasure in telling him that I had no booking but would like a suite. He smiled politely and dryly informed me that such rooms were booked before any potential walk-ins.

"I'll take any room then."

I set my bags down and slowly opened the new wallet, placing the Manhattan Chase credit card on the glossy counter. He smiled thinly as he swiped it, and for a moment, I felt foolish at my naiveté. After all, he probably handled these cards every day.

"I'll need to see some ID, of course," he said officiously, his head still turned to the computer screen. I held my student's I.D. card up for him to see, but his eyes widened before he even glanced at it.

"Oh. Mr. Aidan Ames. I'm sorry. I see your name and that of Felix Montgomery Ames are flagged as VIP in our system."

"Flagged?"

He glanced at me and then at the screen.

"Yes. You and your, I believe this is your grandfather, have standing executive reservations with the hotel."

All I could manage was a bewildered look.

"Oh."

He seemed to take no notice that I was ignorant of this fact.

"I'm sorry. We didn't know you would be joining us this evening. Unfortunately, your usual suite is unavailable, but we can offer similar arrangements. May we offer you a complimentary evening snack or breakfast on the morrow?"

I tried to appear calm, even aloof, as I imagined a person of wealth would act, but the coincidence was too much. Not only had my grandfather stayed here so often that he had a 'usual suite,' but he had planned on me being with him, even having the hotel add my name to its list of VIP guests.

"Uh, sure, that's good, er, that's fine."

Once again, my grandfather's belief in me and my inclusion in the Windows gave me recognition. I was known because he was known.

I called Bill's phone from my room, propped up by a mountain of soft pillows on the king-sized bed, drinking a bottle of spring water from the wet bar. Home, what an odd thought. Where was home now? Kingston?

Calgary? Enniskillen? Bill answered, and I told him where I was. He laughed so loud that I had to hold my cell away from my ear.

"We wondered where you'd gotten to," he said jokingly. "I have the app ready."

"Great. Was it difficult to design a program for the map?"

"Nah," I could hear the shrug in his voice. It would have been a simple task for him. "Dane has the schematic all worked out for the upgrades on the electrical system. Do you think we can do it this weekend? I mean, it's your money and all, but ...."

"No. Go ahead. We should also consider getting new appliances and air-conditioning, maybe one of those heat pump devices if you guys know how to install one."

The fortress was occasionally too hot during the daytime, even with the ventilation fans.

"Yeah, that's a good idea. We have a couple on the ranch. Are you okay with us spending all this money?" He sounded tense, as if he was speaking to an employer rather than a friend. Was he honestly beginning to view our friendship like that, all because of an inheritance?

"No worries. I have lots. Hey, I went shopping!"

I told him about Manuel, the shoes, the watch, and the hotel. He listened politely, interjecting with questions about New York and the warehouse, but the conversation felt strained and awkward. Finally, he asked what I assumed he'd been thinking while I rambled on about my new life.

"You're skipping a lot of classes, eh? What will your parents think?"

What will my parents think?

"Well, it's not their problem, is it?" I answered sharply. "I don't need to tell them anything."

An uncomfortable silence thundered in between us. When he spoke again, his voice had a much different tone.

"Well, Aidan, I need to finish this paper. When are you coming back?"

He was angry with me, but why, and for what? For skipping classes? For my unexpected new life?

"Tomorrow," I replied, my voice devoid of emotion. It felt like something inside me had just died.

"Okay, see you then," he said quietly.

I swiped the phone off and slammed it onto the end table. Why was I feeling guilty? For the first time in my life, I had complete freedom. I could go anywhere I wanted and could do anything I wanted. I was on my own, and I was enjoying my new life. What was so wrong with that?

I donned my new cross trainers and tracksuit and went to the lobby. The doorman gave me a courteous nod as I passed him and pushed through the revolving doors. It was dark, drizzling, and too cool to run without proper layers, but I didn't care. Crossing the avenue into Central Park, I ran hard for about twenty minutes, looking for that mental place where my brain shuts off and I leave the world's stupidity behind. I couldn't find it. That angered me, so I slowed to a steady, even pace, focusing on my heart rate, breathing, and the path at my feet. The weather was miserable. As I ran, I was aware that there were dark, huddled shapes lurking in the shrubbery around the section of the park called The Pond, people whom I wouldn't want to meet in the daylight, yet I felt no fear. I ignored them, though mentally, I felt some irritation at their presence, almost daring them, in my thoughts, to get in my way. I pressed on, attempting to leave everyone and everything behind me, and with each thud of my rain-soaked shoes, I vowed that I would never return to the old Aidan. He was dead, like my grandfather. Sweat mingled with raindrops as they ran down my face and stung my eyes. When I returned to the Plaza more than an hour later, I realized, almost shamefully, that I had been crying.

I showered and watched the last half of a movie. Then, I drank a vodka cooler from the fridge and fell into a restless sleep. The next morning, I awoke angry and tired. I could feel a head cold coming on, so I skipped the complementary breakfast, checked out, and stepped outside to wait for Manuel. It was another dreary and rainy day.

Manuel arrived early, and I asked him to drive me straight to the warehouse. He tried engaging me in conversation, but I withdrew, answering him only in snippets while I stared out the taxi's window. I barely saw the traffic, barely noticed the massive crowds of people who scurried about like ants, hurrying to wherever it was they were going. When we arrived at the warehouse, I handed him the two hundred I'd tried tipping him the day before and then stepped out onto the curb.

"Everything all right?" His voice sounded concerned.

I turned, stooping to look at him through the front passenger window.

"I'll be okay."

"You need me later on?"

"No, thanks. I'm going home today."

Home, the word was sounding even more foreign today than it had yesterday.

His eyebrows furrowed as he looked first at me, then at the sprawling building hanging over us like a giant, blocking what little bit of sun was trying to pry its way through the wet, grey sky.

"Need a lift to the airport? I'll take you, free of charge," he smiled, "since you've paid enough to put tires on this baby for at least a couple of years."

I reached through the window to shake his hand.

"Thanks, Manuel, but I'll take it from here. You've been a great help."

He shrugged.

"No problem, kid. Give me a call if you ever get back this way."

He passed me his business card. I took it and walked away as he slowly drove off. I could feel his eyes on my back.

I caught the 10:45 to Kingston.

FIFTEEN

The house on Turin Street was quiet, but my mind was buzzing with the possibilities of the unwritten future before me. I had always been a reader, consuming anything fantastic or futuristic, allowing my imagination to be drawn into other worlds and alien cultures. Now, my life has suddenly become one of those stories. I could travel anywhere, and anywhere could now be my home. Whatever that was anymore.

The brothers were out, probably at college, doing what they had come to Kingston to do. I took my old clothes, the *before* ones that reminded me of my life, my other life, stuffed them into a garbage bag and carried them to the weathered, wooden bin in the alley out back. The bag was bulky and awkward and too large for the old metal garbage can inside the bin, so I pummelled it with my fists until I could drop the lid with a satisfyingly loud bang. I felt like I was burying my past and being resurrected as a different person. It was as if I had travelled back in time and would now live the life I had always wanted. My future was wide open and unplanned, an unfamiliar road calling out to me, but I was charting the course, not my Dad, my friends, or anyone else. I had no idea what lay ahead of me or who the new Aidan would be, I only knew that I no longer needed the one that had brought me to this point in life.

Did this new resolve of mine exclude Morgan? Maybe. What was there between us anyway? Circumstances had thrown us together. We had been neighbours and went to the same schools, but what else was there between us? A silly kiss?

I grabbed my toiletries, including a pack of cold medicine from the cabinet in the main floor bathroom, and added them to my suitcase, the suitcase of the new Aidan Ames. An inexpensive tablet was on the study desk, along with a note from Bill. I grabbed both, not bothering to read the note.

I crossed over to the island and grabbed two spare Closet 2 keys, deposited them on the kitchen table, along with a note to the twins explaining that I needed some time alone and that they were welcome to use any spare time they had to do whatever they wanted to the fortress. I called the hardware store the property management agency had used since my grandfather's death and authorized the brothers to charge whatever they needed to upgrade the island's infrastructure.

I wrote *Thank You* at the bottom of the note, I didn't want to appear ungrateful for their expertise or time. I had few mechanical skills, and I certainly wasn't going to hire a local contractor to do what needed doing on the island. My grandfather had written that he thought I was ready for this. I laughed. I doubted I could fix a leaky faucet if I had to.

As an afterthought, I snagged the first-aid kit from the desk and then caught the 3 p.m. Window to London. I stepped into an empty room, pulling my suitcase, dressed in a T-shirt, a lightweight jacket and cargo pants from Sease, and a pair of expensive Sperry loafers, all purchased from stores along Fifth Avenue in New York City, stores I would never have been able to shop at before. My grandfather's fedora rested on my head, a reminder that we, he and I, were travellers, *Explorers of the Old Order*, he used to say. That had been one of his favourite lines as we'd explored the neighbourhood around Turin Street those summers. I wasn't sure what those words meant anymore. As I'd learned, he'd been off exploring the world while he'd left me alone in his house, sometimes for hours at a time. Now, it was my turn to explore.

A security system immediately began beeping sharply.

"For real?" I moaned between throbs in my head.

The keypad was next to the door, and I had no idea what the code was. I quickly pulled my pack off and opened Bill's tablet. Precious seconds danced by as I tried to recognize his app. An icon on the home screen was labelled *Map*. Good. I tapped that as a mechanical voice with a British accent suddenly informed me I had 60 seconds to disarm the alarm. Damn. I tapped the icon, and a separate page popped open. A header of white letters on a black background at the top of the page says *Level One*. What the hell is Level One? There are a lot of squares on this page, each with names and times I recognize from the Map. Okay, find London. There it is. I tapped it as the voice indicated 30 seconds. Shit. Another page opens, and I immediately see that Bill has placed all the important information, like a security code, at the top. What a good friend he is. I punch six numbers into the keypad, and the room falls quiet.

I sighed heavily and finally took a look at the space. It's cast in shadows from yellowish light that bled through a single dirt-streaked transom window above the door. Leaving the room, I followed a hallway on my right until I came to an exit door. It required a code to unlock it, so I angrily fumbled through the Key Wallet until I found another set of numbers and let myself out onto a narrow alley, capped with a brick wall on one end with access to a street on the other. It was five hours later than Ontario in the UK, and it was nighttime, windy, raining, and I felt like the world was moving beneath my feet.

The street beyond the alley was narrow, lined with small passenger cars, and fronted with semi-detached houses on one side and a discreet walled industrial area on the other. The Bluebell Guest House, one of my grandfather's favourite hangouts, according to the journal, was directly across from me. I was in London, Kensington more precisely, and Hyde Park was somewhere near, as was Kensington Palace, a private residence reserved for members of the Royal Family.

I crossed the glistening street under the bluish glow of light standards that stood over one side of the roadway and then turned to survey the building that housed the Window. It was an older two-storey brick warehouse, possibly from the Second World War era, and it sported a well-lit sign: *Felix and Son*. The site had been listed on the address card in the Key Wallet simply as *Warehouse*.

Felix and Son? Was the name a coincidence, or had my grandfather planned on including my father in the Enniskillen legacy at one time? I turned to the Bluebell, and something crunched loudly beneath my shoes. There were dozens of snails about the size of dimes on the sidewalk, marching at an imperceptible pace to who knows where. I gingerly picked my way through them up the flat-stone path to the front entrance of the Bluebell.

An illuminated sign surrounded by creeping vines was attached to the right of the door, indicating a room was available. A plump, older woman answered after I rang the door ringer, a little brass handle I had to flip sideways. She appeared genuinely surprised to see someone at such a late hour and glanced over my shoulder as if she were looking for my vehicle or whoever had delivered me to her stoop.

"Uh, you have a vacancy?" I asked, sniffing while pointing at the sign.

She smiled warmly, squinting at me, curious, I supposed.

"Of course, luv, come in, come in. I'm Mrs. Sellars," she offered with a light-hearted chuckle, "but you may call me Margaret."

She ushered me into a comfortable lobby full of family history and homey smells and introduced me to her husband, George, who sat behind a long, waist-high counter in front of a small TV. It seemed way too loud for its small size.

"Turn down that awful noise, George," she said, and then, as an aside, "Poor dear, my George, he's losing his hearing."

He peered at me over the top of his dirt-specked glasses, frowned slightly, and then turned the volume down. She shooed him aside as she went behind the desk, lifting out a thick registration book with a tattered cover and plopped it matter-of-factly on the counter.

"There now, love, what would you be looking for? We've a small room, just right for you, overlooking the garden out back."

"That'll be fine," I answered.

George arched his head in my direction, frown lines encircling his old eyes. I nodded at him, took the pen that his wife offered, and added my name to the guest register.

"How long will you be staying with us, er – " Her eyebrows formed a question on her smiling face. "Aidan Ames? You be from Canada then?"

I nodded, sneezing almost simultaneously.

"Goodness," she gasped. "It's Aidan, then. Why, you'd be Felix's grandson!"

It was more of an exclamation than a question.

"He said you'd be stopping by this way one day. Welcome, child."

George stood up, pulling his glasses off as he rose, and then reached across the counter for my hand, which he shook vigorously.

"An absolute great pleasure to finally meet you, lad," he said enthusiastically. "Your grandfather spoke quite highly of you and often. Will you be staying at the 'Bells for a while then, as Felix used to?"

"Oh, George, let's not pester the poor lad with all these questions. Can't you see he's all knackered?" Her hand flew to my forehead. "Poor lad has a chill!"

"It's okay, Mrs. Sellars," I stammered, "I just need some rest. My grandfather loved staying here."

"His passing was such sad news," George said earnestly, nodding. "A fine gentleman, your granddad. Me and the missus enjoyed tea with him, many a time, in the garden."

"Please accept our condolences, Aidan," his wife added.

There was a soothing softness to her voice. She reached for my hand, cupped it, and gently squeezed it.

"Thank you," I replied with sincerity. After all, these were my grandfather's friends. I pulled my wallet out, reaching for the credit card.

"I have a Chase Manhattan credit card. Will that do?"

"No, luv," she shook her head and glanced at her husband, "we'll hear no talk of money. Stay as long as you wish."

"The missus is right. Your grandfather was very generous to us, and we never took a single quid from him when he lodged here. It would be improper of us now, wouldn't it, lad, to start such a thing with his grandson."

They weren't about to budge, and I wasn't about to argue. My head throbbed above my left eye, and I desperately wanted to escape into sleep. I would think of something nice to do for them. My grandfather would have done that, too, I reasoned.

Mrs. Sellars led me up a creaky, carpeted staircase to a tiny room with a single rain-streaked window and a bed that I wanted to fall into. She pointed to where the washroom was down the hall and where I could find clean towels.

"Thank you," I said weakly.

"There, now, we'll chat tomorrow then, love," she said, smiling softly, in between puffs of exertion, as she pulled the quilt back to fluff the pillows. "You get some rest now. George and I will be in the sitting room downstairs if you need anything. And we'll have a right proper English breakfast when you wake."

And with that, she was gone. I downed a couple of cold pills, stripped down to my underwear, flicked off the light switch and crawled into the welcoming comfort of the bed.

I slept fitfully, tossing and turning, plagued by dreams I couldn't remember, but I felt their lingering terror. The sound of knocking woke me the next morning. I sat up slowly, damp with perspiration, my head aflame with fever. The knocking was Mrs. Sellars at the door, wondering if I was all right.

"Aidan, it's almost past breakfast, deary."

"I have a cold," I said, loud enough for her to hear me through the old door. My head was throbbing painfully.

"You're cold, luv?"

"No. I'm ill. I need to sleep." I closed my eyes again, and she walked away, the floorboards creaking in time to the jackhammer pulse in my head.

Sometime later, Mrs. Sellars brought me chicken soup and tea. She knocked and walked in. I could barely focus my eyes or thoughts, but she propped me up with pillows, and I ate what I could, tossing back more cold pills with the tea. She checked in on me again sometime during my second night at the 'Bells, and we had a brief chat before I pulled the quilt up around my head again. By Friday morning, I awoke with only a slight headache and a desperate need to shower. I went down the hall to the washroom and realized I had already been there several times. Later, I dressed and found the dining area in the solarium overlooking a narrow garden at the back of the house.

The Sellars were seated there and greeted me like an old friend. It was a strange feeling; I didn't know them, but my grandfather had often talked about me to them and how I would accompany him one day. They were engaging people who loved to talk, interrupting each other the way couples who have lived together for a long time do. They cheerfully described their life at the Bluebell between cups of steaming tea. The house had been George's parents, and when his father passed away, he and Margaret and their two young children moved in to help his mother. 'The Bells,' as they fondly referred to their guesthouse, came about nearly two decades earlier when George was injured while working as a plumber. They needed a way to survive beyond his meagre disability pension and the income Margarette received from her job as a clothing store clerk, so they converted their home into a guesthouse. However, they fell on hard times again. The economy took a sudden dip, and the Sellars simply didn't have the clientele or the advertising expertise required to succeed and were near bankruptcy when my grandparents rang the doorbell one day. That was about the same time the old warehouse across the road had been purchased and renovated, according to the property list in the Key Wallet.

"We're not that posh," George explained. "There's a score of hotels just down the lane with the fancy amenities most Americans and Europeans want. You know, the shuttle and all."

"But, George," his wife interrupted, "we are near the Underground."

"The Underground?" I asked.

George nodded.

"The Holland Park Tube Station."

My grandparents had rescued them but with dignity. They bought the property and asked them to run it as their own. They visited at least once a month after that, sometimes more, and enjoyed playing card games and chatting about their travels overseas and in North America. When Felix's wife passed away, Margaret said, my grandfather would visit even more often.

"Your granddad was like one of the family," George said wistfully, turning to stare out the window overlooking the garden.

"Indeed," Margarette said, squeezing her husband's hand while smiling at me.

Then, one Christmas, six years earlier, my grandfather flew the Sellars' family, including their children, spouses and five grandchildren, and George's mother, who was "now deceased, God rest her," to New York, where they stayed at the Plaza Hotel.

"It was a wondrous Christmas," Mrs. Sellars reflected. "The decorations were a thing to behold."

When my grandfather died, they were surprised to learn the Bluebell had been willed to them along with a generous trust for upkeep as long as they retained ownership. I smiled knowingly at that. He was a generous person, always giving money or food to anyone less fortunate in his neighbourhood. I was with him a few summers ago when he crossed a busy street to give an older man panhandling near a bus stop the sack of groceries we'd just purchased.

"Never forget, Kiddo," he'd said as we walked back across the street to the grocery store, "everyone has a story; some they write with their bad decisions, and others just get handed a Shakespearean tragedy. It's not always their fault."

When I'd asked what he meant, he had replied: "I got handed a good story. I like to help out people who didn't."

Is this what he meant? The Sellers were handed a bad story, and he helped them write a better one.

They didn't earn much money, but they were happy and, as George had said, "The Bell's as sound as a barrel."

I took it easy for the rest of the afternoon, napping and taking time to master the map of the Windows Bill had programmed into the tablet. He had been his usual thorough self. The note he left me meticulously explained how to navigate the software. It was a modern version of the map on the wall on the island, and between this and the multi-time zone setting on my watch, I was confident I could navigate the Windows without too many surprises.

The end of his note read:

We should look at getting this onto your phone. Then you won't have to carry another device around that needs charging. Enjoy your new life, Aidan, but don't forget your friends. — Bill.

Angered by his parting comment, I crumpled the note, tossing it forcefully into the wastebasket beside my bed. Was that what was worrying him? That I'd forget them? Despite how I had felt about their unexpected intrusion into my inheritance, they were a part of what was happening to me now.

I slept well that night, feeling only mild discomfort in my sinuses. The next day, I crossed the road back to the Felix and Son storage facility. I entered the room I had arrived in and embarked on the real reason I had come to England: to follow Reinhold Bonk's suggestion. Of course, Bonk knew nothing of the closet's unique ability, speculating that it would take me at least six months to survey my properties by air travel. I figured I could do it effectively in less than a month.

My navigation tools were Bill's tablet with the digital map, my grandfather's Key Wallet, and my cellphone and GSA. Google Maps would be able to pinpoint wherever I was on the planet as long as I had cell reception, and if I didn't, I'd pull out the GSA and link my phone to it to discover my location. I would return to the Bluebell when I needed rest. The Sellars' had given me a key so I could come and go as I pleased, but I wouldn't return to Kingston until I was satisfied with my knowledge of what my grandfather had left in my trust.

I grabbed my suitcase, inserted the key, turned it, and stepped through into a furnished but small office in a building overlooking the River Spree in Berlin, Germany. The world was mine; I could do anything and go anywhere.

SIXTEEN

Travelling through the Window system was like having magical powers. I walked through doors and entered one country after another as if I had an all-access passport to the planet. I kept my fedora on when I was somewhere public to at least try and protect my face from the pervasiveness of CCTV cameras, not that anyone was looking for me. Still, this was not the world of Willie McPhie. He might have been able to suddenly appear without anyone questioning the legality or the how of it, but the world of Aidan Ames was very different. I was unlikely to walk through a neighbourhood without being recorded on dozens of doorbell cameras or enter a store or restaurant without my image being captured.

I'd never been to Berlin, Antwerp, Fortaleza, Dublin, or Vigo. Every turn of the key opened a new world to me. As I travelled and explored, I felt like I was leaving behind the memory of Aidan Ames, the Aidan Nobody from Calgary, Canada, and was starting to create the new me, Aidan Ames, World Traveller. The Bluebell Guest House was my base of operations, and depending on where I was or how engaging a site was, I didn't return for days. I didn't need to, but I would tell the Sellars that I was sightseeing up North or travelling to the Continent, and they never questioned it. George informed me that my grandfather did as much as well.

The Windows weren't laid out in any logical direction, such as East to West or North to South. My globetrotting took me back and forth across the International Date Line, the equator, from night to day and from one season to the next. I crisscrossed aimlessly around the globe, depending on when and where the Windows were established or, as it must have been in the early years of William McPhie, where the money was to be made. It became a question of just how long it would be before I keeled over with exhaustion from the effects of jet lag or, in my case, Window lag, or caught another head cold from the parade of changing climates. Until now, I had not truly understood the concept of the Earth as in a constant state of change. I had lived my life from season to season, but now, it was always snowing when it was raining somewhere else. Elsewhere, the sun ruled, burning the hard earth relentlessly or causing fields to spring to life. Spring, summer, winter, and fall were happening simultaneously, like a crazy mashup of different genres of music.

The diagram in the Map Room on the island had two circles of destinations, an inner and outer ring. For simplicity's sake, Bill had programmed the tablet to display the map as two levels: Level One, the outer ring, and Level Two, the inner ring. Because of the number of destinations for each level, 48, he didn't add the Windows that opened on Turin Street, reducing the number of squares to 36 per level. Even so, I had to scroll through six screen pages for each level. If I tapped one of the squares, a window would pop up with the related information for that destination, taken from what had been written on the cards in my grandfather's Key Wallet. A tab to the right of the Level One grid opened the Level Two grid. It was a clever way to bring the hand-drawn map the McPhies and my grandparents had used into the 21st century.

As I travelled the system, I discovered that not all the doors were the same size or shape. Nor do all have hardware in the same position. Some had knobs on the left or right or locks higher or lower on one side or the other or even in the middle of the door. This made little difference, as the door of the room I was entering did not physically open. When I had walked through the closet door from Kingston to Victoria that first time weeks earlier, only the door on Turin Street opened. The apartment door in Victoria had remained bolted and chained shut.

According to the information cards in the Key Wallet, several changes had been made during my grandparents' time. From the bare-boned descriptions, it appeared part of the reason for travel involved maintenance of the properties and occasionally relocating a Window, which meant moving an entire door. If the lock was taken apart, the Window would lose its place in the cycle of time, shifting the times for every Window. One such move of an entire door was from a Victorian-age house along the Thames, north of London, to Kingston, which explained the age of the closet door.

Another of these moves was to the sheep paddock in West Perthshire, Scotland. My grandfather had moved an entire door, mounting it in a door frame on a porch he had built specifically for it. He had planned to build a large workshop to attach to the porch, but my grandmother's death had put that on hold. The first thing I did when I stepped through was to replace the missing screws in the lock, ensuring it wouldn't fall apart again. The sheep were still there, and they approached me with the same bleating curiosity as before, hoping, I supposed, that I'd brought something for them to eat this time. I said hello and hopped the fence to make my way around the paddock to the road I'd seen meandering away the first day of my closet adventures. The paddock was in the western corner of thirty-one hundred acres of land leased to several tenant farmers through Universal Holdings. One of these farms was managed by an elderly couple, Wallace and Ann Robertson, whose cottage and outbuildings were just out of sight of the paddock. I could have easily walked to their home had I known this when I'd stumbled through the closet that first day.

I arrived a few minutes after 1 p.m., Kingston time, 8 p.m. local time. When I knocked on the door of their ivy-covered dwelling and introduced myself, they immediately welcomed me in. I apologized for the lateness of the hour, but Wallace smiled broadly and reached for my hand.

"Nah, your grandad said you'd be around one day."

I was no longer surprised by that comment. My grandfather had been excited about including me in his travels and had told anyone he knew I would be accompanying him one day. It was a little unnerving to think he'd had these plans for my life without me knowing a thing about them.

Over tea and homemade oat squares, we chatted about my grandparent's many visits. When Felix and Mariah first showed up on their doorstep, the Robertsons said they had no idea they were the leaseholders.

"They just said they were travellers exploring the area," Ann explained.

Only a few years later, once their friendship had grown, did my grandparents disclosed that they were the landowners.

"Aye," Wallace said, nodding, "your Grandparents didn't make much ado about such things. They both just enjoyed people, and when they told us, it didn't change a thing, no."

They mentioned how difficult it had been for my grandfather when Mariah passed. They knew nothing of his death but suspected something when he quit visiting. It was around the time their leasing fees were reduced by eighty percent. A letter arrived in the post, Wallace said, announcing the change. I told them my grandfather had died of a heart attack. Until I knew the truth, that would be the standard answer to those who might ask.

"We're sorry to hear of his passing," Ann told me, touching my hand. "Your Gran and Grandad were fine folks."

Her husband nodded in agreement.

"Aye, and it was very generous of Felix to arrange for a reduction in the lease after his passing. It was a surprise. Though I have to say, they were both very generous people."

His wife smiled and nodded

"So, you've taken over the family business then, have you?"

I saw and heard the concern in her words and her eyes. Did they think I, the new owner, would increase their lease costs? I didn't hesitate to respond.

"I have, but nothing will change. My grandfather was the kindest, most big-hearted person I know. I'm not changing anything."

A flash of relief passed between them, and I briefly felt what I'm sure my grandfather must have at times. The Enniskillen Group was this enormous money-making enterprise, and obviously, he didn't want that wealth coming from the livelihood of people like the Robertsons.

We chatted for a while, eventually turning to the porch in the paddock. They said their adult children and locals had been speculating about it for some time. I didn't explain other than to shrug and suggest that my grandfather liked a practical joke.

"But please don't tear it down," I said, half joking.

"Oh, no, no, we wouldn't think of it," Wallace assured me.

I was about to leave when they kindly invited me to stay overnight as it was late. I gently refused, saying I had rented a motorhome and had parked it by the paddock. It was close to midnight when I left, and I had to use the flashlight I carried in my backpack to return to the porch. I couldn't help but wonder as I waited for the next Window what lessons my grandfather would have wanted to teach me if he hadn't been murdered and we had toured the sites together. Generosity? Kindness? I glanced at my overly expensive watch and felt a twinge of guilt as I inserted the key and opened a Window.

After several days of travelling through the system, it was obvious that many sites were located in large buildings along waterways. This allowed the McPhies to build their shipping empire. The Window in Dublin Port was set in the door to a private office at the back of a sizeable stone warehouse that smelled like an old prairie barn. The site also had a large secure yard of row upon row of stacked lumber destined for somewhere. I explored Ireland's capital for a few days, touring cavernous old cathedrals and eating in small, local pubs vibrating with music from pickup jam sessions. It was amazing how welcoming the locals were and how eager they were to tell me about their city and traditions, such as swimming at the Forty Foot, a popular spot on Dublin Bay. I didn't take the plunge; it was too cold, but I enjoyed two nights of great food and enthusiastic and often moving Irish music. There were several more Windows in Ireland in weathered stone warehouses overlooking bustling ports, including Cork and Holyhead, but I stayed for only a few hours in each place.

In contrast to the ports in Ireland, a modern storage facility in an industrial area in Nuuk, Greenland's capital city, thousands of kilometres away, looked out over the ice-choked Nuup Kangerlua fjord. There were security personnel stationed throughout the complex, and I didn't bother asking whoever was in charge to go and check for an email from Universal Holdings informing management that I, the owner, would be arriving for an inspection. Besides, it was full-blown winter, and I was dressed for parallels much lower on the planet.

The Window in Naples, Italy, opened onto a boardwalk leading to a wharf and warehouses facing the City's port. I had come upon this site during my first incursion of the system, which seemed so long ago. The Window closed behind me as I stepped out into a muggy evening in what appeared to be a massive commercial shipping area. I found the door's key in the Key Wallet and entered a rattan-furnished, multi-roomed office. According to papers in a desk drawer, the space was for a numbered import/export company, mine.

Like Naples, the Window in the warehouse in Bangkok, Thailand, opened onto an outdoor space, in this case, an alley. I'd been here before, but this time, I stepped through the door and down onto the pitted stone steps I had seen that first visit. As always, the Window shut. I turned to find a reinforced steel door with a passcode-protected security system. I located the key and a passcode and used both to enter the room. It was small, windowless, with two doors, one I had just entered and one opposite. The latter opened onto a narrow hallway that led to a vast, dimly-lit warehouse holding towers of crates and mounds of equipment. My cellphone's GPS revealed that the building was on the Chao Phraya River, a major transportation route. The room was spartan, the only piece of furniture a hammock strung between the two walls of a corner. A bathroom sink was mounted to a wall, with a toilet next to it. Beside it was a sealed plastic container of toilet paper rolls.

I had come to this site to visit the elderly man I had met before, Boon Nam. Leaving the room, I navigated through the stacks of buckets and crates to the door where I'd seen him come out. I pressed a buzzer on the wall and waited. A moment later, a small, older woman answered. The room behind her was poorly lit and cluttered with boxes, crates and buckets, and large commercial freezers. She didn't speak English, so I finally told her the man's name. I hoped I had pronounced it correctly, but then her face beamed. Smiling and nodding, she called over her shoulder, and soon, he emerged from the clutter behind her. His face lit up when he saw me and he spoke excitedly to the woman, who immediately grinned just as brightly, bowed her head and hustled back into the labyrinth.

"Ai-dan, Ames' grandson," the old man bubbled, bowing slightly and then grasping my hand. He pumped my arm vigorously.

"You return, yes?"

"Yes," I replied as he continued to grip my hand.

"I hoped we could talk about my grandfather."

"Ames, yes? We talk very much, Ames and Boon Nam."

He patted his chest with his other hand.

"Ames come visit many times and we play Pok Deng. Ames lose much money, much money."

He released my hand while continuing to grin and shake his head.

I laughed, moved by the joy of his memories of my grandfather. He directed me through the door and around a stack of crates. We entered a smaller and less cluttered room. I could see, hear, and smell the life of a busy restaurant kitchen through swinging doors on the opposite wall. The woman who had met me at the alley came towards us carrying a dark teapot that trailed a wisp of steam. She poured tea into little ceramic cups she had placed on a small table surrounded by chairs of various vintage.

"This is my wife, Hansa," he said.

Hearing her name, she nodded and said something in response that I didn't understand.

"She very pleased to meet you," Boon Nam translated. "And she sorry for you."

I smiled and nodded.

"Please tell her thank you."

He said something to her, and his wife nodded once, left the pot and returned to the kitchen, the doors swinging shut behind her.

"Please sit. Sit," the elderly man gestured.

I sat, and he did as well, his face so full of joy that I wondered if his cheeks were aching. He offered me one of the cups of a hot and mildly bitter tea.

I asked questions about my grandparents' friendship with him, and he talked briskly about how they had met in the alley, much like he and I had, and about the many hours they had spent together playing various gambling card games like the Pok Deng. This was usually over cups of strong tea and sometimes even stronger bottles of jiu, a Chinese rice beer. He said there was a time when my grandfather didn't come around for several months. Then, he showed up one day during the monsoon season.

"Very bad weather," he said, his arms swooping in animated circles, "Ames tell me that his wife died. So very sad. We talk a long time that day, and Ames have much peace after we talk."

He touched his fingers to his chin as his eyes glistened with sadness.

"I help my friend."

I felt tears welling up as he smiled apologetically and wiped his eyes with a cloth. I had not expected such a deep relationship between him and my grandfather. Sitting in this cluttered back room, I felt a moment of adult maturity, and I realized even more that my grandfather had never been mine to claim. I was just six when my grandmother died, and I barely remember anything about it. I remember mostly the emotional reactions of the adults around me. This man, whom I knew little about before today, had a long friendship with my grandparents, and I had been the one to inform him of my grandfather's death.

"I'm sorry," I said after a moment. "I'm sorry I brought such sad news to you the first time we met."

Boon Nam smiled and shook his head, waving his hands.

"No, no, no, death is certain. A loyal friend is a gift. Ames was such a friend, as are you."

"Thank you," I replied, taking a quick swig of tea to drown the emotion rising in my throat.

The diversity of my grandfather's friendships revealed something about his character. He was wealthy and could have easily had other wealthy friends, but he chose not to do that. Boon Nam, the Sellars, and the Robertsons were his friends because he wanted to know about them and their lives. He loved the people he had met on his travels, and they loved him.

"I, uh, I'm making a tour of all the properties my grandfather left me. It's something he had wanted to do with me before he died," I said, hoping to change the subject.

"Very good," he nodded, "very responsible, yes. Ames would be pleased with grandson."

He poured another round of tea, and I couldn't help but wonder why such an elderly man was still working. I asked him if he had plans to retire.

He laughed and smiled as he nodded.

"Ames ask same question. I tell him same as I tell you. This is –" he grimaced, searching for a word, "is not possible. My wife and I work to give children much better chance, more luck. Son is studying to be engineer in Udon Thani, and daughter is doctor here in Yanhee Hospital."

He made a sweeping gesture, indicating the room we were in.

"Boon Nam, Hansa, we, uh, not own restaurant. We lease."

"Oh," I replied, embarrassed that I had asked the question. "Uh, how long do you plan to keep working?"

He shrugged.

"We work until we cannot work."

I was amazed at his calm reply. I was almost nineteen, and because of an unexpected inheritance, I'd never have to work at anything I didn't want to, and yet here was an elderly friend of my grandfather who could not afford to stop working. Why hadn't he helped Boon Nam like he'd helped the Robertsons and the Sellars? I wanted to ask but then thought of what he had said both times we had met. My grandfather lost a lot of money to him playing cards. Anyone else I'd talked to had told me how good he and my grandmother were at card games. Perhaps it would have been offensive to offer his Thai friend a retirement that he hadn't earned, but losing at cards was an indirect way to contribute financially. We talked for a few minutes more, but then I excused myself, promising to return and try my hand at Pok Deng. Of course, I would lose. I suck at card games anyway.

According to the Map, there are several Windows in France, some in buildings from the mid-seventeenth century. A warehouse in Paris facing the River Seine, the one I'd accidentally discovered on my first journey, a lumbering shipping container complex in the port city of La Rochelle, and a small office tucked away in the back of an export company in the ancient city of Calais. But the one that drew my interest was at 2:45 on Level One. The Window opened to a modest, furnished, and immaculate third-floor walkup that overlooked a quiet pedestrian street in the port city of Rouen on the River Seine not far from its mouth at the English Channel. This was somewhere my grandparents had lived. There was evidence of this throughout the high-ceilinged, two-bedroom apartment. Dozens of French and English magazines lay loosely on a wooden coffee table between two loungers, next to a floor-to-ceiling bookshelf that contained volumes in a half-dozen languages from several genres. It was apparent that the apartment was cleaned periodically. I stayed the night and wandered the city streets the next morning, taking note of the many shops and museums and a spectacular cathedral with a central spire pointing like a finger toward the heavens. Walking among tourists and locals alike, I began to feel lost, like I was out of place. Scotland, Bangkok, and now France, every one of these countries was different enough in culture and customs to make me realize that if I was going to be a forever tourist, I needed to learn about the people and cultures of the places I was visiting.

Early the next morning, I caught the window to Knokke-Heist, an exclusive beach city in Belgium on the shores of the North Sea. The

Window was in a storage room in the back of a modest villa. The multi-roomed and fully furnished structure was in a Greco-Roman style. Along with antique furniture in every room, three elegant bathrooms, and a kitchen fit with a hanging rack of pots and a massive refrigerator and pantry, there were real columns, a terracotta roof, elegant ceramic tile on the walls, granite on the floor, and coloured glass shards artfully embedded in walls that separated its many rooms. There was a large water fountain out front, a faerie-tale flower garden that hugged three sides of the house, and a two-car garage with no cars but two scooters. I tried to start one of them and then the other, but no amount of cursing or fidgeting with this wire or that important-looking gadget would make them work. Angry with my ignorance of mechanical things, I left the villa and used my phone's GPS to plot a course towards the seafront.

On the way, I found a restaurant that boasted traditional Belgian cuisine. I hadn't eaten for a while and decided to see if I could get a seat. I was informed by a pleasant host that I was fortunate to be in the city off-season, as I most definitely would have had to make a reservation otherwise. Shortly after ordering fried sole with French fries, two men sitting near my table politely excused their intrusion and asked me where I was from. When I told them I was Canadian and just visiting, they launched into a spirited explanation of how the town came into being. They said the two were longtime friends who often visited this seaside resort. I smiled politely and asked a few questions. As legend had it, according to one of them, a group of Irish pilgrims, monks, and villains settled in the area centuries ago. I wondered if that group included the McPhies. His acquaintance, a thin, bespectacled man who informed me he was from Saint-Raphael in Southern France, respectfully disagreed, insisting that the town owed its existence to the dikes built to protect the area around the Zwin sea arm, a beautiful, natural reserve he encouraged me to visit. After finishing my meal, I left them to a friendly argument, fuelled partly by two bottles of French wine I purchased for them.

I located a bicycle shop and rented an electric cruiser to explore. Knokke-Heist was beautiful, unlike any city I'd seen so far, and I couldn't help but feel that Morgan would have loved being here. Its long history permeated every stately neighbourhood, sculpture, and public garden. Alongside this shadow of an ancient past were golf courses my father would have begged to swing a few irons on, a modern beach and a sheltered harbour with a view of dozens of towering wind generators far out at sea. There was an endless array of fashionable shops, exclusive boutiques, restaurants and bistros. Whether or not the local lore attributed the city's existence to the McPhies or other Irish travellers, I could see why they had placed a Window in this beach resort.

The day before I left, I joined a late-season bus tour of the Zwin Nature Park. It was, after all, the one place the two men in the waffle house agreed I must visit. Despite a cool wind blowing off the North Sea, it was worth it. As we approached the reserve, the tour guide pointed out fields where he said lavender bloomed in August, creating an immense carpet covering this unique ecosystem. I decided I'd have to come back in the summer to witness this, but even this late in the fall, numerous seabirds were foraging in the salt marshes created by the high tides that flow up the sea arms. Again, I wished Morgan was with me; she'd have loved this city.

I had to fix our relationship. Somehow.

After a day's rest at the Bluebells to add some notes to the pop-ups in Bill's tablet about the places I'd visited so far, my sojourn into Australia began with a typical but vast industrial warehouse on Sydney's waterfront, within walking distance of the Harbour Bridge. According to the information in the tablet, the massive building was a transfer point for heavy equipment heading for Southeast Asia. My grandfather's journal listed the warehouse as a point to ship large items to the island, which made sense; there were things in Enniskillen too large to go through the entrance in the study. When I peered out the door of the sparsely furnished office the Window was in, I had to explain my presence to an alert security guard who was passing. I showed him my Canadian birth certificate and the key to the room, which seemed to satisfy him.

Brisbane's Window opened on a dusty but modern boathouse, winch and all, minus the boat. I stayed in the city for only a few hours, purchasing a hand-drawn city map from a street artist and grabbing lunch in a bustling waterfront cafe. The third site in Australia was an office space in an expansive warehouse in the Port of Hedland, on the northwestern coast in the Pilbara region. I had no idea such a port existed, but according to the pop-up note on the tablet, the Enniskillen Group shipped iron ore, lithium and other items from there. By now, I was beginning to understand that most sites were utilitarian and strictly for business, with some having a side hustle of being in an interesting city to visit, like the warehouse in Paris.

The Windows might open up the world to me, but ultimately, they were about the locations that made money for the Group. It was clear that the history of the McPhie's, even under the philanthropy of Marianne McPhie, has always been about generating wealth. Only a handful of Windows appeared to have been installed for the pleasure of travel. I could count them on one hand: Rouen, Knokke-Heist, Zurich, and my latest discovery, a condo in Los Angeles.

The Window opened on a fully furnished condominium in a row of condo complexes in a waterfront neighbourhood on Manhattan Beach. When I stepped through the portal onto a short hallway, a security pad on the wall started glowing and beeping, and a stilted male voice announced I had 90 seconds to deactivate the alarm. I quickly fished the tablet from my backpack and swiped it open, navigating to the LA pop-up, trusting Bill's efficiency. The code was there, and a few seconds later, the security system was happy, and I flopped down on a deacon's bench in the hallway, exhaling in relief. Visions of explaining my illegal presence on American soil to armed police had flashed through my head.

The condo felt welcoming like it might be another home. The kitchen was generously stocked with canned and dry goods and bottled water in the fridge. The spacious living room had large comfortable chairs, a flatscreen television, and a bookshelf jammed with fiction and nonfiction. The second floor had a large bathroom tiled in slate and granite, a walk-in shower, and fresh towels and washcloths hanging from a rack. The bedroom had a queen-sized bed, articles of clothing in two dressers, and separate access to the bathroom. French doors led to a sizeable balcony off the bedroom, where a charcoal barbecue and wooden deck chairs that needed refinishing overlooked the beach and surf. Like the sites in Rouen and Knokke-Heist, the condo in Los Angeles was periodically cleaned.

After finding a small grocer nearby to purchase a few fresh essentials, I sat in one of the deck chairs on the condo's balcony and searched through my emails. I hadn't bothered to check them in several days, partly because I was busy exploring the system but mostly because they increasingly represented a world I was leaving behind. I saw receipts from the hardware store where Bill and Dane purchased material for repairs and upgrades they were doing on the island and a handful of emails from

Amelia. She chatted about her new position at the hospital, complained about her roommate, wondered how school was going, and asked if I'd made any friends at college. College? So much for that, I thought. I was getting something far better: a global education.

An email from Morgan downloaded. My heart jumped. She was on her laptop at that very moment and had written me. I stared at the subject line [hi aidan], my mind racing with excitement and apprehension. I had thought of her often in the various places I had been, and now she was contacting me. I clicked it open.

She wrote:

Aidan. I tried texting, but it bounced back. Kelli told me you called. I wanted to apologize again for reacting the way I did. You know me better than anyone. Trust has always been an issue for me, and I guess I expected things to be as they were in high school. You know, where we told each other whatever was happening in our lives. Those were good times. But that's okay. We aren't kids anymore. If you have a break from classes, please call or email. If you don't want to, that's all right, but I'd honestly like to talk sometime. Morgan.

My hands hovered over the screen, my mind racing, wondering how to answer. The more I travelled and saw my grandparents' friendships, the more I wanted to repair the damage I had caused by lying. And the more I travelled, the more I wanted Morgan on this journey. I needed to tell her the truth; that was the only way back to what we'd had.

I wrote: *Hey. No worries. I have a new phone and number. Things have been crazy lately, but yes, I'd like to talk, too. Give me a few days, and I'll call.*

After I hit send, I sat for a while, my feet resting on the balcony's railing, watching the sun slide towards Santa Monica Bay. There might be hope for us, yet. I left the bedroom window open that night, letting the unfamiliar but welcome sounds and rhythms of Manhattan Beach lull me to sleep.

SEVENTEEN

As I unwound in L.A., looking through the tablet and plotting my next trip, I found my thoughts wandering to the Windows marked off-limits. It was the beginning of the third week of my tour of the Window system, and I had visited thirty-nine of the sixty-nine usable sites on the map. I had been on five continents, in thirty-two countries and had seen and experienced more of the world than most people could hope to experience in a lifetime. However, there were three sites supposedly unavailable to me.

The one marked *under the sea* was obvious, but what about the two listed as *unusable* and *dangerous*? None of the journals in the Map Room specifically mentioned them. Why hadn't they been moved and recycled as so many others had? The mystery of what might lay behind these Windows had been pushing into my thoughts for a few days. It would bother me for years if I didn't try to discover anything about what was behind at least one of these doors. That was the explorer in me. I couldn't say, "Oh, well, can't go there, I guess." I needed to know why.

The 9:30 Window on Level One was one of the sites my predecessors had marked with the cryptic word, *Unusable*. I embarked on a pre-excursion information-gathering mission from the Window in the warehouse in Tasiilaq, Greenland. The warehouse was primarily used for storing shrimp and fish in large freezers awaiting export. If water came rushing through when I opened the Window, well, there was a large warehouse to hold it all. Cautiously, I activated the Window, standing close to the door and easing it open about two hand widths in case I suddenly had to close it. I was met with darkness and a waft of moist, putrid air that caused me to gag. However, nothing leapt out at me, and water hadn't come pouring in. I opened the door fully. From what I could see from the light that poured into the space from my side of the opening, it appeared to be nothing more than a musty, old room with a floor strewn with timbers and a few rocks. Across from me, something glistened. Maybe a window? There were sites like this in the Window system, desperate for renovations. This one just wasn't very hospitable. I shut the door.

I launched the official expedition to *Unusable* from the room in the Felix and Sons facility in Kensington. It was a practical staging area, just across the road from the Bluebell and not that distant from the Cromwell Hospital on Cromwell Road in case, god forbid, I needed medical attention. I needed a store that sold climbing gear, so I went to the one city where I thought there might be one: Zurich. I remembered seeing several climbing shops on my last visit, and I wasn't disappointed. I returned to the Felix and Sons warehouse armed with a rechargeable drill kit, leather gloves, a climber's hammer, a carbon fibre helmet with a built-in 'indestructible' headlamp, and steel-toed rubber boots designed specifically for spelunking – exploring caves. The harness was listed as official Kommando Spezialkräfte Marine gear, the German equivalent of US Navy SEALs. In the warehouse, I drilled a hole in the beam that framed the right-hand side of the door and twisted in a steel eye hook, a spot to anchor the harness. Along with my communications gear, I crammed my daypack with dry food, bottled water, a powerful flashlight, my Swiss Army Knife, a small first-aid kit, and a spray can of graphite lubricant that I had been using on some of the older locks in the system. I was as prepared as I could be or knew how to be.

With the climbing harness securely strapped around my groin, I connected it to the eye hook using a sturdy two-metre lanyard of woven nylon with hardened carabiners on either end. I looped my daypack over a shoulder, and when the time touched 9:30, I inserted the key, took a deep breath, and opened the door.

Nothing out of the ordinary happened – at first.

There was the usual flash of light, followed by a gust of wind, which reeked of decay, and a moist, rotting wood smell mixed with the sea's tangy saltiness. Light lanced through the darkness from the room behind me and the light on my helmet. I placed my hands on the doorframe and leaned forward enough to illuminate a glistening rock wall across from me with scattered timbers streaked with greenish-brown slime and leafy vegetation leaning against it. Something looked odd. At my feet was a smooth rock floor and more timbers. The space looked nothing like a basement apartment, more like a watery cave. I pocketed the key and stepped tentatively forward, stopping at the sill, the toes of my boots jutting into the Window. Was it worth exploring?

Disappointed, I was about to pull back when an invisible force grabbed my body, pulling me violently through the door. The action was sudden, like I had unexpectedly walked off a cliff. I didn't fall far, just the length of the lanyard, and then I jerked to an abrupt stop, hanging face up by the line connected to the harness around my midsection. I looked up just in time to see a startling sight: the room in the Kensington warehouse looked as if it had been turned on its side. The lone stool was poised as though it might plummet down the perpendicular floor toward me, but it stayed put, defying gravity. Then the door above me slammed shut, severing the line. I fell again, a short distance, my upper body landing forcefully on a solid, unmoving object. My breath exploded as the headlamp flickered and went out, plunging me into complete darkness.

"Shit!" I gasped, desperately clawing air back into my chest.

I cursed again, my anger bouncing off the walls of my hollow tomb.

What had I been thinking? Of course, the door would close. They *always* closed. What made me believe the rope would keep that from happening? An image of the sparrow's severed head flashed across my mind. I quickly sat up, angry but thankful for the helmet's protection and miffed that my expensive headlamp would fail after one minor bump.

I tapped the lamp and knocked on the battery pack, but it was useless. Suffocating darkness crowded around me as I quickly slipped off my backpack and dug for the flashlight. I fumbled for the power button and found it, and the high-wattage light dispelled the darkness as I twisted the head for a wider beam. Boulders and large, rotting timbers surrounded me, and what I had thought was the floor had actually been one of the cave's walls. The logs looked like they had been hand-hewn long ago. The water was brackish and foul-smelling. I was in an oblong-shaped cave about the size of a single-vehicle garage, with a rough-hewn door about two metres above my head. It was attached to a frame of dark beams, anchored to a precarious-looking patchwork of boards and timbers that made up what was, in reality, the ceiling. There was also clear evidence that tidal action had recently filled the cave, at least within reach of the door above my head. Groaning and rubbing my shoulder, I rose cautiously and looked closely at what I had falsely assumed would be my safety line.

The lanyard, made from thick nylon and rated up to 2000 kilos, had been cut cleanly just as the desk had been in my grandfather's study. I shook my head in frustration. Whatever happened between places when the connection was broken was violently abrupt. I had first-hand evidence of this, yet I had embarked on this stupid and dangerous quest.

What had happened? Why had gravity suddenly shifted, pulling me through the door? Or had gravity changed at all? The Window above me was horizontal, and the Window in Kensington was vertical. Did that mean a traveller always exited a connection between Windows according to the destination's orientation? If a door were built into the floor of a building, did that mean whenever it was activated, a person would either fall through it or, if returning, be pulled up through it?

I shone the light around. A dozen timbers of varying sizes lay in the rubble around me while others haphazardly braced the uneven ceiling. I was standing at the bottom of a collapse, which I realized was what I had thought was the wall across from me earlier. The house the door had been attached to had sunk or fallen through the ground and come to rest on its side, and all that was left was the Window I came through and assorted rotting timbers. I could be anywhere, at any depth underground. I took a deep breath, calming myself, and pulled out my cell and hooked up the GSA. I waited for it to power up, but when it did, my cell continued to show 'No Signal.' Of course, the GSA wouldn't work underground. It needed line of sight. I stuffed both back into my pack, angry at the assumptions that had led to what might be a life-threatening situation.

As I zippered it shut, I noticed a smooth object in a water-filled depression at my feet. It was a human skull. I plucked it out of the water and swung the light on it. The lower jawbone was gone, but strands of stringy, dark hair were still clinging to patches of skin along the hairline. A quick look around revealed a few more scattered bits of human bone.

A few steps away, I located a dark, slimy mass, the remains of a leather shoulder bag. I gingerly pried it open and removed a pulpy mush that might have once been a book or journal. There was also a rust-encrusted flintlock pistol that crumbled into pieces when I lifted it out. I couldn't find any markings that might reveal a name or how the person might have died. Regardless, *Unusable* had meant death for this individual.

This was not the adventure I had envisioned, and I quickly became concerned about getting out of this dead man's cave. That was assuming, of course, that the skull was that of a man. Dead Man's Cave, that's what I would change the map to say.

It took a few minutes, but I wrestled two larger timbers into a makeshift platform, straddling some boulders to climb on and reach the door. It would have to do. While doing this, I noticed water was filling the space between the boulders at my feet. A tide was coming in, and I wondered if the cave filled up to the ceiling. That would not be good.

Feeling the growing urgency, I balanced on my slick purchase and reached above my head to search the door for a knob or handle. A tarnished oval plate was in the centre of the door with a covered keyhole. I unlatched the key from the metre-long retractable line attached to my belt and wiggled it into the lock. I was about to give it a turn when, with a sickening crunch, one of the timbers beneath my feet shifted. I fell, landing painfully among the boulders and pools of water, thoroughly soaking most of my clothing. I pulled myself up angrily. The flashlight had thumped harshly on a boulder but was thankfully undamaged. The key! Fortunately, it was still secure in the lock over my head. The water around me had risen dramatically in just a few moments, and I guessed that, at this rate, I would be in serious trouble within an hour.

I propped the light on a large rock and dragged more of the timbers together, building a platform of crosshatching layers to give the weakened wood a better chance of supporting me. The frigid water began to slosh into my rubber boots as I finished this, making every movement laborious. Finally, snagging the light, stuffing its end into the top of my jacket so it shone upwards, I carefully climbed onto the hopefully more stable platform.

I stood up and extended my hand toward the key. It wouldn't turn completely. There was movement; I could feel the bolt budging a little, but I didn't want to force it and possibly snap the key in half. I quickly slipped my pack off and rummaged through it, searching for the can of graphite lubrication. Would that work? It wouldn't break down any rust, but it could get into places needing help. I slipped my pack on again and sprayed the entire contents into the keyhole and any little gap I could find, much of the black powder streaming down my hand and onto the sleeve of my jacket. I inserted the key again and began to jiggle it, gently working it back and forth.

The water had reached the soles of my feet, adding an unwelcome slipperiness to the timber platform. I turned my focus back to the key. Several anxious minutes later, it edged slightly to the right with a grinding protest. I shuddered, exhaling in relief. Was that enough to make contact? Nothing was happening. It wasn't working. I glanced down just as cold water sloshed into my right rubber boot. Fighting my rapidly rising panic, I eased the key out, hoping the wormhole would form. It did. A flash of light illuminated the space between the door and the roof of the cave-in. Then, the door lurched open a few inches, just enough for me to see the sparsely furnished office in the Fortaleza warehouse in Northeastern Brazil. The hinges must be rusted. I grabbed the edge of the door and gently pulled it open, its hinges squealing in protest until the sodden wood hung beside me.

I pocketed the key and looked at the room above me, where I'd only been briefly just a few days ago. The office was at the back of a massive shipping complex where everything from beet sugar to auto parts was readied for shipment overseas. It was perceptually disturbing to see the furniture, a desk, chair, and small filing cabinet on a physically impossible right-angle plane to where I was. Ignoring the strangeness, I tossed the flashlight through as a test. It cleared the doorsill before suddenly veering comically to the left, landing on the vertical floor. That's what was going to happen to me if I got through. I grabbed the doorframe, my hands reaching around to the wooden sill on the Brazilian side, but I was too heavy to pull myself up. Seconds passed, and I became terrified that the Window would close and I'd lose the parts of my hands that were through to the other side. And now, both boots were filling with water. Struggling to kick them off, I was suddenly pulled upward through the door. Gravity flipped, and I immediately fell to the warehouse floor in a shower of seawater that had come through with me. The Window closed. Laughing in relief, I flopped over on my back, holding my hands out before me.

I had all my fingers, but my feet were bootless. They would have to remain entombed with the unknown and unfortunate Window traveller. I pulled myself up and sat down on the chair, clasping one wet foot between my hands, trying to rub some warmth into it as I considered the implications of Dead Man's Cave. The crazy flip-flop I'd just experienced between an upright Window connecting to a horizontally positioned Window suggested the two sides of the connection were entirely separate regarding orientation and, I guess, gravity. Wind and debris appeared to blow through from one side to another, but a larger mass, like a human body or an even smaller one like my flashlight, would be affected by any differences between the sites.

My brain began to race with the possibility of what I had just discovered. What if the exit side of a Window was in an airplane travelling hundreds of kilometres an hour high above the ground? Would I suddenly be moving at whatever speed it was travelling if I stepped through from a stationary Window below? Would I be crushed by the sudden acceleration and the massive difference in elevation? The elevation may not be a factor since an airplane would be pressurized, but still, would the acceleration from zero to hundreds of kilometres flatten me?

Dane was going to have fun with the physics of this when I told him.

EIGHTEEN

Six and a half hours later, after navigating through four time zones and three continents back to LA, I finally got out of my damp clothing, showered, and slipped into my jogging suit. I regretted having tossed my old clothes into the trash back in Kingston, I could have gone there after Dead Man's Cave. That act seemed foolish now since all the clothes I owned were in the Felix and Son warehouse in Kensington or my suitcase in LA. I may need to leave a few pieces of clothing at various sites if I ever need a change.

I slid fully clothed under the bed's duvet and attempted to get my mind and body to relax. My core had been trembling since shortly after I'd escaped from Dead Man's Cave. I'm sure Morgan would have been alarmed, as my pulse was high, and every muscle felt antsy. The initial excitement of discovering how the sites were connected in relation to each other was quickly overshadowed by the fact that I could have died. Aidan Ames could have disappeared entirely from the face of the Earth if not for luck. Morgan was right: I don't plan things well. However, it was safe to say that my curiosity for what lay behind the sites marked with warnings was satisfied.

I awoke a few hours later in the dark, my heart beating rapidly, with fleeting images of a nightmare lingering at the edges of my mind. I switched on the bedside lamp, grabbed the tablet, and swiped it to the map. I needed to do something completely different and not dangerous. My eyes fell to the Window in Chicago. The information pop-up on the tablet said it was located at 875 North Michigan Avenue, formerly the

John Hancock Center. A quick browser search informed me that Chicagoans still affectionately called it the Hancock. It was situated on the Magnificent Mile, the city's shopping Mecca. The building was one hundred stories tall, with retail and residential floors. Surrounded by a popular plaza with a fountain and gardens, the centre had restaurants, boutiques, high-speed elevators, and an open-air observation deck on the ninety-fourth floor.

An open-air observation deck? That sounded like something completely different.

It was just after 3 a.m. in LA, and Chicago is two hours ahead, so I figured I could catch the 5:30 a.m. Window. Choosing the early morning time would hopefully mean few people would be around, like that security guard who had tried to enter the room the first time I'd come to Chicago. The observation deck didn't open until 9 a.m., so I'd have time to look around the building and figure out why my grandfather had an unfurnished office in the heart of Chicago.

At 5:30, I opened the Window and stepped through. The door shut, and I turned, searching for and flicking on the light. Simultaneously, I noticed a red light flash on a compact surveillance camera mounted to the right of the door, level with my head.

Had someone been expecting me, or was this a new security precaution because of my sudden appearance a few weeks ago? I saw that the camera had a wireless broadcast setup and was plugged into an outlet at the base of the wall. I quickly unplugged it, slipped the device from the mounting bracket, and stuffed it into my backpack. That would keep whoever had put this here guessing. However, the camera's presence meant that someone had a key to this room. How was that possible? The Enniskillen Groups leased this space; I alone should have access.

I reached for the door to the hallway but stopped when a key rattled in the lock. Alarmed, I reacted instantly, pressing the doorknob's locking button as I had done the last time. I wasn't quick enough. The door pushed towards me, but I managed to force it to a stop by leaning in and firmly planting my left foot at the base.

A man's voice blasted through the door.

"Hey! Who are you?"

I didn't reply. He pushed a shiny black boot into the gap between us, and I could feel his weight would overwhelm mine.

"Open… this… door." He demanded as his meaty fingers curled around the edge of the door near my head, incrementally moving it forward with each word.

This was a struggle I wasn't going to win. I was too small, too light, but I could use his weight against him. I waited for his next push, then suddenly jumped back as he shoved, dropping to my knees as the door flew open, its edge narrowly missing my shoulder. Physics happened as his momentum drove him into the room. I was flat on the floor, but one of his boots caught me in the ribs, causing me to gasp in pain as he fell over me. I turned my head in time to watch a uniformed man crash to the far end of the room, a massive blast of air escaping his lungs as he hit the floor. Ignoring the pain in my side, I grabbed my backpack and launched to my feet. Without seeing whether he was about to grab me, I shut the door, drove the key into the deadbolt, turned it, and flung it open to wherever the second site at 5:30 would take me. In my rush to escape, I couldn't remember if the next Window was safe or dangerous.

I saw a single narrow step on the other side, leading down to a wooden plank floor. I jumped through, skipping the step. The Window slammed shut, enveloping me in darkness.

NINETEEN

Where was I, and what the hell was that about?

My heartbeat was thundering in my ears. I took several deep breaths and pulled the flashlight and cell from my backpack. I was in a windowless room dominated by an antique four-poster bed and pieces of smaller furniture likely from the same era. I turned around and jumped, my skin crawling with fright as the beam flashed off a mirror. I angled it slightly down and saw my reflection in a long mirror. It was mounted to the door of an ornate wardrobe with a sculpted spire that stopped just shy of the low ceiling. The Window was in a wardrobe.

I swiped my cell on and watched the digital time jump from 5:36 a.m. to 11:36 a.m. as its GPS located me. Wherever I was, I had travelled East. A minute later, I knew my location: the north of Ireland, in Fermanagh County, in a township named Enniskillen, and undoubtedly the namesake of Willie's island fortress. A web search revealed that the town was on a natural island which separated the Upper and Lower sections of the River Erne.

Leaving the bedroom, I entered a murky room. Dark curtains filtered out most of the daylight, but enough was leaking through to reveal white-shrouded mounds of furniture. It was a living room with an entry to a small kitchen off to the side. Like the island, this site felt like it had a history well beyond that of my grandparents. A quick scan of the pop-up for the site on the tablet revealed that the father of the Windows, Willie McPhie, had lived here.

I unlocked the front door and stepped outside into the late morning sunshine. A weathered brass plaque mounted to the left of the door named the building the *McPhie Cottage on Church Street* and the year it was constructed – *1729*. A low hedge and a half gate separated the property from a residential street of other historic cottages and some newer in-fills. I walked out onto the narrow sidewalk and turned to view Willie's cottage. Ivy reached up the sides of the squat structure, a frilly carpet covering most of the walls and wrapping around a handful of windows. The window frames and the front door had a weathered texture but had been recently painted. I returned to the porch and sat on the edge of the stone steps, letting the warmth of the Irish sun wash over me. Daylight hadn't even touched Chicago's skyline yet.

Chicago. What the hell was going on in Chicago? Why was the room under surveillance, and why had that guard been so intent on getting in? I called Reinhold Bonk, but his voicemail picked up. I left a message saying I was in Chicago and asked if there were any problems with the lease.

As I wandered through Willie's cottage, I realized how calm I felt being here, so I decided to stay for a few days. Besides, I needed a break after Dead Man's Cave and Chicago. Throughout the rest of the day, I brought the historic dwelling back to life, opening the painted shutters that covered the windows, removing the furniture coverings, and making up the bed with relatively new bedding I found stowed in zippered mesh bags. They smelled of mothballs and lemon. The property wasn't large. Besides the living room, the small kitchen, and the bedroom the Window was in, there was another bedroom and a very small bathroom, which had most likely been added sometime in the last century. The front garden was barely larger than the main bedroom, with pockets of flowers and concrete ornaments. The garden behind the cottage was slightly wider than the house but was long and felt like an oasis. Carefully placed flat stones led to an ornate concrete bird bath at the centre of a small flower garden. Beyond this, an old shed with brightly painted gables and moss-covered shingles huddled between two birch trees whose leaves had already made their fall journey to the groomed grass beneath them. Tall hedges gave the garden some privacy from the houses on either side. Everything was well cared for, and I determined I would complement the property management company.

As I puttered around the place, neighbours along the street began to notice, some even stopping by the gate to chat when I was out front. They offered advice on what local shops to visit and how to keep the snails out of the house. One of those visitors, an older man, stooped and supported by a carved wooden cane, remembered my grandfather. He recalled how much he had loved a pint of stout at a local pub.

After a restful sleep, I woke early the next morning and headed out to find a small family-run grocer that one of my neighbours had told me about. The crisp morning air hinted at the coming winter as I walked along a tree-lined road that followed the river's edge. After about 20 minutes, I reached the grocer, a historic stone building at the edge of the city centre. I purchased a few items for breakfast and lunch and walked leisurely back to the cottage, enjoying not feeling like I had to be somewhere.

Later, I began exploring the surrounding area of stone cottages and old winding streets and taking photos of several plaques and monuments celebrating a history I knew nothing of. I soon discovered that Willie's home was a short transit ride from the castle Enniskillen, Ireland's northern home of the Gaelic Maguire Chieftains. Early on the third morning, I joined an advertised tour of the medieval Castle Keep and was impressed by the richness of its ancient and colourful history and well-maintained edifice.

While I was there, Reinhold Bonk called. The Enniskillen Group did lease the space in Chicago's tallest building under a numbered company. My grandfather had arranged this early on in their business relationship, Bonk informed me.

"Felix and Mariah had plans to expand their real estate interests into the American Midwest, but, as you know, your grandmother passed. Your grandfather kept the lease, but it is the extent of your company's connection to Chicago."

"Do you know what their plans were?"

"I'm sorry, Aidan, this was not discussed with me."

He was unaware of any problems with the lease and asked what I might be referring to. I made up a story about a damaged lock to avoid the reason for my call. However, I wondered if this persistent and intimidatingly large guard could somehow be connected to my grandfather's murder. Did he know about the Windows, had shot my grandfather without retrieving the key, and was now waiting for another closet traveller to show up?

Feeling foolish about my conspiratorial musings, I caught transit into the market area of the town and located a regional farmers market a neighbour had told me about. Local producers had set up stalls laden with fall vegetables and pastries. I had fun picking out fresh produce and an 'Authentic Irish Meat Pie' for my supper. While there, I began having that feeling you get when you're being watched. I didn't know if it was just paranoia after Chicago, but a man kept glancing at me often enough that I felt I was more than just a passing curiosity. He had an expensive camera slung around his neck, which he held with one hand and a camera bag with a Canadian flag stitched to it hanging from a shoulder. He looked like a tourist but seemed more interested in me than the market.

A few minutes later, I noticed he was beside me at a stall filled with heaps of potatoes and cabbage. I turned towards him and nodded.

"Hello."

He seemed startled and smiled uncomfortably. A beep sounded in his jacket, and he retrieved a cell phone. He swiped it open and turned away, talking in a hushed tone.

"You're being paranoid, Aidan," I mumbled.

On my fourth morning in Enniskillen, I felt so relaxed that I realized I now had at least four places I could call home. It was an odd feeling, and I wished I could have shared it with Morgan. She would have found my situation amusing, as neither of us had ever felt like the houses we grew up in were what we'd call homes in the sense of feeling like we were welcome or, as in her case, safe.

This would be my last day at the cottage, so I decided to locate the pub my grandfather had frequented. The place was a short walk from the cottage through narrow streets. It was lively, with dark panelling and groups of locals enjoying ale on-tap while watching a soccer game on a wall-mounted TV. The match was causing occasional outbursts of cheers or boos. I could see why my grandfather liked the pub.

As I relaxed on a stool at the bar, waiting for an order of fish and chips, I kept hearing what I thought was my name in snippets of conversation behind me between the cries of the soccer fans.

"You're sure it was him?"

"Ames, yeah. Unmistakable."

Sudden jeering from a bad referee call swept the next bit of conversation away, but then I heard: "He's at the cottage. It's just a recon."

Was someone talking about me? I surveyed the room and saw two men sitting at a table a couple of metres away. One of them was the man from the market. Our eyes met, and he flinched but quickly masked the surprise on his face.

"Hello, again." I offered. Had I heard correctly? Had he spoken my name?

"Uh, hello."

"Are you Canadian?"

The soccer fans suddenly roared, thumping their tables as one of the teams scored.

"What?" he said, looking like he wasn't keen to talk.

I waited for the din to subside.

"Your patch, are you from Canada?" I pointed to the maple leaf flag on the camera pack, resting in an empty chair at their table.

The other fellow, dark-haired and pale like he hadn't seen much sun, glanced down at the bag as if it was the first time he'd seen it. The other man narrowed his eyes but met my gaze unflinching.

"Uh, sure."

"Where from?"

"Canada."

I smiled.

"No, I mean, where from in Canada?"

"Up North," he replied awkwardly.

He lied, and he knew I knew. He was obviously not from Canada, probably from the US, judging by the hint of a Southern American accent when he spoke.

He suddenly shoved his chair back and stood. His partner did so as well.

"Nice meeting you. Maybe we'll see each other around," he said as he grabbed his pack.

"Wait," I said, "do we know each other?"

His dark eyes turned to mine.

"No. I don't think so."

I shrugged.

"I thought I heard you say my name."

"Is that so?"

I slid off the stool and extended my hand.

"Yeah. Aidan. Aidan Ames."

The man smiled tightly but did not reach for my hand.

"No. Can't say I've heard that name before."

"But, I heard – "

"Musta heard wrong."

He glanced at his watch.

"Sorry, we have a train to catch."

I returned to my stool and watched them leave, wondering if I'd misunderstood the conversation.

What had happened in Chicago was definitely making me paranoid.

TWENTY

Feeling unnerved, I left the pub, returned to the McPhie Cottage and packed up my belongings, choosing the next available Window, a site labelled Whitby I hadn't visited yet. I barely made it, stepping through the portal at 12:13 p.m. Kingston time on the Map. Whitby was a centuries-old North Sea port, according to the tablet and was as good a place as any on my list of ports of call. I was in an uninspiring and curtained basement bachelor apartment. Daylight was slicing through where the heavy curtains didn't quite meet in the middle. The only piece of furniture was a single padded kitchen chair that sat forlornly on pristine carpeting facing ground-level windows. A rolled-up sleeping bag and pillows were in a closet, and the usual paraphernalia was in the bathroom. I plopped down on the chair, pulled out my cell, opened the maps application, and waited for the built-in GPS to find me.

I was stunned as the app zoomed in on my location. The McPhie map indicated only two Windows were in Canada, Kingston and Victoria. But, according to the app, there was a third site on the same street as my parent's home in the Calgary neighbourhood of Edgemont.

Surprised, I jumped up and walked over to the apartment's door. It was solid wood, was painted a robin eggshell blue and had the usual two sets of locks. It looked like it originally belonged in a Victorian-style house, not a basement apartment in a not-very-old Calgary neighbourhood. It had also been modified, with matching wooden strips added to the top and bottom to make it fit the height of this door frame. I opened the tablet and navigated to the Whitby listing on the map. Whitby was a seaside town in North Yorkshire, England, and the Window had been there since 1856. Sometime in the past, my grandfather had moved the door to Calgary, and the information had not been updated in the Map Room or his journal.

I pulled the curtains aside and saw, directly across from me, the house I had grown up in, with both my parents' vehicles parked in the driveway. My father's sleek, black, career-fitting sedan sat beside Mom's dark blue minivan. Morgan's old home would be immediately to the right of where I was standing. Her parents sold the house in the spring as part of their divorce settlement. I vaguely remembered an older couple living in this house, but I had no idea a separate basement apartment existed.

I gazed out the window at the house I had not thought I would see again so soon. My grandfather may have stood in this same spot. He would have seen his family without being noticed and might have seen me and Morgan lying on the sloping front lawn, watching the few stars shining bright enough to punch through the city's light pollution. Had he been watching us with the lights off from this window? It was a disconcerting feeling. Why hadn't he ever made himself known? Was protecting the secret of the Windows that important to him?

An early October frost had singed the lawn, turning it brownish-yellow, and I could see that my mother had already prepped her flower beds for winter. The first heavy snow would likely bury everything in just a few weeks.

It was almost 12:30 on Saturday, and I knew my parents would be preparing to leave on their separate paths, the same ones they'd travelled nearly every weekend for years. My father would head off to join a group of fellow accountants and bankers for their usual eighteen holes at the Calgary Golf and Country Club, and my mother would head off for her weekly grocery run. Their relationship was old-fashioned and very gender-role-specific. My father was in charge; he made the money and the rules, and my mother seemed okay with that, assuming the role of domestic slave for her family.

Despite this, my mother was elegant and graceful and seemed out of place and time. She worked part-time in one of the city's last non-chain bookstores, read novels written by classic authors like Proust and Beckett, and was fond of art exhibits or poetry readings. I loved this about her. On the other hand, while always well-dressed and quite capable of sounding educated and world-wise, my father seemed to only care about success, or what he believed defined success. I never seemed able to fit into his view of what was important. At least, that's what it felt like. It was difficult to think otherwise when my passions, which did not include a white-collar job in a downtown office building, seemed of little interest to him. I propped my elbow on the window's sill, rested my chin in my hands, and sighed heavily. Was I being too harsh? Had I become my father, holding him to the same impossible standards he held me to? They weren't terrible parents. My privilege was painfully obvious. I hadn't experienced racism or poverty and had everything I could ever need, even before the inheritance. Why couldn't my father accept that I had plans for my life? Why couldn't he get that?

His sudden appearance at the front door startled me from my thoughts. He was striding purposefully and should have had his golf bag, but he didn't. My mother was behind him, shouldering her bulging and seemingly bottomless bag.

I ducked but realized I hadn't turned the lights on, so seeing into the apartment from across the street was unlikely. I watched, hastily retrieving my cell from my shoulder bag to record them. I was surprised to see them drive away together in my father's car. I waited a few minutes, left the apartment, and walked across the street. The spare key was in its usual hiding place, inside a fake rock among real rocks beneath the cement birdbath in the backyard. The alarm code was unchanged.

I wandered through the rooms, feeling like an intruder. I was living in Kingston, and as far as my parents were concerned, I wasn't expected back unless I decided to visit at Christmas or next summer. I had only been gone a few months, but already, my room had begun to be used for storage. The shadow of my past life here had already been reduced to a room for discarded items.

My grandfather's last visit to Calgary, the Christmas before he died, had been a bitter-sweet mix of joy and tension. Morgan had unexpectedly gone off to visit an ailing aunt in Saskatchewan and missed meeting him, but Amelia had managed to get a few hours away from the hospital to join us for Christmas Day dinner. My grandfather and I made several trips during the week he was with us to various malls, hunting for post-Christmas bargains, but mostly to escape the unpleasantness that lurked behind every conversation at home. Those moments in the mall were the joyous bits; the tense bits were when we'd return, and my father would say something demeaning about what we'd bought or where we'd gone. My grandfather would comment, and Mom, feeling tipsy from too much wine, would join in, and suddenly, there was this triangle of heated words.

I poured a glass of orange juice from the carton in the fridge as sunlight peeked over a neighbour's roof, filtering through the ocean-blue sheers over the sink. I left the empty tumbler on the always-spotless kitchen island. Neither of my parents would leave a dirty dish anywhere in the house, especially in the kitchen. For my father, it would be a matter of protecting his investment; for my mother, it would be about having a spotless Martha Stewart-like house. When they returned, they would see the tumbler and my father would check the security alarm's log and notice someone had entered the house while they were away. He'd call Amelia, and when he learned it wasn't her, he'd probably change the code, and this would be the last time I could penetrate the defences of *his* house.

I laughed loudly in the oppressive silence of the house. His son owned more property than he could ever imagine.

Grabbing a framed photo of Amelia and me from atop the gas fireplace in the living room, I left the way I had entered. The picture meant something to me; my mother had taken it during Easter last year as Amelia and I huddled arm in arm in front of the 12-metre tall bent-wire head art installation in front of Calgary's The Bow skyscraper. It would be perfect for the condo in LA, I reasoned. Was I stealing a little piece of home? Maybe.

The next-door neighbour, a retired transit bus driver, watched me leave as he hauled recycling from his cluttered garage to the curb. He must have recognized me because he called out a greeting. I pretended not to hear as I escaped into the basement apartment. I had hoped no one would see me. He'd surely tell my parents, but they wouldn't believe him. After all, I was, or so they thought, in Kingston, thousands of kilometres away.

TWENTY-ONE

I spent the rest of the evening in Lisbon before returning to the LA condo at 6:30 p.m., going out shortly after for a meal at Chico's, where I wrestled with the memories of my grandfather. I was beginning to realize that my image of him was distorted. He was a much more complicated person than the one who had filled my head with stories and taken me on adventures in his neighbourhood. My grandfather had been a stone's throw away from the house where I had felt so unwelcome, yet he had never made his presence known, not even to me.

I returned to the Bluebell the next day, aching inside. I felt betrayed and confused and welcomed the distraction the Sellars offered. After a pleasant discussion about the weather and the Royals over tea and biscuits, I excused myself to my room. Sitting on the edge of the bed, I checked my watch. It was 7:30 a.m. in Victoria. I dialled Morgan's number.

She answered after the second ring.

"Aidan?" Her voice was like a balm to my loneliness. Still, I could detect a hint of cautious reservation. "Hi."

"Hi," I replied, feeling stupid, like a teen on his first date. "I got your email."

"I know. Thanks for calling the other day," she said. "Kelli wasn't very happy about the early wake-up. She couldn't get back to sleep."

I groaned.

"I'm sorry. I had just returned from Zurich and had forgotten about the time difference."

"She'll get over it. Zurich, huh? How'd that go?"

"It was weird. I own a lot of buildings and stuff."

"Oh," she said.

The emotion in her voice was difficult to decipher. Should I have told her that? Did it make her uncomfortable? I changed the subject.

"Uh, it's my birthday tomorrow."

"I know. Remember your fifteenth?"

I laughed. I had a scar on my left knee from a memorable day of biking in Bragg Creek.

"Uh, yeah."

What was wrong with me? Why did I feel so awkward? I wondered if she thought I would ask her to join me.

"Where are you calling from?" she asked.

"London."

"Ontario?"

"No. England."

"Oh. Wow. England. What's it like there?"

I hadn't seen much of London yet, just the 'Bells and the inside of the Felix & Son warehouse, but I couldn't tell her that.

"Rainy, I'm staying at a bed and breakfast where Gramps used to come." I answered. "The couple who run it know – uh – knew him."

I couldn't believe how immature I sounded, I might as well have been talking to a stranger rather than the one person who knew me better than anyone else.

"Uh, how are you doing? How's school?" I asked.

"It's going better than I expected, thanks. I spent last weekend volunteering at a walk-in clinic, giving flu shots. Next week is all in class."

She paused, but I could sense a question in the silence. Finally, she asked: "How are you handling your new life, Aidan?"

"S'okay."

Stupid reply. How could I tell her I'd spent the last three weeks travelling the world in a way she would only perceive as a delusion?

"Is college on hold?" she asked.

"I dropped out," I said without thinking and quickly tried to explain. "I mean – I'm just too busy trying to figure all this out. I'll go back next session, probably."

I hadn't wanted to tell her I'd quit; we had spent dozens of hours plotting and planning our separate post-secondary journeys. Like her, she knew how much I wanted to get away from home, and school had been the way out. Unfortunately for our friendship, her heart had been set on the University of Victoria, and while I would have loved to join her there, I owned a house in Ontario.

"I understand, Aidan, I really do. It's okay. You need to take care of yourself before anything else, right?"

I knew she'd understand, and for a moment, our friendship felt normal, like before the Windows. Morgan was a fierce advocate for self-care, a frame of mind that carried her through the tumultuous years of her childhood as her parent's marriage imploded.

"Thanks, Morgan."

Then, there was a grating silence that stretched on far too long. I couldn't see her face, and I couldn't tell if she was happy to hear from me or if she was just politely tolerant because we had been friends. But then, she spoke.

"Aidan, I'm glad you called. We didn't end things so well that day, did we?"

I let out a quiet sigh as she broke through the weirdness. She couldn't stand the feeling of not saying anything substantial, either. The volume of history between us couldn't bear the awkwardness.

"I know. I'm really sorry."

"I'm sorry, too. I'm sorry I pushed you to be open about everything."

"Don't be. I want to tell you everything and I will, but I need some time. I'm a little freaked out about all of this right now."

"I understand," she replied quickly, her words filling me with hope. "And I'm glad you still feel you can talk to me. You've had a big change in your life with this inheritance."

Bigger than you know, I thought, but said, "When I get back to Canada, do you still want to get together?"

There was the slightest hesitation, and my heart felt a stab of fear.

"I'd like that very much," she said, the eagerness in her tone pushing the worry away.

"I'd like that, too."

I exhaled in relief and thought I heard a slight chuckle.

"Well, I should go. Would it be okay if I called you in a few days?"

"Yes, definitely, I'd like that," she said.

I ended the call and collapsed onto my bed, exhaling the tension that had built up in my body. We had taken a tenuous step back toward each other, and the truth of my life would have to wait until we met face-to-face.

I celebrated my nineteenth birthday alone. It was appropriate, in one sense, as I felt at odds with myself and everything I thought I knew about my life and my grandfather. I sorely wanted Morgan to be there but knew I would have been poor company.

I went to Paris. I arrived in the early evening at the site in the secure warehouse. I wasn't exactly sure where a restaurant was located in relation to the location, but I was determined to eat someplace expensive. My office space in the warehouse was partially furnished with a desk and chair. The desk held nothing except some age-yellowed writing pads and the usual assortment of orphaned pens and pencils. One of the walls held a large, framed photograph of the Eiffel Tower during a vibrant fall day, but even its once brilliant hues had faded with time.

The warehouse was a small affair compared to the one in New York City or Brazil, but large enough to house towering stacks of boxes and pallets of machinery and important enough to require cameras and security. I had avoided the various guards on my previous visit, but this time, I caught one's attention the moment I opened the office door. My office was next to the staff entrance hallway, facing the security station. The grey-haired older guard saw me and lurched to his feet as I opened the door. I was dressed formally and looked and felt out of place.

I immediately stepped back into the room and was about to shut the door and leave when I saw his face transform into an apparent look of excited recognition. I paused, my hand on the edge of the door. He smiled hugely as he strode from the booth, extending his hands toward me as he approached. According to the tag on his uniform, his name was Phillipe

Robuchon. The same Phillipe my grandfather had mentioned several times in his journal.

"Aidan'!" he said with unexpected exuberance.

I tentatively offered my hand, which he shook vigorously, using both hands like we were old friends. Then, his broad grin broke into laughter as he acknowledged my confusion.

"Your grandfather, he tell me you are coming dis way one day. I am Phillipe," he said, tapping his name tag, "I am an old friend of Felix and Mariah."

"You were expecting me?" I asked, only slightly surprised, as I stepped out into the hall and shut the door behind me.

"Oui, et non." He shrugged in an animated gesture, pointing to the door behind me. "The only person with key to dis office is Felix, and he say Aidan, one day. No one else come and go in dis room."

Then he leaned into me and winked, his eyes casting a conspiratorial look away from us, "Also, Phillipe 'av learn never to ask question about how you come to be in dat room."

I stared at him, uncertain as to his implication. Did he know about the Windows, or was he accepting that the Ames had a habit of mysteriously dropping in? I pushed the thought aside. My grandfather told me once that if you meet someone new, ask them about their lives. People love talking about their lives, he'd said.

"So, uh, you were friends with my grandparents?"

Phillipe nodded vigorously and launched into a lively explanation. He was seventy-six, semi-retired, and worked only as often as he desired, a situation my grandfather had arranged, he told me, with sadness in his watery eyes. He had heard that my grandfather had died but had been unable to talk with anyone about his friend until now. He had told Phillipe he could stay working as long as he still enjoyed it. When I mentioned that I was in Paris to celebrate my birthday, he immediately directed me to the internationally known, though unknown to me, Taillevent.

"Your grandparents much loved de, uh, ambience, uh, de atmosphere," he said with certainty.

Phillipe used the security office phone to call the restaurant to secure a reservation, talking in rapid French. He winked at me.

"Impossible to get reservations, non? Taillevent bien, bien, very busy. But, Phillipe know people, 'ave connections, non?"

He called for a taxi, and while I waited, this friend of my grandfather continued to talk enthusiastically about their times together. He described how he met Felix and Mariah shortly after being hired at the warehouse, leaving the same office I had come out of. He knew of the Canadian owners and was surprised that my grandparents paid him any attention. Phillipe was, after all, just an employee, but that didn't seem to matter to them. It wasn't long before they visited Phillipe and his wife, Marie, every month. The Robuchons introduced my grandparents to La Ville Lumière, the City of Lights. They took them to the places few tourists ever saw, the out-of-the-way restaurants and niche art galleries, and introduced them to the best wines.

After my grandmother and Phillipe's wife passed within months of each other, their friendship became a way for them to work through their grief, he said. My grandfather continued to visit, and as I listened to this man talk of his affection for him, it became clearer that the only adult I had ever thought of as my friend had intentionally built friendships wherever he went. Boon Nam in Bangkok, the Robertsons in Scotland, the Sellars in Kensington, and Phillipe, and I was sure there were many others out there who missed him probably as much as I did. The Windows were more than just a quick end run around a country's borders; for my grandparents, they existed to make friendships with a very diverse group of people.

This realization troubled me as the taxi deposited me at the impressive entrance to Le Taillevent. The restaurant, with its panelled dining rooms, was nestled in a mid-nineteenth-century mansion along La Rue Lamennais, and definitely not somewhere I'd ever thought I'd spend a birthday.

On my server's recommendation, a young, formally dressed woman who looked barely older than me, I ordered Lobster Boudin and lamb with cabbage. I followed this with another of her recommendations, a Nougatine Glacée aux Poires, a delicate dessert made of thin layers of nougat, pastry, and pear sherbet.

I attempted to appear as sophisticated as other patrons who were obviously wealthy, sitting straight, holding my fork and knife as a mature couple did to my left, but I was acutely aware that I was the only person in my area of the restaurant who was by themselves. Conversations in French bubbled around me, and even though I understood little of what was said, I imagined they were probably exchanges of love and friendship and life.

My solo evening cost over five hundred Euros, which, for some reason, didn't feel expensive anymore. When I went shopping in New York City with Manuel Rodriguez as my hired help for the day, I felt conspicuous and out of place. I was there to prove I had wealth, and I willed myself not to look at or ask about prices, but every swipe of my credit card felt like a final exam in high school. Every purchase filled me with anxiety, and I wondered when a clerk would look at me with pinched eyes and announce that I had insufficient funds. Now, only a few weeks later, I felt comfortable with money not being an object to whatever I might want.

As the waiter silently removed my dessert dish, I watched her navigate smoothly between tables, deftly depositing my dish on a cart. I wondered what she thought of me. Could she tell I was nouveau riche, that I had the appearance of wealth without the heritage and gravitas that should come with it? Did she know I was a fraud? My fear was realized when she returned with the bill. I took it from the ornate silver tray, scanning the list of items. When I didn't see a line for a tip, I asked her about this. She smiled politely and patiently explained that a gratuity was not expected nor desired. I was embarrassed and apologized, but she assured me that she was not offended and that it was her pleasure to serve patrons of Le Taillevent.

I appreciated her kindness in softening the sting of my ignorance, but it strengthened my feeling that I didn't quite belong. I was a stranger in a strange land, a city dweller from the vast open spaces of a sparsely populated country, and I didn't know how to fit into this unfamiliar world. My head was filled with images of the many places I'd been, the different foods I'd tasted, and people and cultures so unlike mine, and yet I might as well have read about them in books. I was alone in the wonder of my experiences.

When I returned to the warehouse, I pressed the video intercom button next to the staff entrance door, and a different security guard let me in. He told me that Phillipe had gone home but had informed him I'd be returning. This guard was about my father's age but happier. I could see it in his eyes. We talked briefly, but I quickly excused myself, waiting an hour in the silent office to grab the Window to the empty condo in L.A.

TWENTY-TWO

I called Morgan from Los Angeles the following day.

Her phone went to voice mail, so I hung up and paced around the condo for a few minutes, feeling antsy. A few minutes later, I called her number again.

This time, she answered.

"Aidan?"

"Hi, sorry to bother you – "

"That's all right. I was just in the shower. Give me a sec to towel off."

A clunk followed this – Morgan putting her cell down – and then muffled sounds – Morgan drying off. I tried not to imagine her naked.

A moment later, she picked up her phone again.

"Sorry about that. Where are you calling from?"

"LA."

"Oh, my God. Didn't you just call me from England a few days ago?"

I grimaced.

"Uh, yeah, but I caught an early flight."

"You must be exhausted?"

"You get used to it."

I changed the subject.

"Uh, Morgan, could we get together on Saturday?"

"And talk?"

"Yes, and I'll tell you anything you want."

She didn't hesitate.

"I'd like that. What time?"

"How about shortly after one."

"It's a date, then. I'd like to know everything about your new secret life."

"Okay," I chuckled. That was my plan, too, though I doubted she had any idea what my secret life actually involved. I used to be plain old Aidan Ames, the kid next door, but now I was a globetrotting traveller.

"I gotta go, Aidan. My hair's dripping wet, and I have a hot date with a lab book."

"Okay, Saturday then."

Near the end of grade twelve, our high school sponsored an overnight camping trip to Drumheller for the track and field students. It was a reward for the team's exceptional medal haul at the Southern Alberta Track and Field meet in Red Deer. We set up our tents at a campground on the edge of Drumheller and then visited the 'World's Largest Dinosaur,' or so the sign said. A menacing, outrageously oversized T-Rex towered over the town's visitor information centre as if it were its next meal. There were two T-Rex displays, but the taller monument had a viewing platform jammed between the jaws of its mouth. All of us took turns, in small groups, climbing up the stairs inside the belly of the beast to appreciate the toothy perspective of a victim of this King of the Dinosaurs. We also took a long and exhausting hike along some of the trails that crisscross the Drumheller Valley badlands, poking at fossilized bones, dodging garter snakes, and reading signs that explained the multi-coloured layers of sandstone and mudstone that date back to the late Cretaceous Period. As campfires burned low that evening and the chaperones nodded off, Morgan and I stole away in the twilight with our sleeping bags. We found a spot on the side of a hill that offered a panoramic view of the valley and a glowing half-moon nestled in a magnificent ocean of glittering stars.

We lay side-by-side, stretched out on our bags, enjoying being alone.

"You excited about St. Lawrence?" she had asked.

I shrugged, my hands laced behind my head as a makeshift pillow.

"Yeah. I'm probably more excited about moving into *my* house."

She hummed.

"Still set on the field of athletics?"

"Yeah. It's a pretty good college, and they have a decent program. Maybe, you know, I'll start the big journey to becoming a teacher or something. You?"

Morgan sniffed, a sure sign that this conversation was going somewhere other than how it started. She had a way of bringing up deep subjects.

"You know I'm moving to Victoria right after graduation."

"Yeah," I said quietly. I knew this but hadn't wanted to think about it. We were going to be on opposite ends of the country.

"The start of the long road to a medical career," she said with a mock sigh.

We lay for a moment under the stars before I responded.

"You'd make a good doctor or whatever you'd want to be."

"Yeah? Why?"

"Because you care about people."

"And you don't?"

I smiled in the growing darkness.

"No. Well, I'm more selfish than you. You actually care."

"Thanks, Aidan, but that's not fair to say that about yourself."

I didn't respond. Several small meteors streaked across the night sky as Morgan shuffled a little closer to me. I could feel the heat of her body against my side. It was exciting.

"I know why you don't think much about tomorrow, or the next day, for that matter," she said after a while.

"Oh?"

"Should I tell you?"

"Can I stop you?"

"No."

I chuckled and shrugged.

"So, tell me."

"Well," she began, clearing her throat, "it's your dad."

"My dad?"

"Uh-huh."

"How so?"

Morgan cleared her throat again. She sounded nervous, though I couldn't recall her ever being afraid to say anything.

"You don't get along. You're like two Olympic runners, always trying to outdo each other."

"Yeah, well, what's your point?"

"My point is, you don't think of the future because your dad does."

"You've been thinking about this for a while?"

"Maybe."

"Well, I don't get it. What do you mean?"

She sighed.

"What I mean is, if your dad bought Adidas, you'd get Nikes. If he ran, you'd walk. He obsessively plans for tomorrow, so you obsessively don't. Am I right?"

I drew in a long, slow breath before answering.

"Maybe," I breathed out, looking up at the stream of stars overhead.

She was right, of course, though to admit to it meant I'd have to do something about it. Her insight bugged me.

"Is that your final analysis, Doctor Vogel?"

She elbowed me, and I play-coughed and unwrapped my arms from underneath my head, pushing them down my side so our hands touched.

"I care about you, that's all."

I took her hand in mine, squeezing it gently.

"I know. Thank you."

She squeezed it back before letting go, the backs of our fingers continuing to touch.

"Don't give up on finding a purpose, Aidan. You only have one life."

Purpose.

Morgan's words from that night were haunting me now. I had travelled to places I never thought I would see and had experienced cultures that I'd only ever touched vicariously through books. The Enniskillen inheritance had changed my life in ways I could not have imagined, but now I faced a challenge: the complications that affluence and privilege had brought to me and what they were doing to me as a person. I could easily live the rest of my just travelling and spending, losing touch with the reality that most people don't live like this. Everywhere I had travelled, I had seen both wealth and poverty, and it could be quite easy to insulate myself from the latter and never have to think about another human being except for myself and those I invited into my journey. I felt lost and needed to know what to do.

I found the beginnings of an answer in a safety deposit box in Dublin, Ireland. A dozen or more of these secure boxes were scattered around the globe in various banks. I knew from the information in the Key Wallet that they held valuable items, including, in Dublin, the personal diaries of Marianne McPhie. I took a cab from a mid-sized warehouse in Wicklow, south of Dublin, to the bank, which the cabbie informed me used to be Ireland's Parliament House. He felt he needed to educate me since I lied and told him this was my first visit.

The Bank of Ireland is a large, imposing edifice, oozing history and is part of a three-sided plaza the cabbie called the College Green. However, my little piece of it, a long, narrow safety deposit box, held two items more valuable than the gold coins and fifty thousand American dollars it contained. In the box were Willie McPhie's first key, tarnished and blackened with age, and Marianne McPhie's diaries. The key was simple but well made, without any ornament, wrapped in purple velvet, and securely enclosed in a polished wooden box. Tucked underneath the key was a small, yellowed slip of parchment with a single line of text in cursive handwriting.

Willie's key.

Marianne's thoughts and notes about her life were in three palm-sized leather-bound diaries. I had a feeling these would be important to me. Within them was a history that might give me a broader, more meaningful sense of what my grandfather had given me. I left Willie's key in the deposit box, carefully placed the journals into my backpack and didn't examine them until I was enveloped in the solitude of the condo in LA.

I began reading, and when I grew hungry, I snacked on bread and cheese I had brought with me from a quaint bakery in Rouen, France, and on an assortment of meats and cheeses from a personable older couple who ran a wonderfully fragrant delicatessen hung with traditional hams and rings of salami in Naples.

It quickly became apparent that Marianne's thoughts were the story of the salvation of Enniskillen, taking it from a financial empire that exploited and took advantage of the world's cultures and resources to something that endeavoured to improve the condition of those who lived in the many places where the Windows were located. She and her sisters funnelled staggering amounts of resources into schools, orphanages, and hospitals, using established charities as fronts while always remaining in the shadows. They were like ghosts; you didn't see them, but their influence was felt. They were well-educated and spoke several languages, and when Marianne's son, Ian McPhie, took over, he carried on the same philanthropic philosophy.

Throughout their story, there was the constancy of friendship and caring for those less fortunate. The McPhies knew they led privileged lives yet chose to use that station to change their world. Such was the secret mission of the Enniskillen Group, to use the family's wealth for more than personal kingdom building.

I was both amazed and troubled by what I read. Hours later, as I closed the final diary, I realized I had been crying for some time. This was the McPhie history, one that only a select few had ever known. I was overwhelmed by the privilege of what I had been given. They did not waste their lives on frivolous pursuits. This selfless willingness to improve the lives of friends and strangers alike must have led her son Ian McPhie to give Enniskillen to Felix and Mariah Ames.

My grandparents were the most generous people I had ever known. When I was old enough to spend those four summers with my grandfather, I realized now that he had been teaching me the same principles: people matter. We don't get to choose where we're born or who our parents are, but we do get to choose how we treat the people we meet on our journey.

This may be why my grandfather skipped over his son and gave the legacy to me instead. My father was obsessed with the perceived privilege that wealth brought. It mattered to him that his coworkers saw him as successful and wealthy, so he pushed me to be something he thought would continue this impression. Pursuing a degree in physical education was low on his list of approved careers.

I sobbed deeply as I anguished over my hotheaded arrogance and my spoiled childish grab of the sacred trust that had been given me. I was standing on the cusp of my future, and I finally understood what my grandfather must have hoped for me at that moment.

The fate of Enniskillen rested expectantly in my hands, a treasure as delicate as the Faberge eggs I'd seen in Zurich. I could crush what Marianne McPhie had turned the McPhie legacy into with my selfishness, or I could protect it.

TWENTY-THREE

Morgan was in her apartment.

I knew this because I had been eavesdropping at her door, listening intently to a sporadic conversation over the background din of a television.

I glanced at my phone. It was 1:25 in Victoria, and I was late. I had set the television up in the apartment to receive the stream from my phone of the jumble of video clips I had hobbled together during my first days in the Window system. But that had only taken a few minutes, and now I was pacing back and forth, indecisive, debating with myself, sometimes winning but then losing again in the internal heated argument inside my head. Morgan had eagerly agreed to meet today, so why was I so anxious? I sat at the foot of the stairs leading up to the second floor and then walked softly over to the door, my hand poised to knock, but I pulled back in uncertainty, or was it a feeling of terror? I felt like a teenager on my first date. Well, it sort of was a first date. We had always been great friends and hung out together, but we had never had what one would call an official date. That would have meant we were a couple, right?

Still, date or no date, couple or no couple, I was ready for this moment and prepared to tell her everything. This was why I was here: to show her what my life had become, to give her the opportunity to understand why I had been evasive and had lied. Morgan was more than just a friend; I needed to let her make her own choice about this crazy part of my life. My grandfather was the one adult I felt I trusted, but Morgan had always been there, always listened to my complaining, and always offered advice whether I wanted it or not, much like my grandfather.

"Damit," I said, my teeth clenched, "knock."

I knocked.

A moment later, Morgan answered, balancing an open medical book in one hand and her cell phone in the other.

"Hi," I smiled weakly.

"Oh," I could tell she was fighting hard to keep her expression neutral. "Hi."

Seeing her again felt exciting, but the words I had carefully rehearsed stuck in my mouth. Steady green eyes watched me, her lips slightly curled at the ends, her beautiful face delicately framed by straight, glistening black hair. I knew every inch of that face and had watched it grow into a young woman. Everything about her was smothering, and I had to remind myself to breathe. It had been different talking with her while separated by time and distance, but you couldn't hide when you were face to face, at least not with her.

Kelli and Brittany suddenly appeared, frowning at me over Morgan's shoulders. Immediately, there was an awkward silence as the three of them looked at me.

"Is your invitation still open?" I asked apprehensively, wishing her roommates weren't adding to my discomfort.

Morgan's eyebrow shot up.

"That's a little formal."

I grimaced.

She smiled.

"We made a date, didn't we?"

"I know, I was, uh – "

" – Afraid?" she finished for me.

My shoulders dropped visibly in relief. Her face softened. I had been tense and stiff, imagining the worst.

"Have you eaten?" she asked, with a hint of a smirk.

"Well," I began. I had another idea. Enniskillen. "I want to show you something first, if that's all right?"

Kelli's forehead furrowed in concern, and Brittany glanced at her partner, but I ignored them, focusing my eyes and heart on Morgan.

"Show me – what?" Morgan asked, her eyebrows slowly arcing.

"A video I made. We can watch it upstairs in my apartment."

"Okay, lead on."

She handed her book to Kelli, who took it, her disapproval unmistakable.

I gestured towards the stairs.

"After you."

"I'll follow," she insisted, slipping her cell into a side pocket of her skirt. I shrugged and headed for the stairs.

"You want us to come?" Brittany spoke up.

"I can handle him," Morgan said, giving me a little push towards the stairs.

"You look nice," I said, casting a quick glance back at her as we ascended the stairs. She was wearing a knee-length, dark blue skirt, grey leggings and a floral top I remembered from high school.

She shrugged and smiled mischievously.

"I dressed for a date."

Morgan did not comment as she entered the apartment, but her eyes took it in.

"Did you call me from L.A. and London, England?"

Did she think I had lied?

"Yes, and I celebrated my birthday in Paris."

"Wow, that's amazing. Were the twins with you?"

"No, I was alone."

"That would be a first."

I shrugged.

"It was okay, expensive, but – well – it was Paris."

"Happy Birthday, by the way. I'm sorry I wasn't there."

"Thanks. I'm sorry you weren't either. How was yours?"

Her birthday was in July, the only one I'd missed since we'd known each other. She had moved to Victoria immediately after graduation, and we had talked over video chat a few times, but it wasn't the same. Our paths had already begun to diverge.

"It was okay, too. It wasn't the same without you, though."

She blushed, and I felt my face flush.

"Thanks," I said, feeling adolescent.

She grinned as I pointed to the couch.

"Should we sit?"

She sat, folding her hands on her lap, her emerald eyes watching me expectantly, a hint of our old, less complicated friendship in them. I sat beside her, facing the TV.

I picked up the remote and turned it on. The screen flared to life. I swiped my phone open and found the video I hoped would change her world – our world. I connected to the TV's Bluetooth.

"I've wanted to tell you about what's been going on, but I needed to be sure of a few things first."

Her eyebrows arched.

"Sure of what?"

"Can I ask you something?"

She shrugged, her black hair swaying across her shoulders. My hands were sweaty, and I desperately needed something wet to quench the choking dryness of my mouth.

"We've known each other for a long time, right?"

She nodded.

"I, um, I've always appreciated you as a friend, and maybe I want to know you as more than just a friend."

She nodded slowly.

"And – ?"

"Do you feel the same way?" I blurted out.

Her expression twisted, cartoon-like.

"Do I feel the same way? Are you finally asking me to be your girlfriend, Aidan Ames?"

"What? Uh, I mean – "

I blinked.

"Uh —"

"Well, what then?" She deftly crossed her legs, the loose fabric of her blue skirt flowing over her knee.

I stood up and walked over to the window, groaning inwardly. November winds were stripping the deciduous trees bare. There was already a skiff of snow in Kingston, scorching heat in Brisbane and misting rain in London, and I wanted Morgan to experience it all with me. If she wanted me. I turned to face her.

"I want to share something with you that will change your life just like it has changed mine."

She rose and joined me at the window.

"Enough of the mystery, already. You said you had something to show me. Just tell me what's going on, Aidan."

The force of her words surprised me, and she saw it in my eyes. She reached out and touched my arm.

"I'm sorry. I've always been your friend, and yes, I think about you as more than just a friend. You're definitely weirder than usual, but it's growing on me. It makes you mysterious, maybe even alluring."

"But why?"

"Why do I like you?" She asked, frowning.

I nodded, hardly daring to believe I was pushing the issue, but it mattered. It mattered greatly to me and the future, especially the future of the next few minutes.

Morgan gazed out the window momentarily, pursing her lips before fixing her eyes on me.

"I'd be lying if I didn't say that I haven't wondered what a future with you would be like." She took a deep breath, letting it out slowly. "I'm not exactly sure what I feel about us, Aidan. I do know that when I'm with you, I feel safe. I always have. Nobody has ever made me feel that way."

Her eyes narrowed.

"And whatever happens here today will depend on what happens next."

"Next?"

"Yes. Are you going to explain yourself, maybe even tell me the truth?"

The truth.

I crossed to the couch and sat down, motioning for her to follow.

She sat next to me, our knees bumping up against each other, and I hit play on my phone, then paused it. The face of a harried-looking Aidan Ames froze comically on the screen, my mouth open, my eyes wide. I shivered with the memory of the fear and excitement of the initial moments of discovery.

"What I'm about to show you is the reason for all my weirdness since September – "

"Just since September?" She interrupted, a sly smile playing across her face.

I grimaced.

"Yeah, I deserve that. Okay, here goes, my grandfather left me this system of Windows, er, they're like portals, I guess. He thought they might be wormholes, I'm not sure, and they connect to locations around the planet. I don't own a private plane or even have a passport. I walk through these Windows, that's what they're called, and that's how I was here in Victoria when we ran into each other, and later with Bill and Dane, and how I called you from Los Angeles, and how I celebrated my birthday in Paris."

She was frowning, clearly confused about the direction our date was suddenly going.

"Windows? Portals? Aidan – "

"Uh, look," I stammered, understanding what she was feeling, "let me play the video. It'll show you what I'm trying to tell you."

She shrugged.

"Okay."

"The first time it happened to me was when I walked through my grandfather's closet door. I had my phone, and I recorded everything. It was too fantastic to be believable."

"Your grandfather's closet door?"

I nodded.

"Yeah, I know it sounds crazy, but here, take a look."

I pressed play on my phone, and her face slowly turned to the TV. I could already feel her skepticism.

"Morgan, I'm recording this because I don't know what the hell is going on, and you're not going to believe me without seeing what I'm seeing."

The recording was sometimes jerky, and my babbling dialogue was a bit crazy sounding but convincing, I hoped. I could have just told her what had happened to me, but seeing what I had been seeing and experiencing was worth more than anything I could have said in a long, wordy explanation.

I watched her face from the corner of my eye as the video played. Scotland, Bangkok, New York, Chicago, Denver, and then the island; I had included what I thought would be convincing clips of my first accidental visits to each place. As the recording played, I realized I sounded afraid at first, but that quickly turned to amazement and awe as I figured out how to get back to Turin Street. Despite the images on the video and my unscripted, excited-sounding narrative, Morgan was passive, with no hint of emotion slipping from her face. Her hands lay clasped in her lap, her thumbs occasionally tapping against each other.

"Wow. Apartments and storage rooms, those I get, but I didn't expect anything like this."

The video ended with stills of Enniskillen and the Seagull resting in the cove and a handful of selfies from places like Zurich, Lisbon, and Knokke-Heist. I could have added much more, but a five-minute explanation was already uncomfortably long.

I turned the TV off, and our eyes met. Her brows were knit, and that familiar squint was focused on me.

"I don't get it," she finally said.

"Um," I said, unsure of what she meant. "I've been travelling – around the world – for the last month using these portals my grandfather called Windows."

"Windows?"

I nodded.

"Yes, they're not windows like in a house. The McPhies and my grandfather called them that because when one is open, you can see into other places, like on the video when I was standing on that porch in Scotland and could see the Brooklyn Bridge through the door, or I mean, through the Window, which is in a real door."

The squint continued for a moment, and then her face grew dark.

"What is this, Aidan? I thought you were going to tell me the truth?"

"What?" I stammered. "I am telling you the truth. This," I pointed at the TV, "this is what I've been doing. My grandfather left me this system of Windows – "

Her eyes grew wide as she lifted a hand, cutting me off.

"I have to hand it to you. That's a clever piece of video editing, but why? Why continue to lie?"

Morgan stood up, smoothing her skirt as she looked down at me.

"What?" I stammered, shaking my head.

"Obviously, you've spent a lot of time doctoring that video. I guess it was too much to expect you'd spend as much time telling me the truth about what you've actually been doing since," she made air quotes, "you inherited all that money."

I stood up, and she backed away, her hand blindly reaching for the edge of the couch.

My heart sank. Was she afraid of me?

"No, look, I'm sorry. I'm not lying."

I glanced at my watch.

1:43.

"I can show you."

Her mouth opened, then closed, and then I saw the muscles of her jaw setting. I'd seen that look before. She was angry, and I could see her pulling her emotions back to where she could protect herself from further hurt. I'd seen her do this when her father came home drunk and angry, looking for someone to blame for the troubles of his life. Withdrawing and protecting herself was how she had survived.

"I think I should go," she said, her voice low and flat.

She began to turn away from me but stopped, her face shrouded with disappointment.

"I trusted you – once."

"No," I said, reaching into my pocket for the key.

I quickly crossed to the door and inserted it into the lock. The lock that would prove my incredible story.

1:44.

She slowly walked over to me, placing a hand on my arm.

"No more, Aidan. I don't know what game you're playing, but we're not children anymore."

I glanced at my phone.

"I know you don't believe me. I can understand that. I didn't believe it either, but just let me show you. I'm not lying."

"Aidan, please," she put her hand over mine.

1:45.

I turned the key and opened the door

The flash of light.

A ripple of air between two slightly different altitudes and Morgan stifled a scream.

She was like a deer caught in headlights, wide-eyed and unmoving. I pulled the key out, slipped my cell into a pocket, and grabbed her arm, pulling her through. We were alone in my grandfather's study on Turin Street, and fortunately, the light was on, painting the spartan room in muted tones. Beyond the room's only window, the wind blew as light from a street light angled through the window. The door shut behind us, and the third floor was still, except for the rustling of a few papers on the desk from the disturbance caused by our entrance. I turned to Morgan.

Her eyes were filled with terror. She stumbled backward, bumping into the closet door, looking wildly about.

"What – where am I?" She demanded. "What have you done to me?"

"It's all right. We're in Kingston," I said, reaching out to take her hand.

"Don't! What have you done to me?" she reached an arm around, fumbling for the closet door handle. She turned as she pulled it open, revealing its emptiness. She leaned into the closet, looking down its dark length before spinning around to face me.

"Aidan? What did you do to me?"

I was stunned and confused. I thought she'd believe me if she saw what the Windows could do, but she was afraid. Afraid of me.

"Uh – I'm sorry. I thought …"

I paused, watching her frightened face, unsure what to do next. How stupid of me. Of course, the sudden transition from Victoria to Kingston would be alarming, evening frightening. Morgan was intelligent and cautious, and a jittery video would not become a lightbulb moment for her. She would need time to process what had just happened to her.

"Here," I said as I crossed to the wall where the keyhole for Closet Two was hidden behind the fake light switch.

I saw her lurch back, raising her arms slightly in self-defence.

My heart was pounding in my ears, my stomach twisting in knots of anguish.

"It's okay, Morgan. I'm showing you the truth, the truth about my life."

I twisted the light switch cover aside and inserted the other key that opened a Window to an island on the other side of the planet. I turned it and then yanked the key out. The door flashed, and I quickly pulled the panel open wide.

"This leads to the island you saw in the video."

"A hole in the wall?"

"What? No. I'm going to walk through this – uh – hole in the wall and go there. You are welcome to follow."

The fluorescent lights flickered to life, revealing a hallway carved out of volcanic rock.

"I don't think so, Aidan."

She had positioned herself behind the desk, posturing herself for protection – from me. She cast terrified glances at the window overlooking an unfamiliar street and then painful, accusing looks at me. I stood motionless, my eyes frozen on her frightened face.

"Aidan, where *am* I?"

"We're in Kingston. This is my grandfather's study in my house in Kingston, Ontario."

She continued to cast quick, anxious looks out the window.

"That's impossible. I don't know what you've done to me, but l want to go now!"

"Morgan, I'm not lying to you. I want you to see what my grandfather left me."

The distress on her face remained unchanged, so I persisted.

"The video wasn't enough to convince you, so we walked through one of the Windows. We have travelled from my apartment in Victoria to here, my house in Kingston, by stepping through the door back in the apartment in Victoria and coming out through that door."

She quickly looked at the open closet, then back at me. The anger in her eyes was crushing.

"You asked for the truth. This is it."

She didn't move. I turned away from her, my dreams crashing to the floor of my foolhardy expectations, and pointed at the study door without looking at her.

"Over there is the door that leads downstairs. If you want, go to the kitchen. You'll find a landline there if you don't want the charges on your cell, and you can call your friends."

As an afterthought and a challenge, I added, "Or, dial 911 if you want."

Then, feeling foolishly melodramatic, I crossed into Enniskillen. I hadn't been on the island since I had left for Kensington, and the fortress was ablaze with light from a tropical day. I walked briskly over to the high-backed lounger I had pushed over beside the ship's wheel and bell to face the wreck of the Seagull. I slid into it, hating myself.

I was hurting Morgan – again.

TWENTY-FOUR

I heard the door to Enniskillen open, and I fought the urge to turn and look. I heard a gasp, and then Morgan's footsteps echoed on my island for the first time. I hoped it wouldn't be the last. I didn't rise to greet her. It had taken her several minutes to follow me, and it had been the most nerve-wracking wait of my life. I had sat there, anguishing, fidgeting, and twisting uncomfortably around the edge of the wide chair to sneak glances, wondering if I had made a mistake. Morgan was the smartest person I knew, but the Windows were far outside of anything she had experienced. I had brought her this far, and the rest was up to her. I could hear her walking slowly, halting and then taking more steps. The sheer enormity of the fortress, with its powerful sense of history, was overwhelming, not to mention the improbability of taking a simple step through a doorway in Canada to set foot directly on an island in the South Seas.

Breathless seconds later, I felt her hand rest on my shoulder.

"Oh, my god, Aidan," Morgan said, her voice so hushed I could barely hear her. "How is this possible?"

I looked up. She was crying, which immediately made me cry, and suddenly, the world was as it should be.

"How, how did you do this?" She sat beside me on the broad arm of the chair, allowing her body to lean against me.

Before I could answer, she pointed out to the cove.

"That's the ship. The one on the video."

I laughed as I wiped my tears on the sleeve of a seven-hundred-dollar shirt I had bought from Saks Fifth Avenue in New York. The amount I had paid for it seemed foolish now. Life could not be measured by the things I owned or could afford. It was moments like this one, knowing there was someone you could share life's journey with, wherever it led.

I began talking, starting at the beginning, from discovering the closet door and the paddock in Scotland, how Bill and Dane found out, and about my meeting with Bonk. I talked about the places I had been and of my grandfather's friends, who had all been expecting me. I shared with her what it was like to have the ability to buy whatever service or thing I wanted, wherever I was, and how childish my thinking had been at first. Morgan listened thoughtfully, her eyes occasionally resting on me and sometimes out toward the never-ceasing avian busyness of the cove. She took my hand as I talked, holding it on her lap.

I held nothing back. I told her about the Dead Man's Cave, the mystery of Chicago, and my grandfather's basement apartment across from my parent's home in Calgary. She was especially intrigued by that, thinking it odd that my grandfather had been so physically close but had never made his presence known.

"Was he watching your family?"

I shrugged.

"I think he was, and I think he was watching yours, too."

"What do you mean?"

I told her what Bonk had told me, how my grandfather had made arrangements for one of his apartments in Victoria to be available when she went to school.

Morgan leaned back, her eyes narrowing.

"How could he have possibly known I would go to Victoria? He passed away before I ever met him."

I nodded in agreement.

"Yes, but he also owned the house next to where you grew up. I still do. He was using the basement as a way to be near us, and, I guess, now that I think about it, maybe he never actually flew into Calgary when he came for a visit. We never picked him up or dropped him off at the airport. He always insisted on taking a taxi."

"You know," Morgan said, "an older man did live next door. He and my mother sometimes chatted over the fence. Maybe that's how he knew what my plans were."

"Do you think it was him?"

She shrugged.

"The timing would be about right. I remember we were in Grade 8 or 9, and I think I saw him sometimes from the kitchen window. It might have been your grandfather."

"It was," I said confidently. "I found out that house has been on the property inventory for over ten years."

Morgan frowned.

"But why me? Why arrange to rent an apartment to me long before I would actually go there for school?"

I chuckled.

"Because he knew how much I liked you."

"Oh, really? How so?"

I could feel my face heating up.

"Well, I talked a lot about you around him. He always listened and asked about you."

Morgan smiled and elbowed me gently.

"That's so cute. Though, why do something like that for me? I'm not family."

I had an answer for that.

"I think I might know," I began. "As I've travelled and met people my grandparents knew, I've discovered a remarkable kindness in how they treated people. They used the wealth from Enniskillen to help people out of tough situations or simply to make their lives easier."

Morgan squeezed my hand.

"And living next door to us, he would have known how my parents constantly fought. Do you think he felt sorry for me, and this was his way of trying to help me?"

"I think so. It's what he would have done."

"Hmm, this is an incredible secret. Still, even with the video you made, I didn't believe anything you said, Aidan."

I knew exactly what she meant.

"That day, when the three of you bumped into me outside the apartment in Victoria, I had just discovered the Windows that morning. I wanted to tell you, but I couldn't. I didn't know what I had gotten into, but I hated being dishonest. I'm sorry."

She gave me a nudge.

"I understand."

"I'm not asking you to do anything you don't want to or change any part of your life, but you know everything else about me, and I wanted to share this with you, too. It's a little late to apologize, but I'm sorry I did it so dramatically, pulling you through the Window like that. I'm glad you didn't call the police."

She squeezed my hand.

"I almost did, you know."

"Yeah? That would have taken some explaining. Do you want to call your friends and tell them you're safe?"

"I can call from here?"

I stood up, causing her to slip into the chair. She hooked her legs over an arm of the chair and straightened her skirt. I pulled my cell from my pocket.

"Do you want me to dial?"

She swung her legs around and stood up.

"You can call from here? From the Solomon Islands?"

"Yeah, there's a satellite communication system on the island, and I have a roaming package that works from anywhere on the planet."

She shook her head in disbelief and smiled sheepishly.

"I already called Kelli back in — over there."

She gestured towards the hallway.

"That's why I took so long to follow you — here."

I grinned. She was experiencing the same difficulty with orientation I'd had that first time. It was amusing to watch it from this side of the experience.

"I thought as much. Did you run into the twins?"

"No, I don't think anyone's home. Nice house though, from what I saw back there – in – uh, it's yesterday there, right?"

She pointed again, though it made little sense to do so.

"Should I tell them? Kelli and Brit?" Morgan asked as she walked over to the Windows, placing a hand on the glass as she gazed out to the cove. Another handprint on the Window. I grinned. Now, I could never wash that pane.

She answered her question as she stared out at the cove.

"I'm sorry, I shouldn't have asked you that. This is your story to tell, not mine."

I nodded. She is amazingly sensible.

"What did you tell them when you called?" I asked, moving to stand beside her. It was a bright, nearly cloudless day, and the crystal waters were alive, sparkling in dazzling hues of turquoise and jade.

"Only I was in your apartment, and everything was fine."

"Why only that?

"Are you kidding me?" she grabbed my hand. "When I went downstairs, I ran out the front door. It was obviously hours later in the day, and I recognized the house from the photos you'd shown me, but it still didn't make sense. I stood out on the street, freezing, wondering what to do, then thought of what you'd said about the phone in the kitchen. I called Kelli's cell. That's when I noticed the time on my cell had jumped ahead to Ontario time."

I couldn't help but relish the expression of wonder filling every curve and feature of her face and asked, "What did you think was happening to you?"

"I didn't know what you had done or how. That's why I came back upstairs and followed you through that hole in the wall. I was going to drag some answers out of you. Then, I saw all this," Morgan gestured to the cove and the Seagull. "I'm still having a hard time believing it."

She reached over and took my other hand.

"But, thank you."

"For what?" My heart was pounding at her nearness.

"For trusting me and inviting me here." She let go of my hands and tapped me on the arm, laughing, "Willie McPhie, huh? Sounds like a pirate."

"He was – sort of. He used the Windows to steal from anyone he could."

She leaned up against the window frame.

"Why do you – why are they called windows? Aren't they doors?"

I chuckled.

"When a Window opens, its natural shape is rectangular, like a door, and it makes more sense to call them that, but when Willie first discovered what the two ores could do, the effect was like a window had opened. Calling them Windows is an Enniskillen tradition, I guess."

"Amazing, and these Window things give you access to places you own worldwide?"

"The Enniskillen Group has investments all over the world. Many are properties with buildings, but only seventy-two have Windows."

She laughed, shaking her head.

"You're like an international illegal immigrant."

"A what?"

"Well," she explained, forming a globe shape with her hands, "you arrive illegally in all these countries, right? You're like an illegal immigrant, slipping across the border at night."

"An international illegal immigrant," I said, nodding in mock seriousness, "I like that. I wonder if there's an immigration department for people like me?"

She laughed and reached for my hand again, and we gazed at the Seagull resting in her watery grave. Morgan was here, on my island, and it felt wonderful. Sunlight reflected like a million floating diamonds on the water as palms and thick foliage along the cove swayed in the light breeze. Air whistled in the fireplace, playing my song of Enniskillen.

"It would be nice to take a day and see nothing but sunrises all around the world," she said softly as if sensing my awe.

"We could do that, you and me."

She squeezed my hand.

"I'd like that."

I took a moment to shut the door between Enniskillen and Turin Street. Then we wandered around the fortress, opening trunks and handling various antique objects loaded with a history I was only beginning to appreciate. As we did, I told her about the epiphany I had experienced as I read through Marianne McPhie's diaries. I wasn't sure yet what to do, but I knew I had to use Enniskillen in a way that honoured her memory and what she had tried to do with the Windows.

"But how?" Morgan asked. "Revealing them would create an international crisis in national sovereignty and security, and economically. What you do poses a substantial security risk for sovereign countries, making the use of them something I doubt you would be able to hold on to."

"I agree. The McPhie family did all this in secret, which might not be so easy anymore," I said.

"But how do they work?" Morgan asked.

I shrugged.

"There's no software, no space-age hardware. Sometimes, I feel like a caveman who's stumbled onto some magical, futuristic technology, but it's basically two types of rock Willie McPhie found right here in this cave. He was the Seagull's first mate with smelting experience and used that knowledge to create what still exists today. The Windows are activated using a lock and a key, each crafted from the two ores. That's it."

"You said before you showed me the video that you thought they might be wormholes."

"There's a brief discussion on wormholes that my grandfather had with Ian McPhie in a journal," I gestured towards the Map Room, "there in that room over there, but I'm unsure how two pieces of rock could do that. They're powerful cosmological events, aren't they?"

Morgan nodded, her brow furrowing.

"Distance means nothing, right?"

"Between the Windows? No. You experienced that when you stepped from Victoria to Kingston and then to the island."

"I felt nothing. Nothing indicated I had just travelled thousands of kilometres," Morgan continued. "It's like the two places touch each other, like walking from one room into another. If these connections are wormholes, then they are unnaturally stable."

"How so?" I asked, my eyes watching her mind work over the same questions I'd already wrestled with.

She nodded, her lips pinched in thought.

"The science is constantly evolving with research, but wormholes, at least in theory, are notoriously unstable unless stabilized by something with a negative energy density."

I chuckled.

"Yeah, you lost me there."

"Well, you say the whole thing happens when these two metals are brought into contact?"

I nodded.

"It's possible the molecular interaction between the two ores creates a wormhole, and then one of the ores or the two of them together also act as a stabilizing force, keeping it open for, uh, how long did you say?"

"They collapse automatically when a large mass moves through, like you or me, but I've seen them stay active for about 15 minutes if I don't walk through. Then, bam, it closes all by itself."

She nodded slowly.

"Right, but that doesn't explain the doorway to the island. It had to have been open for more than 15 minutes before you closed it."

I nodded in agreement.

"It's outside of the system. The only way to get to the island is through the Window in the study."

She frowned and said, "It could be the hallway that makes it different. Maybe it's composed of a mash-up of those ores and acts as a super stabilizer, so the Window stays open longer and is undisturbed by mass passing through the portal it creates."

"My grandfather speculated that this whole area," I lifted my arms, indicated the cave, "was super-charged by the impact of the meteorite with the volcanic rock."

Morgans nodded, looking back to the entrance.

"He was probably right. The wormhole that the key and lock form may only be stable enough to last those fifteen minutes or until you walk through, causing a large enough disruption in the field they create."

"Wow," I said, laughing, "how do you know all this?"

She smiled, her eyes sparkling.

"I'm studying medical science, but I'm interested in all kinds of science, even something as complicated as wormhole theory."

Then I told her about the strange flip-flopping of gravity and orientation as I had entered the Window that opened on Dead Man's Cave. I told her how it felt like I had been 'pulled' through the Window, how the lanyard was severed, and then how I was 'pulled' up through the horizontal doorway when I escaped. I explained my idea of putting a Window into a moving object like an airplane or a train and what that might mean regarding the effects of inertia and elevation. As I talked, her eyes grew wide.

"What?" I asked.

She walked over to one of the wide wooden structures that supported the huge arch-topped windows and separated the glass panes on either side. She placed her hand against its dark, aged wood and spread her slim fingers, barely covering its width.

"I think what you just described might prove that a Window is a temporarily controlled wormhole."

I stood beside her and tapped the support beneath her hand.

"How so?"

She placed her left hand against the left pane of glass and her right hand against the right, with the support structure between them.

"The Window is the wooden structure between these two panes of glass, connecting two separate sites, wherever they may be. The point is, just like these two panes of glass, the sites are not physically touching each other. The support structure, the Window you make with the lock and key, connects, so either side of the connection could be anywhere, at any elevation or orientation. You wouldn't know the consequences until you stepped through."

She waited, her eyebrows raised, her head tilted slightly.

"Do you see it?"

"Oh," I said, smiling broadly as she pulled her hands away from the panes of glass.

"So," she said with a nod, "to answer your question, yes, I think you could put a Window in a moving airplane and, as long as the plane was pressurized to something similar to sea level, you could step through a Window and experience few to no ill effects coming out the other side. You are essentially stepping from one position of physical reality to another."

I stared at her in awe. Nothing as clear as what she'd just said to me was in any of the journals in the Map Room. Based on my observations from Dead Man's Cave, she had probably figured out how the Windows did what they did.

She grinned as I told her this.

"Well, Einstein only theorized about wormholes in the 1930s, and most scientific discoveries supporting his theory have only happened recently. Science theory often has to play catch up to science phenomena."

"So, you're okay with this?" I asked, indicating the sweeping expanse of Enniskillen, although I was really including something else, her inclusion into everything my life had become.

"Were you all right with it from the beginning?"

I shrugged.

"Yes, and no. At first, it was exciting. It still is, but it has changed my life in ways I'm still trying to figure out."

She smiled her lopsided grin at me.

"Well, this is one of these sudden left turns in life no one is ever prepared for, but I'm not unhappy about it."

At that moment, I was struck with an overwhelming feeling; the chair across from me wasn't empty anymore. I felt like crying.

She saw my look and reached out for my hand, taking it.

"Are you all right?"

I smiled at her, sniffing.

"I've felt so alone in all of this."

"Alone? What about the twins? They knew before me, right?" she asked.

I cupped her hand with mine and nodded.

"Yeah, they found out because I left the door to the island open. But, I wanted you to be a part of this, to be a part of whatever it becomes."

Morgan leaned into me, her eyes fixed on mine.

"You've always been so emotionally honest with me, Aidan. I love that about you. Now, before you make me cry, show me your island."

So, I shared my island with the young woman whose love for me filled my heart with incredible joy. It was exciting to watch her curiosity as we looked through a few rooms, rode the elevator to the garage, and climbed into the Lookout. We trekked to the other side of the island, where I hadn't gone yet, following the dirt road that flowed out of the volcanic basin, winding its way through trees swaying to the touch of a gentle trade wind that made the heat and humidity somewhat bearable.

The road opened onto a sizeable and sheltered bay that protected a smattering of old sheds and a long, weathered dock that stretched into the bay, silently waiting for a vessel to moor to it. We walked out to the end and sat for a while, our feet dangling high above the crystal waters. We could see little fish swarming through the water as gulls magically appeared, perhaps hoping for a handout.

It was late evening in Victoria on a Saturday, with the island just a few minutes from Sunday's sunset, and we both suddenly felt exhausted. We walked back to the garage, revelling in the wonder of the starkly different life that buzzed and hummed around us.

As we approached the garage, Morgan pointed to a series of propane tanks with odd-looking tops.

"Those mosquito catchers are a great idea, but we'll need typhoid, malaria, and a whole range of inoculations if we're going to make coming here a thing, Aidan. Especially malaria, I believe it's a serious issue in this part of the world."

"Huh," I said, "I hadn't thought of that."

I had been lucky so far, but she was right. We needed to take this aspect of Window travel seriously. I glanced at my watch. The sun was about to do its dramatic drop into the equatorial Pacific.

"Let's go back up to the Lookout and watch the sunset. It lasts about twenty minutes, and then boom, it's pitch black."

Morgan laughed.

"I'd love to see that."

The twilight period was about half over when we scrambled back into the Lookout. We waited in silence, her arm in mine, our heads touching lightly, watching the amazing transformation from blue sky to star-studded night as the sun, ablaze in reds and oranges, melted like an ice cube into the sea. After a few moments, we ascended into the garage and shut the doors, throwing the crossbar in place.

As I slid the elevator door open, I caught Morgan staring at me in the dim light from the cage's overhead bulb. There was a sweet smile on her face. She reached out and took my hands in hers.

"There's something I need to tell you, Aidan."

"What?"

"After that kiss – after that track meet – I guess I sort of gave up any hope of being with you."

"You were hoping to be with me? I thought, uh – "

She frowned, her eyebrows knitting together.

"Well, yeah, I thought it was obvious. I didn't kiss you for kicks. You've been more than just a friend to me for a long time."

The kiss. I felt my throat tightening. How had I misunderstood that kiss?

"Are you all right?" she asked, letting go of my hands and jabbing me. "What're you thinking? Spit it out."

I looked into her eyes, trying to fathom how I could have been so clueless about what our relationship was or could be. I had dreamed of being in a romantic relationship with her probably since Grade 10, but I never went there, never took that step, even after the kiss.

"I'm sorry, Morgan. I didn't mean to hurt you. I thought you were just fishing, you know. Seeing what it would feel like to kiss me, your best friend. And, when you laughed, I laughed because I thought maybe – I don't know what I was thinking, except now I can see I should have kissed you – I mean, I should have kissed you again."

She smiled and gently brushed my cheek with the back of her hand.

"You should have then, and you should now."

I stared at her, aware of my heart thumping in my chest. Time seemed to slow as my hands slid around the small of her back, and our eyes locked in the rising emotion of the moment. Our lips touched, and she pulled me closer, her breath hot against my face, as I reached up and brushed my fingers along her cheek, slipping them into her hair, pulling her close, our lips melding in the hunger of the embrace both of us had longed for.

The kiss felt like an eternity, but we pulled apart, and I saw the happiness and the tears in her eyes.

"I don't want to hurt you, ever," I said.

Her entire face glowed with the love and hope of the moment.

"Just be honest. I'll be honest with you. If I don't like something, I'll tell you. If I like it, I'll tell you that too. We don't have to be anything other than what we are comfortable with. That made us great friends in the first place, remember?"

"Honesty is what I want. You're safe with me, you know."

I pulled the elevator doors open, and we stepped into its cage.

"I believe you, Aidan." Her green eyes glistened, and she leaned in and brushed my cheek with a delicate kiss. I thought my heart was going to burst through my chest.

I was about to slide the door shut when she grabbed my arm.

"Hey, can I try it?"

I stepped back, and she pulled the door shut, latching it and pressing the down button. The Otis elevator responded without hesitation, and we descended through the garage floor into the volcanic strength of the fortress.

We spent the night holding each other under the thickness of a quilt on a king-sized four-poster bed in the largest of the bedrooms in the West Wing. Small night-light pucks were attached to the smooth rock walls, and we turned a few on. The glow from these created an almost surreal ambience. We had slept out under the stars many times back home, but cuddling in a huge bed in a cavern on a small island in the South Pacific was irresistibly romantic. We kissed for a while, our hearts beating with the joy of realized love, but we were also tired. Morgan fell asleep first. I fought it off for a while, watching her serene face on the pillow and feeling happier than I'd ever felt. I didn't want this day to end. Bringing her to Enniskillen had gone far better than I had hoped.

In fact, it was perfect.

TWENTY-FIVE

I awoke alone in another unfamiliar bed, one of many I had slept in since I'd begun travelling. For a moment, I was afraid I had dreamed everything that had happened the day before, but I could still feel the lingering memory of Morgan's body next to mine as we lay in each other's arms through the night. I sat up in bed, throwing off the quilt. No, this was happening.

Morgan, me, and Enniskillen.

I slipped on my shoes and made my way to the main cave. The fortress was cast in shadows from the glowing orb of a South Seas moon peeking through the windows and from the bank of lights over the kitchen I had left on before we had explored the West Wing for a place to sleep. Morgan wasn't keen on sleeping alone in one of the bedroom caverns, so we shared the king bed in a room labelled Mariah's Den.

I caught sight of Morgans's outline, a lithe figure sitting in the lounger by the ship's wheel. She turned when she heard my yawn, smiled, and pulled a hand out from under a blanket to give me a small wave. I smiled back and pointed to the bathroom. She nodded and pulled the blanket back around her. A few minutes later, I shoved a wingback chair over to where she was sitting, its hardwood legs scraping and grating noisily as I bumped it beside hers. I grinned apologetically as I slid into the chair. Morgan reached her hand out for mine, her eyes sparkling as I slid mine into hers. Together, we basked in the tranquillity of a Southern

Hemisphere night, and for a moment, I could think of nothing else that could make our world feel exactly as it should be.

Morgan broke the silence.

"I woke up, and it took a while to realize where I was and that it wasn't a dream. This is amazing, Aidan. That bathroom could use an upgrade, though. It's a bit like camping."

I laughed, nodding.

"Yeah, I'm not really into emptying port-a-potties. My grandparents probably just crossed back to the house to use the bathroom there."

Morgan smiled lovingly at me.

"Life will never be the same again for either of us."

I nodded in reply as I squeezed her hand.

"Yeah. Not exactly your average birthday present, eh?"

"No kidding. Your grandfather trusted you. He must have seen something in you that even you didn't."

Her comment brought tears to my eyes. I had thought this about my grandfather and why he had believed I was ready for Enniskillen, but hearing someone else say it made the reality of his gift all that more special. His risk was paying off. I wouldn't disappoint him or Morgan.

"I need to get back. I have two twelve-hour, back-to-back practicum days this week, and I need to let the girls know I'm okay," she said. "They'll think I've spent the night with you."

I laughed and smiled slyly.

"Well, you did."

She gave me a playful push with her elbow.

"Yeah, they're a couple. They'll be thinking something else."

My eyebrows shot up.

"And that's a bad thing?"

Morgan rolled her eyes.

"Oh-ho, one little kiss, and now he wants his cake."

She rose from the chair and looked towards the kitchen area as she grabbed my hand, pulling me up.

"Speaking of cake, I need food."

We searched the fridge and found some croissants, a jar of strawberry jam, and the last few cups of milk from a container. We ate just as the sky erupted with brilliant light from the sunrise. At 4 p.m. Kingston time, we returned to the study, then left immediately for Victoria. We talked a while longer in my apartment while I waited for the next Window.

Morgan wanted to know everything about where each Window led, to experience the connection to the world they offered, but she wasn't willing to give up on her schooling either. I certainly didn't want that. All through high school, she had been carefully mapping out her future. A career in medicine was something she had always wanted, even when we were in middle school. It wasn't just a way to escape the chaos of her family life. I had never felt pulled in any particular direction, so it hadn't been a difficult decision for me to drop out of college and immerse myself in the affairs of the Enniskillen Group.

We arranged to meet on Wednesday afternoon for a four-day around-the-world trip, chasing sunrises or sunsets. If I planned our trip carefully, we could experience at least four of those in one day and possibly all four seasons. Back in Kingston, I could hear the brothers laughing at a television program in the bedroom they shared below. I was about to head down but noticed several overlapping notes taped to the closet door. The topmost note read:

Aidan: Have you heard from your parents? Dane.

Had I heard from my parents? Were they trying to contact me? It wouldn't be because I had dropped out of school; the college had no obligation to inform my parents of this decision. Ignoring the note, I grabbed my suitcase and cellphone gear from the island and caught the next Window.

Two days can feel like a very long time, especially if your heart is filled with anticipation. I hung out in Zurich and Lisbon on Monday, touring a museum in the former and an art gallery in the latter, just doing tourist things, and then on Tuesday in LA, I read a few chapters of a classic science fiction novel, *Doorway into Summer,* by Robert A. Heinlein. With the life of Manhattan Beach and the surf pounding in the background, I soon drifted off. When I awoke, I caught the Window to Kensington and took a taxi to a little pub in London called the Golden Eagle, one of the places my grandfather had frequented, according to his journal. A bartender recognized my accent and announced cheerily to the pub's patrons that I was a Canadian. This was met with a round of clapping and inebriated cheers marked with references to how nice we colonials were. A group of older men and women sitting in a corner booth invited me to join them. I pulled up a chair, and after sharing my name and a little history, I was astounded to learn one of the couples was sure they had known my grandfather. As the evening wore on, the group gathered around a battered and sorely out-of-tune upright piano and broke into a strong but ale-slurred rendition of *O Canada* and *Four Strong Winds*.

I bought everyone in the pub several rounds, this too receiving further cheers and hearty applause. Just before closing, we raised a glass in memory of my grandfather. It was one of the most surreal moments of my travels, and I struggled to hold back the emotion I kept hidden away in that place that deeply missed him.

Later, I navigated my way back to LA, where it was early Wednesday morning. I slept for a few hours, jogged to the pier and back, moved a few pieces of furniture, ate a bowl of cereal, and fussed impatiently around the condo until it was time to meet Morgan at her apartment.

She was waiting for me, but she wasn't alone. A tall, muscular man in a dark uniform with a tool belt around his waist was talking with her. He paused when he saw me coming down the stairs. I immediately felt that I recognized him but couldn't remember from where. I thought a flicker of surprise passed before his eyes, but he quickly averted his gaze, searching for something in his tool belt.

Morgan used my sudden interruption as an opportunity to excuse herself. Grabbing my arm, she ushered me back up the stairs.

"Who's that," I whispered, turning slightly to catch another glimpse of the man. He had crossed to the bottom of the stairs and was watching us while talking into a cell phone.

She shrugged, shaking her head.

"Oh, that's the guy from the cable company. He's a bit of a creep."

We entered my apartment, and I shut the door, locked it, and then asked, "Have you ever seen him before?"

"He was here last week. He showed up after the cable went out. Why?"

"He looks familiar. What makes him a creep?"

"Well, when he was here last week, he insisted on entering our apartment, which, I suppose, was fine. He needed to check the router. But then I caught him snooping around my bedroom. I don't have a TV in my room. Then, he showed up a few minutes ago, buzzing our apartment and asking to talk with me. That's when you showed up. I think he wanted to ask me out."

"Yikes."

She laughed, grabbing my hand and meshing our fingers together.

"Well, I've only ever wanted one man, and I think he understands that now."

I almost cried again as she looked into my eyes, but I quickly kissed her, pulled away, and grabbed a shopping bag I'd set on the couch earlier.

Morgan's hair was swept back into a ponytail. She wore two-tone purple sweats and had a tattered Northface shoulder pack strapped to her shoulders, the same backpack she'd had since grade ten. I wore my black Armani tracksuit with a matching rip-proof trekking backpack, perfect for travel. I bought one for Morgan but in dark green. I presented the bag to her.

She regarded it ruefully, slowly lifting the pack out of it.

"Uh, thanks? I know you're rich, Aidan, but I don't want you just to buy me stuff. That's never been a part of our relationship, and I wouldn't know how to handle it if you started doing that."

Her statement took me aback.

"What do you mean?"

She shrugged and grimaced.

"Oh, god, please don't misunderstand me." She touched my arm apologetically. "You know my parents fought over money; more than anything, it added to the end of their marriage. Having as much as you do frightens me."

"I never thought of it that way. I just thought – "

She dropped the pack on the couch and grabbed both my hands, pulling them close to her.

"I did need a new backpack." She smiled broadly and let my hands go. "Thank you."

That was fair. I didn't want her to feel like she might owe me something. Still, I didn't want to be afraid to share this new financial part of my life with her. She was right, though; our relationship had been built around friendship and trust, and the kind of money I had at my disposal added a layer we'd have to navigate.

"Okay," I agreed, "but I need to feel free to take you out on the most amazing date you've ever been on."

She grinned and laughed.

"Oh. I'm ready, but I never said I was a cheap date."

As she transferred the contents of her old pack to the new one, I told her about the Golden Eagle and its patrons and how one of the couples remembered my grandfather.

"I wish I had met him," she said, frowning with amusement. "How you talk about him and the generosity he's shown to so many people, even me, I think that level of humanity would be something to aspire to."

I nodded.

"Yeah, that's what I want. Imagine leaving a legacy of people missing your kindness and generosity."

I handed her a bottle of water and inserted the key.

There was a knock at the door.

"'Ello."

"It's that guy," Morgan whispered, clearly shocked. "He must've followed us."

The voice sounded familiar, but I couldn't place it. I glanced at her face. I'd never known her to be fearful, but this guy's pursuit of her was unnerving. He knocked again, more challenging.

"'Ello. Cable guy."

"Aidan?" Morgan grimaced.

I held a finger to my lips and smiled, winking at her. Turning my head away from the door so my voice would sound like it was coming from farther back in the room, I called, "Just a minute."

Then I turned the key and opened the door, and Morgan laughed as we stepped through to the study, leaving our unwanted visitor knocking at the door of a now empty room.

We entered Brisbane, Australia, through a boathouse a few minutes later. It was almost 8:30 a.m. there. It was a boathouse, but there was no boat. My grandparents used this one to visit the capital of Queensland, where, according to the pop-up on the tablet, they often rented a room in a nearby hotel.

"I'm sorry you have to put up with crap like that," I offered as we stepped out into the fresh morning air.

Morgan smirked.

"That guy? Don't be. I get hit on all the time, just not often enough by the right guy."

"Oh?" I managed, but she shoved me away and took off running, her laughter challenging me to follow. I did, feeling overjoyed that she was so relaxed and happy.

Once I caught up to her, we settled into a comfortable stroll, holding hands as we followed a broad path along the banks of the meandering Brisbane River, enjoying the brilliance of the morning sun. The promenade along the South Bank was alive with joggers and blurry-eyed pedlars preparing to spend another spring day offering trinkets and food to the droves of tourists who had already begun to arrive in coach buses. After a while, we crossed the river on one of the many bridges to trek along a mangrove boardwalk. From there, we caught the city's water ferry system for an impromptu tour that took us under the Captain Cook Bridge and to New Farm Park, where we disembarked. The gardens in the park were so well-groomed that it was the kind of place my mother could disappear into for days. We didn't have days, but we wandered the paths for an hour or so, taking photos with our cellphones of flower species that neither of us had ever seen in person. From the park, we followed paths that paralleled the river until we found a nice spot under the shade of a giant fig tree to eat bagel-like breakfast sandwiches we'd bought from a street vendor as the city roared to life around us. Every moment with Morgan was wonderful, I could hardly believe this was my life now. It felt more perfect than I could have imagined.

Later, we caught the Window to Los Angeles, stepping back in time and season where the sun held sway over a cool November afternoon. Morgan laughed as we entered the living room from the entryway. I had left the curtains parted, but the sheers closed, and sunshine gently bathed the space, creating a feeling of welcome.

"This feels like a home, not just one of your empty rooms. Did your grandparents spend time here?"

"Yeah," I replied. "I guess it was their snowbird destination in North America."

She smiled and grabbed my arm as I led her upstairs to the bedroom and its balcony. From there, we could see the near-deserted beach and the white-capped waves crashing in from the churning ocean. Only a few people in hoodies and jackets were huddled against the wind on the boardwalk that followed the shoreline.

"I could get used to this, you know," she said wistfully.

I smiled and pulled her closer.

"We could stay for a few days if you want."

She shook her head and smiled broadly at me.

"No, as much as I'd like that, not yet. I want to see more of your fabulous Windows."

We planned to stay the night in LA, but first, I took her to Chicos, the Mexican restaurant I had frequented. The restaurant may not be large, but the food is authentic and has three levels of spiciness for the various dishes: Bebe Gringo, Hombre Picante, and Mucho Locura. Of the three times I had been there, traditional Mexican music always played in the background over a decent sound system, and customers loved hanging out, eating, and chatting over pitchers of beer. We did all that until the sun began its daily collision with the Atlantic. Holding hands, we walked back to the condo, chatting as we strolled along the boardwalk.

"You know," Margin said as we stopped to look at a kiosk with a map and information about Manhattan Beach, "all of this, the Windows, all the places they take us, the wealth, it's wonderful, but based on what you've told me about the McPhie history, it exists because they stole it and exploited the resources of other people and countries. What they did was no different than the large-scale colonialism most developed countries engaged in for centuries."

I was surprised by her sudden comment, but the reality of the history of my inheritance had been lingering at the edges of my mind since reading Marianne McPhie's diaries. She'd recognized this, too, and had made an effort toward restitution, but what more could I do?

"Yeah, I know. Every time I purchase something or go somewhere like here, where I own a not-so-cheap waterfront condo, I wonder about that."

Morgan touched my arm.

"Hey, I'm not trying to make you feel guilty. You can't change the past, but you can change the future. It's your inheritance now."

I laughed.

"I think you said something similar that night in Drumheller, but I get it. Marianne McPhie changed the legacy of Enniskillen as much as she was able or knew how to do, but what else can I do?"

We started walking again, the condo just in view.

"Well, there's things like, where's the wealth coming from? Is anyone being exploited? Are you one of those business people who doesn't pay a living wage?"

I shrugged, grimacing.

"I don't know. Reinhold Bonk works with the various properties, I spend the money he makes for me."

Morgan clasped my hand tightly and bumped her hip against mine.

"There's somewhere to start. Find out how your wealth affects the people who make you wealthy."

We arrived at the steps to the condo. I fished the key out of my pocket, and we stepped in.

"After I read Marianne's diaries, I knew I had to do something other than what I had been doing, travelling and spending money on nice shirts."

I laughed, and she ran a hand over my sleeve.

"But, I wasn't sure how to do that. I think you can help me."

I shut the door, and Morgan slid her arms around me, pulling me close as she looked into my eyes.

"I love that you have money and all of this, I really do. I can't imagine what it's like not to worry about money, but it's not worth having if it hurts other people."

I nodded. At that moment, I loved her even more. Morgan had always grounded my thinking, pushing me to imagine possibilities I would never have normally. This was one of those moments.

We filled tall glasses with iced tea from the fridge and then crashed side by side on the wicker couch, munching on green grapes and talking, our feet on the coffee table. Morgan reached across me and grabbed the photo off the end table I had borrowed from my parent's house, the one of Amelia and me.

"Wow. You've always been in such good shape, Aidan."

I grunted.

"I'm too skinny."

"You're perfect," Morgan argued.

"Perfect? I don't think anyone has ever used that adjective to describe me."

"Well, you're the right height for your width. You're lithe, supple, and designed to move. Not like me and my big hips."

I frowned in sincere confusion.

"You're a lot faster than I am, and you do not have big hips."

"Now that's what I call being hit on," she said, laughing before leaning in to kiss me. The warmth of her breath caressed my cheek as her lips pressed against mine. My heart raced at what was quickly becoming a familiar gesture between us. I felt like crying.

She pulled back.

"Are you all right?" she asked, smiling tenderly while placing a finger on my trembling lips.

I don't deserve this, I thought, but said, "Thank you for not giving up on me."

"I think you're worth it," she said, kissing me again, longer this time. I put my arm around the small of her back and pulled her closer, our bodies pressing together. I had never felt so emotionally close to anyone, and I didn't want to let go. Morgan moaned softly and gently pulled away, her glasses rimmed with condensation.

"I like where our relationship is going," she whispered.

TWENTY-SIX

Morgan fell asleep in my arms on the couch, her head resting on my chest, the fragrance of her hair strong and alluring. I couldn't sleep.

She was happy. How could I have been so stupid not to see how she had begun to think of me romantically somewhere in the course of our friendship? How could I have been oblivious to the invitation to do the same in that first kiss? I knew why; it was simple – really. I was afraid we'd end up like our parents. Our friendship was comfortable, something to be cherished for sure, but not something either of us worked hard at. We were friends first and foremost. We grew into puberty together; she watched me grow facial hair and teased me about it, and I noticed the day she started wearing a bra and secretly marvelled at how she transformed from a skinny girl to a young woman who made my heart flutter. But I hid those feelings because allowing our friendship to become romantic might wreck what was comfortable and easy. Our parents couldn't make their relationships work, so how could we? There was less possibility of a broken heart if I kept her, in my mind, as the good friend next door, who happened to be a girl, but nothing more.

I brushed the warmth of her cheek with the back of my hand and gently lifted her head as I let her lay on the couch. I grabbed a pillow and the quilt from the bedroom and covered her, slipping the pillow under her head as I brushed a strand of hair from her face. She was asleep, but she smiled just slightly, and I cried.

Her voice calling my name woke me early the next morning.

"Did you sleep in that chair all night?"

I had curled up in one of the loungers; my smaller stature had advantages. I smiled a yawn at her.

"Yeah."

"You could have used the bed. I slept well here."

I shook my head slowly.

"I wanted to watch you sleep."

She stood up, crossed over to my chair, and eased onto my lap, kissing me firmly as she drew me close.

"Man, I *love* this romantic side of you," she said, smiling and biting her lower lip.

After breakfast, we wandered the beachfront, checking out local shops as a slightly cool wind reminded us of the encroaching winter in this hemisphere. At nine o'clock, I took her to the villa in Knokke-Heist, and then we trekked along the sandy beach following one of the dikes as a blustery wind came rolling off the water. We had to escape to the warmth of a small cafe a few streets from the Lippenslaan, Knokke-Heist's long and usually bustling shopping area. We were the only customers, and the waitress seated us at one of several white, wrought iron tables facing rain-streaked windows that framed a view of the wild Flemish coast.

We ended up engaging the lone server in conversation. She was about our age and spoke excellent English, even though she had been raised in a small rural town in southern France. She was excited to meet Canadians and politely peppered us with questions, and we answered each one. She was a fellow traveller.

We held each other against the wind as we left the cafe and walked the narrow streets back to the villa.

"It's amazing how friendly and open people are to strangers," Morgan commented along the way.

I had noticed the same thing during my initial travels.

"Yeah. Mostly. There were a few places where people were suspicious, like Rio Gallegos in Argentina. I was the only English-speaking person in this sketchy dock area. Rusting tankers and freighters, mountains of garbage, and hordes of street kids, I show up dressed like some rich influencer trolling for Likes. For the most part, though, I've had no problems getting helpful answers to some fairly stupid questions."

"Stupid questions?"

I laughed.

"Yeah. Like, 'Where am I?'"

It was shortly after 2:15 p.m. Kingston time, so we decided to take the Window to the house and drop in on the island to walk along the beach under the dawning of a South Pacific day before heading off to Duggan's Ranch in Australia. I opened the Window to Turin Street and nearly tripped over Bill. He was sitting in a lawn chair, facing the closet door, a textbook resting on his knees. He looked surprised but bolted upright as we came in, the air whipping around his face, ruffling his mop of hair.

"Aidan?" he exclaimed as the door shut behind us.

"Bill? Why are you sitting here?"

He rubbed his eyes and then flinched with surprise as he saw Morgan.

"Uh, hi, Morgan."

"Uh, hi, Bill," she teased.

"What's going on?" I asked.

"Where have you been?" he demanded, his voice growing taut as his gaze shifted back to Morgan. She was gripping my arm, snuggling into my side.

"Why? What's wrong?" I asked, feeling a knot of fear in my gut.

"Your parents, they're missing."

"Missing?" Morgan stammered. "What do you mean, missing?"

Bill breathed sharply in and shrugged.

"They're gone. They left home, um, last Saturday, and they haven't returned."

"What are you saying?" I demanded.

"They haven't come back. They're gone. Their vehicle was found east of Cardston, abandoned. You haven't answered any emails, and your phone kept going to voice mail, so we left notes on the closet door. I know you've been here. Stuff was blown about."

Uh, I'm sorry, I have a new phone. What do you mean abandoned?"

"Have the police been contacted?" Morgan interrupted.

Bill nodded.

"Yeah, Amelia's been dealing with them and trying to contact you, Aidan. She's freaking out, and since you didn't leave her a way to get in touch, she thinks you're missing too. We couldn't tell her the truth. We didn't."

"What about the police?"

"She says they're calling it suspicious."

"I only just saw my parents a week ago. I recorded them as they were leaving the house," I said.

I grabbed my cell phone from my bag and dialled Amelia's cell. It rang several times and then went to voice mail. Then I called my parents' landline, and she picked up on the first ring.

"Hi," I said.

"Aidan?"

I could tell she was angry.

"Hi, Amelia," I said again, feeling small.

"My god, where have you been? You're not answering emails or texts, and your little buddies there, I can tell they're hiding something about you, though god knows what or why."

"I'm sorry," I offered, sounding pathetic.

"You're sorry?" She mocked. Her anger felt like a slap across my face.

I sighed, pushing the feelings back to where they had surfaced from.

"What happened? Bill says they're missing."

"Well, they're officially missing, that's for sure. They didn't take any luggage and haven't touched their bank accounts. The RCMP have Dad's car."

I heard her sob, and I felt terrible.

"It's only been a week, Amelia. Are you sure they didn't go on vacation or something?" I knew this was unlikely, but who would want to kidnap our parents?

"Vacation? You know them better than that, Aidan."

She was right, of course. They could hardly tolerate living in the same house.

"But, why would someone – "

She cut me off.

"Where have you been?"

I hesitated, trying to think of something believable to tell her, some lie that would explain my absence and let the brothers off the hook for lying to her. I looked at Morgan, who could hear both sides of the conversation.

Her eyebrows were raised as she whispered, "You have to tell her the truth."

I nodded. My sister needed to know.

"I was travelling overseas."

"Travelling overseas! Aren't you supposed to be in school?" she exploded.

I didn't need her anger, least of all her judgment.

"Look, Amelia, I'm sorry. I'm coming home. I'll be there around noon, 12:30."

"Where? Here? Today?"

"Today."

"Where are you?"

"In Kingston."

"Here, in less than an hour? That's impossible!"

"I'll be there."

I ended the call. Impossible? It wasn't impossible.

An awkward silence settled in the study as Dane joined us, his eyes wide with curiosity as he caught sight of Morgan. I knew the brothers were wondering how and when I had let her in on the secret. Morgan sat down on the edge of the desk, placing her hand on my arm. The whole situation felt unreal, like a badly written movie.

I looked at my watch. I'd be in Calgary in less than an hour, and my parents were missing. How could that be? I cupped Morgan's hand with mine.

"I need to take care of this. You can go to Victoria today if you want. There's a Window at four this afternoon, Kingston time."

"I don't want to leave you. Not now," she answered softly as she looked intently into my eyes.

I squeezed her hand as Bill folded the lawn chair and said, "I'm sorry, Aidan. We were taking turns sitting here waiting for you to show up."

"Yeah, me too," Dane added. "We didn't tell your sister anything."

"Thanks. I don't think she's too happy about that. Do you know anything more than Amelia?"

Bill shrugged, shaking his head. Dane answered.

"Only what your sister has said, and it isn't much. They were going to a marriage counsellor but never arrived there. A farmer near Cardston found the car near his private runway last Monday. The police said everything looked normal, except the keys were still in the ignition. No ransom note, either. Nothing else. That's all we know."

My parents were going to a marriage counsellor? Really? That was as unlikely as them being kidnapped. I didn't think they cared enough about their relationship to try and save it.

The brothers kept eyeing Morgan. I knew they were wondering what was happening, so I told them about my decision to tell her. Morgan laughed, reassuring them she was happy about it, though she had wanted to slug me for how I had gone about it.

"Well, he forgot we were coming a few days after him and left the door to the fortress open," Dane nodded. "That's how we found out."

"I didn't think he could keep the Windows a secret from you for long," Bill said, "knowing how you two were all over each other in high school."

"'All over each other?'" I stammered, embarrassed, but Morgan was grinning.

Bill laughed, nodding his head.

"It was obvious you two had a thing for each other. You practically divorced Dane and me. We got over it, though, eh, little brother?"

"Oh no, not me. I never got a kiss," Dane feigned indignation.

Morgan burst into laughter.

"He told you about the kiss?"

"Yup."

"Uh, well, it was, uh – " I sputtered.

"He's still a good kisser," Morgan offered, smiling and winking at me. I felt my face turning red, but we all laughed as if nothing bad was happening. Then we grew quiet, the moment surreal. We were teasing each other while our thoughts were clouded by the uncertainty of what may or may not have happened to my parents.

We grabbed our winter coats, Morgan borrowing one of mine, then caught the Window to Calgary at 12:30. Exciting the apartment, we climbed the concrete steps to the backyard to follow the snowy sidewalk to the gate and then along the house to the street. Amelia's blue sedan sat beside my mother's snow-covered Neon in the driveway.

I rang the doorbell, and my sister answered the door a moment later. I was shocked when I saw her. She looked haggard, like she hadn't slept in days. I had seen her a week before I left for Kingston, and she had been bright and cheery then. Now, her face looked thin, and her eyes were hollow with dark shadows under them. Her usually well-kept auburn hair was in disarray, pulled back in one of her quick top-of-the-head knots. Her mouth dropped in surprise, then quickly shut as she looked us over.

She didn't offer a greeting.

"You weren't in Kingston."

I ignored the accusation.

"May we come in?"

She stepped aside, directing us to the kitchen, where I'd stood weeks ago, smugly leaving a glass tumbler on the island. Posters were scattered across the table, each with a portrait of our parents and the word *MISSING* beneath in large handwritten block letters, along with a description and a number to call. I flopped down onto a chair and picked up one of the posters, holding it as though it were all that was left of my parents.

Missing. Our parents were missing?

Fatigue hung like a cloud over Amelia's face. She was angry with me, and I couldn't blame her. I would have been livid had she been the one who had gone communications dark.

"What happened?" I asked as everyone took a seat around the table.

My sister struggled with her emotions as she reviewed the details surrounding our parents' disappearance. Eight days earlier, they had left together on Saturday morning to meet with a counsellor. That much had been determined by the message left by the counsellor on the answering service when they hadn't shown up. A credit card transaction confirmed they purchased gas in Southeast Calgary a few minutes before their meeting. That sounded like my father. Why put off for later what you can do right now? Then they just disappeared. No one realized they were missing until the Nissan was found a few days later on a farmer's private airfield outside Cardston. There was no blood, no sign of a struggle, just an abandoned vehicle. The RCMP officer assigned to the case was suspicious, she said. The car had been meticulously cleaned inside, not a single fingerprint could be found, they had told Amelia. As a result, they were tentatively calling it suspicious, and they suspected that if it were a kidnapping, the perpetrators were either unknown individuals or one of my parents.

Dad, kidnap Mom? The alternative was even more ludicrous. Still, why would anyone abduct the two of them? None of it made sense. There was some evidence of recent use by a mid-sized aircraft on the airfield, but nothing else was uncovered. The police, she told us, were hesitant to pursue anything further as there was nothing to support the kidnapping theory.

"That's all I know."

She glared at the brothers.

"And these two have been completely unhelpful, lying about where you've been."

Dane grimaced, and Bill cast a pleading glance at me. Neither had said a word since arriving, shying away from my sister's frustration with all of us.

"Amelia, it's not their fault," I said. "They didn't know where I was. I'm sorry I wasn't here. I should have been."

"Well," she replied, her expression growing dark again, "if you actually cared about anyone else except yourself, maybe you would have known what the hell was going on."

I felt my skin bristle at her anger, but I sighed, pushing the feeling away, and nodded. She was right, of course. I had been traipsing around the world, revelling in my unearned inherited wealth and what I had thought was freedom while my parents had vanished.

"I'm sorry. I deserve that. It's been hard, you know, this being an adult thing," I said.

She graciously nodded, accepting my feeble attempt at an apology, and I stood up and gently pulled her out of her chair. We held onto each other desperately, searching for comfort, aching for resolution, our tears washing each other's shoulders. It felt like the times after one of my fights with Dad when Amelia would hold me as I tried hard not to give in to the tears but often did anyway.

"There is something you can tell me, Aidan," Amelia said quietly as she sat back down and dabbed her eyes with the sleeve of her sweater.

"Where were you when you called?"

Her eyes bore into me.

"And don't give me that overseas bullshit or tell me you were honestly in Kingston an hour ago. Where have you been?"

I stared at her. Bill coughed. Morgan gripped my hand and said, "Tell her. You need to tell her."

Amelia's head tilted inquiringly toward Morgan, then back to me.

"Tell me what, Aidan?"

I sucked my breath in, stretching my hands out before me. For some odd reason, it felt as if I was about to confess to some heinous crime. Perhaps, in a way, not telling Amelia sooner was a crime. Of all the people in my life, I should have immediately included my sister in the legacy of the McPhie Windows. I could have called her that very first day or anytime since. I should have introduced her to what my grandfather had kept hidden from our family all these years. I owed her that much.

"There's something I should have told you weeks ago," I began, preparing mentally for the onslaught of questions I knew would follow my fantastic explanation.

I gave her the abbreviated version, touching on all the essential moments and showing her the credit cards. She didn't believe me, of course. The story, even paired down, was too fantastic, too unbelievable.

"Aidan," she finally cut me off, her voice dripping with the exasperation that I could see was welling up in her the longer I rambled on. "Why are you doing this? Who told you Grandpa killed himself."

"Arnold Silverstein. Dad."

"Dad? He never told me that."

I shrugged.

"Why does this Reinhold person, your financial manager," she said this last phrase while making quotation marks in the air, "think he was murdered?"

I listed off the inconsistencies Reinhold had told me about.

"He hired a private investigation firm, and they determined Gramps was shot somewhere other than the study but died there. Bonk doesn't know about the Windows, so I believe he was shot somewhere in the system and made it back to the study before he died."

"Right. Somewhere in this Window system?"

I nodded, but Amelia shook her head slowly, not trying to hide her anger.

"Why would you do this, Aidan? Windows? Why would you make up such a ridiculous story?"

She threw her arms up, flopped back in her chair, and glared at the four of us.

"I'll show you."

"Right. You'll show me?" Amelia leaned forward, turning to squint at Bill and Dane and then at Morgan. "I can't believe you three are a part of whatever game he's playing. Our parents are missing, for god's sake."

"Bill and I have used the Windows loads of times," Dane said, sounding like he was confessing. Bill nodded vigorously in agreement.

"Oh, finally," Amelia smirked, "they speak."

"I've travelled through them, too, Amelia," Morgan insisted. "We were in Queensland yesterday, then Los Angeles this morning."

"Ho, ho," Amelia mocked and then stabbed a finger at me, "didn't you say you were just all in Kingston? Why are you doing this?"

I was hurting her, and that angered me. I pushed away from the table.

"C'mon! I'll show you right now."

The intensity and conviction of my response must have surprised her because she followed my quick exit from the kitchen. Of course, it might have been that I didn't wait for further protest, which I could hear the start of as I headed for the front door. Morgan and I and the brothers grabbed our coats and left the house.

"Lock the door," I called over my shoulder as we stepped out into the cool air. "I can't bring you back for twelve hours."

"Shall I bring extra clothes and a toothbrush?" Amelia shot back as she snatched a set of keys from a hook and locked the door. Morgan took my hand and squeezed it, smiling sympathetically at me.

With my sister reluctantly in tow, we crossed the street, following the sidewalk and stairs to the back entrance, where I opened the door to the basement apartment of *my* house.

"You say Grandpa bought this house ten years ago?" she demanded as she looked around the bachelor suite.

I nodded, sensing the beginning of that fragile moment of belief.

"And you own it now?" she asked, sounding slightly dubious.

I swept my arms around the room.

"This is one of my houses. I have several hundred properties worldwide, but about seventy have Windows."

"Why are you doing this?"

I smiled sympathetically.

"Believe me, I know how you feel."

"Okay," she conceded, "you obviously have a key to this apartment. I can maybe believe you own this, but these Windows, these things you say you travel through, you're making that up."

"You just walked through one," Morgan interrupted, gesturing at the apartment's entrance.

Amelia nodded mockingly, pointing to the view beyond the partly open curtains.

"Uh-huh, right. We're still in Calgary."

"It doesn't work like that," I said, reaching for her hand.

She let me take it; her palm was cold, and her fingers felt thin. The last week had been difficult for her, and I regretted my part in adding to her worry over our parents.

"I'm sorry I wasn't here, Amelia."

She nodded resolutely as she closed her eyes and breathed deeply.

"I'm surviving. I always have."

I knew what she meant. She had been the good child, at least in our father's eyes, but it had cost her. I had fought against the shadow of my parents' withering relationship, eventually fleeing to Kingston and as far away as the Windows could take me. Amelia had remained physically close to our parents, feeling responsible for their failing relationship and trying in some way to help them, to save them, even if only her love for them. And now, they were missing. The fear of losing them hung over us. We had all sacrificed in this dysfunctional dance in one manner or another, even my grandfather. It struck me how a single decision to place conditions on love can drastically alter the course of a family's history. Now, I had an opportunity to make Amelia's selfless love, a daughter's love for her parents, worthwhile. I wondered if anything would be the same if our parents were no longer alive. Despite my strained relationship with my father, his safety mattered. This was my family, after all.

I checked the time on my watch, inserted the key and opened the Window to Turin Street. The effects made Amelia jump. She let go of my hand, grabbing my arm as our grandfather's study presented itself to us where concrete steps should have been leading up to a snow-covered backyard.

Moments later, we took her to Enniskillen. Life would never be the same again for any of us.

TWENTY-SEVEN

Enniskillen had a fantasy-like quality, with light from the end of a blazing South Sea day pouring through the windows, igniting the otherworldliness of the fortress in stark contrast to the dim light of my grandfather's study. Amelia was quiet as I introduced her to the inheritance our grandfather had left me. Her questions were short and direct as if she were assessing a patient. I had forgotten how methodical she could be.

Later, she slumped into one of the two chairs by the ship's wheel and kicked her shoes off. I sat in the other chair, Morgan sliding onto its wide armrest, leaning into me.

My sister turned to me.

"Aidan, this is insane. How could anyone keep something like this a secret for over three hundred years? Surely someone would have heard about a family that used these Windows to travel, and surely someone would have talked, even unintentionally."

I nodded slowly.

"I agree, but there's no historical record of the Windows, not even as a myth. It was a carefully guarded secret until I came along. I haven't done a great job of following in their footsteps. Even Gramps was more careful."

"You had no idea, though," Morgan interjected, "he wasn't around to explain anything."

I leaned into the warmth of her body.

"Still, I just can't help but wonder if this is why Mom and Dad were taken. Someone must know about this."

Amelia shrugged and shook her head.

"Let's not get ahead of ourselves yet. That someone has not made contact, there may be another reason."

A crackling sound coming from the fireplace drew our attention. Bill and Dane had been building a roaring fire. Its flames leapt and danced, throwing a golden light that embraced the fortress in comforting warmth as the sky outside quickly grew dark. I could imagine my grandparents or generations of the McPhie family relaxing or eating in the glow of this massive hearth. Realizing we were probably hungry, I searched the kitchen for something to eat. There wasn't much we felt like preparing, so I suggested that Morgan, Amelia and I catch the upcoming 2:30 Window to New York and order pizza from Fat Tony's Pizza (they deliver in thirty minutes, or it's free). We went to the warehouse in New York, ordered the pizzas (they arrived in less than 30 minutes), caught the three-quarter-hour Window back to the house and then crossed over to the fortress with our fragrant pizza order.

Afterward, as Amelia and I walked barefoot along the beach holding flashlights, she stopped, turned off her light and looked up at the stunning menagerie of stars above us.

"I'm on a South Sea island. I was in Calgary only a few hours ago, then New York City; this is like something from one of those science fiction novels you read."

It was a breezy but warm evening, and the Southern Cross and constellations she would never have seen from her apartment balcony splayed across an unfamiliar sky.

"I understand why you didn't tell me. I can forgive you for that, but you should have kept in touch."

I nodded, angling the flashlight so that reflected light touched the curves of her face.

"You're right, of course. I've been very selfish since I found out what the inheritance really was. Ask the twins. I honestly didn't know what to do with all this."

I gestured to the fortress with the flashlight, the beam streaking across its towering, glowing windows like a searchlight.

Amelia nodded.

"This – your island, these Windows, they must have something to do with Mom and Dad's disappearance."

Facing this possibility, we crossed back into the study, where Morgan suggested we catch the Window to Victoria; it was almost 4 p.m. We could do little in Kingston or anywhere else, but she wanted to check in with her friends. The brothers decided to remain behind but made us promise to contact them immediately if anything developed. I assured them I would, but it didn't alleviate the sorrow or the fear that permeated everyone's thoughts.

Morgan called ahead to let her friends know she was returning. Shortly, in my Victoria apartment, we gathered at the window, gazing out at the afternoon busyness of the street, lost in our troubled thoughts.

Morgan mercifully broke the silence.

"I'm going down. I'll grab some clean clothes and say hello to Kelli. Brit's in class."

We held onto each other and then kissed softly.

"Everything'll be okay," she said, hugging me before leaving the apartment.

Amelia turned to me and smiled.

"I'm glad you two are finally together. I've always liked her. I could have slugged you when you dumped her."

"Dumped her? I didn't dump her."

My sister laughed.

"Oh, yeah, you dumped her, all right. She kissed you, Aidan."

I sighed.

"I know."

"She let you know how she feels about you, and then a few weeks later you let her go off to Victoria, while you catch a bus to claim your house in Kingston."

I remembered how shocked Amelia had seemed at my response to the kiss when I'd told her about it a few days after. She had cautioned me not to take it lightly, but I laughed and said something about Morgan and I only being friends.

"It was obvious she wanted to be more than just friends, yet you treated her like she was, well, like me, like a sister."

I reached out and took my sister's hand.

"I understand that now. I've always loved her. I guess I just complicated things. I didn't really know how to transition from friendship to what we have now."

Amelia pulled me in for a hug.

"You live in your head, little brother."

Suddenly, we heard Morgan scream. Something in her voice gripped me with fear, and I lunged for the open door, emerging in the hallway in time to hear a scuffle on the first floor.

"Aidan," she screamed.

Then, I heard a strangled cry followed by an ominous silence.

I bounded down the stairs, my hand barely skimming the handrail for support. The foyer was empty, Morgan's apartment door was open, and her backpack lay on the hallway carpet. I glanced towards the building's entrance and saw through the glass doors that a man was shoving her into the back seat of a two-tone blue SUV out on the street. She looked limp, possibly unconscious. Her glasses tumbled from her face, bouncing off the man's arm and landing in the mulch along the sidewalk. I pushed through the door, aware that someone was behind me and darted a quick look over my shoulder. It was Kelli. Amelia was right behind her.

"What's happening?" Kelli shot at me, her eyes following my gaze to the SUV. "Where's Morgan? Was that her yelling?"

I ignored her questions and sprinted towards the SUV, my fists tight balls of apprehension. I wasn't going to make it in time, and even if I had, I doubt I could have stopped him. He was much larger than me. As he leapt into the front of the vehicle, the man's face swung challengingly towards me. His eyes were unwavering, and his lips were a tight line. He laughed and pulled his door shut. The vehicle rocketed away from the curb, tires squealing on the pavement and spitting loose gravel along the street's edge.

I knew that face from somewhere.

"Oh my god! What's going on?" Kelli demanded, casting a distraught glance after the speeding vehicle.

"Aidan, what happened?" Amelia demanded.

"Who are you?" Kelli asked as she became aware of Amelia's presence.

I'd seen that face before, but where?

"Amelia, Aidan's sister."

"Oh, great, that's all Morgan needs, another Ames," Kelli said, her voice dripping with sarcasm.

"Excuse me. Is that a problem?" Amelia shot back.

I retrieved Morgan's glasses. They were undamaged, and I slid them into my shirt pocket. Suddenly, I knew who the man was. He was the cable guy from a few days earlier, the guy Morgan thought was trying to pick her up, and – I felt my chest constrict sharply – he was also the security guard from Chicago. That's why I felt I recognized him.

What was going on?

"I don't like him." I felt a finger jab my shoulder. I turned to look. Kelli was glaring at me.

"Oh?" My sister shot back.

I focused on Kelli, ignoring her insult and the jab.

"I need a car."

"Why's that?" Amelia asked.

"Why do I need a car?" I asked incredulously, unaware I'd been caught in the crossfire between two conversations.

"No, Aidan. Why doesn't she like you?"

"He's loose with the truth – " Kelli said harshly.

"Hey!" I yelled at them as I gestured toward the SUV that had careened onto Bay Street. "Some guy just grabbed Morgan. Do you have a car?"

"What?" Kelli stammered. Then it hit her. "Someone took Morgan?"

"Was she in that SUV that just ripped out of here?" Amelia pointed.

"Yes. A vehicle, Kelli. We need a vehicle, now!" I yelled, frantically casting glances down the street.

"Oh my god! We should call the police."

"There isn't time. Do you have a vehicle?"

"It's out back," Kelli answered, gesturing frantically.

We quickly followed her around the side of the building to an older two-door silver Tercel.

We piled in, and Kelli pulled out onto the street.

"Which way?"

"Left. No, right. Go that way!" I pointed.

Traffic was heavy, and the roads were slick from an earlier rainfall. I wasn't clear about which way the SUV had gone, but I had an idea.

"If you wanted to get off the island, how would you do it?"

Kelli threw an angry look at me.

"You're kidding, right?"

"Just tell me how."

"Only two ways," she said, shaking her head, "Ferry or by air unless you own a boat."

Ferry or by air. What had a security guard from Chicago been doing in Victoria, posing as a cable repair person, talking to Morgan last week? Had he been waiting, looking for the right moment to abduct her? Kelli cranked the wheel, and Amelia suddenly yelled as she gestured.

"I see the vehicle! Look, there, ahead to the left. It's blue, right?"

Kelli swerved, barely missing a turning delivery truck as vehicles honked at us. I saw the SUV, its unmistakable two-tone colour, more than a block ahead and moving faster than we were.

"Where do you think it's going? Ferry or by air?" I asked again.

Kelli swore as she threw the car into a lower gear and sped past a minivan, cutting back into our lane just in time to avoid colliding with a taxi.

"If he doesn't own some kind of watercraft, then probably air. The road we're on suggests he's going to the harbour, maybe Shoal Point."

"Is that an airport?" I asked.

She nodded as we slipped past a slow-moving van.

"Yes, float planes, helicopters."

"Who was that guy?" Amelia asked from the back seat.

I shook my head.

"I don't know, but he talked with Morgan in the apartment building last week. She said he was the cable guy."

"That guy?" Kelli said with a groan.

"And," I continued, "in Chicago. I think he was the guard who forced his way into my office."

"You didn't tell me about that," Amelia said.

"Oh."

"What happened?"

"I left."

"How?"

I looked back and grimaced at her.

"Take a guess."

Kelli interrupted us.

"Why would someone from Chicago come all this way to fix our cable and kidnap Morgan?"

"I don't think he was here to fix your cable. It was a ruse to get to her — or me."

"What have you gotten her involved in?"

"Nothing. Just drive."

"Aidan, answer her." Amelia punched the back of my seat. "I'd like to know as well. Does this have something to do with Mom and Dad?"

"What about your parents?" Kelli said as she threw a glance back at Amelia.

"They're missing."

"Get off the road!" The car jerked us sideways as we avoided a cyclist on what had turned into a narrow street bordered by tall trees.

"Your parents are missing?"

"They were kidnapped," Amelia offered.

"Well, we think they were kidnapped," I cut in. We weren't sure what had happened to them.

"By whom?" Kelli asked.

"We don't know. There's been no ransom, and there's been no contact of any kind," Amelia answered grimly.

The car swerved, and my head glanced sharply off the window as Kelli narrowly avoided another cyclist.

"We're gonna get killed doing this. I'm calling the police," she barked as she pulled a cell phone from a shirt pocket.

She cursed again and threw the phone on the dash. "It's dead. Do you have a cell?"

"No," I answered.

It was a lie. My phone was in my back pocket, but inviting the police into the situation would complicate things for me.

She quickly turned to Amelia.

"You, do you have a cellphone?"

I glanced in alarm at my sister, but she shrugged and grimaced.

"Sorry. I left it in Calgary. I didn't think I'd actually be travelling today."

I smiled at her in relief, but Kelli scowled at me.

"What is wrong with you people?"

I gave her my best I'm-pathetic-look as we sped around a sharp corner that opened onto an intersection. The car skidded, but Kelli managed to keep it under control. Her driving ability was impressive, and I told her so.

"My dad's RCMP. He taught me to drive defensively."

"Oh."

The SUV was at least a dozen car lengths ahead, and its more powerful engine was allowing it to put some distance between us. If traffic let up, it could pull ahead out of sight quickly.

"Why would someone take Morgan?" Kelli asked.

"I don't know."

I didn't know. None of this made sense. The camera in Chicago might have seen me, but why Morgan? What was the connection?

"Why don't you like my brother?" Amelia asked from the back seat.

"He lied to Morgan."

"Oh?"

"Yeah – yikes! That was close."

A driver gestured angrily at us, and another lay on his horn as Kelli deftly missed yet another vehicle.

"He couldn't tell the truth about his inheritance or something, but Morgan kept babbling on about him like he was the best friend she'd ever had."

"What did you lie about, Aidan?"

I turned to look at her, scrunching up my face, pleading.

"What do you think I lied about?"

Amelia frowned for a moment until understanding touched her eyes.

"Oh, of course."

"What?" Kelli demanded.

"Do we have to talk about this now?" I pleaded.

"I want to know. Morgan loves you."

"It's about my life, what I, uh, really do, what I am – "

"And what is that?"

"It's complicated."

As a pickup pulled out before us, Kelli yelped and stood on the brakes. I braced my hands against the dash as the car skidded to the right, tossing us like rag dolls. She cranked the wheel, and we slid sideways into the shallow ditch alongside the road. Grass and water flew up around us in a fountain that cascaded over the car as we came to a stop. The motor stalled. As the SUV sped from view, Kelli angrily slammed her hands on the steering wheel. She repeatedly tried to start the engine, but it took far too long before it finally fired up, and we managed to get back on the road. The SUV was out of sight now, but we knew where it was going – I hoped.

She quickly navigated city streets to reach Dallas Road, which snakes along Victoria's harbour. We had lost time, but she was confident that whoever had taken Morgan was most likely leaving the island from there. As we swung off Dallas Road onto a side street, she pointed to a fenced compound facing the harbour. The SUV was parked next to a squat building near a helipad with three helicopters parked on it. One of the helicopters, its black paint glistening even in the gloom of the overcast skies, looked like it was preparing for take-off.

"There they are," Kelli said, her eyes wild with anger. "Now what?"

"Uh – " I stammered.

We sped up to the heliport's gated compound, stopping with a squeal at a secure gated entrance. The SUV was parked about twenty metres from us, near the terminal. Past that, on the helipad, the guard from Chicago, along with another man, was carrying Morgan up into the black helicopter. He saw us and scowled.

A security person stepped out of a small booth near the gate and approached our car.

"Are you dropping off or picking up?" he enquired as Kelli hastily rolled her window down.

"Neither," she barked, pointing in frustration toward the helipad.

"The people in that helicopter just kidnapped my friend!"

The guy looked toward where she was pointing.

"Excuse me?"

"They're getting away!" Kelli growled and then swore. She turned to me.

"Do something. Where's your airplane parked? We can get the flight plan of that helicopter, but we'll need – "

"I don't have one."

"What? But Morgan said – "

"I don't have a plane."

I grimaced as the helicopter's engine rose in pitch and its long blades grabbed the air. A ground crew member dressed in an orange and yellow safety vest backed away from the aircraft, waving glowing batons.

"You don't have a plane? How do you get here from Kingston every damn weekend?" Kelli demanded as she pushed her way out of the car. I followed, leaving the door open for Amelia to crawl out from the backseat.

Confused, the heliport's security guard stepped back from the car, looking from us to the helicopter.

"I told you. It's complicated," I answered as we ran to the gate.

"Try me!"

"You wouldn't understand."

"Understand what? That you're an asshole, after all?"

"I – "

The sleek helicopter suddenly lifted off its pad and rose quickly above the terminal, angling sharply away from us with Morgan onboard. I watched it rise, rain pelting my face, causing me to blink, but I no longer cared. I no longer felt anything except an awful dread as the receding aircraft climbed higher in the sky. Morgan was in that disappearing place, rapidly leaving us behind.

I had never felt so helpless.

TWENTY-EIGHT

We were able to obtain the flight plan for the helicopter from a flustered heliport security manager who seemed both worried and not entirely convinced our story was true. It's not illegal to ask for a flight plan in Canada, but they can be a confusing jumble of letters and airport call signs. Still, it didn't surprise me when we learned the flight plan's termination was at ORD, O'Hare International Airport, in Chicago, with a stop at YYC, Calgary International Airport, for customs clearance.

"I'm calling 9-1-1 as soon as we get back to the apartment," Kelli fumed as she hopped back in the car with Amelia and me following her.

Her frustration was evident as she drove us back to the apartment building. I understood her anger. Her friend from high school, my girlfriend, had just been kidnapped in broad daylight, and I was positive it wasn't random. The look in the man's eyes was as if he had just secured a victory, which I was fairly certain was somehow related to our missing parents. I tried to assure Kelli that I didn't think Morgan was in danger yet.

"You can't possibly know that," she fumed as we pulled around behind the apartment building. "If anything bad happens to her, I will, I will, I don't know what I'll do, but it'll be terrible — for you."

I nodded, meeting her angry stare with as much contrition as possible. We left her at her apartment door. She was going to call the police and her father, she had said. I didn't want to be around if either showed up. Amelia and I excused ourselves and hurried up the stairs, caught the current Window, which happened to be the warehouse in Kensington, and then waited for the Window to Turin Street.

It was well past midnight in Kingston, but Bill and Dane were still working on college assignments in the living room. Amelia and I sat on the couch and took turns explaining what had happened. As we talked, I felt a growing numbness inside. My flippant attitude toward the camera at the Chicago Window had put Morgan and my parents in danger. This person must have suspected something fantastic was happening and wanted in on it. But how did he know where to find Morgan and me? Had he been surveilling us?

"Has anyone been in the house in the last couple of weeks?" I asked Bill.

He shrugged.

"Uh, I don't think so. I mean, we've mostly been in school or on the island."

Dane nodded in agreement but then held up a finger.

"Wait. There were those guys who hooked up the new cable system a few weeks ago."

I sat up.

"A few weeks ago? When exactly?"

Dane scrunched up his face.

"Uh, maybe a week ago. Yeah, I think it was a Thursday."

"I didn't order cable. We already have it."

Bill suddenly looked worried.

"Uh, it was a cold call. He said his company was going through the neighbourhood, upgrading existing systems – for free."

"Did he have an accent, Irish maybe?"

They both shook their heads.

"Not really," Bill said, "but there were two of them; one might have been an American. Now that we're talking about it, I did catch one of them upstairs. He said he was looking for the bathroom."

"It seemed legit," Dane said, but he, too, looked concerned. "Do you think they were looking for Morgan here?"

"No, but it might be connected."

I told them about the two men I was sure had been talking about me in the pub in Enniskillen. What were they doing in Kingston only days after I had seen them in Ireland, and how would they have known I lived here?

These and more questions filled my mind as Amelia and I returned to our parents' home shortly after 12:30 a.m. in Calgary. Amelia checked the house's landline for voice messages while I slumped wearily onto the living room sofa, mentally replaying the events in Victoria. My eyes ached, and I felt like I was suffering from permanent disruption to my circadian rhythms.

I heard my sister gasp.

"Aidan. Dad left a message."

I was beside her in seconds. She pressed the button for the speakerphone.

"Amelia, this is Dad. Listen very carefully. Get in touch with Aidan and tell him to be at the house – my house – tomorrow, Wednesday, at 8 a.m. I know he's in Kingston, but I understand he has a, uh, special way to get there quickly. You must do exactly what I ask, please. Your mother and I are doing fine, what – ?"

My father's voice became muffled, and we could hear a harsh, unintelligible male voice in the background. Then he spoke again, haltingly.

"Do not contact the police, and tell him, tell him if he doesn't do this, you'll never see us alive again."

I stared at the phone, barely taking a breath. My mind was racing. My father knew about the Windows, and someone threatened to kill him and my mother because of that knowledge.

Amelia spoke first.

"Okay, Aidan, now we have to call the police."

I shook my head.

"No. We can't."

"But, Aidan – "

"No, Amelia. This has to do with me and the Windows. Someone knows about them, and they're using our parents to get to me."

"How can you be sure?"

"You heard him. He knew. He knew I could get to Calgary quickly."

I felt even more anxious than I had a moment ago. My father knew about the Windows. Feeling like my world was crumbling around me, I glanced at the small screen on the telephone.

"Is there a number on the call display?"

Amelia swiped back to the list of recent calls.

"The number's blocked. It's probably from a cellphone."

"He could have called from anywhere, then."

My sister looked at the wall clock with the stylized bluebirds painted on it. My mother loved the colour blue.

"It's almost one; what should we do?"

I rubbed my forehead, exhaustion and fear pressing into my mind.

"Wait, I guess. I'm so tired."

Amelia reached out and took my hand.

"We should still call the police."

I looked at my sister's face and saw how exhausted she was. I placed my other hand on top of hers and squeezed.

"No, we can't. Please, trust me. You heard Dad, they're okay. Let's not jeopardize that. Whoever this is, they'll call in a few hours, and we'll know more then, okay?"

Amelia smiled weakly and nodded.

"You're right. I'm not sure I can sleep, though."

Amelia lay down in our parent's bedroom shortly after, and I collapsed onto the cushy comfort of the couch, longing for Morgan, holding her glasses to my chest as I attempted to fall asleep. I had gotten used to the warmth of her hand, her lips on mine, and the hope of a life together.

I didn't sleep well.

A ringing phone woke me. I launched off the couch toward the kitchen and snagged the receiver as Amelia entered the room, turning on the lights. I pressed the speaker function on the phone.

"Dad?"

There was a pause, and then an unfamiliar voice spoke.

"Ah, Mr. Ames. How good of you to consider your father's instructions."

"Who is this?" Amelia demanded.

The voice had a strong accent. East coast? Irish?

"Ah, the lovely Nurse Ames. In time, young lady, in time. First, your sibling and I must meet. Truly, he holds the key to what belongs to me."

The key?

"Where are my parents? Let me talk to my mother," she demanded.

The voice chuckled.

"In time, my dear. Unfortunately, she, as well as your father, is unable to join us at the moment, but they are safe – for now. That could change, my dear, for the worse if your brother does not follow my instructions exactly. Understand, Mr. Ames?"

"Where and when?"

Did he have Morgan?

"Aidan," Amelia began, but I held up my hand.

"Ah, excellent. Perhaps there is more honour in your heart than in your contemptuous granddad."

He knew my grandfather. My jaw clenched.

"Just tell me where."

"Chicago. You know where, lad."

"Chicago? It will take time to get an airline ticket and – "

"Rubbish. Do not spar with me." The voice rapidly rose from calm to seething anger in seconds. "I know all about the Windows. You just go through the one to Chicago. You've been there a few times already, lad."

This was it, this was why he'd taken my parents and Morgan. He was after the Windows.

"The camera? That was you?"

He chuckled in short little snorts.

"Ah, it is becoming clear to you. You see, I know all about the blessed locks and keys. I tracked your granddad to this building in Chicago. Our last meeting was, shall we say, rather unfortunate in its conclusion. I know where the Window is. You've been there, lad. Captured your image on camera and, indeed, almost caught you, didn't we? How do you think I found you, Mr. Ames? Found where your parents lived? Technology has been such a boon in my quest."

I felt a surge of fear at the back of my throat. This was the man who had shot my grandfather. Whoever he was, he had gone to great lengths to find me.

"You killed him, didn't you?"

The voice chuckled ominously.

"We will talk of these things, I'm sure. You just be here half past the hour."

"I can't," I responded, not bothering to disguise the anger in my voice.

"Ah, well, that'll bring considerable misfortune to yer mum and dad, then."

"No! Wait! You don't understand. The Windows are at specific times. The one you are talking about is at five-thirty."

"I have no faith in your words, lad. You're merely stalling."

"No," I shot back, "think about it. I've only been in that room early in the morning or evening. The Window opens at five-thirty Eastern Standard Time. So, that's like four-thirty Chicago time."

He didn't reply immediately, but I could hear him sigh heavily.

"As you say, Mr. Ames. I'll be waiting, then. Do come alone."

"Wait. I have a friend. She was taken this morning – "

He chuckled again.

"Ah, yes, the young lass. Feisty, that one. I determined a measure of extra insurance was necessary, lad. Do you think I'd wait this long for this glorious resolution without envisioning every eventuality? I know everything about you, Aidan. I couldn't risk that you might not care for the whereabouts of your parents, especially your father, who seems to know precious little of your life."

You don't know everything.

"If you hurt her – "

He ended the connection abruptly. Amelia and I stood for a moment, lost in our fears, the dial tone buzzing loudly over the speaker until I shut it off.

"What are we going to do?" Amelia asked, her voice barely audible but echoing the words in my head.

I didn't have an answer. I sat at the table and began gathering up the posters of our parents, which Amelia had carefully and dutifully made. She was a good daughter and an even better sister.

"Well, we won't be needing these anymore."

"What?" My sister exploded, "What's wrong with you? Some crazy person has Mom and Dad and your girlfriend!"

"I know," I said with a laugh. "Gramps wouldn't have been this careless. This is all my fault. I should have been more cautious. I should have kept the Windows a secret like he had."

Amelia huffed.

"Not much of a secret. It sounds like it got him killed, and now this."

I looked at her, seeing the anguish and the anger in her eyes.

"That's not going to happen. No one else is going to die."

I had nine hours to prepare. I needed a plan.

TWENTY-NINE

I slumped into the soft lounging chair with the blue floral pattern in my parents' immaculate living room. It was my mother's favourite chair. I ran my hands over the delicate material of the armrest covers, feeling the intricate detail and the sorrow in my heart.

Amelia walked in and sat across from me on the couch.

"How are you doing, little brother?"

I couldn't look at her, staring instead through the sheers covering the windows that looked out toward my house across the street, the house my grandfather had watched us from. I fought the emotion climbing up my throat but gave in, sobbing while trying to speak but only succeeding in sounding incoherent.

My sister rose and sat on the armrest of my mother's chair, wrapping an arm around me.

"I can't do this," I finally managed to say.

"You're not alone. I'm here, Aidan."

"I know, but I feel alone. All of this, the inheritance, the money, it's been too much. And now, how am I supposed to deal with whatever this guy wants?"

She pushed me back and levelled her stress-filled eyes at me.

"There you go again. You are always trying to carry the big, bad world yourself. *We* can deal with this. *We* will get through this together."

Sniffing between a laugh, I said, "You sound like Morgan. She always says I'm like Atlas, carrying the entire world on my shoulders."

"Well, maybe you should listen to your girlfriend *and* your sister."

"You're right, as always. I need your help. I need everyone's help."

Amelia squeezed my shoulder, pulled me closer, and laughed.

"Welcome to the human race, Aidan."

A short while later, we passed through the Window to Kingston, where Dane was waiting for us in the study.

"Hi, Amelia," Dane spoke as the gust of wind from our entrance settled. He was dressed in his usual attire, jeans and a T-shirt, and held a large mug of coffee.

I nodded at my friend.

"I'm glad you're here, Dane."

The study door opened, and Bill entered the room.

"Aidan, what's happening?"

I described the alarming phone call to them.

"I have less than nine hours to come up with a plan. This guy has my parents and Morgan in Chicago. He knows where the Window is in the building and will be waiting for me. I need to have something up my sleeve, something he won't know about, some way to rescue everyone without getting us killed."

"You think he would kill you?" Bill asked.

I nodded.

"Yeah, he sounds serious."

"What did you have in mind then?"

I shrugged and slowly shook my head.

"I don't have any ideas at all. That's why I need your help."

Bill shrugged, his face revealing his frustration. But Dane smiled, his blue eyes almost as big as his smile.

"I have an idea," he said, nodding slowly.

For the first time in hours, I felt a glimmer of hope.

THIRTY

A few seconds after five-thirty in the evening, Kingston time, I opened the door to Chicago. I crossed the threshold into the empty room on the thirty-second floor of the hundred floors that make up 875 North Michigan Avenue, one of the tallest buildings in the US. I carefully examined the space, something I hadn't done before in my careless and reckless use of the Window system. Mounted high up in the left-hand corner of the room was a small black tube about the size of a lipstick container. It was a camera and had probably been there all this time, capturing my remarkable appearances.

I realized this might have been the last Window that my grandfather had used. Had he stood here, shot in the chest, struggling to turn the key in the door so he could return home? Anger rose inside me. I pushed it back, fighting to keep control. I needed to remain calm.

I placed my grandfather's fedora on my head, which, it suddenly occurred to me, brought its story full circle to whatever had transpired between him and the man waiting for me. I took a deep breath and opened the door. The security guard who had taken Morgan was sitting casually on the edge of the table I'd seen weeks ago when my journey through the Windows had begun. His eyes were on a small monitor, angled up so he could catch my entrance into the empty room. He nodded slowly and turned to me, a smile spreading across his broad face.

"That is surely something to see."

I felt much like a mouse cornered by a hungry cat. He rose, his lips tight, standing at least a quarter-metre taller than me. I guessed he was in his mid-twenties, well-muscled, with cropped fair hair and a menacing but intelligent-looking face. A gun sat in the holster on his hip, and his right hand gripped a sturdy black baton. I reached around and pulled the door closed behind me. Over his broad shoulders, down a wide hallway, were tall windows that looked out onto the growing Illinois twilight, turning the closest building, which seemed like a stone's throw away, into a patchwork quilt of dark and light rectangles. The moisture on the windows, from wind-driven sleet, reflected light like countless diamonds. I was in the heart of Chicago, and it was a stormy ending to a miserable winter day.

He continued to grin tightly.

"Well, me Da was right about you, after all."

His voice was thick and heavily accented but understandable.

"You were in Victoria; you took Morgan," I said harshly, trying to sound menacing.

"Sorry about that, mate. As you Americans put it, it's just a game, and you lost. Turn 'round."

"I'm Canadian."

"Don't care. Turn 'round."

"Why?"

He gestured with his baton.

"Just do it! I need to search you."

I was dressed in a grey, tailored Armani suit, a dark purple silk tie, and loafers that would suffice should I need to run. Except for Morgan's glasses, my pockets were empty. I'd brought no ID. I turned around, raising my arms halfway, and he patted me down. I'd hung the key on a leather string around my neck. He found the glasses and lifted them from my jacket.

"Those are mine," I said.

He turned me around roughly and handed them back.

"That's a fine watch you have there. You don't have a pocketbook?"

"A what?"

"Wallet."

"No."

"Where's the key?"

"I believe you already have one."

He jabbed me sharply in the chest with the baton.

"Look, don't be an ass. He wants the key, the key what makes it happen."

"I have it."

"Give it here."

"I don't think so. I want to see my parents and Morgan."

He raised the baton slightly.

"The ol' man wants the key. Either you give it, or I take it."

From the look in his eyes, it was plain that he was itching to hit something, perhaps me, with that stick. He'd probably been sitting at that table since my grandfather's death, waiting for someone to appear.

I unhooked the key from around my neck and handed it to him. He took it and cradled it in his muscular hand like I had passed him the last drop of water on Earth. He held it up, peering at it closely.

"Bloody hell. All my life, all that has been done, for this key."

He shook his head and sighed as he slipped it into his pants pocket.

"I never believed him, you know. It was just ramblings, like leprechauns and such. Not until you did that little trick of yours."

"Believed who?"

He grunted without answering and pointed toward a bank of elevator doors to our left. A group of well-dressed people entered an elevator, but they took no notice of us, and the guard prodded me through to another set of doors as they whooshed open. We entered, and he pressed a keycard to a panel beneath rows of floor numbers. The doors slid quietly shut, and the elevator travelled up. His eyes, which I could see in the reflection in the polished brass door panel in front of me, never left my own as European techno-rock played softly overhead, offset periodically by a gentle musical ping as we passed each floor. When the door opened, he prodded me into a wide hallway with several doors and a sign that read, *Residential Condominiums*, with a row of numbers and left and right arrows beneath this. He pointed to a door across from us on the right, and we entered a short hallway that led to a large and brightly lit room.

I lurched to a stop. Old steamer trunks and wingback chairs rested on the floor, and tall, dark tapestries hung from two of the room's walls. Two high-backed leather loungers flanked a stone gas fireplace on my left. Flames danced mutely over its fake logs. Above the mantle hung a large, impressive painting of Enniskillen – *my* island. The scene, viewed from inside the fortress Windows, was of a much less decayed but still derelict Seagull. The wall space around the fireplace also showcased several smaller paintings of varying scenes and styles. Some were depictions of various parts of the island, or people engaged in one sort of activity or another *on* the island. It was clear these artists had visited Enniskillen on more than one occasion.

How was this possible?

I turned to the security guard, searching his hard face for answers. He smiled grimly and continued to prod me onward as he gestured toward the floor-to-ceiling windows across from us, separated by a thick, dark, x-shaped beam, part of the outer support structure of the building. A heavy-set man, stooped over a cane and dressed in a dark business suit, was looking out at Chicago's stormy skyline. The glow from the city gave him an ethereal outline, making him look even larger. I heard him exhale heavily as he turned toward us from across the room, using a cane to steady himself.

"Dia duit, Mr. Ames, and welcome to my Enniskillen," he offered formally, with a slight wave of a hand.

A chill played across the back of my neck. This was the man who had killed my grandfather. He looked like he might be in his late sixties or older and was balding with streaks of grey, making a crown that framed his almost neckless head. He smiled thinly, and light from the dancing flames of the fireplace revealed two hard lines carved like canyons, one on either side of his nose, streaking down past the edges of his mouth, disappearing into the tightly buttoned collar of his white shirt. He took laborious steps down a small set of stairs, crossing over to me, his cane making little clicking sounds until he stopped, a circular throw rug separating us. He extended his right hand. His dark eyes were alert, sizing me up like an opponent. A nudge in my back indicated that I should approach him. I took a wary step, but I stopped short, not willing to shake the hand of the man who had killed my grandfather.

"Where are my parents?" I demanded, trying not to look around a room that was disturbingly similar to Enniskillen.

I also wanted to ask him a thousand other questions.

He blinked, raising his bushy eyebrows as he lowered his hand, then frowned and looked me over.

"Dia duit. Good day to you. I speak to you in my mother tongue, a language you and your grandfather may not be familiar with, I should think, considering your fraudulent use of the great Irish inheritance Ian McPhie delivered wrongly into your hands."

He paused, frowning almost comically as he lifted his hand again, jutting it towards me.

"Are you unaccustomed to the pleasantries of civilized men, Mr. Ames?"

I glared at him, my anger bristling, my skin tingling with the confrontation. Where were my parents? Where was Morgan? And what did he know about the inheritance? And why was this room patterned after an island he should know nothing about?

"Ah, well, perhaps you are not as civilized as you believe your stolen inheritance makes you."

He reached out with his cane as if he were going to tap my chest. I recoiled, connecting with the guard's baton as I stepped back.

"I see your ill-gotten wealth fits you well, Mr. Ames."

Stolen? Ill-gotten?

"Who are you? Where are my parents?"

He waved a hand and then sighed noisily as if annoyed.

"In time, lad."

Then he gestured to the hulking figure hovering behind me.

"You have it?"

The guard stepped around me and handed him the key. The older man grasped it firmly by the string and held it close to his face. Light danced in his eyes as a sneer curled the corners of his mouth.

"Maith thú, well done, m'son."

And then to me.

"I trust my son, Reilly, has introduced himself to you. He's been waiting for you, Mr. Ames. Yes?"

"He didn't have a pocketbook with him, Da." Reilly said.

The older man pursed his lips and nodded.

"Afraid of being robbed, are you?"

His voice was thick with sarcasm, and his eyes narrowed as he leaned forward, his hand gripping the cane as if he might fall over.

"You're the robber. You're the thief."

"Who are you? What do you want?" I burst out.

My confusion was threatening to sidetrack me from our plan. I had expected a ransom demand, but not what this room represented. Something was not right here.

He smiled ominously and gestured to the wall behind me.

"Look," he said with glee, "look at yer not-so-secret life."

I slowly turned, and Reilly flicked a light switch, illuminating a large corkboard panel with dozens of glossy images and pieces of paper tacked to it. There were images of me in Kingston and of my grandfather's study, including the open closet door. But, I noticed, not of the opening to Enniskillen. The Window to the island had been closed when the brothers had been tricked into letting the so-called cable guys into the house. There were shots of me in the office space in Chicago, of the brothers disembarking from a city transit bus in Kingston, and several photos from various angles of me inside Willie's cottage. That's why those men had shown up a few days after my arrival. There were pictures of Morgan walking into the apartment building in Victoria, one emerging from a hospital entrance, and photographs of Kelli parking her car behind the apartment building and of her and Brittany walking past a fabric store holding hands. There were several pictures of my parents outside their home, one of my father entering his office in downtown Calgary and Amelia frozen in mid-stride along a path near her apartment. There were names, addresses, and phone numbers circled in red pen and then ticked off with check marks like tics on a shopping list. The timeline in these photos suggested that I, and everyone close to me, had been under surveillance since a few weeks after that first visit to Chicago.

"What is this?" I managed to croak as I turned to him.

The old man laughed, though it sounded more like a gurgle that oozed from somewhere deep within him. He didn't answer, just directed me to the lounge area, and when I refused to move, Reilly jabbed me sharply in the back. I ignored him but slowly sank into the chair and placed my grandfather's hat on my lap. The old man slid his wide girth into the chair opposite me, propping his cane on a stand beside it. The two of us were separated by a wide glass coffee table with a vase of garish, fresh-cut flowers. Reilly circled around me to hover near his father, lightly tapping the baton against his leg as he fixed his eyes on my face. It was a disconcerting stare, and I had to remind myself that I was not a victim.

My host rested his hands on the arms of his chair.

"You should know me, lad. Your grandfather did. My name is Nollaig O'Shannon."

He paused, studying me as if looking for some sign that I recognized him, but he was right; I didn't know who he was.

"My mother named me Nollaig. It means to be happy in Gaelic, Mr. Ames, but I have not been a very happy man. As to what I want?" He looked away momentarily, gazing at the considerably smaller replica of the Fortress's fireplace. Then he smiled at me. It was a thin-lipped, disturbing smile that transformed quickly into a sneer.

"What I want, lad, is what belongs to me and my son. I want Enniskillen. I want the riches, and I want the Windows in the doors. If you do not give them to me, I will exact vengeance upon you, your parents, and your lovely lady friend. I will kill you all. It's that simple, lad."

Reilly slightly turned his head towards his father, his brows knit together. O'Shannon leaned forward, the reflection of amber flames from the fireplace dancing in his eyes as his face grew dark.

"I've waited a long time for this day, lad. My son and I are the last of the O'Shannons to accept as true the legacy, and it be only by the Blessed Virgin Mary, Mother of God, and by her blessed hand, I may finally exact revenge upon the bloody McPhies."

I could not hide my confusion, and he saw it and smiled gleefully as he twisted his bulk in the chair toward his son.

"He doesn't know, Reilly, m'boy. He doesn't know. His precious, dear, departed granddad never told him. He has three hundred years of blood guilt on his hands, and he thinks they're as clean of sin as the day his mother gave birth to his wretched arse!"

He sucked air into his lungs, turning his blazing eyes upon me.

"Do you not wonder at this room, lad? Does it not remind you of the island?"

"What are you talking about?" I erupted, my hands gripping the fedora.

"You really don't know, do you, lad?"

I felt like a drowning man gasping for breath as I pushed back into the chair, its stiff leather creaking. I gazed around the room again. It was all too familiar.

"What do you mean?" I asked, turning my face back to the sneering O'Shannon.

He smiled rapturously and leaned forward.

"None of it belongs to you. Not a single sterling pound of it!"

"I, I, don't understand."

"You see, lad, it wasn't that bloody Willie McPhie who discovered the miracle of the Windows. It was Miles O'Shannon. That godless Willie was an evil man, a murdering thief, clean through to his blackened heart. He stole Enniskillen from us, the O'Shannons!"

THIRTY-ONE

O'Shannon's countenance looked as happy as I'm sure it ever had. Indeed, his face was aglow with what he must have felt was the end to a centuries-old injustice. I had to remind myself to keep focused. As sure of his grievance as he sounded, I had to watch the time. We had a plan. Plan A. I was prepared to make it happen, but I couldn't have possibly anticipated any of this. Was it possible that O'Shannon was speaking the truth?

"You just sit there, lad. I have a story to tell. I tried with your granddad, but he was as greedy as those McPhies. He attempted to kill me. Did you know this?"

"My grandfather would never do that," I answered sharply.

He only guffawed.

"Ah, my young thief. You don't truly know a man's heart until he is faced with the kind of wealth that your ilk stole from us. Yes, riches truly are the root of all kinds of evil, including murder."

I could feel the anxiety in my stomach churning as I listened to Nollaig O'Shannon paint an even darker picture of Willie McPhie.

Miles O'Shannon had been the first mate aboard the ill-fated Seagull, and it was he who understood the magic of the rocks in the cave and how their unique qualities could be used to provide a way for the crew to escape. Being clever enough to realize this, Willie joined him in his quest to escape the island, using his skill as a locksmith to assist Miles. This part of the story was no different from what I had read in the journals, except for who were the villains and the heroes. However, in Nollaig O'Shannon's version, as the crew rushed the Window the two men had built, Willie McPhie struck Miles with a stone, leaving him for dead. However, Miles survived and soon escaped the island, returning home with enough of the ore to change his family's future and wealth.

That would have been the end of it, and there would have been a significantly different history in the O'Shannon clan had it not been for a chance encounter several years later between the two on the docks of Portsmouth. Since escaping the island, Miles had created a global shipping empire. Using the secret of the Windows to transport goods at a fraction of the cost and time compared to land and water-based transportation. McPhie wanted in on the venture, claiming part ownership of the Windows because of his work on the key and lock when they were stranded on the island. But Miles refused, not trusting Willie's motives.

"Just think of it, lad," O'Shannon raised a hand, "we weren't the thieves; we would have changed the world for good. We would be the wealthy ones."

He angrily slapped his hands down on the arms of his chair.

"Loscadh is dó McPhie! Cursed be that loathsome, black-hearted pirate. He destroyed what the future could have been, the glorious future of the O'Shannons."

O'Shannon sneered and continued his tale. On a night in February of 1782, Willie and his compatriots attacked the O'Shannons in their sleep, shooting Miles, his wife, and their two sons. He stole the keys to the Windows and Enniskillen and took the raw ore, the journals and Miles' detailed diagrams and maps of where the Windows had been installed. Miraculously, as had happened on the island, Miles survived, but his wife and sons had not shared his luck. After he recovered, he attempted to locate Willie, but the scoundrel had vanished, and Miles' wounds prohibited extensive travel. In time, he remarried, sensing that he may not have the strength or time to reclaim what belonged to him. He knew he would need an heir to fight for Enniskillen's return. The family quest to find Willie McPhie had begun.

"And search they did, lad, but the murderer hid his tracks well. He moved the Windows Miles had established and built his system based on thievery and evil intent. Miles O'Shannon passed from this life, but his second wife had borne him a son who carried on the quest followed by his children after that."

O'Shannon snagged his cane and, with great effort, rose and crossed over to stand in front of the fireplace, his heated gaze on the painting of Enniskillen.

"You see, Mr. Ames, Enniskillen is mine. Willie McPhie stole it from the O'Shannons on the night he left m' ancestor for dead. All we have of the legacy is these bloody, useless paintings!"

He raised his cane and tapped it sharply against the frame of the painting over the fireplace.

"Miles had kept them for those who would come after him. His first wife painted them on the island while he built their new home. They are a reminder of what is rightfully ours!"

Then he drew the cane back and stabbed its tip into the centre of the painting, twisting and pulling the cane away and the painting with it. He roared in rage, the cheeks of his face flushed and moist, as he flung the painting towards the windows. It twirled and bounced and smashed against a dining table shrouded in darkness. I saw Reilly flinch from the corner of my eye. He stood, his eyes on his father.

Nollaig turned to me, sweat streaming down his face.

"I hate those damn paintings, every one of them. I will take back the real island tonight."

O'Shannon hobbled back to his chair, coughing and muttering, and eased back into it, not taking his disdain-filled eyes off me. He loosened his thick black tie and continued.

"You simply do not understand the history of the stolen inheritance you have been given. You cannot understand the depth of treachery that has befallen my family. You," he raised a finger, brandishing it like a sword towards me, "you have no right to the legacy. My family has passed the knowledge of Enniskillen down from generation to generation, hoping that one day we would have our revenge, to take back what belongs to us from those murderin' McPhies. And saints be praised! The day of revenge has come!"

He reached into his coat and withdrew a handkerchief, which he used to wipe the glistening perspiration on his forehead before continuing.

"My granddad was in the Irish infantry during the Great War and learned of a woman who'd helped soldiers escape mysteriously from behind enemy lines. He found her, but she became suspicious of his enquiries and refused his friendship."

It had to have been Marianne McPhie.

O'Shannon continued his story. Every penny his grandfather had, every possible resource he could muster, had gone into finding the woman. He learned of her name, but she and her family were elusive. O'Shannon explained that after his grandfather had passed, his father carried on the search, but it was time-consuming and cost-prohibitive, and few O'Shannons continued to believe in the myth of Enniskillen. The McPhies were like ghosts, phantoms whose presence was felt but not seen until he saw a small one-line obituary in the London Times announcing the philanthropist Marianne McPhie's death. Using this information, he managed to find the young Ian, but again, as with his mother before him, the claim was denied. Because Ian held the keys to the Windows and had enormous wealth and resources at his fingertips, he could fade into obscurity.

A teenager at the time, a vengeful Nollaig O'Shannon listened as his father cursed the name of Willie McPhie with his last breath, and he vowed that the generation of his children would be the last to suffer the indignity.

O'Shannon's quest for Enniskillen led to the formation of a successful European security company that used high-end surveillance technology and well-trained teams. Over time, an elaborate web of worldwide security contacts was forged so that when Ian McPhie died in a hospital in Dublin, O'Shannon knew of it within a few days. Only two people had attended the quiet funeral in the town of Enniskillen on the River Erne, and O'Shannon was very interested in who they might be. He tracked the couple to a hotel in London, where he introduced himself and presented his claim.

"They listened, all smiles and sunshine, and led me to believe they were of a different sort. But, no, they were as full of thievery as the cursed McPhies; they didn't even use their real names. How dishonourable is that? And picture this, lad, when it seemed I had convinced him, your granddad would still not recant. He offered to share Enniskillen. Imagine that? Share with me? The rightful heir?"

He fumed, his teeth again clenched, and I felt the flame of his entrenched bitterness and knew that the generations of hatred would make any negotiation with him impossible. The drive to have all or nothing was such an overpowering force that it must have frightened my grandparents, and like the McPhies, they, too, disappeared.

"Your granddad was careless, much like you, lad," he said, glowing with satisfaction, "but then again, neither of you have claim to the McPhie name. Your deviousness has not been engrained into your blood like it was in theirs. I had one grainy security photograph of your granddad. I sent it to all my operatives, and by a stroke of blessed luck, one of them spotted him entering this very building. I flew here hoping I'd catch him, and eventually, I did. He was a fool, popping in and out of that room like he was the master of all things. I waited, and when he stepped out one morn, I confronted him again. Oh, he was surprised, he was, that I'd found him, but much like you did with Reilly here, he turned and fled through the door. I had a small fortune of me own saved up from investments and my security business, so Reilly and I secured this flat in this cursed dwelling."

He gestured towards his son.

"You see, my company manages security for this building, and I have access to every floor and every room. Your granddad did not much like that, especially with Reilly standing watch outside his precious door. We even had a key constructed to fit the door's working lock, so if the old man returned, we could seize him."

He laughed, his eyebrows arching.

"Reilly almost had you."

I glanced at Reilly. He wasn't smiling, which seemed odd, considering how thrilled his father was.

"Your granddad didn't much like that we had a key to that room," the elder O'Shannon continued. "Then, one day, he shows up and demands to see me, but I was ready for his treachery, and I shot him. We struggled. He took my own pistol and managed to shoot me. Imagine that, will you? Shot me in the leg, the rightful heir? The coward managed to escape, and he never used that door again."

"You killed him, that's why," I retorted.

He smiled coolly, nodding. Reilly cast a quick glance at him. Did he not know?

"Aye, I suspected as much. I have no regrets. I only seek to take what is mine."

He leaned back, stretching his short neck, its bones popping unpleasantly, and cast a glare down the hallway on my right.

"Thanks to your carelessness and some hi-tech facial recognition software, I learned of who you were and of the true name of your grandad. The rest, where you live, your family, the young lass you fancy, all of it was a matter of patience and waiting for all the pieces to fall into place. I led you to this moment we are having, lad, like a rat to cheese."

He smirked at some thought and turned his face to Reilly.

"One will do anything for family, anything at all."

He slowly rose again and walked stiffly to the sleet-spattered windows, where he slouched over his cane and gazed out into the night.

"I'm getting old, and I hate this country. I long for the green hills of home."

He turned to face me.

"My childless sister died three years ago in Dublin. She never saw the fabled Island. I vowed again then, on her grave, that my son, my only child, a direct descendent of Miles O'Shannon, would not be denied what is rightfully his."

Reilly had been studying me intently as his father rambled on. It was hard to tell, but he looked like someone unsure of what was actually going on, like the bus he should have taken might have already come and gone. It was that kind of look. He realized I was scrutinizing his face and quickly set his jaw, narrowing his eyes.

"Have you nothing to say?" he asked.

His father chuckled. I took a deep breath, my heart thumping violently in my chest.

"What do you want me to say? Even if any of what your father says is true, you've kidnapped my parents and my girlfriend, violated my privacy, illegally entered my home, and have probably broken a dozen or so American and Canadian, if not international laws and – " I gestured towards the elder O'Shannon, " – he murdered my grandfather. You two are nothing more than common criminals. All you want is the money."

The elder O'Shannon erupted.

"Dún do bheal! Shut your mouth!"

The old man's face transformed with rage as he limped back towards the sitting area. His cheeks crimson with anger, his nostrils flared, and his shoulders hunched as if the weight of his hatred was pressing down on him.

Reilly reached out to help him, but the elder O'Shannon slapped his son's hand aside as he attempted to lunge past his chair. He stumbled, and his bulk and instability caused him to stagger into its back edge, pushing the chair forward into the table between us. The table skittered forward with the impact. I jerked my feet off the floor and raised my legs to keep them from being pinned between the edge of the table and my chair. O'Shannon's lips curled in anger, and I shrank back, clutching my grandfather's fedora as if it were the one safe thing I had left in the world. He grasped the back corner of the lounger and leaned toward me, spittle oozing from one corner of his hard mouth as he sputtered through trembling lips.

"You accuse me of thievery and murder? You, who has the blood of the innocent on your hands!"

"How could I've known?" I blurted, forcing myself to breathe.

Stay focused.

"Bah!" he roared. "It makes little difference to me if you did or did not know. Today, you know. Today, you will pay. Today, you will return Enniskillen to its rightful heir, me!"

He sucked in a long rasping breath of air and clenched his teeth together. Was it true? Had I inherited a stolen legacy? O'Shannon had only done what he felt compelled to do if it was. I could accept that, but it made me a bully or the heir of bullies. I couldn't accept that. If this were the skeleton in my grandfather's closet, my conscience couldn't let me leave it there.

THIRTY-TWO

I placed my feet against the edge of the table and managed to push my chair back, making room for them on the carpet. I sat up straight and swallowed the fear rushing up my throat.

"Let me call my lawyer. We'll work something out," I said, fixed on his scorn-filled eyes. This was Plan B if I couldn't immediately execute Plan A. The lives of my parents and Morgan were worth far more than Enniskillen.

O'Shannon's lips flared over his teeth, and the look on his face sent shivers through my chest. His voice was low but deliberate, like the warning growl from a tiger.

"There's nothing to work out, lad. I will have it, all of it, or you and your family and your girlfriend will die here, all of you, tonight."

"Da," Reilly suddenly said to his father, "we don't want to be killing anyone, do we?"

I glanced at him, searching his face. The younger O'Shannon was clearly alarmed. Maybe I had misjudged him. Did he fully realize how far his father was willing to go to get what he felt was his?

"We don't have to do this," I spoke quickly and directly to Reilly. "My grandfather is dead because of this."

"It doesn't belong to you!" The elder O'Shannon bellowed. "The legacy is mine!"

I continued looking at Reilly and responded to him.

"That may be true, but I have it, and I'm willing to work this out for everyone's benefit. Believe me. There's more than enough."

"Do not ignore me! I will have it!" O'Shannon roared, pulling my attention back to him. Spittle had escaped from between his lips and spattered the coffee table as he smashed his fists on the back of the chair. "I will have it all. You will not deprive me."

"Da?" Reilly said, his face growing angry. "Your heart, da."

What was going on between them?

The old man jammed his lips tight and held his hand up. His son flinched back. I recognized the fear on Reilly's face. My father had never hit me, not even a slap, but his words and the threat behind those words had been like slaps.

I focused on Reilly, pleading.

"We can share Enniskillen."

But the elder O'Shannon couldn't contain the centuries of injustice any longer. His fingers, their beefy knuckles glaring white, dug deep into the chair's leather while the other strangled the cane in a death grip.

"I will not be denied! I will take back what belongs to me."

He brandished a trembling finger at me.

"Call your lawyer. Call him now, but you'll have none of it! Not one stone or timber from the O'Shannons' Enniskillen!"

"Da?"

"Shut your mouth, Reilly. Now is our time. Now is our inheritance at hand," he hissed between clenched teeth, and Reilly turned his head away, his countenance darkening.

"Well. Mr. Ames, what is it to be?"

It became alarmingly clear at that moment that I would die, even if I gave him everything he wanted. He could not afford to leave any of us alive. We knew too much, no matter how brief that knowledge had been. He would kill anyone who knew about the Windows. He had no choice. His need for vengeance far exceeded his need to regain Enniskillen and the Windows. His bloodthirstiness had to be quenched. Three hundred years of a perceived wrong could not be satiated. He had to erase the memory of the McPhies and the Ames from his reality, just as the

O'Shannons had been struck from Enniskillen centuries ago. There was simply no other way for him to conclude his quest.

It was time to revert to Plan A.

I took a deep, terrified breath, every inch of my body tingling with apprehension. Cold rivulets of sweat coursed down my back beneath my shirt. I cleared my throat, my lips sticky with fear, and leaned forward in the chair. I spoke firmly but calmly. I needed to disarm him and make him believe he had won.

"All right, we'll do it your way. I'll call my lawyer to make the arrangements, but first, I want to see my parents and Morgan."

I leaned back, sighing loudly, doing my best to sound as if I were defeated.

"Or kill me and get nothing, no money. You might have the Windows," I pointed to the key he had strung around his neck, "but you'll have no legal right to any of it. You won't get one cent."

O'Shannon blinked several times as if he could hardly believe he had won, then snorted and recomposed himself as he patted his lips with his handkerchief. He adjusted his tie, smoothing his jacket over his expanse as he nodded slowly, believing perhaps that his all-consuming quest was finally ending.

His voice was controlled when he spoke, and it was clear that I had convinced him.

"Brilliant, young Aidan, brilliant. You have a small measure of my respect. You shall have your visit. It required a concerted effort on my part to persuade your father to talk of you, lad. He's almost as stubborn as you, but he cares deeply about your mother's safety. Indeed, you shall have your visit, and then we shall talk of the completion of our affairs. This evening shall culminate in the glorious victory of the O'Shannons over the McPhies."

"I'm not a McPhie," I said firmly.

The old man sniffed, his head tilting back as he eyed me through narrowed eyes.

"Aye, you're not. I'll give you that much."

He pointed toward the hallway off the living area, and I eased out of the chair, placing my grandfather's hat on my head as his son led the way. Reilly stopped before a door, fumbling for a key, and then unlocked it. I heard my dad mumble what sounded like a complaint, and as I entered, I saw my parents sitting on a bed in a relatively large and stylish bedroom. The room's one tall and narrow window was partly covered with plywood. To my right was another door. This had been their prison, and the room smelled of it. Morgan was not with them. Damn. That would complicate the next few moments.

Plan A was simply to get the hell out of Chicago, but not without Morgan.

My parents rose, rushing to me, and we embraced and cried. Even my father, always so controlled and self-assured, was sobbing. We held on to each other as though it might be the last time we would ever do so. In any other circumstance, I would not have been hugging my father, much less telling him that I loved him. This felt oddly wonderful and even normal after listening to the sordid and bitterly destructive tale of the O'Shannons. It would have been a remarkable moment in our family had I not been faced with the certainty that O'Shannon intended to kill us.

I was about to turn to him and demand to know where Morgan was when the other door in the room opened, and she stepped out. Her green eyes glared proudly and defiantly at the O'Shannons, but looked exhausted. She saw me, relief flashing across her face as she slid into my arms.

"Are you okay?" I asked.

She held on to me, and we kissed desperately.

"I'm sorry, Aidan," she finally said as we separated, "the Neanderthal was waiting for me in Victoria."

"I know. Amelia and I – and Kelli – chased him to a heliport, but he got away. Did he hurt you?"

She shook her head.

"You guys tried to rescue me? That's so sweet."

She kissed me again.

I pulled her glasses from my jacket pocket and handed them to her.

"Oh, thank you, I can see again. I thought they were lost."

"Are you hurt?"

"I'm all right," she said as she slid them on her nose, "but he sprayed something in my face, and I lost consciousness. Otherwise, I would've kicked in his thick Irish head."

She said the last words much louder while sneering at Reilly over my shoulder. I heard him snicker.

I turned to my dad.

"I'm so sorry I got you into this, and I'm sorry I didn't tell you about what's been happening in my life."

Mom whispered that it hadn't been all that bad, but she looked frazzled. Her clothes were dishevelled, and her eyes were cradled in dark circles. She straightened my tie, brushed my shoulders, and regarded my face as though she wasn't sure I was her son.

"I've always liked her," she whispered, smiling at Morgan.

Right there, in the prison of their captors, my mother had given her official approval of my romantic relationship with Morgan. It was surreal.

My father looked rough. A large yellow bruise was under his left eye, and a small butterfly bandage was over his right eyebrow. He leaned into me.

"Have you dropped out of college?"

I stared at him, unbelieving, and then laughed.

"Dad, I'm here to secure your release. I don't think that's important right now."

He shrugged, acquiescing in his usual manner as he stepped back.

"Fine, but is anything these people have to say true?"

He jabbed a finger at the O'Shannons.

I nodded in reply, but it was impossible to know what my parents had been told, although I assumed it was everything the O'Shannons knew or thought they knew.

I caught him looking at the fedora, his father's hat. He looked away. It was the old familiar jealousy, the painful realization that his father had not shared Enniskillen with him. It was one more reason for him to dislike me, one more thing to widen the gulf between us. I touched his arm and felt a surprising amount of compassion, but I needed to stay in the moment. Time was of the essence.

"Don't, Dad. Not now." Then a little more loudly, so the O'Shannons would hear.

"I'm here to negotiate your release."

I turned my head to both O'Shannons with a look of contempt.

"Negotiate?" My father fumed.

I grimaced and tried to calm my voice as I leaned into him.

"Shut up for once, and just trust me."

"Thank you, lad," the elder O'Shannon interjected from the doorway. "He's done nothing but complain and demand his rights since his arrival. I've been a gracious host, have I not? I've fed you and given you adequate accommodations, have I not?"

"I would prefer not to be here in the first place, and what about this?" my father shot back, pointing to his face.

My mother cut him off.

"Charles. Shut up."

O'Shannon laughed riotously, savouring the moment.

"Listen to your dear wife, Mr. Ames. Your son has what I want to ensure your release, and the sooner he and I resolve our differences, the sooner this will end."

My father clamped his lips tight, his eyes wishing something terrible upon his captor. I had seen that look many times before. It was a relief to see it directed somewhere else.

I turned toward the O'Shannons.

"Can I talk with them for a moment, alone? I need to explain what it is you want from me."

Reilly turned to his father, and the latter shrugged and sneered.

"By all means, shed a few tears. It'll be the first of many, lad, as I take back what's mine."

He laughed and turned to leave, placing his hand on Reilly's shoulder.

"Remain out here, by the door."

Reilly leaned against the wall in the hallway, the baton tucked under his arm as his eyes followed his retreating father. I turned back to my parents and Morgan as I slid my grandfather's hat off my head.

Dane and I had removed the lock from a site in Ireland, an ancient stone barn southeast of Derry, and secured it inside the elastic inner lining of the hat. The real key was also there, on the opposite side. Amelia had modified the lining, adding a strip of spandex cloth to accommodate the bulky lock. About the size of a fat wallet, it had been almost too unwieldy, bumping against the top of my head when I had it on. Fortunately, while O'Shannon had been rambling through his revenge-driven tale, I could hold the fedora in my hands, keeping the pieces firmly in place. I slipped the lock and key from the hat.

Removing the device from the barn rather than building a new one from spare parts on the island would allow the Window's position to remain in the system. There were at least one or two places in particular that I wanted to open it on, and the time was fast approaching to make that happen. I, or rather, the brothers and I, had a plan.

I slid my grandfather's hat back on my head. I didn't want to leave it behind, and I had no intention of returning, no matter what the truth was, at least not while our deaths at the hands of the O'Shannons were possible.

I nudged my parents and Morgan, directing them to the corner of the room by the washroom, as far as I could get them away from Reilly's occasional glances. Dad was looking from me to the apparatus in my hand. Mom started to speak, but I tilted my head, hoping she'd understand. She raised her eyebrows and remained quiet.

Morgan's eyes lit up as she realized what I was about to do, and she mouthed, "I love you."

My mother caught Morgan's silent words and glanced at me with an amusing expression.

"This is going to be fast," I whispered. "Do exactly as I say."

I let my eyes drop to the items in my hands.

"When I put these two things together, a Window, uh, a door — "

"I know," Dad interrupted. "Morgan's explained it, and Nollaig has been ranting about these Window things and their stolen inheritance since they assaulted us."

"Good," I continued, "that'll make this easier. A Window will open. Walk through it. Don't hesitate. I don't care how weird or impossible it looks, walk through."

"What about you?" Dad asked.

"Morgan will follow right behind you, and I'll come once she's through, okay? Now, on three."

I glanced at Reilly. He was frowning and fidgeting with his baton while looking down the hall, away from us. I turned so the lock was pointing away from us, counted quietly, and, on three, inserted the key into the lock.

I had only opened a window outside of the usual door-mounted lock method twice before, once in the study in September when I had taken the closet door off its hinges to figure out how it worked and now hours earlier in an interior storeroom in a barn on a small patch of farmland slowly being surrounded by the growing city of Derry. Both times, it had startled me enough to realize how eerie and strange it must have been for the crew of the Seagull. When the key was inserted into the lock and turned, the Window formed instantaneously, a few centimetres from the back of the lock. Without a doorframe to define the opening, you saw something you'd see with a picture-in-picture effect on a television: the old Irish farm where we were standing and the door-sized view provided by the Window, a stationary rectangular hole in the air. You could walk around it, watch it completely disappear when looking at its razor-thin edge, and be totally unaware that it was open from behind it. The effect was bizarre.

Earlier in Kingston, Dane's plan had been simple and elegant: make a portable Window.

"We've been thinking inside the box," he had said. "We have assumed the McPhies had the technology figured out over the last three hundred years, and there was nothing else to learn."

"Think outside the box, or in this case, outside the doorframe of the original superstition, the sailor's fear of an unframed Window," Dane had said with more enthusiasm than I had seen from him in a long time.

"Make a Window anywhere, anytime, and carry the key and lock components in separate pockets. They're still part of the system, still just one of the Windows, only now you're carrying it with you. In fact," he said, barely containing his thoughts, "it doesn't even have to take the form of a lock and a key. It's just a switch. That's all this is, a switch that creates a temporary wormhole, connecting one place to another in a network of connected wormholes."

Dane and I had chosen the old barn outside of Derry to remove the lock because it was a piece of property that didn't have much purpose. A local farmer planted and harvested various crops on about ten acres of rich black soil. Other than that, it was an insignificant destination in the Window system. Perhaps the McPhies had used it in their long history, but time had marched on, leaving the little farm behind.

It had taken us two nerve-wracking hours to cut the lock from the barn's storeroom door without destroying the aged components and possibly losing the Window's spot within the system. We even used it to return to Turin Street. On the island, Dane had carefully chiselled away the excess wood that had fused over time to the outer edges of the lock and then managed to reinforce it with wire, a rancher's best friend, he'd said. The stripped-down components had been small enough to hide in my grandfather's fedora, though I had been aware of its hope-filled weight every second since I'd stepped through the door in Chicago. The plan wasn't foolproof, but it provided a way to escape.

I held the lock and key at arm's length away from me towards the window and turned the key. A brilliant light enveloped us, and the air moved explosively as two sites connected. The wind whipped around my mother's dress, and she stifled a scream. My father's mouth dropped open as our ears adjusted. Reilly bellowed behind us.

It was 6:35. The Window, a perfectly rectangular hole in the air, opened on the condo in LA. I backed away to make room for my parents to pass through. Bill and Amelia had gone to LA and were waiting for us, waiting for this moment if all went well. I'd left Dane in Kingston after returning from the old barn. He had the key etched with *Closet 2* in case I failed, though none of us had planned for anything else if Plan A suddenly went sideways.

Amelia's eyes widened as she saw us, and Mom croaked Bill's name in surprise.

"Oh, hi, Mrs. Ames," he said, gesturing to us to come through.

"Mom! Dad!" Amelia called.

Dad grabbed my mother's arm, and they rushed past me. Amelia caught my mother, and my father stumbled through, quickly turning around, his eyes on me. Suddenly, his gaze flinched past me and his face filled with alarm. I craned my neck just in time to see Reilly launching himself at us, his baton swooping toward my head. Morgan grabbed my shoulder and drove us toward the Window. I stumbled, my leg catching the corner of the bed, dragging us both down. We stumbled towards LA and freedom.

I pulled the key from the wire-bound lock, knowing the Window would remain open only a few seconds after we passed through the portal. But Plan A suddenly went sideways. The jury-rigged lock fell apart in my hands, its pieces spiralling away towards the carpet at our feet. I wasn't worried about that; it took both key and lock to make the Windows work, but I hadn't wanted to leave anything behind.

I saw Reilly's huge hand and black baton from the corner of my eye. I braced for the blow while a panicked thought rushed through my brain: he would also fall into LA with us.

The Window suddenly collapsed.

We were still in Chicago.

THIRTY-THREE

The next few moments were chaotic. Reilly's head glanced off my shoulder as he fell screaming to the floor at the foot of the bed. Something warm and wet splattered across one side of my face, and Morgan gasped sharply. I stepped back from the bed, frantically searching for the key. It had fallen from my hand in the collision with Reilly.

Reilly's horrible screams pulled me away from my search. He was slumped against the bed, gripping the wrist of the hand that had been holding the baton a moment ago. His fingers were splayed wide, strange-looking, and glistening with blood. I realized the tip of his thumb and fingers were severed in a diagonal line as if made by a razor-sharp chef's knife. He pulled his good hand away and began desperately grabbing at the bottom edge of his jacket, trying to pull the fabric up in an effort to staunch the flow. I reached a hand to my face; his blood was on my cheek. I looked at Morgan, crouched over, slipping her feet into her shoes. There was blood across her back and left side. My mind flashed to the severed lanyard in the Dead Man's Cave and the sparrow's head. This was the danger of having anything in a Window when it closed.

Reilly was struggling to his feet, calling for his father in a tight, strangled voice. Nollaig O'Shannon lurched into the room, his face flushed with the effort it must have taken to run down the long hall. I saw a pistol in his hand and murder in his eyes.

O'Shannon aimed the gun's silver barrel at me. I had been very naive to think everything would go as planned. I braced for what I thought would be the last breath of my life, wondering if this was how my grandfather had faced this exact moment.

It didn't come.

Out of the corner of my eye, I saw a blur of movement, and Reilly, who was standing hunched over near me, was suddenly driven into the wall at the head of the bed as Morgan used his bulk to launch herself into the air. Reilly grunted in pain as he bounced off the wall to land hard on the floor, knocking over a small end table. Morgan flew past me and dropped and rolled, coming up directly before one very startled old Irishman. Another incredible flash of motion, and the gun went airborne. It spun upward, glanced off the ceiling in a shower of stippling, and landed on top of the dresser, shattering a small glass lamp. However, I only noticed this in my peripheral vision. My attention was focused on Morgan.

She twisted to the right and, without showing the slightest interest in where the gun had fallen, reached across the stunned O'Shannon's neck with one arm, using her other to grab the back of his coat. Then she swung her legs up, arching above his head and, coupling this move with his suddenly off-balance weight, she tipped him backwards toward the floor. His feet shot out from under him, and as he slammed into the floor with a loud thump, the air exploded out of his lungs. Morgan rolled away and twisted toward me in a half crouch, her hair whipping about in a crazy cinematic flourish. It was like watching a pro wrestling match on television. I half expected her to leap up, grab a chair, and start beating him over the head.

"God!" she snarled, "I've been waiting all day for the chance to do that. Let's go!"

I looked where Reilly lay on the bed, whimpering like a wounded animal, his lifeblood ebbing out onto the bedding. I could hear his father wheezing, struggling for air behind me. I turned to him. His face was purple, one hand gripping his chest. And Morgan, my wonderful, bespectacled Morgan, had just saved my life!

"Aidan," she said, gesturing for me to follow, "grab the key and let's get the hell out of here!"

Then I saw her eyes fall on Reilly.

I spotted the key lying on the quilt at the foot of the bed. Pieces of the lock were scattered like shards of broken pottery on the carpet.

"The lock fell apart! I think I just screwed up the timeline."

I snatched the key, slid it into my pocket, then scooped up the remnants of the lock and tossed them into my hat.

"Quick," Morgan instructed me, "I need something for a tourniquet!"

She was at Reilly's side, kneeling beside him and holding his wounded arm above his head. The blood flowed over her hand to her elbow and then dripped onto the carpet.

"Just a second."

I set my grandfather's hat down on the floor and flung back the edge of the bed's quilt, pulling back the linen top sheet and trying to tear a strip from it. It wouldn't tear. I glanced at Reilly. He was conscious, but his face was as white as the bed sheet. I grabbed one of the bed's pillows and pulled the cotton pillowcase covering off with one swoop. I knelt beside Morgan, and we pulled off his jacket. He began to shake uncontrollably.

"He's going into shock," Morgan said as she twisted the pillowcase into a tourniquet, which she tied tightly around his upper arm.

I glanced at the elder O'Shannon. He had rolled onto his side and glared at us between rasping gasps.

I grabbed a second pillow case, and Morgan wrapped Reilly's wound with that and instructed him to hold it high. She started to rise when he reached out with his good hand and fiercely gripped her arm. I went for his hand to pry it loose, but Morgan drove her thumb into the flesh between his forefinger and thumb, and Reilly gasped and released her.

"Hold your arm up, or you'll die," she said without a trace of compassion in her voice.

He swore as he grasped his wounded hand. Grabbing my grandfather's hat from the floor, I headed for the bedroom door, Morgan ahead of me.

"You better call an ambulance for your son," she said sharply to O'Shannon as she knelt beside him and checked his pulse. O'Shannon was sucking air in short, gurgling gasps, but his eyes were narrow and hard.

"Go hifreann leat!" he hissed, jerking his head away from her exploring hand.

"What's he saying?" she asked, casting a questioning look at me.

"Go to hell!" he croaked in answer, feebly pushing Morgan away. She stood up and stepped over him. I followed.

"They're Irish," I explained as we rushed down the hallway and out of the condo, its door automatically slamming shut behind us.

"Kinda' figured that. Over here!" Morgan replied, pointing to the elevators.

She stabbed frantically at the down arrow button while I sorted through the pieces in the fedora. None of them looked like the bolt.

"Is it true, Aidan, what he said about Enniskillen? About it belonging to them?"

"I think so. Gramps was killed because of the Windows. That room, O'Shannon's knowledge of the Windows, and the island, it's not a coincidence. He was going to kill us, Morgan, all of us."

"Even if you gave him what he wanted?"

I nodded in reply. I had expected a glitch or two, but that was not what had just happened. We'd had to improvise. Plan A, part two. At least my parents were safe. One of the elevator doors slid open, we rushed in, and Morgan punched the close button. I dropped to my knees and flipped the fedora over, dumping the pieces onto the floor.

"Will we be able to open a Window with all the parts lying on the floor like that?" she asked.

"It'll work, but the timeline will have shifted with the lock falling apart."

"Shifted?"

"Yeah. Gramps always moved an entire lock if he was relocating a Window. That way, it might be physically in a different place, but it kept its place in the system. I think I just messed that up.

"What does that mean? Will it still work?"

"Yes, I'm just not sure where we'll end up."

I took the key out of my pocket and reached for her hand, gripping it.

"Get ready; it'll be a little weird like the Dead Man's Cave I told you about."

I touched the key to each piece, expecting a Window to open beneath us. Nothing happened, so I touched each one again, no matter how small. Still, nothing happened.

"I don't think it's here."

"What?"

"It's not here. The key touching the bolt activates a Window. The bolt must still be in the bedroom somewhere!"

"Well, we can't go back for it. What floor was the Window on, the one you came through?"

"Thirty-two. Press thirty-two."

Morgan stabbed the button, but nothing happened.

"It's key carded."

"What?"

She punched the panel.

"It needs a secure key card to activate it. Reilly had one."

I jumped up from the floor.

"Wait here."

I jabbed the button to open the doors and squeezed through before they parted completely, only then remembering that the condo's door had shut behind us. The door was propped open with a rubber wedge. I stood at the entrance listening for a few seconds before quietly entering. It was eerily silent as I slipped down the hall to the bedroom. I peered through the door. Reilly was still slumped against the wall, his good hand holding the tourniquet. His father and the pistol were nowhere to be seen. I searched around and under the bed but could not see the bolt. Maybe it had gone through the Window to LA with my parents. Reilly watched me through half-closed eyes but said nothing.

"Your key card, Reilly," I demanded.

Where had the elder O'Shannon gone? I wondered if his father had called an ambulance or if he had left his son to fend for himself.

Reilly lifted stricken eyes to me.

"It was all true. Da was right all these years, wasn't he?"

"Yes, but it didn't have to be like this. I don't want it to be like this."

His eyes bore into mine as his lips trembled with the shock of his wounds.

"I don't either. All we have done to you has been very wrong."

That was it, wasn't it? Reilly was his father's son, but he wasn't his father. We had that much in common.

"Look, give me the key card. We're leaving. I'm not interested in dying here, and I hope your father called 9-11."

Really sighed heavily, his eyes dropping.

"I doubt he did. Enniskillen is all that's ever mattered to the old bastard," he sobbed and turned his face away from mine.

"Do you have a cellphone?"

He turned his eyes back to me.

"Me back pocket. I can't – "

I reached around behind him, felt it, and pulled it out. The home screen flared to life, revealing a photo of a red-haired woman holding a toddler with hair as bright as hers. I held the phone up to Reilly's face to unlock it, swiped the phone app open and dialled 9-1-1.

"Here," I said, laying the phone on his chest. "I'm sorry this happened to you."

I saw an edge of white plastic sticking from his shirt pocket and snatched it. It was a keycard. Morgan was holding the elevator doors open, waiting anxiously for me. As they shut, I tapped the card against a sensor on the control panel, and we began our descent. I told her about calling EMS for Reilly.

"His father didn't call?"

I shook my head.

"I guess not. Only one thing matters to him. Getting control of Enniskillen."

Morgan sighed and shook her head as we watched the screen overhead as floor numbers lit up, each followed by a chime. There were rows and rows of buttons listing floor after floor, several sub-basements and an observatory on the 94th floor. The doors opened, and I froze.

Nollaig O'Shannon was leaning heavily against a wall a few metres across from us, his pistol gripped in one hand. The hall was deserted. A yellow-handled fireman's axe leaned against the wall next to him. The fake key and its chain were lying at his feet. Off to his left was the door to the storage room where the Window had been, but it was hacked to pieces, shards of wood hanging limply from its hinges. I could hear O'Shannon's tortured breathing. He was hunched forward, his face swollen and purple. He must have recovered enough to take the other elevator down in hopes of entering the Window system with what he had assumed was the real key, but I had not brought the key I used to activate the Window to Chicago. I had pulled it out of the lock and tossed it to Dane in the study on Turin Street before I crossed over. I knew I would be under surveillance as soon as I entered the room in Chicago.

The old Irishman slowly stood up, his expression changing from weariness to a disturbing look of hope. He seemed to draw strength from some deep inner reserve as he gestured with his gun and raised his other hand. He was holding the lock. He had hacked it from the storage room's door, knowing I would need it to activate the Window.

"Need this?" He hissed between clenched teeth.

"Close the doors," I shouted to Morgan, but O'Shannon fired his pistol, and my ears reverberated with the concussive sound. The bullet zinged dangerously close to me, impacting with a crushed-egg sound against the elevator's back wall.

"Give me the key, the real key, damn you!"

O'Shannon spanned the distance between us with surprising quickness. I lurched back, but he struck me with the side of the pistol, causing me to stagger further into the elevator, my legs buckling beneath me as I felt blood trickle down my face.

"Stand back!" I heard him scream. "I have no revulsion at killing a woman."

I forced my eyes to open. I saw Morgan backing away as I lifted my head. She was defiant, glaring at O'Shannon as he stood over me.

"I will have what is mine. I will have it! Give me the key, damn your soul."

Fire shot through my shoulder as he gripped it and hauled me to my feet. I rose, blinking through tears of pain, trying to separate myself from it. Morgan was crouched, tensed like a cornered animal, her back against the elevator wall. O'Shannon slammed me into the wall, and I flinched, reaching for my pounding head. He slapped my hand away with the gun and then pressed the barrel against my forehead, just above my right eye.

"The key, Mr. Ames. I wouldn't want to spoil the nice shiny walls of this lift with your brain matter, but if you deny me what is mine for one moment longer, I will gladly splatter them all over these walls!"

I struggled, but his grip was that of a desperate man, and he smacked me again with the pistol. Then, just as quickly, he levelled it at Morgan. The barrel hovered so close to her face that she could have leaned forward and touched it with her forehead. Her eyes were wide and defiant.

"Or perhaps you would like to watch this young lass die. I don't need her. She's worth nothing to me. You have the key and the money."

His laugh was raspy, like he was strangling on his anger, a raging fury causing the prominent veins on the sides of his head to pulse like undulating worms.

"No. Wait!" I pleaded, plunging my hand into the pocket of my slacks.

He pulled away, and the gun swung back to my head. He watched me fumble for the key, the maddening gleam in his eyes heightened as he caught sight of the object of his family's three-hundred-year-quest, the key to Enniskillen.

He placed the lock from the door in his jacket pocket and reached out to take the key from my shaking fingers, but the elevator suddenly stopped, and my shaking hand lost its grip on it.

"Damn you," he growled and shoved me to my knees, the gun barrel painfully digging into the top of my head.

"Pick it up."

I fumbled for the key, blood stinging my right eye, blurring my vision. Long, terror-filled seconds passed until I grasped it. He snatched the key from my raised hand, laughing maniacally, and hauled me to my feet again as the elevator doors whisked open. Morgan made her move then. She dropped low as he pulled me up, forcing her body between mine and the elevator wall. Using O'Shannon's and my shifting centre of gravity, she managed to tip us out into the hallway, where we crashed heavily to the floor. O'Shannon grunted explosively and cursed as I rolled off him, wrenching the key from his beefy fingers. Morgan saw me do that, grabbed my hand and my grandfather's hat, and pulled me up.

"Come on!"

"Wait! The lock! We need the lock!"

O'Shannon was gasping for breath, but his hand was in his pocket, on the lock. He wrestled it out, laughing between wheezes. I kicked out, connecting with his hand. The lock spun away, landing a short distance from us, where his gun lay. I grabbed the lock from the carpet while kicking the pistol further away. As I turned to reach for Morgan's hand, the prone O'Shannon struck out with a leg and tripped her. He slammed an elbow into the back of her head as she fell. She screamed and slumped to the floor, her eyes closing. Cursing, he struggled up, his face red and streaming with perspiration. Groaning with the exertion, he grabbed her around the waist, lifting her as if she weighed nothing.

"You can't win, Mr. Ames. Enniskillen is mine, and I will have it," he bellowed as he turned and limped towards a door marked with *Skywalk Maintenance - Authorized Personnel Only*. He slapped his key card against a reader. The door popped open, and he carried Morgan through with him.

I dove for his gun and brought it up just as the door shut. Fishing Reilly's keycard from my pocket, I unlocked the door and pushed through. O'Shannon was just ahead, hunched over in the dim glow of a single pot light, gasping for breath, Morgan still trapped in his grip.

I was suddenly aware of what floor we were on. He hadn't been taking us back to his condominium. This was the 94th floor, the 360 Chicago Observation Deck, according to a sign with an arrow pointing to my left. We were in the hall leading to the building's famous viewing area, three hundred metres above the plaza.

"Stop!" I shouted, raising the gun. I wasn't sure I knew how to use it, but he wouldn't know that.

He roared insanely in defiance, pressed his card against another reader, and opened a door behind him. O'Shannon stepped through, and I caught a glimpse of an outdoor walkway. Sensors reacted to his presence, bathing the walkway in brilliant white light, revealing a nightmare of gusting wind and swirling snow. The door began to shut, but I was there in seconds, pushing through onto a narrow service walkway, where a bone-chilling blast of winter air and the dull roar of city noise hit me. A sign attached to the walkway's railing had the ominous words *Safety harness must be worn beyond this point* stencilled in large yellow letters. Chicago was naked around us, a frighteningly long way down. I cautiously approached O'Shannon as the freezing wind clawed at my clothing and skin with icy fingers.

He was a few metres away, leaning against the railing. Morgan had recovered and was struggling furiously as he gripped her around the waist, holding her close to his side. She was driving an elbow repeatedly into his lower back. He swore and swung her around in front of him, grasping her by the neck with one hand as he pushed her upper body precariously out over the dizzying chasm beneath us. Only her flailing legs remained on this side of the railing.

"Throw me the gun, Mr. Ames."

"Shoot him," Morgan cried, but O'Shannon squeezed even harder.

I tossed the gun. It skittered over the walkway's rough grating, stopping short of his feet.

"Hand me the lock and key, Mr. Ames, or I'll send your lass to her death!"

"Let her go first."

"I think not."

I saw Morgan struggling for air as her eyes widened with fear, and his hand gripped her throat fiercely.

"You'll kill us anyway!" I screamed over the noise of the wind and the city.

"Give me what is mine!"

"Let her go. Then I'll give it to you!"

"Give it to me now," he shouted, pushing Morgan further out over the abyss. She was desperately trying to get some purchase on the railing with her feet.

I held the key out to him and shouted over the roar of the wind and my fear.

"Pull her back, and I'll give it to you. I promise."

"Wrong decision, lad," he howled as he pushed Morgan over the railing and let go. Her hands clawed fruitlessly at the air, and then she was swallowed by the night; her horrified scream mingled with O'Shannon's blood-curdling laugh.

THIRTY-FOUR

"**N**o!" I screamed as my mind filled with the horror of what O'Shannon had just done.

"Go dtachta an diabhal thú!" he screamed as he leaned over, reaching for his pistol. He stumbled and fell awkwardly to his knees. Curses erupted from his mouth but were quickly swept away by the relentless wind. His veins bulged alarmingly large under the ruddy flesh of his head as he gripped the weapon with both hands. He swiftly angled it toward me, and I could see in his eyes that he intended to kill me.

I lunged toward him, my mind racing with the madness of what I knew I had to do. He grunted in surprise as I used one of his broad shoulders as a springboard and launched my body over him and the railing, delivering a stinging blow to my right knee against its steel pipe. A part of my brain registered the shock of bone connecting with the unforgiving metal, but I ignored it. I had the lock O'Shannon had violently hacked from the door in one hand and the key in the other. His gun fired, its sharp crack whisked away by the deafening rush of air as I plunged toward the street more than three hundred metres below.

The air was brutally cold, assaulting every bit of my exposed flesh. I couldn't see Morgan at first, but then I saw her twisting helplessly as she flailed. Light and terror filled her face as each floor lit her descent. Unbelievably, she was holding onto my grandfather's fedora. I angled my body toward her, head first, like a missile. Fall like a rock, I willed. I had to reach her, but I might shoot past her if I wasn't careful.

I should have been terrified, but there was no time for fear. I could open a Window from anywhere. It didn't have to be done through an actual physical door. Dane had said so, and we had proven it. But could I do it while plunging from this height? How much time did we have? If I activated a Window, would we be splattered against the room's far wall wherever it opened?

No. My thoughts came in split seconds. Dead Man's Cave had proven that two separate places, each with its physical dynamics, are connected by a Window. How I entered a Window on one side was not how I existed on the other. Did that include full-on bone-crushing speed from falling off a very tall building? It should work, right?

She saw me and screamed my name, but her voice was swept away. She called my name again, and this time, I heard her, shrill, full of fear and surprise. The air violently pummelled my body, and snow pelted me like stones, forcing my eyes to flood with tears. I blinked profusely, desperately trying to focus on the woman I loved. It was happening too fast. We were about to collide. I attempted to flatten myself out, to slow my ferocious fall.

"Grab me!" I shouted as we collided, a windmill of arms and legs.

Morgan's fingers clawed my side but then secured their frantic hold on my belt with one hand. My head and shoulder brushed painfully against one of the windows we were falling past, bouncing us out and away from the building's massive cross beams. Morgan kept her grip, but her glasses were swept from her face, spiralling out into the darkness, their lens reflecting light from the building like little beacons. Her other hand grabbed my shirt under my jacket, pulling herself up along my body, sliding her arms around my chest, and locking her legs around the small of my back as we tumbled dangerously close to the building again.

"Hold on," I yelled unnecessarily as I fought to see past the mass of her hair whipping me in the face.

I pointed the lock and key away from us, towards the plaza. I wanted the Window to be open beneath us because once it opened, it would be stationary in space. We needed to fall through it. I slid the key into the lock, turned it, and had a fleeting, terrifying glimpse in my peripheral vision of the pedestrian-jammed plaza rushing madly toward us. We had only seconds left before impact. The flash of the portal temporarily blinded me. I pulled the key out, holding onto it and the lock for dear life, my vision recovering just enough to see startled faces looking up at us, mouths gaping in horror, and I knew I had failed.

We were going to die.

THIRTY-FIVE

We rocketed through the Window, the stone-cold death of the plaza's concrete a split second away from ending our lives.

We had been falling at a horrific speed when I opened the Window. As we passed through it, dragging a blast of Chicago winter with us, we were suddenly flipped horizontally, coming to a complete and mentally jarring stop. My brain thought we were still falling, but whatever momentum we had had when we entered the Window had been stripped from us. However, just that sudden reorientation, coupled with the weight of Morgan clasping desperately to the front of me, was enough to throw us off balance. We fell forward, but I had the presence of mind to twist sideways, allowing us to share the impact of falling onto a painfully solid surface.

The Window closed at our feet, and, except for the rasping sound of our tortured lungs and pounding hearts, we were cradled in silence. I turned my head and saw a single window framing the glow from a street light, and I instantly knew where we were. We were wet, terribly cold, but alive on the floor in my grandfather's study.

I laughed and cried and then laughed some more.

"W-we're alive?" Morgan stammered.

Her Herculean grip remained around my chest and waist, her face tucked into the crook of my neck. She wouldn't let go, and I could voice nothing intelligible. The spontaneous madness of what I had just done and that we had survived was almost incomprehensible. Her hold finally relaxed as she pulled away, flopping onto her back. I took a deep, shuddering breath as I rolled painfully onto my back, dropping the key and lock before trying to feel if anything was broken. One arm was still under Morgan's neck, but didn't feel injured. I heard her mumbling something through the hiss in my eardrums as a trembling and chilly hand found my face. She placed my grandfather's hat haphazardly on my head and then let her head flop onto my chest. I grunted and blew welcome strands of her hair from my face. An arm draped across me, pulling me closer for warmth, and I wrapped my arms firmly but gently around her, both of us shaking, neither wanting to let go.

"Let's not. Do that. Ever. Again!" she gasped.

Our fall from the 94th floor lasted a little more than twenty seconds; that's how long it takes for a body to fall from three hundred metres if conditions are favourable. Favourable, as in a strong updraft caused by the infamous winds along the Magnificent Mile. We had fallen from Chicago's tallest building and landed where this journey had started.

"We're in Kingston. We're safe," I said, still holding her tightly.

"Kingston? How?"

Good question. I could barely think clearly, but my mind began pulling all the pieces together as we lay on the floor. The lock I'd used to help my parents escape was from a site on Level Two, and when it fell apart in O'Shannon's condo, it would have caused it to lose its spot, shifting all the times on that level by fifteen minutes. The window back to the study on Level Two was at the forty-five-minute mark of the hour. I had a theory, but I wasn't sure about it since I hadn't been checking my watch as things were a little crazy a few minutes ago, but O'Shannon might have thrown Morgan off the Open-Air Observation Deck shortly after 6:30, and we'd plummeted through the Window twenty or so seconds after that. Did that mean the Window to the study was now at the half-hour mark on Level Two? Every other site on that level would be fifteen minutes earlier now. It hurt to think about it.

Suddenly, the light bulb overhead flared to life. Dane was standing at the study door.

"Oh my, god," he gasped, "are you okay?"

He helped us up, rolling the chair around from behind the desk to let Morgan sit in it before running downstairs for blankets and bandages. I sat on the edge of the desk and began feeling for injuries. My nose was broken, my right knee and shin were scraped, blood was soaking through my pants, and my left shoulder felt wrenched. Morgan's right hand was bruised from punching O'Shannon, and her left thigh had a long scrape that she said had come from when O'Shannon had thrown her off the building, and she'd glanced off one of its support structures, but otherwise, we were remarkably okay.

After nursing our wounds as much as possible, which included Morgan pushing my nose painfully back into place, I borrowed Dane's phone to call my phone in LA. I had given it to Bill when he and Amelia went to LA. My hands shook so severely that I couldn't punch the numbers on the screen, so Dane did it. There was an ear-splitting cheer on Bill's end when I confirmed that Morgan and I had escaped. I didn't disclose all the shocking details. That could wait until we were all together.

As I ended the call, Dane shook his head and asked, "How did you escape? Bill said the Window collapsed."

Morgan laughed, grimacing in pain as she did.

"He improvised."

"Improvised?"

I chuckled.

"I used the lock from my office door in the building. O'Shannon took an axe to the door and chopped it out, but we managed to get it from him. I still had the real key, so I used it to make another Window —"

"As we fell off a hundred-story building!" Morgan cut in.

Dane blinked.

"You made a second portable Window while you were falling off the building? It worked?"

I stared at him. He wasn't joking.

"You," I stammered, "you thought it might *not* work?"

He grinned and shrugged.

"Well, we hadn't planned on you suddenly improvising a second portable Window. We knew the lock we took from the farm outside Derry worked, but would they all do that?"

I stared aghast at him as he grimaced.

"Really?"

He laughed, and Morgan playfully slugged his arm.

"We could have died."

Dane nodded thoughtfully.

"Yes, but you didn't, which means my theory is correct. You can use a portable device anywhere, and I mean anywhere."

Morgan and I looked at each other and then laughed.

"Yeah, we're not doing that ever again," she said, squinting at her watch, "I need to call Kelli and let her know I'm okay."

After taking showers, we changed into clean clothing, Morgan borrowing a pair of my jeans and a t-shirt that was a little tight in places. At 2:30 a.m., Kingston time, we caught the Window to LA. My parents, Amelia and Bill, were waiting at the condo's entrance when we walked through. My mother was on the deacon's bench, looking anxious, with my father beside her. As the Window shut behind us, I was overwhelmed with unexpected compassion for them, especially my father. Maybe we would never be the closest of friends, and perhaps he would never be all I had wanted him to be, but he was not the dark, revenge-driven father of Reilly O'Shannon.

We held onto each other, and my father openly wept. It was a surreal moment. Right there, in a condo where we were all illegally on US soil, I felt something change between us as a family.

THIRTY-SIX

We gathered in the condo's living room, where my parents and Bill wanted all the details of our escape. As I was explaining the insane twist our rescue plan had taken, Amelia came into the room holding a plastic sandwich bag.

"I need to get these to Chicago right away," she said briskly, holding the bag so we could see the severed fingers of Reilly O'Shannon.

She had responded as any experienced ER nurse would. She'd placed the digits in a plastic sandwich bag, which she put inside the refrigerator's vegetable crisper. She knew they weren't my fingers; they were too big. Even before Morgan and I had arrived, she had tracked down which hospital specializing in trauma injury and limb reattachments in Chicago had admitted a man with missing fingers.

It must have been a mystery to the surgical staff at Northwest Memorial Hospital when Reilly's fingers showed up by FedEx express from Manhattan less than four hours after they'd been severed. I used a made-up name and return address.

The next day, my parents returned to Calgary with my sister. Dad contacted city police and the RCMP and, after some creative explaining, managed to convince them that they had chartered a private plane for a spontaneous getaway vacation in Victoria. I owned an apartment there, so it wasn't beyond the realm of possibility.

Morgan and I returned to Victoria later that day. Kelli had been in contact with the local police and her father, but there was no actual evidence of a crime, just her story, which, to be honest, sounded like an episode from a TV police procedural. Of course, Kelli was angry with me; our various bruises and scraps didn't help either, so we had a conversation with her and Brittany that went as well as expected. They didn't believe us, so we took them to Kingston and the island. I was concerned about the growing circle of people with knowledge about the Windows, but these were Morgan's friends and besides, Enniskillen and what it was and had been was evolving. Marianne McPhie had taken it from a den of thieves. Now, it was my turn to transform it again.

I just wasn't sure what that would be yet.

In the weeks leading up to Christmas, I obtained a Canadian passport and made plans to fly to Chicago. It would be the first time since discovering the Windows that I would legally enter the United States. My purpose was to meet with O'Shannon and his son on my terms. I could have repeated what the McPhies and my grandfather had done, run and hide from past grievances, but I believed O'Shannon, and my conscience could not let his claim go unanswered. The old Irishman might not like what I would offer him, but I was determined to end the injustice his family had suffered.

I found his security company's phone number through a web search. After negotiating my way through a frustrating automated answering service, it became clear that no human being was answering calls. I tried contacting O'Shannon through his suite's phone number, but again, there was no answer, and the number did not go to a messaging service. Finally, I left voice mail messages at the cell numbers of the only two Nollaig O'Shannons listed in Chicago. I kept it simple in case neither was the correct O'Shannon, inviting him to meet in person to discuss the future of Enniskillen. A few days later, Reilly replied by, in turn, leaving a voice message on my cell.

"Where?" was his monosyllabic response.

I called the number back immediately, but it went to voice mail. I hung up and tried again, with the same result. I waited for the beep this time and suggested meeting on Monday, December 3, at a popular bistro along the Magnificent Mile. It was within walking distance of 875 North Michigan Avenue. After ending the call, I wondered if the O'Shannons would come armed since Illinois has a conceal-and-carry law.

My parents, my father especially, were concerned with my plan. I was attempting to bargain with the man who killed his father and who had attempted to kill Morgan and me. He didn't say it, but I could tell he was worried O'Shannon might finish the job. On the other hand, Morgan felt attempting to reconcile a past grievance was the only option.

"You can ignore the past, but it'll catch up to you," she said one evening as we sat before the fireplace on the island, "then you get what happened to us. They may have attempted to kill us, but it didn't work out that way – this time. You have the power to bring something good out of this situation."

She's always impressed me with her ability to see a future beyond what's happening in the present. I only hoped I wasn't naive; the O'Shannons had already shown the extent they'd go to restore their legacy. Throwing somebody off a building looks a lot like murder in any country.

I arrived an hour early outside the bistro by taxi from my hotel and sat huddled in my winter parka on a bench across the street, watching the restaurant for any signs of surveillance by the O'Shannons. A quarter before the hour, I cautiously entered the restaurant. I removed my parka, placing it on the back of my chair at the table I had booked over the phone the day before, securing a spot in a front corner near the street-facing windows where I could keep an eye on the entrance a few tables away. This was as safe as everyone thought I could be. I was worried Nollaig might try something again, but I hoped not in a public place. Besides, I wasn't suicidal. I had Dane's ingenious and completely portable Window switch tucked in the front pouch of my Calgary Stampeders' hoody. I'm not a huge football fan, but the Stamps' hoodies are warm and comfortable with a big front pouch. The control was a repurposed TV remote, and all I had to do was point it away from me and activate it by simultaneously holding down two side-by-side buttons with my thumb. Doing so pulled pieces of the two ores together, opening a wormhole. Releasing the buttons was like pulling the key out of a lock. As much as I didn't want to believe it, I suspected I would have to use the switch to escape. O'Shannon was bitter, and despite what I felt for sure was his son's hesitancy to take the inheritance by force, I didn't believe either would be willing to share Enniskillen.

I was sure of this because there was no hint about that miserable night on American TV or social media news channels. O'Shannon and his son had not told authorities what happened. Who would have believed them, anyway? A centuries-old quest? A nineteen-year-old kid who traipses around the globe by travelling through wormholes? It sounded like the stuff of science fiction.

Ten minutes after one, Reilly entered the bistro. He was alone and clearly wary as he paused to scan the thinning lunch crowd. Our eyes met, and he began to walk slowly toward me. His right arm was cradled in a sling, and I could see a portion of his hand and bandaged fingers protruding from behind the cloth. Without saying a word, he pulled out a chair and sat across from me, continuing to survey the other tables through narrowed eyes. Was he expecting a trap? I let my left hand slip into the hoodie's pouch to cradle the Window switch.

"Hello, Reilly," I said.

I'd thought of a dozen things to say, but seeing him again made what I had rehearsed seem inadequate. The Window I had opened had hurt him, and it could have been much worse.

His eyes levelled with mine, and I saw his father's hatred for me.

"Have you come back then to finish the O'Shannons, Aidan Ames?"

"What? No. I didn't want this, any of this," I stammered. "We saved your life. Your father left you to bleed out. You should be thanking me."

He smirked and raised his bandaged hand toward me. The fingertips were puffy and dark with bruising, and I could see small black pins sticking through the bandage.

"They sewed them back on, and the pins are holding the bones together. The surgeons say I should eventually have most of the use of them."

His eyes examined my face. I was still sporting a yellowish shadow around my healing nose.

"You have an injury."

"Your father tried to kill me."

He blinked rapidly, his eyes watching my face.

"You stole from us," he said with little emotion.

"I had no idea. Your father murdered my grandfather before he could tell me anything about the Windows or Enniskillen."

He didn't reply. We just stared at each other, a vast, unsurpassable gulf of suspicion between us. I considered pulling out the Window switch and getting away before the situation became dangerous, but then his shoulders suddenly slumped, his anger seeming to deflate. He spoke quietly.

"You know, I grew up with his stories, the family's story, the stolen inheritance, the fantastic Windows, the despised McPhies. Before me Da moved here to America, I left home as soon as I found work. I wanted nothing to do with his anger or our family's stupid quest. He was always angry, as if life had cheated him even before he was born. How was I to know the stories were all true?"

He paused and looked away, blinking rapidly, his good hand clenching.

"I believe your family was cheated, Reilly," I said quickly, seizing the opportunity, saying what I had rehearsed as I'd prepared for this meeting.

He looked at me, shaking his head slightly, a glimmer of something different forming in his eyes.

"You do?"

I nodded.

"Yes. I want to make things right."

He blinked and exhaled, the fingers of his good hand unclenching.

"I still didn't believe any of it when he came to me after he'd been shot in the leg and telling me he had shot the man who had stolen our inheritance."

He looked down, tears catching the overhead lights of the bistro at the edges of his eyes.

"He invited me to move here then, to work for him, to sit and watch that bloody door in the Hancock building. His company had done well, and he paid more than a fair wage for doing very little. By god, though, before the day you magically appeared in that room, I was ready to quit. It made no sense, the stories, the myth of Enniskillen, until – "

"Until I showed up," I interrupted.

He nodded as his eyes lifted back to mine. He seemed different. The anger I had sensed moments ago was simply not there anymore. I let my hand ease off the switch.

"Where is your father?"

Reilly drew in a long breath.

"You don't know? You were there."

"Don't know what?"

"He didn't get his wish. He died because of you, because of your granddad, and because of the bloody McPhies."

I curled my fingers around the switch again.

"I didn't kill him. He was alive when I jumped off the building to rescue my girlfriend after your father threw her off the maintenance platform on the observation level."

I shivered with the memory of the frigid, pulverizing air that had pounded every part of my body and the unforgettable image of Morgan's terror-filled face as we fell.

Reilly flinched, groaned and shook his head.

"Bloody hell, old man."

He bit his lower lip and slowly shook his head.

"He threw her over the railing, and you jumped after her? I don't understand. How did you survive?"

"I had the key and the lock from the door you had been watching, and I opened a Window to escape before it was too late."

"While you were falling? You can do that?"

I nodded.

"Christ," he muttered. "I hadn't believed he would go that far."

I didn't know what to say. Angry people do stupid things.

Reilly groaned again as he slowly shook his head.

"Don't worry yourself. You didn't kill him. He put a bullet in his head by his own hand."

I was stunned. My mind flashed back to the seconds after he had thrown Morgan into the darkness. Nollaig was kneeling, his countenance a terrifying image of rage as he reached for the pistol where it had fallen on the deck. He had bellowed in surprise as I used his shoulder as a springboard. Had he believed I had deliberately jumped to my death, robbing him of the only means to get to the financial inheritance? I recalled the sound of a shot as I leapt into the darkness. Had he accidentally shot himself? I looked out the window facing the city, anger churning inside my gut. The battle for Enniskillen had robbed us all of the ones we loved.

I turned my attention back to him.

"I'm sorry. I truly am. I knew nothing about you, your family, or what Willie McPhie had done. I didn't want it to be like this."

A waitress came to take our orders, and I asked for tea for both of us. Reilly and I sat in silence until she returned. Reilly pushed his cup away and narrowed his eyes at me as she walked away.

"My Da is dead. His security company has been dismissed from the Hancock because of what happened, and in this business, one breach of trust can destroy your reputation. I am scrambling to retain what is left of that, to keep what little remains to take care of my wife and child. Do you mean what you just said, that you wish to make things right?"

Suddenly, I knew that the distance between Reilly and I had been reduced to the one thing that mattered: loving and doing your best for the people you were fortunate enough to call your own.

"I'm sorry all this has happened. I'm sorry your father and my grandfather are dead. I'm sorry the McPhies stole Enniskillen from your family, but you and I are alive, and we can turn this into something that benefits both our families."

Reilly's jaw tightened, and I could see the anger creep back into his eyes. Was it too much to hope he would agree to what I had planned? Didn't he understand that we could end centuries of injustice?

"Why would I want to have any sort of alliance with you?"

"So we don't end up like our fathers," I blurted out angrily, stunned by my words.

A rush of emotions swept over me. So much of what had happened had been unnecessary. Reilly's father had died; anger had killed him as sure as the bullet from his gun. My grandfather, my friend, had been murdered because of the Windows and had died without ever reconciling with his son. I didn't want to walk down the same road for any reason.

Reilly raised his good hand, his palm open.

"Hey, mate, I am here."

He lifted the edge of his coat.

"I have no gun. Unlike me Da, I am here to listen."

"Good," I said.

I could feel the tension slipping away.

"I believe your father's version of Enniskillen's history. I believe that Willie McPhie inflicted a terrible crime upon your ancestors. Your family may have a claim, but the last three hundred years of the history of Enniskillen is that of the McPhie and now the Ames families. However, I am willing to share everything that is Enniskillen. I want to share the Windows, properties, and money with your family."

I pulled my hands out from my jersey and laid them palms down on the table.

"This is the only reason I contacted you. I want to restore your family's place in the story of Enniskillen."

Reilly continued to gaze steadily into my eyes. He was appraising me. He might not be his father, but like his father, he had been raised to view the McPhies as murderers and thieves, and my grandparents, who had taken Enniskillen over from them, were no better in his mind. Would he trust me, or was it too late?

When he finally spoke, it was with a steady voice.

"Aidan Ames, my Da would not have wanted to share our family's legacy, but I am not my Da. I despise the hate that did consume him and has consumed the O'Shannons for generations. I have known very little else in my life. It has been a curse upon every dream and wish for a good life. From the time I was but a lad, I have known only hatred for a people I did not even believe existed."

He lifted his damaged hand and gazed down at his bandaged and swollen fingers.

"There has been a bitter price to pay, and I have become someone I am ashamed of."

He turned his face back to me.

"I abducted your family and your Morgan, and even my own five-year-old son learned to curse the name of the McPhie's from my Da. This has not been good."

He looked at me, his eyes wet with tears, and I knew Reilly O'Shannon wanted something different for his family.

"Vengeance," he spoke, shaking his head, his jaw taut, as he tried to control his emotions. "The Irish are not known for their forgiveness, Aidan. The god's truth is we hold our grudges long and dear to our hearts, but the honour of the O'Shannon family name has been sullied by this thirst for vengeance over something that happened hundreds of years ago. I wish this to end."

I could see in his face that Reilly was sincere. This was the outcome I had doubted would happen, but as he'd said, he was not his father. This was no longer about the money or the Windows but about reconciling a wound inflicted long ago by a violent man neither of us knew except by his choices.

I reached around and pulled a thick letter-sized envelope from an inner pocket in my parka. Reinhold Bonk had prepared a concise overview of the company's financial assets at my request. I felt euphoric as I offered an equal partnership with Reilly and his family. He listened carefully, looking through the document. I offered what I hoped would be an acceptable working relationship administered by Reinhold Bonk of Universal Holdings, one company, two separate divisions, the Ames and the O'Shannons. It would require months of working out the logistics, I explained, but this would be the next step in the evolution of Enniskillen.

Reilly placed the document between us as I finished and placed his undamaged hand on it.

"Forgive me; how do I know I can trust you? That you will not try to cheat my family?"

I nodded.

"I understand, Reilly." I gestured toward his wounded hand. "You've seen the dangers of the Windows firsthand. There are a couple of the older sites that, if you went into them, you probably wouldn't be able to get out. You would disappear forever. I could just be luring you to your death, and then I could keep everything, right?"

He blinked, his gaze not leaving my face, but I saw his concern.

"Here," I said, reaching back into my parka to pull out the small polished wooden box that supposedly contained Willie McPhie's first key. I'd retrieved it from the Bank of Ireland in Dublin, removing the slip of paper inside it that claimed it was Willie's key. I was sure it was Miles

O'Shannon's first key, possibly crafted by Willie but later stolen in a terrible act of violence and greed.

I slid it across the table to him, opening it for him.

"I believe this belonged to your ancestor before it was stolen from him. It's the first key."

Reilly slowly lifted the old, dark key from its soft cradle. He held it close and then carefully placed it back.

I retrieved a folded sheet of paper and the second repurposed TV remote switch Dane had made, identical to the one in my hoodie. I slid both across the table to him.

"And this is the modern key to Enniskillen and a map of the Windows and times. You don't need a door and a lock; point this away, make sure the Window won't open inside furniture or a wall, because – " I pointed to his hand, "as you know, that doesn't go well. Press the two top buttons simultaneously, and you can access the system. You can go anywhere you want."

He looked at me and then at the remote, touching it cautiously. The memories of that fateful night and the scars that would form on his hand would long be with him. He picked up the folded paper and flipped it open, letting his gaze traverse the page. After a moment, he set it down and lifted his face to me, tears sliding down his cheeks.

"I'm sorry. Thank you."

I sniffed and wiped a tear from my face.

"It's okay. I am not my grandfather or the McPhies. What we're doing here today can't change the past or centuries of grievance, but we're making a different future for our families."

We talked for more than an hour about the Windows, how they operated, and the various sites and the countries they were in, and as our conversation felt like it was coming to a natural end, Reilly suddenly offered his left hand to me. As we embraced the promise of a brighter future, it was clear the quest for vengeance was over.

"Tell me, is the island as beautiful as the paintings?" Reilly asked. "I've grown up on tales of Enniskillen and the lost inheritance, but it's difficult to know what is true and what is family myth."

"Enniskillen is like nothing I've ever seen," I gestured to the window beside us, "certainly no snow storms. You're welcome to come there and stay as long as you wish. It's your inheritance, too."

I pulled out my phone to show him a few photos. Reilly was quiet as I swiped through the pictures. I wondered what he was feeling, being the first O'Shannon to see images of the island in over three hundred years. Finally, he spoke.

"I would go with you to Enniskillen for my Da's sake and to spread his ashes in the place of our ancestors. I would not want to live there, though. It's not my home."

He glanced out the window beside him, the snow pelting softly against it, as Christmas shoppers, huddled against the wind, passed by, unaware of the historic moment between Reilly and me.

"I miss Ireland."

I understood what he was saying. I had struggled with where home was even before the inheritance, and I still wasn't sure where that was, except maybe for me, home as a place was the people I loved and who loved me rather than a physical space. As the Windows opened up the world to Reilly and his family, they would have to figure that out for themselves.

I gave him my email and cellphone number. I promised to arrange for him to fly to New York in a few days to meet me at the warehouse to take him to Zurich to begin formalizing our partnership and to set up immediate access to the various bank accounts. Unless he began experimenting with the Window key I had given him, it would be the first time he would travel through them. I hoped the magic of the wormholes would capture his imagination as it had mine.

We stood and shook hands again, our meeting ending far better than I had hoped.

"A Merry Christmas to you and your family, Reilly," I said. "I truly am sorry about your father."

Reilly nodded once.

"Thank you, and I am sorry about your granddad."

I could tell he was not the same person who had entered the restaurant a few hours ago. Our families had suffered unnecessary losses, and it would be some time before the events were just memories, but today was a start.

"By the way," he said, pulling his coat tight, "Nollaig Shona Duit is how you say Merry Christmas in Gaelic."

"Knoll-lag-shauna-duet?" I replied, grimacing apologetically.

He laughed.

"Aye, mate, if we are to be partners in Enniskillen, you'll have to be practising your Gaelic."

Reilly smiled warmly, nodded, and then pushed through the door into the cold Chicago night.

THIRTY-SEVEN

Silvery, wet sand squished between my toes as the thinning edge of a wave of warm Pacific water splashed across my bare feet. My mother, also barefoot, laughed, lifted her colourful ankle-length sari, and skipped along the water's edge, splashing and running further up the beach. I smiled as I watched her. Seeing the gradual return to the carefree person I remembered as a child was a welcome change. Wealth, especially the kind of wealth I had thrust upon me, can make people shallow, frivolous, and blind to the plight of those less fortunate. However, I wanted the financial power of Enniskillen to be a window of opportunity for us to make a difference beyond the physical needs of our lives. Reilly and I agreed on this: the legacy of Enniskillen, as it was intended through Miles O'Shannon, was not to make us ridiculously wealthy but to use the phenomenon of the Windows to bring the world together. None of us knew how that might happen, but that purpose seemed to spark something in my parents, giving them a new direction.

It's the first week of June, seventeen months since I'd met with Reilly in Chicago. Since then, Morgan and I have become friends with Reilly, his wife, Ellen, and their young son, Ryan, and have done several excursions together. Reilly and I have travelled extensively throughout the system. In a way, I've been doing for him what my grandfather had planned to do with me: mentor me and introduce me to the many people the Windows connect us to. The O'Shannons have shown a great interest in the philanthropy of the Enniskillen Group, and Reilly has been keen to work with Bill and Dane on the upkeep of the locations. The one place neither he nor his wife has travelled to yet was been the island. He has stood in the study and seen the open door to Enniskillen many times, but he could not bring himself to step through Closet Two and see what Miles O'Shannon had built. He'd said it had been too emotional for him to know that his father's quest was only a few steps away, but today was different. Today would be a reckoning, a coming full circle, where the first O'Shannon in more than three centuries would step foot on the island where the evil intent of one man had caused so much grief. It was a perfect day for a happy ending.

The weather in the South Seas in early summer was far less muggy than the rest of the year, with cooler trade winds blowing in from the southeast. It gave lower daytime temperatures, making long walks along the beach slightly more comfortable and tolerable.

My mother suddenly did that thing with her hair, flipping it up at the back of her head and magically tying it in a knot.

"I still find it difficult to believe any of this, Aidan."

I laughed, stopping at the water's edge to let the next wave caress my toes.

"I'm getting used to it, but, yeah, it's still a bit crazy. I often wonder what it would have been like if Gramps had just invited all of us to begin with?"

She hummed, her eyes following a flock of seabirds trekking toward the lagoon's inlet.

"We'll never know. People often make decisions without honestly considering the consequences of those choices. Charles and Felix grew apart years ago, and I'm not sure either would have been able to tell you what caused it. They were two very different people," she laughed gently, "just like you and your father."

I nodded, feeling the familiar sting of my grandfather's death. I still miss him, but time, as cliche as it sounds, has a way of bringing healing of sorts. He was gone, but he was also all around us on the island and in the many people he had befriended in his travels.

"He had his reasons, I guess," I said after a moment.

"He did," she said, touching my arm and smiling in that motherly way, like no matter how hard something was, it would be okay.

She stooped to retrieve a speckled, golden-coloured shell, about the size of an ostrich egg, from the sand. She brushed grit from its highly polished, flat underside, then held it for me.

"Oh, look, honey, a Cowrie shell. Not long ago, these symbolized power and rank for chieftains among the Solomon Islands."

"Really?" I replied, genuinely surprised. "You've been doing some research?"

She smiled, squinting at the shell as she turned it over.

"Well, you know how much I love gardens, and the island is just a different kind of garden."

I chuckled.

"You and Dad settled in?"

My mother lifted her gaze from the shell to look at me and smiled broadly.

"We are. Knokke-Heist is a beautiful city, and Belgium, well, who could complain about Belgium? Thank you again, Aidan."

I shook my head.

"It, they, the Windows, needed to be shared, at least with family and friends — for now. I couldn't live like Gramps' did, hiding out across the street from our house, having this whole other life apart from us."

Mom placed the shell back on the water's edge and lifted her face to the infinite blue sky.

"I'm glad you made that choice, and your father is more relaxed than he's ever been."

With some hinting from me and a strong suggestion from my mother, my parents took possession of the villa in Knokke-Heist. Reilly agreed as he and his wife's interests tended more towards the British Isles and South America than Belgium. The villa was close to boutiques, art galleries, and sidewalk cafés, all places my parents enjoy. About six months ago, with the financial freedom the Enniskillen Group provided, they both quit their jobs and moved to Belgium. My father eagerly became the financial officer of my share of the Enniskillen investments. Zurich is a little more than an hour's flight from Knokke-Heist, and he had already met several times with Reinhold Bonk, putting his accountancy skills to good use. It keeps him busy, and oddly, this has led to another healing of sorts between my father and the memory of his father.

Nollaig O'Shannon had taught me an invaluable lesson. Bitterness is destructive, and he and my grandfather had proven it. O'Shannon had lost his perspective and life, and my grandfather had lost the chance to reconcile with his son. The families of Enniskillen won't let that happen again.

"What do you think of the villa?"

My mother reached out and pulled me to her as we walked, linking her arm in mine.

"I fell in love with the city the first time you took us there. The garden is fabulous. It's a lovely city, and your father quite enjoys the golfing. You've been very kind to him, you know. He never understood the relationship you and Felix had. He was quite jealous of it, and I know that wasn't good for us — as your parents and as a couple."

I glanced at her. Her blue eyes were moist. We hadn't talked much about their couple counselling sessions, which had resumed a month after the incident in Chicago. A new and different relationship was taking shape between them. Whenever we got together, which was quite often now, there was a growing affection between them that I vaguely remembered from my childhood. A playful brush of hands, a sly smile, and a quick kiss were cute, but in a weird way. They're still my parents, after all.

"I used to wish you two would split up, you know. But I'm glad you're, uh, finding your way back to each other. You deserve happiness."

She squeezed my arm and kissed my cheek.

"You've really become quite the romantic. I like this side of you."

We came to the stone steps that led to the fortress towering above us in all its enduring strength and sat down together. We had left our shoes on the first step. I brushed loose sand from between my toes, tipped my loafers up in case something had decided to take up residence while I was away, and slipped them on. My mother gazed wistfully at the cove as she slid her feet into her sandals. Even at the height of the monsoon season, which we had only just come through, there was always a dazzling chorus of sound, motion and colour playing out in a never-ending display. Today, the skies were rich with fathomless hues of cobalt and magnificent statuesque clouds. The water was translucent like German crystal, disturbed only by the occasional egret diving for food, their slim bodies puncturing the surface like arrows shot from heaven.

"Knokke-Heist might be a beautiful city," she said softly, "but Enniskillen takes your breath away."

"It does, doesn't it?"

At that moment, I felt a twinge of sorrow for the first O'Shannon who had stood here, perhaps on this very spot, on this tiny island, just as we were now. He'd had no idea the centuries of grief that would be visited upon his family.

"Do you think Amelia is back yet?" my mother asked, disturbing the quiet contemplation that had settled over us.

"She should be."

The Siblings of Enniskillen, as Bill was officially calling the Windows side of the Enniskillen Group, were gathering for what had become a monthly tradition, a feast, to be followed by a meeting to discuss the Windows and any necessary repairs, excursions, and the like. Working with Reilly and his security knowledge, we implemented ways to minimize our visibility as more of us used the system. This meant we all had passports and occasionally flew to locations to provide a legal reason for being in a country like my parents had when they began the immigration process for their move to Belgium. We also made a rule to wear sunglasses and nondescript hats to keep our images from being easily recognized if and when captured by CCTV cameras that may be using face-recognition technology.

It was understood that if governments knew what the Windows could do, their control would be wrenched from our hands. The secret would eventually come out; the planet was just too connected, but we had to be in control. We had to do the revealing. Until then, we had a few years to figure out how to present the phenomenon of these small wormholes to the world.

Recent meetings of the Siblings of Enniskillen involved serious discussion on how this might look. Bill had suggested renting space on a private spaceship and sending a self-contained human habitat with a Window built into it to the Moon or Mars and then revealing the device to the public and governments as a once-in-a-century technological breakthrough of a transporter-type technology.

Dane, as usual, was a little more practical and imagined a scenario where we do something closer to Earth, presenting the breakthrough as a way to move people and goods between select locations. It would be one of those once-a-century societal sea-change moments and offer humanity a way to lessen the impact of fossil fuels from shipping and air travel. It also, as Morgan pointed out, would help to tear down the inequality endemic in travel.

Maybe we were naive; humans don't have a great track record for doing what's best for all the Earth's inhabitants. Still, the science of the Windows needed to belong to everyone; it needed to continue moving from its colonial roots, as Marianne McPhie had begun, to something that benefitted all of humanity.

I glanced at my watch. Morgan was meeting the O'Shannons at the Window in Dublin in a few minutes. They could have come to the island on their own, but Ellen had asked Morgan to meet them. It was a powerful and emotional day for all of us.

My mother and I climbed the steps and pushed the door open to the fortress. The aroma of foods from a dozen different countries teased our senses. Roast lamb from Brazil, various types of sausage and meats from around the Mediterranean, vegetables from Spain, Canada and the US, and platters of fruit from Australia, South America, Africa and the Middle East. This inviting cornucopia of the Earth's culinary offerings was displayed on an elegant dining table Reilly and I had purchased from a furniture artisan in Istanbul and had shipped to the island through Australia. My parents had already brought bottles of chardonnay from a small family-run winery outside of Rouen.

Today, there would be much laughter and conversation, but it would end with Reilly O'Shannon and his family spreading his father's ashes on the South Pacific that caressed the shore at the foot of the fortress.

Soft jazz was coming from the entertainment complex in the common area, and Amelia was mounting another of our mother's newly framed paintings near the fireplace. It was a strange thing, my mother, an artist. She was pretty good at it, and the fact that she had begun doing this since first travelling to the island was fitting. Many inhabitants of Enniskillen had done the same before her, and, in a way, it was a wonderful continuation of the remarkable history of the Windows.

"Hey, you two," Amelia called when she saw us.

"Hello dear," my mother responded as she crossed to the fireplace.

My father was reading a novel in the common area. He glanced up and nodded as I approached.

"You ready for this?" he asked, closing the book as I sat across from him.

"For Reilly and his family?"

I was nervous but not unprepared.

He nodded.

"This is a very kind thing you've done, Aidan."

"Thanks, Dad."

He had already told me this many times and even met Reilly and his family, seeming to hold no ill will towards him for his father's actions. He held up a hand.

"No, I mean it sincerely. I know I've said this before, but I wouldn't have been able to do what you've done. When they kidnapped your mother and me, I only wanted to see both of them dead. And when I learned that Nollaig had murdered my father, I, well, you've done the right thing, son. I'm proud of you."

I smiled awkwardly – this new dad was as surprising as my reemerging mom. After so many years of being at odds with him, the warmth between us was almost disturbing, but I welcomed the change.

A half-hour later, the door to the hallway to Turin Street opened, and Morgan ushered in the O'Shannons. My heart leapt in my throat as I saw her. We visited just once a week, an agreement we'd made before she flew to Brisbane, Australia, from Victoria for an international student medical program at the Royal Brisbane Hospital. My heart was also pounding because of the reality of the return of the O'Shannon family to Enniskillen.

I could only imagine what they must be feeling. I didn't have to wonder long, though, as Reilly's face flooded with emotions when his eyes fell on me and then tracked slowly around the cavernous room. Then he began to sob, and Ellen, a kind-hearted and petite woman with flaming red hair, gripped his arm and wept. Their son Ryan, five years old and who'd become my buddy, clung to her leg, casting anxious glances at his parents.

Morgan hugged Ellen, then picked up Ryan as I walked over to them and extended my hand. It was reminiscent, I suddenly realized, of the night the elder O'Shannon held out his hand as he welcomed me to his sad parody of Enniskillen.

"Welcome, my friend," I said, trying hard to keep from choking up, "to the real Enniskillen."

He took my hand, gripping it firmly with the one that had experienced first-hand the potential dangers of Window travel. The strength of his handshake was a matter of pride, I felt. He was still strong, still proudly an O'Shannon, and still the rightful heir to the legacy of the Windows. This was the moment his father and the generations before him had sought to reclaim, and Reilly and I had made it happen.

"Dia duit," he said briskly.

"Dia is Muire duit," I answered, nodding slightly. I had been practicing Gaelic using an app, as Reilly had jokingly suggested I do at the end of our first meeting, but it's a tough language, and I generally mangle the words more than I make sense.

Reilly grinned and nodded in appreciation.

"Very good, Aidan."

Once again, everything was as it should be. My grandfather had said that everyone has a story. Some write their own with bad decisions, and others just get handed a Shakespearean tragedy. The ancient grievance between the O'Shannons and the Mcphie's had taught me the value of his words, if you want a better world, then tell a better story. Today, we were doing that. We had closed the book on centuries of injustice and had begun to write the new story of Enniskillen. The moment's emotions were almost incomprehensible, and I wept with them.

Bill and Dane, who had travelled to Victoria to bring Brittany and Kelli, arrived soon after, and the cave was filled with the conversation of friends and explorers. We weren't explorers so much of some Old Order but of a New Order, the Order of Enniskillen.

"What a wonderful day this has been," Morgan sighed later as we lounged side by side in the Lookout.

The O'Shannons had gone down to the cove with Nollaig's ashes, and we excused ourselves from the rest of the group, slipping away for a few moments of quiet as myriad stars dazzled the Southern Hemisphere.

"Yeah, quite something, eh?"

"Pretty emotional, too."

I nodded.

"Are you okay?" Morgan said quietly as she reached out and took my hand.

I didn't answer immediately. My thoughts were elsewhere.

"Aidan?"

"Huh? Oh, yeah. I'll have to write this one in my journal for sure."

Morgan kicked the leg of my chair with the side of her foot.

"You've been acting weird since the O'Shannons went to the cove. What's up?"

Her head was tilted, her brows creased, her mind trying to decipher my thoughts.

"Nothing… um, just tired." I averted my eyes and then stole a glance at her. She watched me keenly, her green eyes slowly pinching behind her glasses.

Whisking unruly strands of hair away from her face with a slim finger, she arched an eyebrow at me and persisted.

"What's going on, Aidan?"

"Uh …" I looked away, focusing on the flashes of lightning from a far-off storm, to look anywhere else but into that face, but I couldn't. Her eyes probed mine, and I struggled to remain expressionless but failed. My mouth was suddenly feeling parched.

"Um, I know we've never talked about this, and, you know, considering your parents and all – "

My throat tightened, and my love for this woman who had seen something worthwhile in me burned like an irrepressible fire in my chest.

"Aidan Ames, are you about to ask me to marry you?" Her eyes grew almost as wide as her grin.

I blinked rapidly.

"Um, well, yeah, well, I know maybe marriage isn't something you, well, we're still pretty young, um, but I was hoping maybe someday, after you're done your residency, maybe, um…."

"Done my residency? That's five years from now."

I stared at her, my heart beating wildly as if I had just leapt off the John Hancock building again, and I was falling, rushing madly, headlong to certain death.

"Oh – uh, well, I mean, you know – maybe –"

Morgan's face blossomed into a grin, her eyes beaming with love. I groaned, and tears blurred my vision, but she grabbed my arms, pulling me up with her as she stood. The heat of her breath was on my face.

"About time you asked me," she whispered as our lips met.

About the Author

Wyatt Tremblay is perhaps best known for his three decades of political cartooning for the Yukon News. Born in Jasper, Alberta, he spent much of his life in the Yukon but now lives in Airdrie, Alberta. He is the father of four children and the proud grandfather of nine.

His first novel, *Medusa Gone*, and a short story collection, *iDead and Other Short Stories*, are available online through Amazon, Barnes and Noble, and anywhere great reads are sold.

The Key to Enniskillen is his second published novel.

Look for his third novel, *Below*, coming out in December 2024.

Acknowledgements

The idea for this story came from a dream I had in 2002. I spun it into a novel, had my friend Josephine Holmes, a budding freelance editor at the time, look at it, and promptly put it on the shelf. I had never travelled outside North America, and I felt I couldn't authentically write a book like this without at least having some first-hand experience about how vast and diverse our planet is. Years later, I have experienced the smallest of glimpses of a world that would take several lifetimes to explore. However, having travelled overseas, I now feel slightly knowledgeable enough to release The Key to Enniskillen into the wilds of speculative fiction readers.

I owe a huge thank you to Cheryl Fountain and Raspberry Press for accompanying me on another publishing journey. Without the guidance and knowledge my association with Raspberry Press has brought, I'd still be holed up in my second-floor studio, happily writing away for no one else but me.

I am greatly indebted to the many writers I have had the privilege to know who have encouraged me to keep writing and the many readers who've purchased, downloaded, and borrowed my previous works. Sharing what crawls out of my imagination with others has been the most exciting adventure of all. Also, a special thank you to my daughter Brittany, who loved the idea of portals that made travel affordable.

Most of all, I wish to thank my best friend and partner in life, Bonnie, for believing in me and encouraging me to "go upstairs and write."

Thank you for reading!

Please add a short review on Amazon.ca, or write me at wyattsworld@me.com and let me know what you liked or didn't like!

Also by Wyatt Tremblay

iDead and Other Short Stories

(2013. Updated and reissued 2022)

From a co-worker whose endless dialogue is an analog blog in the workplace to the sad idea of a completely human-less way to pass from life to death to a disturbing encounter with a baby on a sidewalk, these ten stories come from my imagination and my dream life. The plots may be varied, but they carry a similar theme: reflections on life's joys, sorrows, and hopes.

"This book really brings the reader to an emotional level, and that is a true art! Highly recommend the book!" - Blue/Amazon Review

Medusa Gone: A Novel (2022)

Life isn't easy. Getting old, for instance, or finding the right costume that expresses your magnificent maleficence, or battling your mortal enemy for more than a century without destroying him. If that weren't difficult enough, how about being transported to another dimension to find yourself forced to share a body with an insufferable, younger, and powerless version of yourself? Perhaps worst of all is having to deal with your younger version's girlfriend. Indeed, that may be the most difficult thing of all!

"Wyatt Tremblay presents us with a refreshing story complete with drama, tension, stress and humour. This is one of the better books I've read over the past long while. I recommend it." - Norm Hamilton/Amazon Review

Available through Amazon, Barnes and Noble, Chapters, and anywhere great reads are sold.

Raspberry
Press

www.ingramcontent.com/pod-product-compliance
Lightning Source LLC
Chambersburg PA
CBHW061640190726
48289CB00006B/1674